MEDWAY

Medway
Published by The Conrad Press in the United Kingdom 2019

Tel: +44(0)1227 472 874
www.theconradpress.com
info@theconradpress.com

ISBN 978-1-911546-58-0

Typesetting and Cover Design by: Charlotte Mouncey, www.bookstyle.co.uk
The Conrad Press logo was designed by Maria Priestley.

Printed and bound in Great Britain
by Clays Ltd, Elcograf S.p.A

MEDWAY

DAVID CRAMER SMITH

PART ONE

'The rain falls hard on a humdrum town.'

1

Soon, I will flee Manchester.

Soon, I will forcibly dislocate myself from my own life, a shoulder popping itself out of its socket, loosening itself free.

Joyous, burning pain.

It's July 2008. I'm almost twenty-five years old.

It's been nothing but Manchester since starting university at eighteen and that's too much.

I no longer love/like my girlfriend.

My boss and most of my co-workers are a bunch of shitfucks.

I've finally realised that Morrissey is… no longer the Morrissey of The Smiths.

Kill your idols.

So I will relinquish my dignity and return to my parents' place in the Unitary Authority of Medway.

I could go anywhere in the world.

I could go and live in the desert in New Mexico and become a student of the wind.

Live like a shaman in the jungles of Peru, learning how to listen to the plants.

Leave society and become a hermit, to try and fix my broken, bipolar brain.

But no.

I'll be going to Rainham, my dead-from-the-neck-up home-town, in England, my dead-from-the-neck-up country.

Soon.

2

Alice and I have increased the frequency of our loud, drunken, public arguments.

Our relationship has decayed.

Three years we've been together, renting a tiny, bland flat fifteen storeys up in a modern high-rise block.

Bleak, uninspiring architecture.

Shoddily built, cheaply appointed, over-priced.

The grubby Manchester rain quickly managed to besmirch the facades of the building, ageing it beyond its years, like the sallow face of a sixty-a-day chain-smoker.

But Alice and I were happy there for a while.

When we moved in we set about cosying up the place with all our stuff. We put fairy lights around the headboard of our bed; blu-tacked unframed posters of bands we loved all over the walls; plastered the fridge with photos from our student days; put fancy, artisanal handwash in the bathroom.

We bought houseplants. So many houseplants.

We nurtured them like children.

We were pretending to be grown-ups and it was fun.

3

It was a mutual friend from university, Deb, who match-made us.

I was a year older than Alice and had almost finished my Politics degree; Alice was in her second year.

I wasn't looking for a girlfriend.

When Deb broached the topic I told her I was knuckling down to my dissertation. I didn't tell her that I was still hung up on my ex-girlfriend from the sixth-form, Caitlin Gilberthorpe.

But Deb was persistent.

'She'll civilise you,' Deb said. 'She's out of your league but somehow you've caught her eye. She saw you the other day at the student union and asked me about you. I lied of course. If she knew the truth she'd run a fucking mile.'

'I'm not a monster,' I said.

'You're a gentle savage,' she said, patting my head.

'Exactly. A rough diamond.'

'Charcoal, then.'

'Same difference. Carbon-based.'

'Just remember to shower before you go out with her, that's all I ask. And maybe get an STI check.'

I stood up and looked proudly into the distance. 'I won't change who I am for anybody!'

'I will hose you down, Jamie, so help me.'

4

I met Alice at a 'Chav Night' in a nightclub in the city.

I didn't know it was Chav Night so I wore my usual lack-lustre clobber.

Everyone else was dressed up. A lot of boys had on 'Burberry' baseball caps, Ralph Lauren polo shirts with the collars turned up, heavy gold chains around their necks, sleeper rings. Girls had 'Croydon Facelift' hairstyles, hypertrophied gold hoop earrings, velour tracksuits.

Garage music pulsed through the club, rattling my ribcage. People were mindlessly grinding against each other.

It was like I was back in Medway at Bar Rio with my old friends from school. Except this was 'ironic'. This was middle-class students taking the piss out of the commoners.

Deb screamed and hugged me when I found her on the dancefloor with some of our friends. She held me at arm's length and looked me up and down. 'Babe! What the fuck are you wearing! It's supposed to be fancy dress! Nevermind. There's someone I want you to meet.'

She yanked me off the dancefloor towards a group of people idly moving to the music and sipping drinks with straws.

'This is Alice Green. She's in my International Relations class. Alice, this is Jamie Sinclair.'

'Hi,' said Alice. 'I see you're also against the idea of dressing up to mock the underclass.'

'Yaaawn,' said Deb. 'It's just a bit of fun. And I make this shit look good.'

She struck a pose.

'At the expense of those less fortunate than us,' said Alice.

'All right, all right, I'm an evil bitch,' said Deb, stabilising herself by holding Alice's shoulder and leaning in to plant a wet-looking peck on her cheek. 'I'll leave you two humourless babes to get to know each other. I'm gonna bag me a hooligan.'

She put her empty glass on a nearby table and moseyed back to the dancefloor.

I faced Alice. 'I didn't actually know it was fancy dress,' I said. 'If I had, all I would have needed to do was raid my old wardrobe back home. This is how I used to dress.'

'I hope you're not being flippant,' said Alice.

'I'm being... serious,' I said.

5

The next time we met was by chance at a house party.

A friend of a friend of mine was also a friend of a friend of Alice.

I was already tipsy when she arrived, but at least the venue was more conducive for conversation, unlike last time.

She came over to say hi. Full of uninhibited bravado I told her I wanted to kiss her before the night was over.

She touched my arm and laughed, then went to talk to some friends.

Drunken idiot. I'd blown it.

Except I hadn't.

She found me towards the end of the night and led me upstairs to an empty bedroom, where we lay on the floor and kissed, and that's it, because we didn't have protection.

It was okay though.

I knew we'd meet again.

We had an immediate, intense connection, and for the next few days I thought of nothing else but her.

6

And Alice had thought of nothing else but me, apparently. That's what she said when we met for coffee in the student union later in the week.

I was unlike anyone she'd ever met, she said.

I told her the same thing. It was almost true.

Alice wasn't anything like Caitlin.

Which is to say she looked a lot like Caitlin (undeniably beautiful) but had blonde hair rather than brown.

Which is to say she'd also been head girl at her high school (but had gone to a private school rather than public).

A few things set Alice apart: she had dimples; she went on protest marches; she wore a Yo La Tengo t-shirt that she'd stolen from her older brother.

I focused on these differences as much as the similarities.

'What are you doing for the rest of the day?' she said.

'I was going to stay here and drink coffee all day, reading this beast.'

I drummed a brief tattoo with two fingers on the hardback library book on the table before me.

'Want to read it at mine? The coffee's free there. Nescafé finest.'

'That sounds… pretty good.'

'Is that a yes then?'

'Are you sure I wouldn't be in the way? What about your housemates?'

'Hundred per cent. They've both gone home to visit their clingy boyfriends and convince them they haven't been sleeping around all this time. Come on. There's a bus soon. We'll make it if we go now.'

7

In those early days the sex was there, was good.

When we were alone together, in a kind of comical way almost all physical contact between us culminated with nudity.

We might be in Alice's lounge on the settee, reading our respective textbooks, then one of us would rub the other's knee, and then we'd be naked, doing it right there, hoping her house-mates wouldn't come downstairs for another few minutes.

In bed, if I was big spoon, Alice would do this kind of super slow-mo twerk against me to indicate that it was time. I could never resist, even if I was half-asleep and had to get up early for a lecture.

She would do the slow-mo twerk thing in the middle of the night.

I would respond by dreamily nuzzling the place between her neck and shoulder.

Would sneak a sleepy, questing hand between her arm and ribs to find a terrific breast, then she'd reach behind and start rubbing me through my boxer shorts.

We knew how to make each other come.

Sixty-nine.

Ninety-six.

Fifty-five.

Pi.

All the sex numbers.

We skipped lectures to be together. We were hindering the growth of our minds and it felt great.

My fragile ego was boosted. I'd never been able to consistently satisfy another person before Alice: Caitlin found it difficult to climax and brought a lot of adolescent anxiety to sex (she wouldn't take her top off and didn't enjoy receiving oral sex); with other women it was hit and miss. So Alice and I kept doing it and doing it, delirious with youthful exuberance, and passion, and joy, and relief.

8

There was all the other stuff as well.

I loved the smell of her Herbal Essences shampoo (it reminded me of Caitlin).

I enjoyed that she was smarter than me, and how equanimous she was about her intelligence.

We helped each other discover new things: new bands, new artists, new writers. I introduced her to Billy Childish, Amy Hempel and The Smiths; she introduced me to Georgia O'Keefe, Sebastian Faulks and Death Cab for Cutie.

It wasn't a fair swap but I let it slide.

Long into the night we talked earnestly about politics, spirituality, science, travelling, music, literature, art, philosophy, history, the future. We lay together for hours, listening to album after album. I wrote poems for her, about her, because of her, all of which I shared with her then immediately snatched back and threw in the bin.

We put a lot of thought into each other's birthday and Christmas presents.

We had pet names, and spoke to each other in baby voices in private.

We told each other we were in love.

But eventually, ineluctably, our love commingled with our respective mood/attachment disorders, and the rows started.

I think it began when I accidentally called her Caitlin one evening. It was a (relatively) honest mistake, but something broke in Alice's mind.

We had our first screaming match and the relationship never recovered.

From then on, if we were out with Deb and our other friends, Alice would have no problem talking to me like shit in front of them all.

She'd home in on all my physical insecurities to emasculate me. Imply that she might have slept with other people. Accuse me of pretending to be less posh than I was (when it was absolutely the other way round).

Sometimes, her progressive mask would slip and she would describe my drunken behaviour as 'chavvy'.

She insulted my parents: called them 'The Little Englanders'.

She was right, but how dare she?

In retaliation I flirted with women to try and make her jealous. Accidentally-on-purpose sent her texts that were meant for imaginary female friends.

We were both petty and childish.

Awful.

Many evenings were ruined by our fights. It was all perfectly convivial to begin with, but as we got drunker we'd get louder and more belligerent, which made everyone awkward.

It was stressful and energy-sapping.

The make-up sex, which in my mind was supposed to provide a counterpoint in this deranged composition, was underwhelming.

For 'underwhelming' read 'non-existent'.

Sometimes after an explosive argument, once we were home and I'd had a cigarette, I would lie on the bed, roll up onto my shoulders, cup my buttocks and hold my legs straight up in the air in a botched yoga pose. I'd do this for like ten minutes. It felt good to stretch and to have my blood squeeze downwards and into my face.

Then I'd stand up like I was about to high-dive off the bed.

I wanted my chest to burst open and my groin to burst open and the top of my head to burst open, and have blinding rays of plasma beam out and incinerate everything.

Flushed in the cheeks, I'd silently shout 'Raaaaaaaaaaaar!' over and over again until I thought I could go out to the front room and be civil.

9

It was around this time that I had my first major episode.

I'd not long started work at the insurance company as a 'graduate'.

I got my first pay cheque and accidentally went on a three-day bender.

Ended up being hospitalised on the Sunday evening because I thought Alice was plotting to kill me.

She wasn't.

It was all in my head.

I managed to spend almost three thousand pounds in one weekend.

A lot of it went on booze – 'The drinks are on me! Everyone in here, listen! Put your next drink on my tab!' – but other purchases included a replica samurai sword (for protection) and a nine hundred pound three-piece suit, all of which maxed-out my credit card.

I was diagnosed with bipolar disorder by the hospital's psychiatrist, and shortly afterwards began a course of lithium carbonate.

Mum and Dad paid the credit card bill, which is one of many reasons Dad isn't really talking to me. I sold the samurai sword (I couldn't sell the suit – I vomited down it, which left a permanent stain) and paid them back over the next few months, but Dad couldn't get over it.

As for Alice, she temporarily called a truce.

She was gentle and lovely with me for a few weeks. Our

relationship almost healed.

The mould flowers soon blossomed again though.

We were like a punnet of raspberries.

The ones on top looked pink and ripe, but underneath was where you'd find the rot.

10

Alice often looked through my emails.

No-one suspected she was the sort of person to do this, but she was.

She emotionally blackmailed me into sharing my passwords. The first few times she asked I refused to tell her, but she sulked for hours, days even, suspicious that I was hiding something.

'It's not that I want to read your emails,' she said when I called her out on it. 'It's about trust. If you trust me, I'll trust you.'

I caved in, hoping for a quiet life.

I caught her doing it again earlier this week.

I got in from work and as I walked into the front room she closed the laptop lid too quickly.

'It's okay if you're looking at porn,' I said, slipping off my backpack. 'Don't be embarrassed.'

I collapsed next to her on Saxtorp, our tiny oatmeal-coloured Ikea settee, and kissed her shoulder ironically.

She kept her fingers arched on top of the lid. She was looking straight ahead.

'What's wrong,' I said.

'Who's Karla Simulija,' she said.

'My mistress.'

'That's not funny, Jamie. You better not be cheating on me.'

'We're not having this conversation again.'

'Yes, we are. '

I got up, walked the three steps to the kitchen and grabbed a bottle of beer out of the fridge.

'You shouldn't be looking through my emails.'

'You shouldn't be emailing people like Karla Simulija.'

'She's a colleague. We were discussing work.'

'How do I know you won't sleep with her when you're fucking manic again and out drinking?'

She slumped sideways on Saxtorp. She was already in sulk mode.

I necked the beer, wiped my mouth with a wrist.

'I'm going to the pub,' I said.

'What a surprise,' she said, her voice muffled by Vargyllen, a black-and-white-striped cushion.

She stopped sulking a few of days later, a Sunday.

She told me she wanted to study for a Masters, having only just finished as an undergrad the previous month.

She missed out on a first-class degree by a paltry/significant 1%, but she was confident she'd be able to get onto a course.

I was sitting next to her on Saxtorp, matching pairs of clean socks from the laundry basket and balling them up, feeling anally retentive. Feeling like the 'system' had beaten me because I always wore matching socks.

Alice was sitting cross-legged, reading a prospectus, flicking through it like it was a lifestyle magazine.

Rare afternoon sunlight was beaming into the flat from the wall-to-wall window that offered views over Salford.

She announced that she wanted to study again.

This is how she said it: 'I want to do my Masters in September', with that possessive pronoun, like she owned the qualification, like it was something she was destined to do.

Her Masters.

It was some bullshit course that would help her further delay going to work. She needed the structure of being graded again, of regurgitating what she'd absorbed and being told she was clever by people who also thrived on being seen as clever.

Her parents would pay for it.

Her masters.

'Deb's in London doing her LPC,' she said. 'Tim and Sarah have gone to India to do conservation work. It's time for me to do something with my life too.'

Disgust - a yoghurty, phlegmy disgust - welled up in my throat. I looked at her, with that taste in my mouth.

I thought about her brainless, wealthy, baby-boomer parents, with that taste in my mouth.

I thought, This situation is fucked.

This person is fucked. I'm fucked too, but at least I know I'm fucked. This person doesn't have the faintest idea she's fucked.

Fuck this, I thought.

So I ended it with her there and then. I'd been planning on doing it for a while but hadn't yet summoned the courage.

'I think we should break up,' I said.

'What?'

'We bring out the absolute worst in each other,' I said.

She dropped the prospectus on the floor and stormed into the bedroom.

I sat down again and reclined on Saxtorp. The spot where she'd been sitting was still warm. I took out my phone and watched the 'Large Hadron Rap' on YouTube, which had received over a million views in only a few days.

When the video finished I looked up 'quantum physics' on Wikipedia.

Felt stupid the whole time I was reading; I know nothing.

I closed the tab and thought for a while about protons, and how stable they are. I learned that a proton's half-life is at least 10^{31} years, which is longer than the lifespan of the universe.

Which means, for all intents and purposes, protons don't decay.

Good for protons.

12

Alice is crying and screaming at me as I chuck my stuff into a suitcase.

I do my best to ignore her but now I'm crying and screaming at her too.

I'm revolting.

I say disgraceful things.

I try hard to destroy her self-confidence.

But relief spreads through my body all the same.

I clomp my suitcase down the concrete stairwell.

I go back up and grab the rest of my meagre belongings: my electric guitar, a tiny Marshall amp, a box of books and CDs.

Alice is sitting on Saxtorp now, no longer crying.

'I'm sorry to do this but it's the right thing to do and we'll be better people eventually,' I say, trying to stand appropriately.

'I know,' she says. 'It's so hard though. It hurts. Like, it actually, physically hurts.'

She clutches her stomach. Her eyes are red and puffy and I want to go over and make her feel better.

I want to go over and make her cry some more.

'I'm really sorry,' I say. 'I'm not sure what happened.'

'We got into a relationship and our relationship happened. It took its natural course.'

'I'm really sorry.'

'I know. I am too.'

She blows her nose with a tissue. 'I'm really worried about you.'

'Don't be. I have the, y'know, the lithium. I'll keep seeing a psych.'

'I know I haven't been as supportive as I should have, but please call me if you need help. Please.'

'That's not true, Alice. You've been good. We're probably better off as friends, that's all. I'm not an easy person to live with.'

She starts crying again, but manages to contain it.

'Sorry,' she says. 'You never call me Alice. It sounds so weird.'

'Yeah, I guess it does.'

I leave before we hug, before we reconcile.

I put my stuff in the boot of my smegma-yellow Corsa and drive in the twilight to the first B&B I find.

A musty-smelling, friendly-seeming lady shows me to a room and leaves me to it.

The room is chintzy, meant for a middle-aged cis couple, probably. Flowery Laura Ashley curtains, cushions and bedspread; kitschy art on the walls.

The musty smell in the room still.

I turn on the cheap pedestal fan in the corner, which hums pleasantly, and yank the curtains closed.

I do my botched yoga pose on the plush carpet for a while.

Then I move to the bed and lie in the dark thinking about what I'm going to do.

I've been umming-and-ahhing about going back to Medway; maybe this is the opportunity to do it. Except I only feel like dissipating now that it's time to act.

All I want is to intergrade into a particulate mist and dissipate through the atmosphere. Float away, never come back.

Or else find Caitlin Gilberthorpe and marry her.

But I don't even know where she lives these days.

Plus she was the one who ended it. I don't really know why -- she used platitudes to protect my feelings -- but I suspect it was some unfixable defect within me that repulsed her.

Maybe she knew, somehow, that I was going to become this crazy bastard.

The day she did it, not long after we got our A-levels results, I felt in that moment as she was gently releasing herself from me that I was floating in space at the other end of the universe.

I could feel her hands on mine, could still see her face, but I was simultaneously light-years away from her.

My phone vibrates on the bed-side table.

Alice again.

It almost wriggles over the edge. I don't try to stop it.

It continues to vibrate, illuminating the entire room with its ghoulish blue light.

I put my hands over my closed eyes to block it out.

It finally shuffles off the table and bounces under the bed, and the room goes dark again, and the fan keeps on with its humming.

13

Walking to work.

Trying to psych myself up for the same old shit.

Already had two cigarettes. Only supposed to have one before work -- that's the rule.

I light my third and ring my mum, a female eunuch.

I tell her a redacted version of what happened last night with Alice.

She enthusiastically reiterates that I can stay with her and Dad, a hysterectomised male, if I need to.

She's been suggesting it ever since I was hospitalised. Plus my elder brother John emigrated to Australia last year and I know she wants her youngest, her baby, closer to the nest.

John has always been a better son than me, but I'll do in his absence.

'You can come home and save some money,' Andrea says. 'We'll only charge you a little bit of board. It will give you a chance to get a deposit together for your first house.'

I shake my damn head, knowing how long it would take to save a sufficient deposit, but it's sweet of her, probably.

'I'll think about it. I might come home for a few days anyway, just to get some breathing space. Would that be okay?'

'Of course, darling.'

I'm reluctant to move home, but my options are... limited.

If I live on my own I'll be broke within two months. And finding new housemates seems too exhausting right now.

It's just that I know Dad won't be happy about my moving home, even if it's only for a week or two. He still hasn't got over that credit card bill. He thinks that I'm, quote, 'a dissolute, drunken layabout who's feckless with money.' The bipolar is just an excuse to rinse him of all his hard-earned cash. 'It's a fashionable diagnosis that means irresponsible pissheads can get away with murder.'

And I should never have gone to university, in Col's view. Students are good-for-nothing, work-shy spongers who contribute nothing to society. Now I want to come home and live in his house, when I should be out there comparing mortgage deals, trying to get on the housing ladder!

Mum will be happy though.

Okay, she can be pretty unbearable at times.

I would never (NEVAAH!) admit it to Alice, but I consider Mum to be neurotic, heteronormative, puritanical, and uninquisitive (all the cups and mugs should face handle-outwards in the cupboard; sex should be performed by one man and one woman and preferably within the confines of a marriage; alcohol is perfectly okay, all other drugs are EVIL!!!!!!; evolution is just a theory).

But in (very) small doses they aren't so bad.

I know they really just want the best for me.

They've had hard lives and aren't the best at expressing themselves, that's all.

Being at home might be a stop-gap that could afford time for reflection, to adjust to the idea of being single.

It might be salutary. A change is as good as a rest, and all that.

As Yogi Bear said, 'When you get to a fork in the road, take it.'

Thus Manchester starts to transmogrify into a place I will henceforth only visit in dreams.

14

My only friend at work is Lee.

We both have the same nothing call-centre jobs in Salford with a totalitarian insurance company that lately made the national news for mis-selling PPI, nice one guys.

We've been working there since we graduated and have barely ascended the 'ladder'.

We work in 'Business Retention', a euphemistic term. We have to convince customers not to surrender their insurance policies, even though the customers have explicitly requested this and it's in their financial interests to do so.

If we don't meet our weekly targets, Mr Pancakes, our jobsworth boss, calls us into his office and gives us a dressing down like we're naughty school children.

Mr Pancakes is not his real name. His real name is Andrew.

Lee named him Mr Pancakes because he eats pancakes every day for breakfast.

Unimaginative, but funny.

There are maple syrup stains all over his faux-pine desk, on his swivelling ergonomic chair, on his cheap suit trousers.

His shirt stretches across his paunch, flecked with maple syrup blotches.

The salary is seventeen thousand pounds a year and Mr Pancakes is constantly reminding the staff to be grateful.

If the weekly figures are looking sour he'll walk among the rows of desks and proclaim, 'We pay a whole two grand a year more than Simmons does, plus you get the free life insurance, so buck your ideas up!'

'We're very lucky,' someone will say, to shut him up.

'We'll be better,' someone else will say.

Then we'll all get back on the phones and collectively imagine a grisly end for him.

There are rules to be followed.

Here are three of the most pernicious.

1. We have to keep our Facebook profiles 'corporate-friendly' so as not to bring the company into disrepute, which means they can sack us if we're ever tagged in a photo and appear to be drunk.

I'm drunk (and morose) in every single one of my Facebook photos, but it hasn't been mentioned yet, perhaps because the company has already brought itself into disrepute.

2. Men have to wear suits and women have to wear skirts, no exceptions.

This seems relatively innocuous, right? But just think about it for more than two seconds.

3. We have to type a special code into our desk phones when we go to the toilet so Mr Pancakes can monitor our productivity.

This last one in particular makes me want to set fire to the place.

I watch Lee arrive at his desk in a Monday morning haze, put his jacket over the back of his chair, switch on his computer, yawn. is the only likeable person in the office. It would be cool in touch with him once I leave. He's funny, and doesn't have Stockholm Syndrome for the company, unlike every other poor sucker who works here.

I log into the company's instant messaging application and tell him I'm leaving.

- what will you do, go and work for simmons like farooq did?
- no, i mean i'm leaving manchester
- oh, right
- i hate it here. hey tit. i hate this job. i hate the cold. i hate having to take vitamin d supplements. i want out
- is alice going with you
- we had a big fight last night, we broke up. i'm staying at a bnb
- sorry to hear that mate. will you go to london then
- thanks. not sure. don't want to, rent is crazy there
- true. one of my sisters moved there last year. she pays 550 a month for a room in tooting
- where's tooting
- not sure. south i think? far south. someone got murdered in the flat next door
- shittt
- where will you go then
- my parents' place first. after that, don't know
- when are you going
- maybe this weekend
- you'll have leaving drinks, right?
- i guess. it will just be you and me mate
- you should invite mr pancakes
- dear lawd
- it will make his year

- haha, ok
- you should tell him that he's been an inspiration to you and that you'll always remember him as one of the greatest people you've ever had the privilege to work for
- yeah, i'll get him a present, a ludicrously expensive one. i will make myself broke for him
- get him a really nice card too. write a huge, heartfelt message
- he will be confused
- then when i eventually leave i'll do the same thing. also maybe pretend i always had a secret crush on him
- he will be confused for the rest of his life
- hahaha
- gotta go, sandra's coming over. delete these messages
- they're encrypted
- delete them anyway
- ok

15

I type the appropriate code into my phone and go to the toilet.

I don't need to go; I'll have to tell Mr Pancakes that I'm constipated again.

It's what I do when I come back and find Mr Pancakes hovering around my desk, ready to admonish me for taking too long.

I always say it nice and loud for the whole office to hear. Something like, 'I'm really backed up at the moment, Andrew. It takes me at least twenty minutes to push out a complete turd. I have to be careful not to exacerbate the piles. If I push too hard my anus literally turns inside-out.'

Mr Pancakes never knows what to say in response; usually he mutters something about targets or office decorum then shuffles off back to his office.

If Lee's on the phone he has to put his hand over the speaker and stifle a laugh.

I lock the cubicle door and pull my trousers and boxer shorts.

I realise I've had this pair of boxer shorts for at least two years. I remember buying them from Marks and Spencer, a pathetic little treat for myself.

I bought a pack of three, size Medium, but this particular pair was erroneously included in the set: they're Extra Large.

They fan out at the sides; from the front it looks like I'm wearing a horrible mini-skirt.

Alice found it funny when I first tried them on.

I walked camply around the bedroom, stopping every few

steps to jut out a hip and look over my shoulder coquettishly, pretending to be a 'sexy, liberated woman from the sixties' or something.

Alice promptly slid them down and we made love.

The last time I tried the 'sexy woman' routine (some time last week) Alice merely tutted and carried on scrolling through her Facebook feed, so I went to the toilet and masturbated, thinking of a composite image of Alice and someone I'd seen in the street that day.

When I was cleaning myself up I had an epiphany: Was it possible that I no longer loved Alice because she'd stopped finding me funny?

I look at my watch. Been in the cubicle for ten minutes already.

I consider masturbating.

Anything to improve the day.

Idly begin to touch myself, but then someone else comes in and enters the cubicle next door.

The person immediately starts making a lot of noise with their anus. It kills the mood.

Semi-turgid, I contemplate staying in Manchester and find this prospect actually makes me wince.

The thought of spending another hour in this place under the strictures of Mr Pancakes is bringing on a case of the fantods.

And without Alice there's no reason to stay in Manchester.

Still sitting on the toilet, still listening to the anus noises from next door, I text Mum and asks if it's okay to come back sooner than planned, i.e. tonight.

She replies immediately.

- Of course darling. Exciting! Let us know when you're about to leave. Love you xxx

I pull up my trousers and flush the toilet. Quickly wash my hands and leave the toilet before the other person in there finishes.

I hate it when I have to make small talk with colleagues after I've heard them farting and pissing and shitting all at the same time.

I get back to my desk and draft a resignation email to Mr Pancakes.

Everyone else is on the phones, politely but stiffly remonstrating with irate customers.

Mr Pancakes will deduct my unserved notice period from my final pay, but I don't care, it's worth it.

I go to my internet banking page and transfer some money to Alice, enough to cover the rent I owe for the short remainder of the lease and a bit extra for bills.

In the reference line I write 'Give Saxtorp a hug from me'.

I message Lee, giving him my private email address and urging him to visit.

- what about the leaving drinks?!
- sorry mate. i need to get out of here now or i'm gonna go on a killing rampage. you'd be spared but no-one else would survive
- you're a sweet man

I send the email to Mr Pancakes and log out before he can digitally or physically assail me.

I hurry across the call-centre floor, out to the lobby and down the emergency stairwell to the faux-marble-floored reception.

It's 2pm and the receptionist looks bored. She's scrolling on her phone, audibly chewing gum.

I approach her and say in a kind of 'wise' voice, 'When peace is made between great enemies, some enmity is bound to remain undispelled.'

I slide my security pass towards her across the kitchen bench-top-esque divide.

In broad Mancunian she says, 'Does this mean you're not coming back?'

'It does.'

She blows a little pink bubble and it pops with a crack that caroms around the reception area.

'See ya,' she says, taking the security pass.

I step outside and take a deep breath.

'Let's do this,' I think. 'Medway, I'm coming home, baby! Medway, sweet Medway, nourishing mother, I will suckle your engorged, pale, veiny teets once more!'

I stride back to the bed and breakfast, full of manic energy.

I grab my belongings and hit the road.

I hit the road with both fists, several times.

Then I load up my car and accelerate away, due south.

I've cut myself adrift like a balloon on the wind: a balloon whose string is still tied to a dismembered finger.

16

En route to Medway I pull up at Grantham services around 8.30pm.

It's already dark; it's already cold. The summer is guttering out.

This is one of the other reasons I'm heading South.

I've been nursing a sense of terrible, irrational foreboding about the imminent winter. There's no way I could last through another nine months of freezing rain in the North.

Especially with so few friends to help me through it.

I think about calling someone to tell them I'm coming 'home'. But who would I call?

My friends from Medway and most of my university friends, including Deb, flocked to London ages ago, summoned by Moloch.

I swiftly lost touch with them all.

I was late getting a Facebook account so I missed out on that time when they were fortifying their virtual networks.

Occasionally I was asked to come to London for someone's birthday, but I would usually make an excuse not to go, and eventually the invitations petered out.

I was still able to click through their photos late at night when Alice was asleep. I could see what I'd forgone. I had a window into their lives, though I was disconnected from it at the same time.

I was a voyeur, nothing more.

Which I liked, at first.

It was a time for me to silo myself, to try out being a kind of loner.

In my mind I was a Hemingway-esque kind of loner. The sort who swims alone in the Bay of Biscay at San Sebastian, drinks whisky and sodas or lemonade with shaved ice in Spanish cafes, and sends telegraphs to people telling them he won't be in Paris for another week.

But deep down I knew I was not this kind of loner and that Hemingway would have hated me.

Hemingway would have wanted to take me by the shoulders and shake me, maybe even fight me.

Nonetheless, I wanted to try and define myself on my own terms, not in relation to others' perceptions of me.

I had to become a proper loner, cut-off from social media.

I knew that Facebook made me uniquely sad. It was full of lies. All the posing and fakery made me feel inferior. It was like being at school again.

I deactivated my account.

Only to reactivate soon after.

Manchester wasn't the same place after everyone left. It had started to give me the cold shoulder. I was lonely.

I would remember someone I'd lost touch with, and a nostalgic memory would percolate to the surface of my mind, and then I'd be back in the game, clicking through endless photos once again.

But the loneliness could not be assuaged. Facebook was as indifferent to me as Manchester was.

I know there's a good chance Medway will be indifferent too.

I sit in my car and scroll through my Facebook feed, peering into friend-strangers' lives.

Eventually I update my status to say, 'Manchester Shitty, Manchester Disunited.'

I get zero likes.

17

I had planned to drive the whole way in one go, but I kept yawning and imagining 'Final Destination'-esque scenarios where I'd fallen asleep at the wheel and caused a gory, gargantuan pile-up on the motorway.

I put my phone away and sit for a moment in the carpark watching the patches of unseasonably icy rain illuminated by my headlights and the orange light from the nearby lampposts, hoping the rain might briefly cease and allow me a dry passage to the Travelodge.

I twist to see if there's a jacket or a hoodie on the backseat.

Nothing but empty Red Bull cans and crisp packets back there.

I shiver and switch off the engine, then grab some clothes and my toiletries out of the boot and leg it to the reception, the sleet prickling my face.

I check in at an automatic terminal.

No musty-smelling lady here. Just lurid purple carpet, lurid yellow light.

The terminal coughs out a keycard.

I walk along the corridor, which smells recently vacuumed.

The room is round a couple of corners.

I insert and remove the keycard; the light goes from red to green with a little bip.

Inside I find the curtains drawn, the lamplight not too harsh, the radiator working.

It's good enough.

I array my toiletries on the cheap dressing table. Lie supine on the hard mattress, sodden and cold.

I try to get some sleep but my mind is alive.

I get up and go to the 'ensuite'.

The mirror takes up the entire wall above the sink.

When I'm down to my mini-skirt boxer shorts I jut out a hip, do a camp limp-wrist gesture, do the whole 'liberated woman from the sixties' bit.

I piss on the seat a little, tear off a few squares and wipe the seat dry.

Decide to masturbate. I think of Alice at her best, but I can't come.

Switch to Caitlin but it's no use.

I pull up the miniskirt and my trousers, still hard.

Wash my hands, splash my face, check for zits.

Change out of my wet clothes, grab my newspaper and decide to go to the bar downstairs.

Time for a drink.

The bar is trying hard for an Art Deco, San Francisco-noir vibe, sort of Casablanca meets The Maltese Falcon.

But the floorboards are laminate, the tables dotted around are over-varnished, and the name of the bar in marquee lettering above the door is a meaningless juxtaposition of nouns: The Frog and Trumpet.

It's like an airport bar, a simulacrum.

I lay the folded paper on the bar, crossword-side up to indicate to any passing strangers my capacity for doing the cryptics.

Reconsider this ('Try not to be so pretentious, Jamie') and stuff the paper into my back pocket.

Now I'm uncomfortable, sitting obliquely.

I read somewhere that you can fuck up your lower back sitting on your wallet. I take the paper out and drop it under the stool.

It's almost dark in the bar, the only light coming from the 'Art Deco' lamps (probably Ikea) above the bar itself and a corner-mounted TV showing 'breaking news' on mute with closed captions.

The subtitles are slightly delayed, so the words are incongruous with the images, rendering everything in absurd juxtaposition.

It goes like this.

Picture: Images of the American consulate in Istanbul.

Closed captions: 'Another Taliban IED has exploded in Afghanistan, killing 3 British soldiers.'

Picture: Images of Jerusalem, a bulldozer, the face of an intense-looking man.

Closed captions: 'Four men believed to be Turkish citizens have attacked the American consulate in Istanbul.'

Picture: Images of Britney Spears, including clips from the music video for 'Hit Me Baby (One More Time)'.

Closed captions: 'In Jerusalem a driver of a bulldozer has driven into cars and pedestrians, as well as two public buses carrying 50 passengers.'

Picture: Images of Manchester United in action.

Closed captions: 'Britney Spears has announced a comeback tour after her mental breakdown earlier in the year.'

It's almost artistic, a kind of video installation.

The bartender appears.

I order a 'good' scotch. It's all subjective -- you get to decide what's good for you, no-one else.

The bartender compliments my choice. I buy her one too.

It's just us in the bar. Bogart and Bergman (ha).

We drink our good scotch together and talk for a while about the breaking news.

She makes witty, sarcastic comments about current affairs. She has an edgy hair-cut and a tattoo of Ren and Stimpy on each forearm. She has a fantastic cleavage on display.

I try with all my might not to stare.

She looks like she has it all worked out. Maybe I should get a tattoo. Maybe that's what's missing from my life.

I imagine myself unzipping my skin along the spine and slipping it off.

Throwing it over my arm like a fur coat and walking into a tattoo parlour, bloody and raw, muscle and sinew exposed, my lidless golfball eyes bulging, serious, funny.

Putting my skin on the counter and saying to the dude, 'Give me a Union Jack in the shape of a heart, with the word 'Medway' in the middle, right here.'

Pointing to a saggy, loose mound of skin that was once a buttcheek. Pushing my finger right into it like it's playdough, making a shallow recess.

I bet that would feel nice.

Perhaps too nice.

I sip my Scotch.

It burns my lips, my tongue, my throat, my innards.

Self-harming in a way that society finds acceptable.

I'm about to ask the bartender what time she finishes for the night when a short, creatine-bloated guy with a bad goatee and too much gel in his hair appears from out back.

The manager.

Her boyfriend.

Victor Laszlo (ha).

The guy puts his hand on her shoulder and whispers something in her ear.

She rolls her eyes, drains her whisky, goes out back.

We watch her leave.

Laszlo begins tidying up behind the bar, wiping surfaces, tipping stuff into the bin.

After a while he pauses and says to me, 'Ding ding, buddy. Last orders.'

'I'll have the same again, thanks,' I say, lifting my glass. 'It was that one.'

I point at the bottle of good scotch with a long, simian finger.

'We do take-away,' says Laszlo. 'Why don't you take it to your room. There's only a little bit left.'

I shrug. Grunt, maybe.

Laszlo detaches the optic from the bottle and manoeuvres the bottle from its position on the wall.

'Everything's coming up Milhouse,' I slur.

Laszlo says nothing and taps at the till. With his knuckles, maybe.

'That'll be 24 of your English pounds,' he says.

I smile. My lips peel back, revealing my gums and my large, curved, yellow canines.

'Ooh ooh ahh ahh,' I say.

I stand up and get my wallet out (from my front pocket),

put my debit card in the machine, enter my pin, sweat it out.

I know I have enough in my account but I always get nervous waiting to be approved. I scratch my head and jump through 360 degrees.

'Thanks buddy,' Laszlo says, handing me the bottle and my debit card. 'Have a great night.'

I clasp my hands together and skip a few times, dislocating my shoulders and using my hirsute, slender arms as skipping rope, like King Louis in Disney's Jungle Book.

'Thanks,' I say. 'You too. Say goodnight to your girlfriend for me.'

'I will,' says Laszlo.

As I'm leaving I hear Laszlo mutter, 'Drunk prick.'

I stop and turn around, grunt.

Take a deep breath: tufted elbows out, furry belly lifted, diaphragm open.

I screech, 'Prick!'

Laszlo stands there looking at me. It's an old-fashioned battle of the apes.

Men do this sometimes.

I screech again, 'Prick! Prick! Prick! Prick!'

'Take it easy buddy. People are sleeping.'

I increase the volume; I jump up and down on the spot; I beat my chest. 'PRICK! PRICK! PRICK!'

Laszlo pretends to do something behind the bar as if I'm not there.

I bare my fangs again, hiss, scratch my armpits, then exit and go up to the room.

I place the bottle of scotch on the dressing table and crash face-down on the bed.

I think about the bartender and consider masturbating. I conjure a fantasy of her sweeping empty glasses off the bar with her forearm, grabbing me and pulling me in, aggressively kissing me, smashed glass on the floor around us, all that sort of stuff, but she quickly morphs into Ingrid Bergman, then Caitlin (more beautiful than Bergman).

I imagine going to Costa Rica with Caitlin.

I could become a bartender at a place on the beach, serve white rum to tourists.

Caitlin could be a doctor at a local ramshackle hospital. She would become the director of the hospital and bring it up to Western standards.

We could get married on the beach, a private ceremony with no family present, just some locals we've befriended there to act as witnesses.

We would have a chance of achieving eudaimonia, an almost untranslatable Greek term.

Then Caitlin morphs into Alice and the fantasy is over.

I sleep solidly, fully-clothed, till morning.

18

wake early to continue my journey to the strange, familiar palookaville we call Medway.

I check out of the Travelodge and fire up on the first attempt the Corsa; set off back to 'square one'. The temperamental windscreen wipers frantically swish away The North's interminable drizzle.

Before I reach the motorway I decide to stop at an off-licence so I don't arrive at Mum and Dad's empty-handed. I select a couple of bottles of Mum's favourite dry white wine and, after pausing to consider the ramifications, a bottle of good scotch for Dad.

Set off again.

As I join the motorway my phone rings. I peek at the screen. It's Alice.

Ignore it.

If I speak to her now I'll only end up capitulating and getting back together with her. For maybe the first time in my life I'm following through with a decision.

I don't know how I feel about this.

Flat and confused, I think.

After an hour or so of monotonous driving I pull into the outside lane without looking, almost smashing into an overtaking Ford Focus.

Daydreaming, driving on autopilot.

The Focus reacts quickly and brakes; I slot millimetres in

front of it, still doing 80.

I glance in the rearview mirror because I'm a masochist. The driver of the Focus mutely curses at me and makes the wanker gesture. His facial expression is furious.

I try to apologise with my facial expression.

I move back to the middle lane (checking my wing-mirror this time) and let the Focus overtake.

The guy makes the wanker gesture again as he zooms past me, which makes me giggle/want to smash him off the road.

After the shock has drained and I can't see the Focus in the distance any more I switch on the radio and try to relax into the journey.

Four hours to go yet.

I notice how green from the rain the trees are on either side of the motorway. They look like giant broccoli, dense with protein, dietary fibre and vitamin C.

I tap the steering wheel to the beat of the song (it's Radio 1 and I don't know the name of any new artists anymore).

Then the news comes on.

'In the early hours of this morning a sinkhole appeared in Manchester city centre. Five people were seriously injured as an entire intersection collapsed, creating a hole twenty metres in diameter and partially destroying the foundations of surrounding commercial buildings.'

I switch the radio off. Sinkholes give me the fantods.

I think about what I might have for dinner later.

Broccoli would be good. Maybe just an entire broccoli.

Maybe two?

No. That would be greedy.

When I finally arrive at Mum and Dad's I notice Mum twitch the lace net and peer out the window.

I breathe in through the nose, out through the mouth.

It's the same semi-detached house I grew up in.

Hardly anything has changed from the outside, though it looks like Dad has recently painted the garage door again.

The front lawn is mown. The bushes are trimmed. Their car is sitting on the sloped driveway, freshly washed.

The flag of St. George is blazoned above the porch in the window of my old bedroom, which is now the 'gym', apparently.

I open the boot and lug things to the front step.

Mum opens the door, steps out, hugs me.

She's dyed her hair again and is wearing fashionable yet age-appropriate clothes, but her face betrays her end-of-term tiredness.

She's a dedicated primary school teacher, a workaholic.

'I'll get your dad. He can help you with your stuff.'

'Thanks,' I say, struggling into the hallway. 'He's still got the flag up I see.' I nod upward.

'It's from when the World Cup was on. They didn't make it to the Euros this year so he's clinging onto it.'

'It's embarrassing having it up there. Doesn't it bother you?'

'No, not really,' she says, firmly. 'It's patriotic, that's all. Anyway, let's not start all that. Col! Jamie's here! Come and give him a hand!'

'Here Mum, this is for you.'

I leave the carrier bag containing the wine next to the shoe rack.

'Ooh, lovely. Thanks darling. Not that I drink of course.'

She winks at me and smiles.

51

'Obviously,' I say.

She tuts. 'Where's your dad got to? Colin!'

'It's all right Mum, I'll get the rest in a bit.'

We go through to the kitchen and she puts the kettle on. 'Tea?'

'Just hook it to my veins,' I say, proffering the vein in the crook of an elbow.

She gets on with making the tea. I rest against the counter by the fridge. I look at the fridge magnets, all of them arranged in rectilinear tessellation, none of them overlapping or crooked.

'Keep calm and have a cup of tea,' one of them reads.

'I would give up alcohol but I'm no quitter.'

'As far as anyone knows we're a nice, normal family,' reads another one.

Mum hands me my tea. The teabag is still in the cup and the milk hasn't been stirred.

'I just need to take the washing out of the machine,' she says, touching my elbow. 'You know where everything is.'

I smile and kiss her on the cheek and she leaves. I pick the teabag out of the cup and drop it in the sink. Wet, metallic thud.

I slurp the tea and look out the window to the garden.

I love this garden.

The house, not so much.

But the garden. The garden has always been special.

Dad emerges from the shed holding a spade.

His remaining hair is almost entirely silver now.

He's clean-shaven and wearing an old England rugby shirt baggy enough to hide his gut.

He rests the spade against the back fence, which is covered in wisteria.

Other shed items are resting against the fence too; more are arranged on the lawn, including the lawnmower and a deflated paddling pool from when I was little.

Dad sees me and lifts his head in greeting.

I put a hand up.

Dad goes into the shed again.

He's having a clear-out, before the first cold snap hits.

19

After a fitful night's sleep I wake up long after Mum and Dad have left the house for work.

I mosey to the front room with a fresh cup of tea and open several tabs in my browser, including The Guardian and multiple temp agency sites, imagining all the amazing things I might do now that I'm 'free'.

Politics students from Manchester are supposed to go into the Foreign Office or the Diplomatic Service or some-such, but I quickly realised these paths weren't open to me, because of both forced and unforced errors.

I imagined instead that I would somehow make my fortune in an unconventional way.

I still imagine this.

I didn't think to apply for any jobs before returning to Rainham; it was all so spur-of-the-moment.

But England is a land of Hope and Glory, thank goodness, so I'm not worried.

All over the country, the streets are paved with fool's gold.

I'll take anything going: cleaner, postman, car-washer, call-centre rep, binman, whatever.

It will only be temporary.

There's a copy of The Sun on the coffee table in front of me.

Dad's.

I'll have to have a word with him about that when he gets in from work.

I pick it up and have a quick peek at page three.

Put it back down, ashamed.

Open a new tab. Google the words 'hope' and 'glory'.

Google tells me that usage over time for these words has steadily declined since the nineteenth century. Google's algorithms also show that higher frequency words and phrases around this time include 'credit crunch', 'generation rent', 'quantitative easing', 'in-work poverty' and 'memeplex'.

The phrase 'friendly fire' has become more fashionable, more prominent in the lexicon.

But I don't care about all this negative stuff.

Don't give a furrrk.

I'm in possession of a P.M.A.

I have a 'can-do' mentality. I'm a 'team player'. I can 'foster positive interpersonal relationships with all stakeholders'. I 'take the initiative with projects, have proven ability to multi-task, and possess sharp attention to detail'.

I fully expect a 'Claire de Lune' ending of birds dreaming in the trees and fountains sobbing in ecstasy.

(Or maybe it will be more like Kerouac's offering to the world in the end: 'a peaceful sorrow at home'.)

Whatever.

Everything will work out fine, I just know it will!!!!!!!!!!!!!!!!!!! !!

However, to defray ongoing sundry administration costs, I've had to whore myself out in perpetuity for ad-revenue, so here's a short pop-up message from an unofficial sponsor, Credit Crunch.

It flashes across my laptop screen:

'Try Credit Crunch, the high-in-cardboard, low-in-fibre

breakfast cereal for those who can't afford real breakfast cereal.

Captain Credit Crunch says: 'Hi everyone, fuck you!'

Captain Credit Crunch is wearing a dirty pilot's cap and has week-old stubble and bloodshot eyes.

The words come out of his mouth in animated, flashing gif form, alternating between 'Hi everyone!' and 'Fuck you!'

I stare at the gif for a long time, mesmerised.

20

Alice wasn't a relentlessly terrible person to be with.
I've fallen head over heels out of love with her, yes. She was a crazy bastard too, in her own way.

But I can still appreciate some of the kindnesses she showed me, some of the care she'd been capable of in the early days of our relationship and after my diagnosis. I'm not a complete arsehole.

I'm an incomplete arsehole.

She was good at calming me down whenever I was on the verge of another panic attack.

She was into 'mindfulness', and taught me how to steady my thoughts when my mind was foundering in an ocean of anxiety.

I try it now, sitting on the floor of the front room.

It isn't working yet.

I want my thoughts to drift by, 'like leaves floating downstream', to use one of her phrases.

But they keep getting snagged on detritus.

Random events from the past year intrude into my consciousness, building up and forming clumps along the riverbank.

I open my eyes, close them again ('Not too tight').

Focus on my breath.

The year is 2008 CE/AD.

Two Thousand and Eight. Twenty Oh Eight. Common Era. Anno Domini.

In the year of our Lord.

Let the leaves float downstream.

Is Barack Obama a good thing? He seems to be.

Our Lord and Saviour.

Breathe.

Maybe we're projecting our desires onto him. We want him to be good.

But we don't have enough information.

About anything.

Inhale. Exhale.

Heath Ledger, Arthur C. Clarke, George Carlin, Albert Hoffman and Grandad Carl, the last of my grandparents, all dead.

Everyone dies.

Breathe.

Need a new phone. Don't want to contribute to Apple, the bastards.

Might have to go to Bluewater.

Bluewater isn't just a shopping centre, it's a portal to hell. Celebrating its ninth birthday this weekend; accordingly there are incredible sales, fantastic savings, mind-blowing deals across many of its stores!

Hell.

We're living in a simulation.

Hello, hell.

Cogito ergo sum.

iPhone therefore I am.

Breathe.

People camp outside Apple stores overnight to await the release of the latest device, what the eff.

Focus.

Gillingham challenging for promotion to League One; Man Utd top of the Premier League, the bastards.

Stop looking at the paper. Focus on your breath.

Noel Gallagher is still annoyed that Jay-Z headlined Glastonbury.

Apparently that's news.

In through the nose, out through the mouth.

The Guardian's better.

Dad should read The Guardian.

The Telegraph, even. Just, no more tabloids dude.

He's scared he won't understand the unfamiliar words.

Dictionary.com, motherfucker.

Breathe.

He's not a stupid man. He used to read all the time. He has a large vocabulary.

Has a lot of 'common sense'.

Too much, probably. Needs more 'individual sense'.

Needs to embrace learning. Embrace uncertainty. Embrace negative capability.

The Guardian isn't perfect though.

Still makes it seem as though the world is burning.

Inhale.

Today The Guardian features a recent poll indicating that the majority of British society won't permit the kind of socialism that helps refugee families in need of council flats; that across the land, everyone but the Occupy movement and its supporters are tacitly permitting the kind of socialism that bails out gigantic, too-big-to-fail multinational banks who, res ipsa loquitur, turned a blind eye to the money-laundering of Russian oligarchs and to collateralised debt obligations' lack of structural integrity.

Exhale.

Features inter alia Paris Hilton and humans who are murdering other humans on behalf of various abstract entities such as the UK, the US, NATO, Al-Qaeda, the Taliban, plus other groups fighting internecine conflicts within Afghanistan and Iraq, amongst other regions.

Features yet more articles on the melting ice-caps, the decimation of the Amazon basin, and the coming extinction of bees.

Things are getting better though.

Float downstream.

Aren't they?

Breathe.

The world is less violent than ever. There are graphs to prove it.

But there is still so much suffering.

Samsara.

Maybe Obama will stop the suffering of the world. Our Lord and Saviour.

Agnus Dei.

There are just too many things to know.

Too many variables.

Too much for the papers to report.

There must be a googolplex^{googolplex} (at least) fractal events unfolding in the 'multiverse' right now, all of them attributable, as far as we know, to the curious traits and behaviours of time-crystals (if they exist) and bosons (force-carrier particles).

Breathe.

Which are in turn connected to the multitudinous stochastic processes performed by fermions (matter particles), agglomerating and separating in Brownian motion -- according to their programming (?) -- into multifarious molecular configurations, creating integrative levels of more complex, self-organising, emergent systems such as ancient forests, pandemics, snowflakes, human consciousness, traffic roundabouts, computer algorithms and flocking birds, in a teleonomic fashion, an infinitesimal fraction of which we are capable of perceiving, let alone understanding, with our limited primate brains.

And we don't have the faintest idea how it all started.

Pratityasamutpada. The interdependent origination of all the forms and phases of life.

The papers aren't going to sell more copies writing about that, are they?

Namaste.

I open my eyes and adopt my famous botched yoga pose. Hold it until my feet get pins and needles.

I roll out of the pose, flex my feet, enjoy the throbbing of blood in my toes.

I sit on the settee, open my laptop again, close the Guardian website.

Open a new tab and watch 'The Pleasure of Finding Things Out' by Richard Feynman on YouTube, which makes me feel slightly better about everything.

This video always does the trick. Thank you, Richard.

Namaste.

Now must go.

Time to make my fortune.

Sat chit ananda, cogito ergo sum, caveat emptor.

Ommmmmmmmmmmmmmmmmmmmm.

21

The novelty of moving back home palls very quickly.

As in, immediately.

Two days I've been back in my old room sleeping on an inflatable single mattress, living out of my broken, sad-looking suitcase, with that St. George's cross hanging in the tiny window and a barely-used treadmill in the corner (the 'gym').

They always called my room the 'shoebox room' and it's only gotten smaller.

I have to leave the suitcase out on the landing opposite my brother's old room, which is now the 'study', and leave my boxes of books and CDs in the car if I want any floorspace at all.

I'm aware, somewhere at the periphery of my mind, that I've hit a new low and this isn't where I'd hoped I'd be at this stage in my life, but I have no idea what I should do, or what I even want to do.

Andrea wants me to buy a house and make her a grandmother.

All I want is to sleep for a thousand years.

I think of Caitlin. Costa Rica. White rum. The beach ceremony. Eudaimonia.

A great tiredness has descended on me; I'm beginning to shut down.

But it's time to get up and look for a job.

I email my CV around to various places.

Decide I should get dressed and wander into town to interact with other human beings.

I take out all my balled socks from my suitcase. I need a pair that will go with my 'smart' trousers.

Mum appears at the top of the stairs. She's smiling one of her neurotic smiles, watching me unpack my stuff.

I know the mess is painful for her.

She'd put this down to her 'OCD', which she doesn't really have.

Everyone says they have OCD these days. It's a way of getting sympathy for being an uptight control freak.

And it devalues the term -- as when people who are merely bored or temporarily sad say they're 'depressed' -- so that those who really do have the illness aren't taken seriously.

Mum is just anal about clutter. Probably because, in a chaotic world, she can at least exert some control over her own house when everything else is mayhem. That's understandable.

Still bloody annoying though.

She manages not to say anything, which I silently give her credit for, though I know in a couple of days the nagging will start. I'm running out of time already.

'Why aren't you at work?' I say.

'First day of the summer holidays. Yay!'

She does a little hands-only celebratory dance.

'Oh, cool.'

'Not that I'll get to relax much,' she says. 'I've got so much marking and planning to do.'

'Take a few days off at least.'

'I don't want to leave it all to the last minute.'

'You've got six weeks off, Mum. You can afford to have some down time.'

'Maybe. Anyway, I was going to ask, will you be wanting dinner tonight?'

I'm planning on sitting in the local pub on my own and reading a book.

'I think I'm going to meet a friend later,' I lie.

Dad hears this from downstairs and yells up, 'He's only been back five minutes and he's already treating this place like a hotel!'

I pull a face.

'Just ignore him,' says Mum.

'Andrea!' yells Dad. 'You seen my toolbox anywhere?'

'It's under the stairs,' says Mum.

'What's it doing there?'

Mum tuts. 'The cleaner must have put it there.'

'What cleaner!'

'I'm talking about me, you daft bugger.'

She half-smiles.

I do nothing with my face.

'Thanks for the offer, but I'll probably eat out,' I say.

'No problem. Don't forget your key.'

'Mum, I'm not a child.'

'You'll always be my baby,' she says, coming towards me and pinching my cheek. 'Goochy goochy goo.'

'Get off me, woman,' I say, reluctantly laughing.

22

head to the bus stop.

It's drizzly. Not quite raining, not quite not raining.

Should've taken the car. Oh well.

I wait with my cheap umbrella for the 132 bus heading to Chatham Bus Station.

Wearing smart trousers with odd socks -- fuck the system!

The 132 is the same bus I sometimes caught to and from school.

I only got it when it was pouring with rain and I couldn't get a lift with a friend's mum.

You took your life into your hands on that bus.

People from my rival school also caught it.

They hated people from our school indiscriminately because they all failed their eleven-plus (or opted not to take it) and didn't get into our school, the grammar school.

We were 'boffs' and the rival kids liked to torture us because of it.

Fair enough.

It's not a cool thing to do to a bunch of kids: separate them based on a single, flawed test.

You're 'bright', go to this school; you're not as bright, go to that school.

As though intelligence is a fixed thing that can't change. As though there is only one way to be intelligent. As though most of the eleven-plus kids weren't merely absorbing all that middle-class cultural capital around the dinner table, getting a head-start.

And there are some among us who want to re-introduce grammar schools to the rest of the country!

Haven't they seen the damage it's done to Kent?

It's a riven county!

I remember when I was maybe thirteen or fourteen and caught the 132 one afternoon.

The lower deck was full so I went up to the top deck.

The bus pulled away and I had to grip the handrail as the g-force kicked in.

I hauled myself to the top. Felt pure dread flood my body as I realised the entire top deck was occupied by students from the other place.

Except for one lad at the back from my school who looked like he was in year 7. He was wearing an oversized blazer and had a gigantic holdall in the aisle by his feet.

A poor little boff on the 132.

There was nowhere for me to sit, so I perched at the top of the steps.

Surreptitiously zipped my coat to the top to hide my blazer and tie.

It was raucous up there. Everyone seemed to be yelling and laughing.

The little boff was being tormented by a group of older kids. He looked traumatised but was trying to hold it together.

They were taking turns flicking his ears.

Aggressively mussing his hair.

One of them, a girl with a 'Croydon facelift' and gigantic

hoop earrings, stood up and booted the boff's holdall down the aisle.

The little boff watched helplessly as it was booted further and further towards the front of the bus by people from each subsequent row.

It eventually reached me. The rival kids on the seats nearest to me eyed me expectantly, like I should kick it down the stairs to keep the demonic game going.

But the bus jerked to a halt and I was off the hook: it was their stop.

Dozens of them left the top deck, stamping on the holdall and barging past me as they went down the stairs.

The bus pulled away again and I took an empty seat at the front.

I turned around to inspect the situation.

The top deck was mostly empty now but the little boff was still at the back, still surrounded by a few remaining kids from the other place.

I reached down and pulled the boff's holdall towards me, brushed some of the mud and dust from it.

I wanted to go and help but was too skinny, too weak, too afraid.

I looked over at them again.

The boff was silently crying now.

I thought, Don't cry little boff. In twenty years it won't matter. Sure, this moment will psychologically damage you forever, but at least you will have learned something.

You have become a man today, little boff.

The boff was still crying and the rival kids were escalating the torture.

They were unremitting.

The girl took out a lighter.

Flicked it a couple of times but it didn't catch.

Shk shk.

Then a flame appeared. She touched the flame to the boff's head and a patch of hair above his ear briefly caught fire.

The boff screamed.

I instinctively stood up but didn't move.

Another rival kid got up, unzipped his trousers and took out his cock.

It was an absurdly big cock. Maybe not that big in the scheme of things, but it seemed big at the time.

It was weird to see someone with a boy's face and a man's cock.

The first word that popped into my head was 'unholy'.

The boy pissed on the boff's head. The fire went out almost immediately but he carried on pissing.

I sat down again.

The rival kid shook the last few drops onto the boff's head and put his monstrous cock away.

They were all laughing and whooping.

The bus stopped again. They got up and walked to the front of the bus, single file.

The pisser was the last in line. Before he went down the stairs he kicked the holdall back towards the boff.

Yelled, 'Don't forget your bag!'

They alighted the pavement and the bus pulled away.

I looked out the window at them on the pavement, getting smaller as the bus accelerated.

To the untrained eye they were happy and innocent and care-free.

The pisser was the happiest of all. A happy kid with a big cock, on his way home from school, probably recounting what had just happened to his buddies, re-living the moment.

What japes! What larks!

I got up and took the holdall towards the boff, trying to keep my balance as the bus rumbled along.

The boff didn't look at me as I sat across the aisle from him.

I dropped the holdall by his feet. The boff was soaked in piss.

Just, utterly wet and defeated.

I silently vowed to avenge him one day. I fantasised about becoming a masked superhero, annihilating all the bullies of the world.

Taking flying kicks at them all and bashing their chests in like empty cardboard boxes. Performing roundhouse kicks and knocking their heads off like car wing-mirrors.

But instead I just got off the bus at my stop and grew up and left Medway and became Jamie Sinclair.

23

And now Jamie Sinclair is back on the 132 at the age of 24. On my way to Chatham to look for a job, any job, in the rain.

Medway, give me a job you bastard!

Medway, give my life meaning!

Medway, touch me, I'm cold!

Medway, oh Medway, I will touch you where you need to be touched!

I will say this for the 132: it has a good pattern on its seats.

Very 'eighties'. Yellow, pink and grey geometric shapes on a turquoise background.

Nice!

I take a seat by a window. I put my soggy umbrella under the seat.

Have to sit almost sideways because the leg-room isn't fit for an average-height human being.

The bus pulls over at the next stop.

A woman, maybe my age, gets on with her baby in a pram.

Followed by Silly Billy. Silly Billy is a well-known local character.

I didn't give him that name, Medway did. He has an intellectual impairment and has been homeless for as long as I can remember.

He always needs 'two quid' for the bus. That's what he asks for if he stops you in the street.

Sometimes you give it, sometimes you don't; he won't hassle you too much either way.

Today he has a little money: he pays the driver and sits opposite the young woman and her baby.

He looks the same as the image I have of him in my memory, though he must have aged at least ten years since I last saw him in person: He's still in need of a good meal, a good bath, a good dentist.

The bus is on the move again, its dump valve hissing each time the driver changes gears.

Silly Billy is staring at the woman, smiling.

I know he's harmless but the woman doesn't. The woman busies herself with her baby, straightening its blanket, using a baby wipe to remove some imaginary muck from its face.

I get up and move closer to them, to try and help the woman feel less anxious.

Maybe the woman will appreciate this and fall in love with me.

Her hair is wet.

Maybe she'll go to Costa Rica with me where it's sunny all year round.

She could stand on the balcony of our apartment and let her hair dry in the morning sun.

Maybe she would overlook my unfixable defect and we could attain eudaimonia.

I stand in the aisle, holding onto one of the dangling grips, swaying to and fro.

I suddenly get a hit of Silly Billy's stench.

I can taste his smell. Like a bin on a hot day.

Silly Billy notices me.

'I like your shoes mate,' Silly Billy says. 'Well nice.'

'Aw, thanks,' I say.

'They're well nice,' Silly Billy says again.

'I like them too.'

I should invite Silly Billy back to my mum and dad's, let him use the shower, give him some food.

Why not?

'Hey mate, you ain't got two quid do ya? I'm trying to get to London.'

He's always trying to get to London. Everyone's trying to get to London.

I pat my back pocket, pull out some change, about 70p.

'That's all I've got I'm afraid.'

Silly Billy takes the coins and stuffs them in a pocket.

'Fanks mate,' he says, then looks at the woman with the pram. 'What about you love. You got two quid? I'm trying to get to London.'

The woman shakes her head and continues fussing over the baby.

The bus pulls over and Silly Billy stands up ready to alight. He puts his fist out for me to fist-bump.

'Boom,' I say, as our fists connect.

I open my hand and make a quiet explosion noise.

'Haha, boom!' says Silly Billy, imitating the gesture. 'Boom!'

Silly Billy gets off the bus.

The woman looks at me and widens her eyes as if to say, 'What a crazy bastard.'

I do something with my face in response, but I'm not sure whether it's a smile or a frown.

The bus pulls into the Pentagon Centre bus station.

Everyone gets off and enters the mall via the service doors that lead to the lifts.

It's quiet. There's half-a-dozen people standing in close proximity but no-one talks. We wait silently for the big silver doors of the lifts to open.

I push the 'call lift' button more than is necessary, causing the neon green halo around it to turn off and on each time. The woman with the baby lines up the pram with the doors, ready to enter.

I feel very at home in this mall, especially when it's prematurely dark and rainy outside, as it is now.

Most people shop at Bluewater now; the Pentagon is a ghost town.

But I feel loyal to it.

Not sure why exactly. Nostalgia, maybe. The look of the floor maybe: polished concrete with exposed aggregate.

Also the fry-up smells from Star Burger drifting in from the food arcade which commingles with the lingering diesel from the bus station that girds the building.

Also the general eighties style of the mall.

I just feel good when I'm here, always have. Is that a crime?

It's an awful place, but I still like it.

When I was young, Mum would take my brother and me shopping with her. I thought of the Pentagon as a strange, giant, complex playground, and didn't understand how adults could be unhappy when they were free to roam around places like this whenever they liked.

Mum always looked so miserable and stressed there, wanted

to get home as soon as possible. I wanted to run around with John, ride on the escalators, hide among the showroom beds in C&A, play Cowboys and Indians, roller-skate across the smooth, exposed-aggregate flooring.

Pentagons were my favourite shape as well.

I was a simple boy.

Later, when I was a teenager, I would come here to hang out with friends.

Mall rats.

We'd go bowling sometimes, if we had any money.

Let's! Go! Bowling!

That's what the guy used to say in the advert for Pentagon Bowling that aired on local TV.

We'd yell it to each other as we ran up the carpeted steps, which were covered in little bowling pins.

Let's! Go! Bowling!

If it was dark and rainy I would pretend I was a successful employee working for a high-flying company in Manhattan, the sort who gets up when it's dark and arrives home when it's dark; the sort who has a stylish umbrella and wears an expensive raincoat and keeps secret documents in a briefcase that his beautiful, knock-out wife can never know about; the sort who goes bowling with friends after work.

Stupid, but the mall reminded me of New York.

Still does.

I haven't been to New York, am pretty sure I'd hate New York (too much like London), but the orange-red brick, the grey concrete and the layers of glass windows of the high-rise office block that house this mall remind me of movies set in

New York.

The interior design of the shopping centre hints at progress – hints at an ambition far greater than it's entitled to – which captures the ethos of the Big Apple somehow.

'I am still a simple boy,' I think.

The lift arrives and everyone steps into it.

I gesture for the woman with the pram go ahead and she smiles.

Inside the lift it's the perfect combination of faux-Art Deco wood-panelling and futuristic chrome that I love.

It's so New York.

I feel incredible. I'm smiling at the buttons as the lift ascends to the top floor of the mall, like we're going up the Empire bloody State Building.

I smile all the way up. I smile until tears come to my happy, optimistic eyes.

I sniff back the tears.

The woman with the pram asks me if I'm okay.

'Incredible,' I whisper.

'Do you want a tissue?'

She offers me a Kleenex from a shelf on the pram.

'Thanks,' I say, taking it. I dab my eyes.

'No problem,' she says, moving herself and the pram ever-so-slightly further away from me.

24

Listen.

My accent's different now.

When I lived in Medway as a kid it was the local accent.

Now it's a version of 'Received Pronunciation'.

I cultivated the new accent at university when I found myself in seminars with students who'd been to private school.

I'd been embarrassed to speak aloud in the seminars; could feel the other students evaluating my intelligence based on my accent; felt 'common', even though I knew I'd achieved better A-level grades than many of them.

So I doctored my voice.

My accent is less jagged now, though I'm just as self-conscious of it. I've done a splendid job sanding down the 'Estuarine' edges and buffing the 'Mockney' surfaces.

My supercilious English teachers would be proud if they could hear me now.

Professor Higgins would approve.

I've nipped and tucked those nasty 'shibboleths' of Medway. Scrubbed all traces of my natural dialect.

No more glottal (gloʔal) stops; no more dropped t's or h's.

I say 'thanks' now, not 'fanks'; say 'isn't', not 'ain't'.

I add yods, as well: 'tishoo' and 'ishoo' have become 'tissyou' and 'issyou' respectively.

Strangers meeting me for the first time often assume I'm intelligent and/or financially stable, even if I say nothing particularly insightful or astute and the subject of money doesn't come up.

In these situations I hate myself for being a complete phoney, but I hate the other person too for being credulous enough to buy into the game so many of us are playing.

25

I walk from the Pentagon centre out to the High Street.

The non-rain has stopped. The smell of burger grease and frying onions hangs in the air.

A lot of Medway smells like that. It's Medway's signature scent.

Alienation, by Calvin Klein.

I pass Argos and Cash Converters and the burger van producing the smell, and enter a temp agency.

A guy wearing a shiny suit and a skinny tie approaches me with intense, aggressive amiability.

He has a giant quiff, but not a rockabilly quiff. It's vertical, held in place by super-strength hairspray. It travels at least six inches straight up from his forehead.

He shakes my hand with gusto.

'Alright boss,' he says in a broad Medway accent. 'Can I help yoo?'

'I hope so,' I say in my bastardised accent. 'I'm looking for a job.'

The guy beams. 'You're in the right place, boss!'

He slaps me on the arm and takes me to his 'workstation'.

'Ave a seat boss.' He sits behind his desk and logs onto his computer. 'Let's get you registered.'

He takes my particulars and inputs them.

We talk for a bit about what I'm looking for, what my goals are.

I make some stuff up, thinking all the while about Costa

Rica, Caitlin, white rum, eudaimonia.

'Wicked,' the guy says. 'Sorted.'

He presses return on the keyboard with panache. 'Next up is the skill-set evaluation. You got time to do a couple of tests? There's a Microsoft Word test, an Excel one and an Outlook one. It'll take twenty minutes, tops.'

'Sure,' I say.

'Awesome,' he says. 'Follow me, boss.'

He leads me into another room where there's a row of old, off-cream-coloured desktop computers. Nothing on the walls. A coat of dust on the grille of the air-vent in the top corner. Dirty grey carpet.

He sets me up and explains what's involved.

'When you've finished, giz a yell. I'll be at my workstation next door.'

'Thanks,' I say.

I complete the tests, which evaluate my ability to do things such as put text into columns, turn a data-set into a pie-chart and send an email to multiple recipients.

I click 'submit' at the end and go back to the guy.

'Whoa, lightning!' the guy says. He taps his desk a couple of times with both hands. 'What I'll do is add the results to your profile and we'll be in touch.'

'Don't you have any openings at the moment?' I ask.

'To be honest boss, there ain't much going right now. But as soon as summink comes up I'll ping you an email.'

'You could have told me that before.'

'It's just the, y'know, standard protocol.'

Protocol.

He gets up, which makes me get up. He shakes my hand.

'Things are bit slow right now but I'll be in touch.'

I suddenly imagine Caitlin in a hospital, marching down a corridor, pulling on latex gloves, getting ready to attend to a patient outstretched on an operating table.

I imagine myself outstretched on the operating table. Numb but awake. Caitlin trying to operate on my unfixable defect.

'Fanks for coming in boss,' the guy says, ushering me out the door.

'No problem,' I say, and step outside.

It's raining again.

I pause under the overhang of the temp agency.

Umbrella?

Shit. Left it on the bus.

I jog along the High Street and into the Pentagon Centre, which, despite being only 50 or so metres away, is far enough to make me sodden.

I stop to window-shop at a men's clothing store just inside the mall. A puddle forms around me on the awesome aggregate flooring. There's a stylish raincoat on one of the mannequins. A stylish umbrella is gripped by its lifeless hand.

So New York.

I peer at the price tag dangling from the wooden handle.

It's more than I have in my current account.

I wander back to the bus station to wait for the 132 to take me home.

26

'Can you go to Tesco for me, love?' Mum asks. 'We need a few bits.'

I'm in the front room again, on my laptop again, looking at Caitlin Gilberthorpe's Facebook profile.

She works at a hospital in London now. She doesn't seem to have a boyfriend.

'Love?'

'I said yes.'

'No you didn't.'

'I did.'

'You didn't.'

'Okay, well, I'll go in a bit.'

'Thanks.'

This keeps happening. Me thinking I've said something when I only thought it.

My mouth can't keep up with my brain. I'm slurring and tripping over words and struggling to finish sentences.

Torpor.

It's like I'm moving across the surface of a planet with very strong gravity.

Everything is

      slooowing

           dowwwn

        and

              greying

                 out.

I log off Facebook, fetch the re-usable carrier bags from under the kitchen sink and get in the car.

It takes me at least three minutes to start the car.

I arrive at Tesco and amble around the store with a trolley.

I get to the frozen aisle and come to a halt. I stand there, myself frozen, looking at nothing, when someone I went to school with comes up and taps me on the shoulder.

Louise Someone. I can't remember her last name. She looks healthy and happy. I'm certain I don't. I've neglected to groom myself for a few days. I have goosebumps from standing next to the frozen pizzas.

'Jamie Sinclair, hi!'

She smiles a friendly smile.

I respond slowly, like my words are trapped in a force-field. 'Oh, hi Louise,
how's it
going?'

'Great thanks. You're looking well. Love the beard.'

'Thanks, I love yours too. What have you
been up to?'

We chat for a bit, and arrange to go for a drink later, to 'catch up'.

When I get home from shopping I put everything in its right place.

I make sure all the tins have the labels facing outwards – no sense in triggering Andrea's 'OCD' – then I go upstairs to the bathroom and think about Louise Someone while half-heartedly masturbating.

But later on when I have to leave the house to go and meet

82

her I feel weirdly shy and devoid of any desire to see her.

It's like someone's glued me to the armchair.

It takes forever, but I text her a flimsy, tardy, greyed-out excuse. She rightly responds with coldness and finality.

I spend the night like a latency-stage teenager playing Tekken on my old Playstation 2 until the early hours of the morning.

27

Mum knocks on my door the next afternoon when I'm still in 'bed'.

I don't answer.

She pokes her head around the door then opens it wide.

'So that's where all the bowls are.'

I glance at the small leaning tower of breakfast bowls near my feet. 'Yeah, sorry.'

'You know it annoys your father when you don't take them downstairs.'

Bullshit, Mum. It annoys you more. 'I know. But he won't have to put up with it much longer. I'll find a place soon.'

'You need to see a doctor,' she says, hands on hips. 'I'm worried about you. Have you been taking your medication?'

'Actually, I've run out.'

'Right, well, we're going to the doctor first thing tomorrow.'

'Mum, I don't need it. It makes me feel like a zombie.'

'I don't care. The doctor in Manchester said you were to continue on it until further notice. And you know this is what happened to your dad. He would stay in bed all day, then he ended up walking to Tonbridge in the middle of the night and then he, well, you remember. He tried to... He took too many of his pills with some of his whisky.'

'Mum, come on.'

'Well, that's what happened. I won't sugarcoat it.'

'This is completely different.'

'Is it?'

'I don't need a doctor. I don't need medication. I need this country to change. I need its people to change.'

'How are you going to make that happen?'

'I'm not, it's impossible.'

'Oh darling, you're so melodramatic. And so pessimistic.'

She strides into the room to adjust the blinds and open the window. Light and air invade the room. I cover my face with a forearm and hiss like Nosferatu.

'Mum, leave the blinds alone. Why are you even in here?'

She flat-out ignores me.

'You have no right to be a pessimist,' she says, folding some of my dirty clothes. 'Where's your get-up-and-go? There are millions of people in the world worse off than you. Millions upon millions upon millions of them. Many of them have no homes, or food, or access to clean water even.'

'Is this supposed to make me feel better.'

'You should count your blessings, is what I'm saying. You should be seizing the day. The world is a beautiful place.'

'You just painted a pretty un-beautiful picture of it.'

'No I didn't.'

'Um, the millions and millions and millions of people? The fucked people? You brought them into this.'

'Don't swear.'

'Sorry. The doomed people.'

'They're not *doomed*. Many of them are happy. You see them on the telly sometimes. They have absolutely nothing yet they're still happy. Puts things into perspective.'

'Mum, that is insane. You're confusing the uncontacted people who've voluntarily lived in the Amazon or New Guinea their entire lives with people who've been fucked -- sorry, *ruined*

-- by war or famine or globalisation. Because those people are definitely not happy.'

'Look, Jamie, all I'm saying is you need to get out of bed.' She bends down to pick up the tower of bowls and cradles them against her body. 'And go to the doctors.'

She closes the door.

I sink back into a powerful sleep.

28

It's one of our silent dinners.

Me, Mum, Dad.

In the dining room, which has been redecorated at least once a year for the last twenty years and always smells like potpourri and new carpet.

Eating my signature vegetarian spaghetti bolognese, which is as 'foreign' as it gets in Col's house.

The only noise the scraping and chinking of knives and forks against plates.

It's like I never left home.

It's Autumn already.

Memories of my life in Manchester have faded like polaroids left out in the summer sun.

After a while Col pipes up.

'You need to stop parking your car so far away from the driveway. You're encroaching on Kevin's space next door.'

'Okay,' I say.

'And would it kill you to put the hoover round the joint?'

'I did, this morning.'

'Well it don't look like it.'

'Mum, tell him.'

'It's true, Col, he did. But darling, perhaps you could go behind the settee next time? There's months of dust back there.'

'Okay. I don't see why that's suddenly my problem, but okay.'

'It's the least you can do, to help out around here.'

'I am helping out, but unfortunately I don't have the same absurdly high standards of cleanliness as you. Clean enough to be healthy, dirty enough to be happy, that's what I say.'

'We shouldn't have to lower our standards for you!'

'I'm not asking you to!'

'Don't yell at me!'

'Sorry.'

'You found a job yet?' says Dad.

'Not yet.'

'Perhaps you shouldn't be sleeping in so much,' says Mum.

'What time did you get up today?' says Dad.

'I don't know. But I've signed up with a temp agency. And I've been emailing my CV around.'

'You should get down the job centre.'

'I will. I've made an appointment.'

'Good. Because I won't have any son of mine signing onto the dole.'

'It's okay, I've got some savings.'

'But that should be for a house deposit,' says Mum. 'Don't fritter away your money.'

'There's hundreds of jobs out there,' continues Dad, talking over Mum. 'There's no excuse for unemployment. Are you ironing your shirts properly? Appearances are important.'

'It's just atoms covering other atoms,' I say.

'You've always been a bit of a scruffbag, haven't you darling,' says Mum, briefly touching my beard.

I grin, cheeks bulging with pasta. I swallow. 'Can we change the record guys?'

Mum and Dad look at each other briefly and the chinking of plates resumes.

'This vegetarian mince isn't too bad really, is it,' says Mum. 'Maybe we should go full-time veggie too, eh love.'

She nudges Dad, who makes a face like he's chewing newspaper.

Mum looks at me and rolls her eyes. I smile as thinly as possible.

Dad pipes up again.

'Well, since you're still dossing about I need you to come and help me at work tomorrow and Friday. You can paint the two remaining bedrooms. The owners get back on Saturday.'

Dad is a home-improvement factotum. A boiler fitter by trade, he also does painting, decorating, tiling and other sundry jobs that the customers need doing.

He's too tight to pay someone to help him, so he's always stressed about getting the job finished on time.

'I'm busy tomorrow. I have an interview with another temp agency. But I can help you on Friday.'

He doesn't say thanks. He's concentrating on putting ketchup on his bolognese, carefully tapping the bottom of the glass bottle.

I stare at Col's shiny bald pate; shiver slightly as I contemplate my own bald future.

That bit more skull-like, that little bit nearer to death.

'How much will I get paid?' I ask.

Ah, I've given Col an opening. Now he can release some of the pent-up rage.

Col puts the ketchup down and stops chewing.

'I'm letting you stay in my house and eat my food,' he says. 'That's your pay.'

He resumes chewing.

'But I cooked your dinner,' I say. 'And I pay board. So how much are you going to pay me for my labour?'

Col points his fork at me. 'You pay a fraction of what it would actually cost to rent this house,' he says.

'I'm not working for you unless you pay me.'

'Fine! Then you can pack your bags and find a new place to live!'

Mum gives her husband a look.

I feel yet again as though someone has turned up the gravity.

We finish dinner in silence.

The next morning I put on my absurdly expensive suit with the faint vomit stain on the lapel.

Col hadn't said anything else about moving out (Mum would have had a word with him after dinner), so I hadn't packed my bags.

I go downstairs to make a cup of tea.

My interview with the agency isn't until this afternoon but I want Dad to see me in the suit.

Col is in the hallway, doing his bootlaces. It looks like he's on the brink of anger already.

'What time's your interview,' he asks.

'In an hour,' I lie.

Col picks up his toolbox. 'Don't forget you're helping me tomorrow,' he says, and bangs the front door behind him.

I go upstairs and get back into bed.

I keep the suit on, waistcoat and all.

When my alarm goes off, I cancel my appointment with the temp agency.

It's 12.30pm. I physically can't get out of bed.
I call them; the person on the phone is indifferent.
I hang up and push my phone across the carpet.
Turn onto my stomach and slip into another deep, dark sleep.

29

At 5.30am the next day Col throws my door open.

'Time to get up! We're going to be late!'

I was having a dream where everyone was absurdly tall and behaving like arseholes.

I can feel the residual cortisol in my veins, tingling like pins and needles.

I cry for a few minutes, then get up.

This is how I start the day now: with a good cry.

Breakfast of champions.

The house is in an affluent neighbourhood not too far from Mum and Dad's.

It belongs to a dentist and her husband.

We arrive while it's still dark.

The hallway alone is roomier than Mum and Dad's entire house.

Col tells me they have a heated swimming pool in a separate building in the garden.

He seems pretty impressed/angry about that.

'Can I swim in it later?' I ask.

'No!' says Col, stomping up the stairs.

'Go and get the stuff out of the van!' he shouts from the landing.

Col bores the shit out of me explaining how to properly apply the paint to the roller, how to evenly coat the wall, how to go around the edges with a paintbrush.

I tell him I already know how to do it, that I helped him out before a few years ago when I was still in the sixth-form.

'Yeah I remember, but I had to re-do the whole room after you'd knocked off early for the day.'

'You weren't paying me anything,' I say.

'You should have pride in your work no matter how much you earn.'

'I have pride all right. It's the motivation I'm lacking.'

'You said it son!'

Around midday I rest the roller on the paint tray and go into the ensuite where Col's working.

It smells good in there. It smells like grout and glue and tile dust and brand new ceramic fittings. It smells like honest work.

I inform Col that I'm going to get some lunch.

Col's cutting a tile. He doesn't look up from his task immediately. This tells me he thinks I'm slacking off.

The tool squeaks as Col scores a line, the tile snaps in two like a broken plate, the excess piece gently thunks to the linoleum floor.

This done, he slides a soggy, rumpled twenty out of his wallet and tells me to get us both a few things from Tesco down the road.

He says I can keep the change.

'Ah, thanks Dad,' I say.

'I suppose you'll spend it on cigarettes,' says Col.

'I was thinking of investing it,' I say. 'I could buy half a share in Tesco.'

Col ignores my wise-assery and carries on snapping

dinner plates.

'They should get exposed aggregate tiles,' I say. 'They'd look good in here.'

'They're expensive,' says Col.

'I don't think that'd be a problem for these guys.'

'Waste of money. They'd get chipped after five minutes and then you'd have to re-do the whole room.'

'More work for you in that case.'

'I've got enough work to do as it is! Go and get us some lunch!'

I walk to Tesco and get us a meal deal each: sandwiches, crisps and a drink.

I have enough change left over for a large pouch of Golden Virginia, Rizlas and a pack of filter tips.

As I leave the store I say out loud to myself, 'Bawler. Neck level bawler.'

An old lady shuffling in with a shallow trolley smiles at me, but I'm pretty sure she didn't hear what I said.

After lunch I get sick of the radio.

It's tuned to the local station Invicta FM and has been all morning.

'More. Music. Variety,' a voice-tracked DJ keeps saying between each of the thirty-two songs the station plays on a loop every day.

Instead of smashing it against a wall, I switch it to Radio 4.

Col calls out, 'Oi, I was listening to that song!'

'That was the third time they've played it today!'

'Change it to Five Live then!'

'All right.'

Every now and then Dad and I can agree on things.
It always gives me a false sense of hope.

I finish painting the bedrooms and ask Col if there's anything else to be done.

Col gives me a handful of screws.

Tells me to get a screwdriver.

Sends me into the main bathroom to put up some brackets for some shelving.

I set to it.

I like working with my hands.

It gives me delusions of manliness.

I fantasise about setting up my own handyman business one day.

I'd bring good music to listen to, some interesting podcasts to keep myself mentally sharp, and could feel satisfied at the end of the day seeing the immediate fruits of my labour.

I'd get paid pretty well too, cash-in-hand.

I feel inspired!

I think, Maybe this is what I'm meant to do!

No boss!

No pointless office drudgery or busywork to pass the time!

No passive-aggressive bullshit from colleagues!

I could set up a handyman business in Costa Rica, and Caitlin could work at the local hospital, and we'd be happy! We'd finally have some of that sweet, sweet eudaimonia!

I'm really getting into the daydream, but suddenly notice I'm in pain.

I've been pushing too hard with the screwdriver and have given myself the beginnings of a monumental blister, the size of a two-pound coin, right in the centre of my palm.

It's bloody sore, and bothers me for the rest of the day.

It's four o'clock, the time Col had said we'd finish for the day.

I tidy up my areas and find Col in the ensuite.

He's tiled most of the walls, but still has one small section above the basin to grout.

'It's gone four o'clock. If there's nothing else to do I'm off home,' I say.

'We haven't finished yet,' says Col, smearing and pushing a blob of white grout with a trowel into a crack between two tiles.

'Is there anything else I can do?'

Col ignores me while he tries to think of something.

I tidy up around him and take stuff down to the van while he carries on grouting.

There's nothing left to do after that.

'I'm going home,' I say.

'Typical,' says Col.

I decide to walk home and go straight to bed for a nap.

I wake up to Mum calling out 'Dinner!'

I see on the floor next to my inflatable bed an envelope with two £20 notes poking out of it.

My wages.

I did a nine-hour day minus half an hour for lunch and about twenty minutes in total for cigarette breaks.

Works out at just over £5 an hour.

Plus the free lunch and cigs.

Better than minimum wage!

I push my blister with my thumb and go downstairs to eat.

Another silent dinner.

Me, Mum, Dad.

After a while, Mum pipes up.

'How did you go at the agency yesterday?'

'Yeah, okay,' I lie. 'They said they'd call me if anything comes up.'

'Where was it?'

'Gillingham,' I lie.

'Aren't there any agencies in Rainham?'

'No.'

We chew our food for a bit.

'And how did you go today my handsome workers?'

Col grunts.

I hold up the palm of my hand to show off my stigmata.

'Ooh, that looks sore,' she says, beaming. 'Must have been a productive day.'

Dad snorts like I was basically swimming in the pool the whole time, goofing off.

'What's funny,' I say.

'Nothing,' Col says, smirking, avoiding eye contact.

'Thanks for the money,' I say.

'Oh, you earned it son.'

Still smirking, still avoiding eye contact.

I silently vow there and then to move out before the month is up.

With a follow-up vow to let my father die lonely and senile in an old people's home if I end up being the only one left to take care of him in his dotage.

30

Just before I go to bed I read a Facebook message from a guy I went to school with.

Tom Pritchard.

'Oi oi Sinbad, looong time no see.

Heard through the Fbook grapevine that your [sic] moving back to Medway soon. This true? I hope so, it'll be good to have you back. Msg me when your [sic] in town and we'll have to go out for a beer or two. Maybe at The Star like the old days!!

Tom :)'

I don't respond to the message immediately.

I haven't spoken to Tom in at least five years.

Which means no-one has called me Sinbad in that time.

Sinbad is dead, buried, exorcised. Tom is resurrecting him against my will.

The message makes me uneasy.

Tom was part of the 'bad crowd' I fell in with for a couple of years during high school.

My chav years.

For a while I thought of that crowd as a posse of roguish miscreants; rebels with multiples causes.

Perhaps we were.

But we were also delinquents.

Selfish, shitty human beings.

I extricated myself just in time to be able to study enough to pass my GCSEs.

As far as I know Tom is still part of that group.

I haven't thought about Tom much, if at all.

I don't want to allow him into my life again.

Tom irked me.

He would always brag about his expensive new trainers.

And he would take the piss out of my no-brand trainers, which cost like £10 from Shoezone, and mock how my parents couldn't afford to send me on any of the school trips abroad.

Tom's stupid mum would buy him trainers that cost £50 or more; she paid for all the school trips.

Nike, Adidas, New Balance, Reebok, he had them all over the years.

Spain, Egypt, New York -- he had the time of his life.

It was insane. Who spends that kind of money on shoes, let alone when their kids' feet are still growing, and especially when they're made in sweatshops by people treated little better than slaves.

Who allows their children expensive holidays when they make their teachers cry on a regular basis.

Why can't my mum be stupid, I used to think.

I tolerated Tom's annoying behaviour back then because he was in our little squad.

I had a sense of loyalty to that squad, a sense of Mafioso honour.

And it was fun to play the role of one the 'bad boys'.

Being a delinquent didn't come naturally to me, but I was getting taller, filling out. I'd started going to the gym and had learned how to box.

Before long I had a kind of reputation, and that was thrilling for a while, even though I had to continually prove it by fighting the various challengers from our rival school who'd heard about this boff who thought he was hard.

It was Tom who introduced me to the drink.

He used to steal the cheap French beer from his dad's garage, enough to get us tipsy but not enough for his dad to notice.

Cigarettes too.

He looked older than everyone else and was able to bolster the stocks with White Lightning and cheap vodka from the off-licence.

He'd hide it all in the bushes near his house, and the whole squad would arrive at dusk with whatever we'd each been able to pilfer from our own parents' drinking cabinets.

From there we'd roam the streets, tanked up and ready to fight.

It wasn't all fights and arguments though.

Tom could make me laugh.

We were in the same English class one term and were seated next to each other by a new teacher who didn't know any better.

Tom would draw doodles on notepaper and slide them in front of me to try and make me corpse.

Would cut up Pritt-stick and throw it at the teacher's back, silently decorating her with little discs of glue while she carried on writing about subordinate clauses, oblivious.

It continued beyond the confines of the classroom.

A lot of pranks happened on the playground, or the school field.

One time Tom streaked, bollock-naked, across an 'important' football game taking place between our school and the rivals.

He got suspended for that.

But I felt utter relief once I detached myself from the group.

Despite his sense of humour, despite all the booze he provided, Tom would always ruin the good vibe somehow, eventually.

We could go all day having a good time when suddenly Tom would turn on me, become a frenemy, seemingly for no reason.

As the school year went on it got worse; the jokes and pranks got crueller, I became a regular target.

We fought.

I had to stand up to Tom (one of countless playground ape battles) and put him in his place.

We reconciled as we always did, but it kept happening, and after school, the extra-curricular activities got shadier.

I could see that Tom and the group were going too far with some of their escapades (eventually two of them ended up in prison for nine months; if it hadn't been for their good behaviour it would've been eighteen), so I chose to 'evolve' and move on from that rebellious teenage state.

As I choose now to ignore Tom's message.

get another one from him the next night, however.

'Hey Sinbad,

Not sure if you got my last msg. I've been really looking forward to you coming back here. I always respected how you got out of Medway. You were always funny and smart, it's good you actually put your brain to use. Tbh I sometimes hate it here. I'm still hanging out with the old squad but their [sic] a bunch of dicks.

Sorry, bit drunk right now, lol.

Just wanted to say that I think it will be good to catch up.

Laters, Tom

Ps, did you hear about Lauren Hitchens?'

I did hear about Lauren Hitchens.

It was all over Facebook.

Lauren is another person I went to school with.

She was recently in the local news.

She didn't know her baby was playing near the open window of their first floor flat.

She was passed out in a heroin-induced coma, that's why.

The baby crawled out and fell onto the awning of the shop below, bounced off it and landed on an old man walking along the street beneath.

Both baby and old man were okay.

Lauren now spends a lot of time on Facebook ranting about Social Services.

I wish she could be okay.

Oh Sweet and Sour Lord, what am I doing back in Medway?

Tom Pritchard, why are you contacting me?

You're not my friend.

None of my actual friends live in Medway. (And would they still consider me their friend?)

There's nothing to do.

I don't want to see you, Tom; don't need you in my life.

I want to be in Costa Rica.

Unemployed in Costa Rica would be better than unemployed in Medway.

It was a stupid idea to go back home.

But I know on some level that I need something to happen otherwise I'm going to implode.

I have a bad case of apoptosis, have had it for a while now.

I'm unhealthy: smoking too much and drinking too much and eating shit.

Skinny-fat. No muscles, no definition.

Little man-tits, almost perky. Gut all squidgy like pizza dough.

Still handsome -- just about.

Okay-looking/reasonable-sized penis and balls. Nothing special or anything.

It is what it is; it ain't what it ain't.

I know my mental health isn't what professionals would describe as 'robust'.

That I'm experiencing something akin to what Nabakov described as toska, an untranslatable Russian word.

Do you know about this, Tom Pritchard?

Can you help me?

It's like I came out of a fugue state in Manchester and realised that everything I'd been doing up to that point was totally wrong.

I thought I'd gotten myself onto the 'right track', thought I'd atoned for my earlier teenage ('chavvy') sins by leaving Medway and attempting to 'better myself' at university.

Except I only feel like a traitor to my true self, whoever that is.

I'm in a fugue state in no man's land. Feel like the whole of England is in no man's land.

And now, in the real world, a graduate with no prospects, I have the sense that, in a recursive fashion, I'm seamlessly entering another fugue state, out of which I will emerge at some future date, only to sense that, in a recursive fashion, I'm seamlessly entering another fugue state, out of which I will emerge, etc...

It feels like 'insanity' is beckoning me, inveigling me, like someone who lives in paradise (Costa Rica?) cajoling another person, someone who's stuck in a rut, to up sticks and move: 'Come on, it's better here; leave all that shit behind and start a new life; new pastures, new you!'

What do you have to say about this, Tom?

I don't want your pity, but at the same time, I do.

Want you to know about my life, but at the same time, don't.

Care about everything, and about nothing.

Can you help me, Tom Pritchard?

Help me out of this no man's land?

Help me along the way from toska to eudaimonia?

Please?

32

I don't know why, but I reply to Tom.

Maybe because his second message made me think he might've changed, might've grown up, might've become less annoying.

Deep down, I know this probably isn't true.

But he's the only person I'll be able to go to the pub with.

I'm not in contact with anyone else in Rainham after all, and I don't go to the pub with Dad anymore.

The pub is still a social place for me: I can't be dismissing potential drinking buddies.

I only enjoy drinking alone at home.

'Hey Tommy,

Good to hear from you.

Yep, you heard right. Well, sort of. I'm already back in the hood, actually.

Would love to go for a beer. Surely there are better places than The Star though? Next you'll be telling me you want to go to The Zone x_x

What's your phone number?

Jamie.

Ps, yes, I heard about Lauren. Will talk to you about it when I see you.'

I press send and adjust my pillow.

I close the laptop lid and lie quietly on the inflatable mattress, alone.

It's dark outside, dark in here, and the laptop is warm on my lap -- gently lowering my chances of being able to have children, no doubt.

I fall asleep in this position: yet again fully clothed, yet again without brushing my teeth.

33

'Describe yourself in three words!'

Filling out another application form, this time for Sainsbury's.

I visualise the simpering, over-enthusiastic tosser who created the document.

I silently hex them, hoping they'll get a curable but agonising growth on their anus.

I decide to hack the question and answer honestly.

Sometimes people appreciate this kind of maverick behaviour.

I envisage someone high-up in the company reading my response and being impressed with my disarming self-effacement, immediately promoting me to a peripatetic senior position with vague, easily achievable targets and a luxury company car.

'Look, I can't describe myself in three words. It's impossible, okay? I might do better with, say, a hundred and eighty-four though. If I had to describe myself in a hundred and eighty-four words I would say that I'm someone who often tries to make myself seem more intelligent than I truly am by using long or obscure words, talking about serious topics at the expense of humour, subtly highlighting how good I am at cryptic crosswords, using non-sequiturs as a defence mechanism, frequently mentioning the things I've listened to on BBC Radio 4, giving the impression that I can speak French at a higher level than I can, and telling people that I'm going to write a book.

I'm sexy in my own way, and funny (I put the 'quip' in 'sesquipedalian', yo) and when someone's talking to me I'm often thinking, 'At some point (before time existed) there was nothing, and then there was something', which has been known to bring on a panic attack before.

I get frustrated that people don't try harder to make life enjoyable for as many people as possible, and I'm fun-loving.

There are other things about me, but they're things I can't tell you. Secret things.

If you want clarification you should email my referees, Mssrs Dunning and Kruger, or consult the Akashic records.'

I never hear back from them.

34

If I had to describe Rainham in, say, thirty-three words I would say that it's part of the conurbation of Medway, a dysfunctional family of several knackered old towns, situated about two-hundred miles south-east of Manchester, forty miles south-east of London and eighty miles north-west of Calais.

This is where I'm living as I enter my mid-twenties.

After filling out another one of these application forms, I drunkenly post the following to my Facebook one night, for no discernible reason.

– JULY 2008

Let's meet the gorgeous Medway family.

Closest to London is Strood, the short-tempered paterfamilias who's charming to strangers but beats his wife in the wee hours.

Living alongside Strood is Rochester, the lonely mother with two black eyes: she was beautiful in her youth.

Meet Chatham, east of Rochester, the smack-addict daughter in her early thirties with hardly any teeth.

Next along the old Roman road is Gillingham, the football hooligan son who aspires to join the English Defence League and thinks Nigel Farage 'talks sense'.

Finally there's Rainham, the quiet, feckless youngest sibling who always gets into trouble because of the others and can't hold down a steady job.

There are few cousin suburbs as well, some of whom are

estranged, but these are the five most prominent family members.

Of course -- they're not necessarily like this.

What I've done is libelled five perfectly respectable English towns via the power of personification to further my agenda.

But they're going to have to work pretty hard to respond to these allegations and restore their reputations, aren't they.

No-one's getting sued any time soon though, so in the meantime (GMT+0) let's continue traducing them.

Because this isn't a tourist brochure; no-one recommends visiting Medway.

No travel agent has ever suggested it as a holiday destination.

You won't enjoy yourself here; you won't feel renewed or rejuvenated after a sojourn; nor will you find what you're looking for.

Or maybe you will, who knows.

I mean, the place has history: it's on Wikipedia and everything.

It has moody streets which conceal stories.

Its depressed buildings -- which were unconventionally handsome when they were first built, except no-one ever told them, and now they're ugly and bitter from neglect -- conceal stories.

The dockyard; the Pentagon centre with its unfashionable shops trying to compete with the parvenu Bluewater; the river (the Thames' precocious/underestimated little sister); the spalled concrete footbridges; the football grounds; the mental wards; the academised schools; the graffitied brutalist council estates greasy and grimy from endless diesel rain; the nocturnal parks ruled by aggressive drunk teenagers; the maritime pubs ruled by aggressive drunk men; the innumerable sodium-lit kebab shops open seven nights a week; the midnight living rooms illuminated only by television screens... they're all concealing its stories.

But are they worth telling?

This isn't Richard Curtis' London, baby.

This isn't Paris, or New York.

Don't people want to hear stories from those places?

Or if they're feeling escapist, don't they want to hear about the exotic at arm's length, in the books of Marquez and Murakami?

Medway is a place with a nightclub called The Zone.

The Zone is in Gillingham.

You can get a taxi there from Rainham for under a tenner.

It has sticky carpets and smells like vomit and chlamydia.

Hope.

They play the same set-list every Friday night and have done for the last fifteen years.

The songs change but the music doesn't, if you see what I mean.

You can eternally re-live your favourite Friday night, dancing the same dance-moves like a moron, knowing all the words and singing along like a fuckwit, week after week.

Chesney Hawkes!

The Macarena!

David Guetta songs!

Beyonce!

Barbie Girl!

Justin Timberlake!

I Will Survive!

Songs from 'Grease'!

It's a diabolical place that can only be survived by getting completely ballbagged.

Glory.

Bottles of WKD and pints of watered-down Stella cost £2 before 11pm.

Getting headbutted on your way home is free.

Plenty of people have found what they were looking for there (entangled with a stranger on a seat in a dark corner, or off the lid of a cistern in a squalid toilet cubicle), and you might too.

Perhaps I'll see you downstairs some time.

Downstairs is where they play the drum 'n' bass, which isn't ideal, but I can't go upstairs to the godforsaken 'cheese' room any more. (Chesney! Macarena! David Guetta! Beyonce! Barbie Girl! Justin! I Will Survive! Grease!)

I just can't.

Once again, zero likes.

35

I join an online dating site on a lonesome, drunken whim.

A targeted ad on my gmail account asks me whether I'm single, tells me that dozens of local singles want to meet me if so.

In the dark of my room while my parents sleep next door I sign up and create a minimal profile, using a picture of myself that's at least three years old.

Over the next couple of nights I 'like' several profiles and message dozens of women, but stop logging in when it dawns on me that I'm essentially shopping for sex.

I sign back in when I get an email notification telling me that 'Neve27' has liked my profile.

My id vanquishes my superego when I see her profile picture.

We arrange to meet up.

She lives in Gillingham, so I suggest we go to Riverside Country Park for a walk to see where our feet take us.

Neve27 is enthusiastic about this.

I park just in front of the grass bluffs and text her to say I've arrived.

A moment later she taps on the window and waves.

I wave back, like a dork, and suddenly feel self-conscious.

I get out and give her a brief, unromantic hug.

'Hello Neve27.'

'Hello Jamie3000.'

'I'm Jamie,' I say.

'Neve.'

We shake hands.

'Jolly good,' I say, like a dork.

'Jolly spiffing,' she says, and laughs, and it's a nice laugh.

She looks better in person than she does in her profile picture.

She's someone who doesn't feel the need to wear make-up, and she's right to feel that way.

She's wearing a suede trenchcoat, burnt copper in colour, and has on a fantastic black wide-brimmed hat.

I wonder whether she noticed that I have a lot more hair in my profile picture.

It's already started falling out.

'I love that coat,' I say.

She twists from side to side and allows the bottom of it to fan out. 'Thanks,' she says. 'Second-hand. Thirty quid from Oxfam.'

'A steal at twice the price.'

'Like the hat?' she says, and pulls the brim down at the sides.

'You're crushing it today with your outfit.'

I crush invisible rocks with my fists.

Crush them to sand.

We walk over the bluffs and down to the path that runs alongside the mudflats.

I'm walking in a strange way, I think.

'Have you texted anyone to say you're with me?' Neve says.

'No...' I say, nonplussed. 'Have you?'

'I texted my mum and brother. So don't rape me,' she says.

'My mum's a cage fighter and my brother's six foot five.'

'Really?'

'Yeah, he takes after our grandad.'

'No I mean, is your mum really a cage fighter.'

'Yeah,' she says. 'She used to be a bare-knuckle champion. We're Roma gipsies.'

'Cool,' I say.

I try to walk less strangely.

'I'm just messing with you,' she says.

'So... you're not a gipsy.'

'I am, but my brother isn't six-five. He's like, six-four, tops.'

'Okay.'

I put my hands in my coat pockets, take them out, put them back in again.

'I like it here,' she says.

'Me too.'

A wading bird is standing in the middle of the mudflats.

It looks proud and defiant, but also kind of dumb and sad.

I pull out my phone and take a picture of it.

'What is it?' says Neve.

'I think it's a sandpiper.'

Further away a man is slowly negotiating his way towards the carcass of an old, rusting iron barge that's half-sunk in the bog, probably to harvest some scrap metal.

We walk for about half an hour and get to the lookout point.

Read the information board and regard the Hoo Peninsula across the estuary, as well as Horrid Hill, poking out from the mudflats, covered in bracken.

Several cranes sit on the horizon like giant, headless robotic giraffes, or diplodocuses.

In the middle of them the Kingsnorth power station chimney, a giant cigarette, puffs out grey smoke.

The sky behind the smoke is a milky, alien blue.

It used to be different around here, apparently.

The information board tells us that it used to be a hub of industry.

The iron barges roamed the estuary.

There was a quarry, which a had a little railway station, and the workers would pour into the pit to dig chalk from the earth, which they would heave onto the barges once they'd arrived again with the tide.

Long before that, there were nomadic neolithic people carving dolmens and other mysterious megaliths, like miniature Stone Henges, out of the local flint.

Now the megaliths are fenced off, the power station runs on a skeleton staff, the quarry has been filled in, and the bones of the iron barges are picked at by vultures in Wellington boots.

'Humans are shit,' says Neve.

'What?'

'Look at that thing.' She gestures to the power station chimney. 'It's monstrous.'

'There's something iconic about it though, isn't there? It's our Empire State Building.'

'I hate it.'

'It's not ideal.'

'Humans don't give a shit about this planet.'

Why does she keep referring to people as humans? Technically correct, but jarring.

'Some do,' I say.

'Most don't. We'll all be sorry one day.'

She says this with an element of glee in her voice.

'I'm optimistic,' I say.

'No offence, but optimism's for idiots.'

She nudges me lightly.

'I guess I'm an idiot then.'

She doesn't say anything.

'There's lots to be hopeful about,' I say. 'I'm not saying this is the best of all possible worlds or anything... but, like I read the other day there's these bacteria that feast on plastic. They also destroy bee colonies... but I'm sure one day we'll genetically engineer them to leave the bees alone.'

'Are you saying you're okay with genetic modification?'

'I am when it works. Like with that dwarf wheat in India. It stopped millions of people starving to death.'

'So you're one of these people who blindly believes in science.'

'I do have faith in the scientific method, yes.'

'Science doesn't have all the answers.'

'No, but we should continue to use the scientific method.'

'You can't explain everything.'

'I know,' I say.

'Science has caused plenty of problems,' she says.

'But what else is there? Acupuncture? Jesus?'

'Coal-fired power stations,' she continues, 'Nuclear weapons, plastic bags, big pharma. I hope the Earth gets rid of us one day. We're a plague.'

'That's a bit nihilistic, isn't it? What about all the good stuff that's happening. And if all else fails the robots will help us one day. They say that once AI surpasses human intelligence thousands of Nobel prize discoveries will happen every day.'

'Please,' she says. 'The robots will destroy us. It'll be like Terminator.'

'But I thought you wanted us to be destroyed.'

She ignores me.

'I'm a 50.0000000001% optimist,' I say. 'I think 49.9999999999% of things are awful. But 50.0000000001% are awesome.'

'I think it's more of a 10-90 split.'

'I'm starting to believe that hanging out with you.'

She gives me a look. 'Bit rude,' she says.

I look ahead, focusing on Horrid Hill. Not much of a hill, but not so horrid either.

'What star sign are you?' she says. 'Let me guess. You're a Virgo. I can tell. Virgos are overly logical.'

I'm not in the mood to talk to an earnest person, especially a self-righteous, superstitious one.

When I was a teenager I used to read my horoscope because my mum did, my nan did, but one day I snapped out of it. It just seemed patently absurd all of a sudden, and I felt embarrassed/furious that I'd been hoodwinked.

How come Neve27 can't see that, can't see things as I do?

'I'm going back to my car now,' I say. 'I'm not feeling too bright.'

'Oh, don't you wanna go for a drink?'

'I do,' I say. 'But I'm going to drink on my own.'

She raises an eyebrow. 'Are you serious?'

'Yep,' I say, walking away.

'That's kind of sad,' she calls out.

'I'm okay with that,' I say.

I leave her at the lookout point, with the low-angled sun behind her.

Her hat and coat give her a top-notch silhouette.

Top-notch.

As I walk along the path I peek back every now and then, very much enjoying her silhouette, as well as the gusts of wind that gently thresh the trees either side of me.

36

Tom Pritchard and I exchanged numbers via Facebook.
It wasn't long before he texted me.

- yo sinbad what u doing fri?
- looks like i'm going out with you bruv. also please don't call me sinbad.
- ok sinbad. let's hit the star
- oh jesus, really?
- it's all fancy there now, trust me. you won't recognise it
- all right. if you say so.
- i do say so. see you there at 7??
- sounds good

The Star was one of the legendary places from our teenage years where we could get served.

We might get declined at first, but we'd simply walk to the other end of the bar and wait for one of the other members of staff who was slack asking for ID.

If we were really unlucky and kept getting refused there was always Bar Rio down the road, God rest its soul: Bar Rio was shut down a few years back because there it was being over 18 that was prohibited, or so it seemed to all us joyful adolescent drunkards who kept the place alive.

The Star was always full of 'hard' people though.

We had to offset the thrill of getting served with the

likelihood of getting in a fight.

And when I used to go there with Tom and the squad, there were plenty of fights.

Tom was right, however: the place has changed, superficially at least.

It's clearly under new management. It's been given a makeover and appears to be trying to attract a more middle-class clientele.

It's all laminate wooden floors and 'funky' cushions on high-backed banquettes upholstered in lime green or Etruscan orange or aubergine fabric. The beer garden has a new smoking deck that looks as though it was installed by the Ground Force team.

The pub has lost all its previous character (the smell of urine, the fug of a million cigarettes, the threadbare Axminster carpet, the peeling wallpaper), but it seems unlikely I'll be getting punched in the face for looking at someone the wrong way, so that's all right.

I can't see Tom yet so I buy a pint of Stella and go over to one of the new quiz machines.

I'm playing Deal Or No Deal when Tom taps me on the shoulder.

I turn around to find Tom, 6'2", grinning, with his arms open ready for a hug.

His hair is styled like David Beckham's circa 2004: shortish, vaguely side-parted yet slightly tousled, approaching a mullet at the back, with blonde tinting throughout.

He still has his ginger stubble, which even as a teenager he was able to cultivate into a full beard within a week. Still wears

Ralph Lauren polo shirts with the collar turned up. Still looks like a chav.

'Come here you big cunt,' he says, pulling me in for a bearhug.

'Hi Tom,' I say, my face in his armpit.

Tom smells like mild b.o. commingled with Lynx Africa (the same fragrances from our teenage years).

He pushes me back, holds me at arms-length, regards me.

'Bruv, what happened? You used to have some muscles.'

'Er, you can talk. What's this?' I poke his gut, which had always been there but has swollen further.

He laughs and musses my prematurely thinning hair, which I've taken to arranging in careful, hairspray-reinforced constructions. 'Aaah, it's good to see ya. Wait here. I'm gonna get a pint in.'

I surreptitiously pick at and smooth down strands of hair while I play out my game on the quiz machine.

'Who composed The Hungarian Dances?' asks Noel Edmonds.

I tap on Mahler, but it's incorrect.

37

We sit near the pool tables.

Tom struts over to one and puts a few fifty pence pieces on one of the cushions to reserve it.

A couple of blokes in their early fifties are in the middle of a game. 'Cigarettes and Alcohol' by Oasis is playing on the jukebox. There's background chatter and the comforting click-clack of the pool balls.

We could be in any chain pub in England.

'So how come you're back in this dump then?' Tom says, sitting on the stool next to me.

'Long, boring story.'

'Okay, I won't ask then.' He laughs and slaps my arm with the back of his hand. 'Nah I'm just kidding. I wanna know. You was in Manchester weren't yoo?'

'Yeah. I broke up with my girlfriend. I hated my job. So I thought I'd come back and take some time to figure out a few things.'

Caitlin. Handyman business. Wedding on the beach. Eudaimonia.

Tom is squinting at me.

'Bruv, I've gotta say, you sound posh.'

He imitates me, repeating what just said to him in a close approximation of my voice.

I stare at him; I've been rumbled.

'I'm just messing with you, you bellend,' he says, intuiting that I might be offended. 'Carry on.'

'That's it to be honest,' I say, trying to sound a bit less 'posh', a bit more 'Medway'. 'I probably won't be around very long.'

'Well I'm glad you're back,' says Tom. 'I'm fucking over Mark Galbraith and all that lot.'

'Yeah, you said in one of your messages. What's the problem?'

'Mark's like their ringleader innit. Whatever he says, goes. And if he wants to give you the cold shoulder, they all will. They're little lemmings.' He swigs his pint, wipes his mouth, rests a hand on one knee. 'They're always taking the piss out of me. It fucks me right off.'

'Can't you ask them to stop?'

'You know what they're like. It don't work like that.'

I nod. 'Why do you think I stopped hanging around with them.'

'Anyway,' says Tom. He pauses for another swig. 'I've been reading.'

'Oh yeah? Reading what?'

'This and that. Mainly history stuff. I've been getting well into it. You like your books, don't you.'

'Yes, I do like my books.'

'That's what I fought. That's why I wanted to start hanging out with you again. You ain't like them lot.'

He smiles and drains his beer.

The two blokes finish their game of pool and wander over to the bar.

'Come on,' Tom says. 'You get the beers in and I'll rack up the balls.'

He grabs his crotch and pretends to lift his testicles onto the pool table.

For the first time in a long time, I laugh.

38

Friday night is getting under way.

The place is heaving with Medwegians. Tom and I have to pause before taking our shots to let people squeeze past us. The sound of hand-dryers punctuates the hubbub as people enter and exit the toilets nearby.

Tom takes his shot, pots the black, wins the game.

'Ah-ha! Four-nil! You mug. That's another pint you owe me.'

I'd forgotten that Tom was competitive.

I lean my cue against the table, take out my pouch of tobacco, start to roll a cigarette, pretending in vain that I'm not a sore loser.

'Yeah yeah,' I say. 'You'll get your drinks. I know you've gotta keep that belly sated or else it gets angry.' I push my own gut out; rub it, pat it.

'Shut it baldy. Giz a fag.'

I put a filter tip between my lips and hand him the green pouch. We head to the smoking area.

'You still like to, ah, shmokey shmokey?'

Tom does a little spliff-puffing gesture with one hand as we step outside onto the deck. The cold air immediately reddens our cheeks.

'Shmoke and a pancake?' I say.

'Pipe and a crepe?'

We giggle. We're drunk. We've sunk to quoting Austin Powers.

'Yeah,' I say. 'From time to time.'

Tom looks at me like I've passed a test I didn't know I was

taking. He pulls out some hash wrapped in clingfilm and dangles it in front of my face like a talismanic pendant.

'Let's walk home via Darland Banks,' he says.

'Yes!'

I'd forgotten about Darland Banks. I used to love going there.

It might be the prettiest place in Medway. There's something about it. Something spooky and, dare we say it, magical, especially at night.

It's a nature reserve of steep chalk grassland, scrub and ancient woodland, with views from the summit ranging out to the south not just of Medway but of greater Kent as well -- that supposed Garden of England.

When I was in the Cub Scouts, my fellow scouts and I would play night-time manhunt with torches and compasses, and throw dried cow-pats at each other; I took my first ever girlfriend there on bonfire night where we sat atop a wooden fence and watched the panorama of silent fireworks popping all over the Medway towns; I smoked my first spliff there.

The place has special significance for me.

'Let's get another beer in first,' says Tom. 'There's still ten minutes before last orders.'

'Perfick,' I say, channelling Ed from Shawn of the Dead, who was himself channelling Delboy.

We walk inside.

'A Little Bit of Luck' by DJ Luck and MC Neat comes on over the speakers as I close the door.

Wid a little bit a luck, we can make it troo de night.

Tom does a little Garage dance, rhythmically miming the action of punching his own chin: one, two, one-one; left, right, left-left.

'Choon!' he shouts, pointing in the air and then dipping his finger to the beat, nodding his head in time as well.

I cringe. Tom sees this.

'What's the matter?' he says. 'Am I embarrassing yoo?'

I shrug. 'No,' I lie. 'It's... I dunno. It's not really my thing anymore, this kind of music.'

'Mate, you think you're well posh now, don't ya. You used to LOVE this song! You're putting on all airs and graces.' He waggles his hand in front of my face as he says 'airs and graces'. 'Why don't you go and put some Mozart on the jukebox.'

'Shut up you div,' I say, dialling down the poshness some more. 'Let's get the drinks before we run out of time.'

Tom puts me in a headlock and drags me to the bar, pretending to punch me in the face as we go.

'Listen,' he says, releasing me and leaning on his elbow at the bar. 'I'll write off your pool debt if you get us both a Navy Rum,' he says.

'Deal,' I say, pulling my t-shirt back down and re-setting my hair.

I imagine I'm at a bar on a beach in Costa Rica.

Sunshine. Rum. A happy disposition.

A little bit a luck.

'It's like the old days, innit,' Tom says, grinning, as the barman places our shots on the bar.

'Yeah,' I slur, picking up a glass and holding it aloft. 'Cheers.'

39

We walk along the lamp-lit Darland Avenue which segues into the moonlit Star Lane.

Eventually the moon is obscured by the tree-tunnel formed by Star Lane's chestnut trees reaching out to each other from either side of the road and interlocking in a continuous canopy.

Gorgeous darkness.

I'm in a nice boozy haze, kicking through the dewy leaves, feeling optimistic; or at least like I'm not a complete loser.

We both clumsily vault a stile at the bottom of Darland Banks and traipse upwards through the soggy scrub.

Tom gets his phone out and turns on its torch. We follow the light up the hill.

It's good to crunch and swish through nature.

I haven't done it in months, maybe years.

I remember how being around other living things helps you feel better.

It's not just the free oxygen, it's something else which I don't understand.

At the top I fall to my knees and roll onto my back.

The ground is damp but it feels good.

'I'd forgotten how steep it is,' I say.

I cough for a bit.

'You need to cut down on the fags mate,' says Tom.

'Sorry but haven't you been bumming them off me all night?'

'I'll have a night of smoking once in a blue moon,' he says.

'But I ain't addicted. I'm actually pretty fit at the moment. Don't let the belly fool ya. I play 5-a-side. I got bare tekkers innit fam.'

He loudly slaps his gut a few times with both hands; kicks a horse chestnut into the night.

He doesn't seem out of breath at all, which annoys me.

'Speaking of blue moons, check it out,' I say.

I point over Tom's shoulder. The moon is out and proud, full and flat and pale blue.

'Cool,' says Tom. 'Why's it blue?'

I don't really know, which also annoys me. 'Light refraction?'

'I reckon it's hollow.' Tom gets out the hash and sits next to me on the ground. 'Yeah, and there's a big light on in there. Coz there's aliens in there sending out radio signals that keep us stupid so we'll believe anything the politicians tell us.'

'Haha, maybe,' I say.

'I'm serious,' he says, sprinkling yellowy-brown hash crumbs into the Rizla on his lap. 'I've been reading David Icke.'

'Oh God, I thought you were joking.'

'Nah, don't be like that. People laugh at him but he's got a lot of fings right.'

'Like what?'

'Like how a lot of people in power are paedos.'

'I thought you said you've been reading history.'

'I have. It is history. He ain't mainstream but that don't mean it ain't true.'

'But he has no evidence for most of the things he says.'

'But there's no evidence it ain't true.'

'That's not how it works, Tommy. The burden of proof is on him, not us.'

Tom imitates me again, to emphasise how posh I sound.

'Let's just agree to disagree shall we?' I say, bristling. 'I don't want to argue about it. I'm too pissed.'

'Suit yourself.' Tom licks the Rizla and seals the joint. 'But you ain't getting any of this.'

He holds the joint like a dart and aims it at me.

'I don't want it if it means I'll start believing in the hollow moon theory.'

Tom manipulates a lighter out of his trouser pocket and sparks up. 'Nah, I'm just mucking about. You've gotta try this stuff. It's hash but it's fucking dank.'

He takes a hit, holds it in as he passes the joint to me, blows a yellow cloud out over the nature reserve.

It floats along the horizon, over the orange lights of the Medway towns, east to west, then dissipates above the shadowy outline of the South Downs.

'Thanks,' I say, taking the joint.

I lie back and look at the sky while I toke, enjoying the breeze on my face.

I imagine everything's inverted, like I'm looking down from on high.

Roughly half the sky is a semi-hemispherical mountain range of imperious clouds. The other half is clear and dark like a black lake, with a sprinkling of stars floating on its surface, avoiding the moon, which is a strange disc-island towards the edge.

'Did you know that when you look at a star you're probably actually looking at two or three, in either a binary or ternary system, but they're so far away it looks like one object,' I say. 'Like Orion's belt there, it might actually be made of eight or nine stars, not three. It might even be a string of supernovae.'

'That's cool,' says Tom.

'And each of them probably has at least one habitable planet orbiting. It's crazy when you think about it.'

'What do you mean.'

I answer Tom telepathically. The weed has kicked in for me, but Tom doesn't answer: he obviously hasn't cultivated this superpower yet.

I go back to using my voice and the air as the carrier-wave of information. 'I mean, right up there above us is space. Bloody outer space, and it might be infinite. It might stretch out forever, in all possible directions. And if not, then there's a void...'

I can't finish what I'm saying. The thought of it all brings up a powerful swell of anxiety.

That's what the Sublime can do.

I become hot. My head's a prison.

I convulse for a few seconds.

Then I black out.

When I come to Tom is kneeling by my head.

'You okay fam? Want me to call an ambulance?'

'How long was I out?'

'Like, a minute or something. You all right?'

'Yeah, I'm okay. Don't call an ambulance.'

'What happened?'

'I have panic attacks sometimes.'

'Wait here a sec.'

Tom scurries over to some bushes.

Comes back with wet hands having shaken some dew from the leaves. Smears the moisture on my forehead, like a Baptism.

'Do you promise to renounce Satan,' I say.

'What?'

'Nothing.' I put out my hand. 'Can you help me?'

'I told you it was dank stuff.'

He sits me up.

I take some deep breaths, do my little post-panic routine. I stand up slowly, using Tom's shoulder as a crutch.

I stretch my arms above me but immediately feel nauseous. 'Oh shit...'

I run over to the bushes and vomit.

'Man you are such a lightweight.'

Tom comes over, rubs my back a few times.

'I had wanted to talk about Lauren Hitchens,' he says.

I vomit some more.

'But it can wait.'

I look up at him. 'What about her?' I say, then yak again.

Tom tokes on the joint. 'You know her kid?'

'Yeah,' I say, wiping my mouth with my forearm. 'The one that crawled out the window.'

I shake some dew from the leaves into my palm and wet my forearm, splash my face.

'Yeah, that one.' He turns away from me. 'I'm his dad.'

I stand up. 'What? Are you serious?'

'Yeah, but let's not talk about it now. How you feeling?'

'All right,' I say. 'Better for having puked. Let's get a taxi.'

'It ain't far to walk.'

'I know, but I really need to sleep now.'

'Come on then.'

We make our way to the Hoath Way exit; Tom calls a taxi.

'Tell me about Lauren tomorrow,' I say after Tom ends the

132

call. 'We'll go and get breakfast somewhere before you go to work.'

Tom pats and rubs my back. 'All right. Thanks mate.'

We hear rustling.

'Shit, there's someone in there,' says Tom.

'Where?'

'Down there. Behind the trees. Past the fence.'

'Probably just a fox or something.'

'Might be a ghost. This place is haunted.'

'Dude you love a bit of woo-woo don't you.'

'I'm telling you, I've seen weird things here.'

'It's because you smoke too much of that stuff.'

More rustling.

We stop and peer through the trees, trying to allow our eyes to adjust to the darkness.

A cow steps forward and stops at the fence.

It's the right height for its head to rest on top of it.

'It's a ghost cow,' I say. 'Mooooooooooooo.'

The cow just looks at us.

Or maybe it's looking at something else.

It's too dark to tell.

40

I don't meet Tom for breakfast in the end.

Mum wakes me up early and asks me to go into work with her.

It's nearing the start of the new term. She's going in to rearrange her classroom and update the displays before school starts again.

Needs my help because her bad back is playing up.

I'm suffering an apocalyptic hangover from last night with Tom, but I still don't have a job so there's no way to get out of it.

I text Tom to explain.

- can't do breakfast now tommy. later in the week for sure
- all good fam. beer later?
- you pisshead! aren't you hungover?
- nah i'm not a pussy like you
- i'll probably skip the beer tonight. maybe tomorrow instead

Andrea is highly organised and great at motivating little kids.

She's determined to become a senior leader in her school and haul herself and everyone she teaches firmly into the middle class.

She's a woman on a mission and is very good at what she does.

However, she also treats other people in her life like children.

I often need her not to talk, especially when I'm hungover. I often need quiet to manage the anxiety, as well as my old friend, existential dread.

Andrea has a habit of clucking on anyway though, offering unsolicited advice.

'I hope we can get through today without arguing,' I think, knowing this is a futile thought.

I put various boxes and bags in the boot, then get in the car. I'm driving on account of Andrea's back.

'You're all clear this side,' Andrea says, craning to see past Kevin's car next door.

We set off.

Andrea's school is in Chatham, about fifteen minutes away. We listen to Invicta FM play adverts for local businesses and the majority of 'I Believe in a Thing Called Love' by The Darkness.

I try to change the station but this action is vetoed by Andrea's firm, moisturised hand blocking the dial.

41

Andrea is putting her students' work onto backing paper and I'm standing on a desk, stretching to tack the corners of a poster about insects onto a pinboard, when the inquisition starts.

'So what happened exactly between you and Alice,' she says.

'I don't want to talk about it.'

'I know you said you'd been arguing but every relationship has its ups and downs. Do you think you might get back together?'

'I don't want to talk about it,' I say again, giving her a look.

'Don't look at me like that, I'm only showing an interest in your life.'

'You're being nosy.'

'I'm your mother, it's my job to be nosy.'

We carry on working for a bit.

'What about Caitlin? How's she doing these days?'

'Mum, I've asked you before not to mention her.'

'Oh for goodness sake, can't I talk to you about anything? That was a long time ago. She was a lovely girl. I just wondered if you might have heard from her.'

'Jesus Christ, I don't know, I haven't spoken to her in years. Let's drop it, please.'

It's one thing to ruminate about Caitlin on my own; to talk about her with Mum might send me into a gyre.

I hold no ill-will towards Caitlin. High school relationships, on the whole, are meant to end sooner or later.

My flimsy young heart (unfixable defect) just couldn't take it; is still frangible all these years later. It's a nuisance but that's how it is.

'What are you going to do for work then,' says Andrea.

I sigh. 'I've been applying for things. I've joined temp agencies. I'm looking. There isn't much around.'

'It doesn't seem like you're doing a lot. You should be applying for at least five or six jobs a day.'

'Five or six? Why not eight or nine? Why not twenty or thirty?'

'Well, exactly, why not.'

I make to leave. 'Okay, let me just grab my things and I'll get down the job centre now.'

'Don't be silly, you know what I mean.'

'I do indeed.'

It's her turn to give me a look.

'Mum, please, I'm hungover.'

'Yes, about that. Your father and I are concerned you're squandering your money on nights at the pub when you don't have a job. Have you thought about commuting to London?' she says.

'Firstly, what I spend my money on is none of your business. And secondly, yes I have thought about commuting but it doesn't appeal to me all that much. I'd spend at least half my income on getting to and from work. Plus it's like two hours each way, door-to-door.'

She tuts and shakes her head. 'Your generation doesn't have any stamina. In my day we took work wherever we could.'

'Oh, I'm sorry Mother, but when exactly did you ever commute to London?'

'I never had to. But I would have.'

'Bollocks.'

'Language! You're in a classroom.'

'There's no-one here except us!'

After a pause, I say, 'Why do you want me to suffer like Dad did?'

Andrea turns back to what she was doing.

Slightly too far, that comment. Probably because Col still isn't completely better.

Who really knows though. No-one in the Sinclair family can talk about anything that matters without arguing and creating a more convoluted mess than was there at the start.

Better to allow the prickle of emotion to settle and pretend these conversations never happened.

Before Col did his home-improvement work he ran an electronics shop in London and commuted on the train for about ten years.

He hardly ever saw his family during this time.

When he did he was angry and low-level violent.

Because This Be The Verse.

He hated the job. Hated the succession of demanding area and regional managers.

The salary was shit, the pay rises were pathetic (if they ever came) and the commute was exhausting.

And he got sacked eventually.

It turned out he'd been stealing.

Not big or expensive stuff. He hadn't been pilfering SLR cameras or tellies. He wasn't getting rich off it.

He'd been collecting negligible little things like the cheap earphones and the SCART cables; stuff like that.

No-one knew how long it had been going on.

He said later that he hadn't realised he'd been doing it. He'd been sorting out the refunded items and hadn't put them through the system properly, and then he'd left them in his office where he was keeping them safe, he said.

The area manager had come in to do an audit and noticed that the books were out of whack; he'd only had to do a cursory search in Col's office before he found the boxes of refunded items, and Col was toast.

Brown bread mate.

Col said that the area manager had harboured a long-standing grudge against him and this was a witch-hunt. The trouble was there was more of the refunded stuff in the boot of his car, which he couldn't account for.

The company didn't press charges in the end and Col was released after a night in the cells, but they still sacked him.

Not long after that, he tried to do himself in.

It was Mum who found him.

Face-down on their bed with empty packets of SSRIs strewn on the floor and a bottle of good scotch on its side.

The last of its contents spilt and puddled like blood from a cracked skull.

Andrea and I carry on working in silence.

I get to the end of the display and wipe my brow with my sleeve.

I stick the ball of blu-tack to the wall, climb down, perch on the desk, check Facebook on my phone.

Caitlin is going on holiday soon, to Santorini.

Is that in Italy, or Greece? Sounds expensive either way.

I look for any evidence of a boyfriend.

None at the moment.

I am not going to Santorini.

I am not going to Costa Rica.

I look up, notice the crucifix above the blackboard, frown.

I scroll through Caitlin's feed some more.

'Oh!' Andrea says after a while. 'A bee!'

She walks over to the window.

I follow her.

A bumblebee is on the window sill, struggling to cling to this existence. It's more or less completely still, occasionally moving an antenna like it's the hardest thing it's ever done.

'Back in a minute.'

She leaves the room.

I quietly observe the bee.

We are all connected, I think.

The tree of life, I think.

Little bee, my brother (or sister).

Andrea comes back with a pipette; teachers have ready access to this kind of thing.

'What's that for,' I ask.

'My class and I learned about this the other day. It's not dying.'

She squeezes a single drop from the pipette onto the window in front of the bee's head.

It stirs, then sniffs (?) the droplet and appears to imbibe from it.

'What did you just do?'

'I dissolved some sugar granules in water,' she says, watching the bee. 'It just needs a sugar boost.

Both antennae are moving now. It pushes itself up like it's been given some kind of magic potion and is stronger than ever, galvanised with mystical powers.

Andrea lifts the sash window.

The bee flies out, reborn.

The thought of the air buffeting its yellow fur makes me feel powerful.

'I saved its life!' Andrea says, beaming. 'Not a bad day's work.'

I nod. 'I'm hungry,' I say.

'Me too,' says Andrea.

I sit in Andrea's revolving chair behind the big teak desk.

Andrea grabs our packed lunches from the fridge. She produces napkins from somewhere. Gives me three and tells me to get my feet off the table.

Mine's a cheese salad sandwich.

Andrea's is a chicken salad sandwich, containing the flesh of a murdered chicken.

'Saving a life, taking a life. You're playing God today.'

I wink at her.

'What do you mean,' she asks.

'The chicken,' I say with my mouth full, motioning at her sandwich.

'Jamie Sinclair, yours is becoming a high horse. Don't become one of those vegetarians who guilt-trips people.'

'I'm not. I'm just saying. You celebrated saving one creature's life but you'll think nothing of eating another one.'

'The Good Lord put certain creatures on this planet for us to eat.'

141

'What?'

'Never mind. Let's talk about something else.'

Andrea knows what I'm like. She knows I'm prone to jumping on her Creationist-flavoured statements.

But this time I don't say anything. I can't say anything. I'm so flabbergasted by what she said I immediately need to go to the toilet and shit.

I drop my sandwich on the desk and rush along the corridor past all the kids' displays about The Ancient Egyptians.

I can't find the staff toilet so I go into the boys'. Crouch above one of the tiny toilets and try to go.

Nothing comes: after all the messing around with Mr Pancakes back in Manchester I'm actually constipated now, have been for a few days.

I pull my trousers up and go out to the playground for a cigarette, hoping in vain that it might loosen me up.

I sit on a swing and gently push myself back and forth while I smoke.

I try to picture Mr Pancakes' face.

Did he have a moustache?

I can't remember.

Andrea and I used to have a lot of theological arguments, but today I can't be arsed to get into it all.

I decide to leave the issue alone.

I finish the cigarette and go back inside.

I put my headphones in and get on with re-covering the children's library books with fresh sticky-back plastic.

I listen to a recording of Terence McKenna talking about

psilocybin mushrooms and DMT, a molecule with a similar chemical structure to psilocybin.

In the recording Terence McKenna says, 'You cannot imagine a stranger drug or a stranger experience.'

He posits the existence of other realities, sort of nether- and supra-worlds, some of which might ingress, somehow, into our own dimension via psychedelics.

A fusion of the DMT with our own DNA, creating a kind of hyperdimensional portal, or something along those lines.

He talks about the peculiar alien entities that people see when they travel into DMT hyperspace.

He speculates about the role magic mushrooms might have played in the evolution of human consciousness with his so-called 'Stoned Ape Theory'.

Panspermia, and mushroom spores travelling across space, hardy enough to withstand electromagnetic and cosmic radiation.

He says a lot of other seemingly crazy stuff.

If anyone else (David Icke or the local vicar) was saying these things I would assume they were unhinged.

But Terence McKenna has this way of speaking that melts away my preconceptions; it compels me to give his ideas some consideration.

Channeling JBS Haldane, McKenna says, 'Reality isn't only stranger than you suppose, it's stranger than you can suppose.'

This statement does something to me.

I pause Terence McKenna.

A lot of people don't like to think about the strangeness of reality. It's just plain old mundane workaday reality, nothing special about it.

Why spend too much time pondering it?

It's not extraordinary. It just is.

Always has been, always will be.

Except, I think it is extraordinary. And I think everyone else does too, but it scares them.

And/or it makes them feel insignificant and/or silly.

They're going out to their jobs every day, some of them so they can buy things they don't really need (manufactured by exploited people and devastating to the environment) to signify their status to their peers or their parents.

Others work because they're casualties of an economic system that forces them to labour full-time yet still not have enough money to eat sufficiently nutritious food and pay all the bills.

Being confronted with the absurdity and strangeness of existence itself is not something they are willing or able to handle. It's not top of the ol' to-do list.

And even if they do take the time to contemplate existential issues, they often don't think reality is particularly strange in-and-of-itself.

If you asked them to share their existential thoughts they might outline things you'll find at the core of Taoism, Mahayana Buddhism, Hinduism, Jainism, or Sikhism. They might lament how we are often too 'materialistic'; they might recognise that nature is beautiful, and make vows to go hiking up hills more often, and declare that a simple life of charity and compassion and community and mindful pleasure is the ideal, because life is fleeting and we must seize the day, which is all stuff I can get on board with.

They've seen The Matrix and found it entertaining.

They've watched Carl Sagan's 'Pale Blue Dot' video on

YouTube and been moved by it.

But they don't think reality is strange.

They are so used to being inside this reality, they are so familiar with perceiving it from within, they can't see how odd it is, how odd everything within it is, and cannot conceive of alternative paradigms or other extraordinary realities.

If they want strangeness they look to the 'supernatural': they get into the occult, search for ghosts, read into astrology, not realising that reality is just as weird as anything supernatural that can be conjured by the imagination.

Weirder even.

They take it for granted.

I don't blame them. I can only see it because I accidentally took a large dose of LSD once and it upended my mind and temporarily broke the lens of my ego.

I saw that reality is a subjective neurochemical state which can shift and twist like a dream.

I closed my eyes, only for new eyes to open in their place, showing me things that were just as real as those seen by my old eyes.

I travelled through different Bardos and repeatedly encountered the terrifying and humbling presence of the Sublime.

Felt like I was in the presence of the Mysterium Tremendum et Fascinans.

Ein Sof.

Felt connected to every single thing in the universe, as one tiny aspect of the fractal godhead suddenly able to perceive all other aspects of itself, which simultaneously elated and terrified me.

I experienced the loneliness of a god.

Now I can't take the pursuit of status seriously.

There are some people doing good things in the world: doctors (Caitlin), nurses, health workers of all stripes; social workers, aid workers, (most) teachers and so on.

I can take that seriously.

Most people, however, are in jobs that exist only because of the scarcity of resources and the unequal distribution and allocation of those resources across populations.

Andrea desperately wants me to get one of those -- a well-paid one -- so she can brag about it at her next Bitch 'n' Stitch with the girls.

It's all so perplexing, I think.

Too much for a primate brain.

But we have the X-Factor and Eastenders and Game of Thrones and Match of the Day, so it's okay guys.

Everything's going to be okay.

After a while Andrea comes over to check my work.

She asks me what I'm listening to.

'Michael Bublé,' I lie, taking an ear-phone out and letting it hang down my shoulder.

'Ooh I like him,' she says. 'He's gorgeous.'

I smell the plastic I've just put around the book I'm holding.

I press the book to my nose and inhale deeply.

It smells great/sad.

It smells like saudade, an untranslatable Portuguese word.

Andrea squeezes my shoulder.

'Thanks for your help today,' she says.

'No worries,' I say, putting the earphone back in.

'I'm ready to leave when you are,' she says.

'Safe bruv.'

She laughs and shakes her head like I'm a buffoon.

As we walk out to the car I text Tom, asking him if he still wants to go for that beer later.

42

I eventually go to see a doctor in Medway, but not of my own volition.

I wake up at 11am and Andrea is waiting at the bottom of the stairs, dressed for the cold.

'I'm taking you to see a psychiatrist,' she says. 'You can call me when you're out and I'll pick you up.'

'Mum, really, I'm fine--'

'Get your coat, put your shoes on, and get in the car. I've already booked the appointment.'

'Okay,' I say.

The clinic's in Rochester.

'I'll be here when you come out,' says Andrea.

'Thanks Mum.'

The doctor appears and calls me into his office.

Andrea sits in an armchair in the reception and begins leafing through a gossip magazine.

The doctor holds the door open for me and gestures to an armchair.

I sit.

The doctor's 'chummy' with me.

He asks how I've been feeling.

I tell him about leaving Manchester and returning to Medway. Tell him I've been finding it difficult to shit. Tell him I read Anna Karenina in a week from all the time I spent on the toilet not shitting.

I recount the recent panic attack and the generally low mood.

Eventually, after a little probing from the doctor, I confess the bipolar diagnosis from a few years before.

The doctor asks me if I've had thoughts of suicide.

I say, 'Not exactly.'

'What do you mean not exactly.'

'I mean, no. I haven't. Just... death.'

'Do you want to die?'

'Precisely the opposite.'

'Have you done anything reckless recently? Drugs, unusually promiscuous activity, high levels of spending, that sort of thing?'

'Not... really. I mean, I left my girlfriend and job in Manchester. I guess that was quite reckless. At the time I thought it was the right thing to do.'

'No drugs?'

'Just weed.'

'Cannabis.'

'Yes.'

'And would you say you've speaking quickly, having racing thoughts, or anything else indicative of an elevated state?'

'Again, precisely the opposite. My brain feels like sludge right now.'

The psychiatrist takes my blood pressure and weighs me. Tells me to exercise. To stop smoking.

He prescribes more lithium carbonate.

Handing me the prescription he says, 'This will put the snap back into your elastic.'

I imagine the psychiatrist pulling the elastic of my underwear and letting it snap against my waist.

I imagine wearing my miniskirt boxer shorts and the psychiatrist giving me an atomic wedgie.

The psychiatrist explains how it is believed the lithium works, when I should take the tablets, why I should also look into CBT.

He says I seem 'unfulfilled' and that CBT with a psychologist might help me formulate some goals.

'Have you ever tried mindfulness meditation?'

'Not formally...'

'I've heard it's rather effective. You could talk to a psychologist about it. They'll be able to tell you more about these so-called mindfulness techniques to deal with your anxiety.'

'I'll look into it,' I say.

'Good man! And good luck. Things will get better; you're young. One has to be patient, that's all! Illegitimi non carborundum and all that.'

'What does that mean?'

'It means, don't let the bastards grind you down.'

'Oh.'

'So, I'll see you in a fortnight, Jamie.'

'Uh, I haven't checked to see if I'm free yet.'

'Your mother has already paid for six sessions. If it's all right with you I'd like to see you every two weeks over the next few months, to monitor your condition.'

'Oh. Okay. But you recommended a psychologist too. I'm confused.'

'See me for prescriptions and general monitoring. See the psychologist for CBT, which they're specifically trained in. All right?'

'I guess.'

'Good man. Take care, Jamie. Stay off the *weed*. It might exacerbate things. And don't forget to take the tablets. We can look at alternatives over the coming sessions, but for now I want you to continue with them. If you stop them abruptly, it can be disastrous.'

Andrea drives us home.

'I'll pay you back for the sessions, Mum.'

'It's okay. I knew you wouldn't go if I didn't book ahead.'

'Are you guys all right for money?'

'The usual. But we're managing. Keeping afloat.'

'I'll pay you back.'

She squeezes my hand. 'I just want you to be okay.'

'Does Dad know?'

'It was his idea.'

'What?'

'I used his credit card.'

'He's going to resent me for that.'

'He cares about you more than you realise.'

'He's got a funny way of showing it.'

She squeezes my hand again, and doesn't let go until we're home.

43

Manchester.

I keep thinking about it.

Keep thinking about my old life, dreaming about it, picturing people I haven't seen for a long time, pondering how things might have turned out had I not broken up with Alice.

Andrea didn't know Alice very well, didn't seem to like her all that much, but for a while there it was looking like she was going to get some grandkids, so Alice was good enough.

Col was indifferent towards Alice, as he has been with all my girlfriends, but Andrea always made an effort to be civil, despite having a strong inkling that Alice believed the Sinclairs to be of inferior 'stock', which is what Alice secretly did believe.

She never had to say as much; it infused every interaction she had with Mum and Dad, and despite finding my parents insufferably frustrating at times I always felt defensive on their behalf, knowing as I did that Alice was a gargantuan crypto-snob masquerading as a right-on progressive person.

But all that is academic now, because we aren't together and won't ever get back together.

Though it would be nice to see her again.

She was a great kisser.

Her vulva and her unkempt pubic hair were glorious. You just wanted to spend all day down there.

It might be nice to...

I reach for my phone to text her, but manage to resist.

I let the phone drop from my hand to the floor.

Twist in my bed and scream into my pillow.

We broke up multiple times throughout our relationship and reconciliation always began with one of my drunken, craven text messages, fuelled by loneliness.

Not this time.

But now, in one of those strange synchronistic moments where the person I'm thinking about ingresses into my life, my phone rings, and I make the mistake of sliding off the bed, plucking my phone from the carpet, and answering.

It's her. She asks if she can come and see me.

'I miss you,' she says. 'I need to see you. We should talk things over.'

'I don't think that's a good idea. And anyway, I'm at my parents' place.'

'We could meet in London. Could stay at my aunt's place.'

'I hate London.'

'Please, Jamie. I want to know you're okay.'

'No.'

I can hear her softly crying.

Kneeling on the floor, I punch myself in the leg three or four times. 'Okay, but this... this is the only time.'

44

We meet at Euston station later in the week.

It's teeming with people.

I wonder how Londoners deal with the constant low-level cortisol in their systems.

Surely the whole city is overdue a nervous breakdown.

Alice appears.

As she comes through the ticket gate and waves at me I think about bolting.

There's just too many people.

But I don't run.

She puts down her suitcase and we hug for a long time in the middle of the concourse.

The hordes stream around us, river rapids around a boulder.

We decide to go for a walk, even though neither of us knows our way around this part of town.

The sky is overcast; it seems closer to the earth than usual.

There are hundreds of vehicles on the Euston road beside us. Smog.

There's smog everywhere. Smog up the river, where it flows among green aits and meadows...

I zip my jacket to the top and tuck my nose inside.

We find a Pret a Manger.

'This looks good,' says Alice. 'I feel like a sandwich.'

'Why are people obsessed with French phrases,' I say, looking up at the signage. 'It's pretentious.'

'Pot and kettle,' says Alice, selecting something vegetarian. 'Moi? Pretentious?'

'I'm only teasing.' She touches my elbow. 'But yeah, you are. Do you want one of these?'

She holds up an egg and cress on multigrain.

I suddenly remember that I didn't have breakfast because I was too anxious.

I nod and offer some money.

'It's okay. I know you don't have a job at the moment.'

'How?'

She goes to the counter and pays.

'There's this thing, I don't know if you've heard of it -- it's called Facebook.'

'I need to deactivate again.'

We sit at a table amidst tourists and office workers on their lunch breaks.

'How's Saxtorp?'

'How's what?'

'Saxtorp. Our sofa. That's its name.'

'Oh. It's... fine.'

'Good old Saxtorp.'

'How have you been? Have you had any episodes lately?'

'Funny you should say that...'

'What happened?'

'Panic attack.'

'Have you been seeing a psych?'

I nod. 'Mum took me the other day.'

'What did they say.'

'He said I'm unfulfilled. He recommended CBT to help me

formulate some goals.'

Costa Rica.

Unfixable defect.

'You always wanted to write a book. That's a good goal.'

'I have no muse. My muse isn't talking to me. I'm getting the cold shoulder from my muse.'

'You need to aim higher. Go back to university or something.'

'You sound like the careers officer from school.'

I recall the careers officer's image and voice: the flat, no-nonsense bowl-cut; the practical clothing she'd probably had since the seventies; her shrill cadence, not unlike Anne Widdecombe's.

I'd said I wasn't sure about university when she asked which one I was going to during my careers guidance interview.

'My mum wants me to go,' I'd said. 'But I might get a trade. My dad says I'll get paid more.'

'Nonsense,' she'd said. 'Graduates earn more money in the long-run. And you don't want to let your brain go to waste.'

She proceeded to sell me the dream of a glorious future in whatever field I turned my mind to, a future in which (I felt she implied, if not explicitly stated) I would cease to feel distanced from my experiences and would become connected with my life; I would somehow 'become myself', and all would be well in the world.

'You're still hung up on your background,' says Alice, bringing me out of my recollection. 'It doesn't matter that you didn't go to private school.'

'I don't care about all that.'

'Good. Because you're destined for better things.'

'I'm destined for bitter things. Bitter batter.'

'A bitter better batter.'

'A little bitter luck.'

'What?'

'I don't know.'

We munch our sandwiches.

'How have you been?' I say. 'Did you start your course?'

'I've... deferred until next year.'

'Why.'

'Because, well, that's why I'm here actually. Why I wanted to see you.'

'Have you got a job in London?'

'No.'

She fiddles with a serviette that has the Pret a Manger logo stamped on it.

'I'm pregnant.'

'Shit.'

'Yeah. But don't worry. I'm not keeping it.'

'It's not mine, is it?'

'Whose else would it be?'

'I don't know. I thought you might have... moved on.'

'I've been on a couple of dates, but that's it.'

'You haven't got in someone's dirty bathwater or anything?'

'Ew, Jamie, no.'

'So what are you going to do?'

'I just told you, I'm not keeping it.'

'Right. I mean, where are you going to get the proce-dure done?'

'The procedure. It's called an abortion. Don't be squeamish.'

'Do you want me to go with you.'

'No. Thank you, but no.'

'Alice, it's fine, I'd be happy to.'

'Deb's going to come with me.'

'Okay. How is Deb?'

'Same old Deb. She's a qualified solicitor now. Anyway, she insisted on coming with me.'

'That's good. Deb's good.'

A woman approaches our table.

''Scuse me my darlings, can I interest you in the Big Issue?'

We both dig out some coins for her. She puts two slightly battered magazines on the table.

'Thank you very much my darlings.'

'Keep this one,' Alice says, giving back one of the magazines. 'We'll pay for two but we can share one.'

'You sure my love?'

Alice nods and smiles with her eyes. A Pret a Manger employee comes over to the table.

'It's all right, I'm going, I'm going,' the Big Issue vendor says, melodramatically. 'See you my darlings. What a lovely couple. Gorgeous. You'll have gorgeous babies.'

She cough-laughs and is led out by the Pret a Manger employee.

'What the hell,' I say.

Alice pulls a face.

We finish our sandwiches and head back towards Euston.

'Where are we going?' says Alice.

'I don't know. We should talk more.'

'Do you want to do something first? We could go to a gallery.'

I look at the time on my phone.

'All right. I've got nothing better to do.'

'You were always a charmer.'

158

'Sorry. It's true though.'

'I've never been to the Tate Modern.'

'Okay. Do you know how to get there?'

'We'll suss it out.'

We enter the station, seek out the information desk, head down the escalators, underground.

45

The Tate Modern is exhibiting Duchamp, Man Ray and Picabia.

There's The Fountain and some of Duchamp's early paintings; Man Ray's Indestructible Object; Picabia's Femmes au Bull-Dog.

It's weird that we should get to see some of these iconic works without having planned it; I remember looking at some of them on Alice's laptop years ago.

We argue over their worth (I like them but think they're overvalued by pretentious art-historians and buyers; Alice accuses me of hypocrisy for the second time in an hour), wandering around the gallery until we get hungry again.

'Let's go and eat. I have some things for dinner at my aunt's place.'

'Where's your aunt's place?'

'Kentish Town.'

'Where's that?'

'It's this way.'

She leads me towards the exit and we walk to London Bridge to catch the Northern Line.

Sitting next to each other on the busy tube we talk about my recent trip to the psychiatrist.

We quietly mock some of the other passengers, the ones who look the most yuppie, the most conceited, the most hipster.

We're playful and gentle with each other.

It's all very comfortable and weird.

When we get to Kentish Town Road I'm struck by how much like Gillingham High Street it is.

The only real difference is the house prices.

You have to be a millionaire to live here in squalor.

Alice's aunt is out of town so Alice is house-sitting for a few days.

No doubt Alice will inherit the house one day. No doubt I will die from an unfixable defect one day.

Alice puts the kettle on and sits on a stool at the breakfast bar.

She opens her laptop.

'It says on the NHS website you can get six CBT sessions for free. You should try it.'

'What if I need seven?'

'You'll only need six. I believe in you.'

'I have these as well.'

I take out from my backpack the oblong box of tablets I recently acquired and show them to her.

'Are they still working?'

'I think they were. But then I ran out.'

'Jamie!'

'I know. But, I have more now.'

I rattle the box.

'Why don't you have one now.'

'What the hey.'

I don't read the list of side-effects.

Best not to think about them. They might manifest psychosomatically.

Alice gives me a glass of orange juice and rests her arm on my shoulder.

I pop a little white tablet out of its foil blister and say a silent prayer to the god of psychopharmacology.

I swallow the tablet with a gulp of juice.

Then Alice kisses me. I kiss her back.

'What are we doing,' I say.

'I'm sorry. It felt natural.'

'This whole day has felt natural.'

'It has, hasn't it.'

'That's why I better go.'

'Have some food first.'

'I'm not hungry.'

'Don't go yet.'

'I can't stay. This is too confusing.'

'Jamie, wait. I just think, you know, you were manic when you left me. Maybe we could try again now that you're back to baseline.'

'It doesn't work like that. And anyway, there were other issues. Also, I have no baseline.'

I go to the hallway and put my shoes and coat on.

'How long are you house-sitting for?' I say.

'Till Friday.'

'Maybe I could come and see you again before you leave.'

Her arms are folded. 'I'm sure you'll do whatever you want.'

'Don't be like that.'

'Don't tell me how to be.'

'I'll text you.'

'I'll keep my phone charged. I'll hold my breath.'

I open the big front door.

It's raining. I hear the sticky wet tyres of a car driving up the road.

'Bye Alice.'

She says nothing and I close the door behind me.

After getting lost on the underground a couple of times I arrive at Victoria station.

I arrive just in time to catch the 20.08 heading to Rainham.

I go through the barriers, board the train, and as the doors close I realise I left my backpack at Alice's aunt's.

I know I won't see Alice again. I can't see Alice again. I consider hopping off the train and heading back to grab it.

My book's in the bag; my pills too.

No, wait -- I pat my pockets.

The box is squashed underneath my phone.

The train starts to pull away and I take a seat.

Oh well. The book wasn't that good anyway.

46

From Victoria it's about an hour on the train.

Rainham is roughly equidistant between Dickens and Chaucer, between Rochester and Canterbury.

But pay attention: the thing to notice when you get past Bromley South is an altered ambience, a change of the wind's direction.

The amnion of the capital breaks and you're no longer protected; the spell is broken.

I first recognised this phenomenon after I'd left for Manchester and started coming back to Medway to visit Mum and Dad, when this previously familiar place became unfamiliar and I felt as though I was seeing it for the first time like a tourist.

The atmosphere becomes slightly more comforting and threatening at the same time. You're heading home but the people don't have the same city mindset anymore.

You can sense the parochialism seep into the carriages, but you can also feel the London stress leaving you.

London is supposed to be frightening and dangerous but it's not. At least, it's no worse than other places in the south-east of England, especially within a particular radius that expands into the Home Counties.

I've witnessed more aggression and violence on Southeastern trains than I ever have in London.

And yet I'm always glad to leave the capital.

It's the London paradox.

There was this time when I was coming home from a gig at Earl's Court.

I must have been seventeen or eighteen.

I was on one of the last trains of the night back to Rainham. It seemed as though every single person on the train was inebriated in some way.

My friends (including Caitlin) had all disembarked at the previous stop, and for some reason I decided to move seats, probably to find a quieter carriage.

As I waited for the automatic door connecting the carriages to open, some bloke, some brass-necked geezer, threw a full can of beer square into my back. I'd had to walk past him and his group to get to the next carriage and the guy threw his can of beer at me, told me to get a haircut and called me a faggot.

This was in a modern, futuristic-sounding year in the early twenty-first century.

The impact of the beer can hurt. Dull throbbing in the centre of my back. I wanted to rub the site of the pain but pretended I hadn't felt anything and went two carriages further down where there were other people.

I located a window seat, sunk into it and closed my eyes, hoping the guy wouldn't follow me.

He did though, of course; he couldn't resist.

The guy stepped into my carriage and shouted over from the doorway that he'd have my wallet off me when I got off the train. He laughed and went back to his own carriage.

I looked around to see if anyone else had heard him but most of the other passengers were asleep, or were ignoring what had happened for a quiet life.

Fortunately the guy and his chums got off at Chatham, two

stops before me, and from the platform, by way of goodbye, they repeatedly slapped my window and yelled incoherently at me as the train pulled away.

These were the sort of people that Alice would call 'chavs'.

I wouldn't defend their behaviour to her. They were a bunch of queyntes, to quote Chaucer.

But that doesn't mean Alice was right to use that word.

They'd been let down all their lives; they'd needed help and never got it. Parents, schools, the government: no institution had fulfilled their duty adequately.

And now everyone had a word they could use to write them off as something almost sub-human.

Despite their aggressive behaviour, these were my people.

Alice had never struggled. Her whole life had been filled with comfort, stability and direction.

The only time she'd ever come close to having a crisis was when she got a 'B' for one of her GCSEs.

Strood passes beneath the train.

I watch Rochester come into focus.

The train rattles gently over the steel bridge, crossing the River Medway. A houseboat bobs on the water near a World War Two submarine being abseiled by outdoorsy types with torches on their helmets.

Rochester castle, now purple, now green, now yellow, up-lit by spotlights at its base, floats past behind the high street; the cathedral follows.

The 20th century disappears. The 12th century and the 7th century disappear.

I'm adrift in time in a clackety old time-machine, unsure of the ultimate destination.

The automated train announcer informs us we're approaching the station.

The doors open and a group of teenage lads get on, all of them wearing baseball caps, puffer jackets and conspicuous gold jewellery.

I look out the window at Rochester. I clench my fists, squeeze my toes together and tense my stomach muscles.

I make sure not to look at any of them in the eye.

47

I decide to get off at Gillingham.

There used to be a good pub just off the high street. The Red Lion.

I text Tom Pritchard to see if he wants to meet me there.

Tom says he can be there in half an hour.

Good. I want to know what Tom thinks of the whole situation.

Tom has no tact and will tell me exactly what he thinks.

I find the pub hasn't changed at all.

It probably hasn't changed since the eighties.

No upholstered banquettes in here.

Apart from a few locals sitting at the bar the place is empty.

I order a beer and sit at a table with ring marks on it. I play with the square beer mat in front of me.

It's black with the Guinness logo on it.

Below the logo it says, 'Good things come to those who wait.'

I flip the mat from the edge of the table and try to catch it mid-air.

Fail.

Try again.

Fail.

Try once more.

Fucking hooray.

The door opens and Tom walks in.

He has a black eye and his arm in a sling.

I gesture at the spectacle before me. Tom makes a meal out of sitting on the stool opposite.

'It's not as bad as it looks.'

'What happened.'

'I had a fight with Mark.'

'What? Why?'

'He was mugging me off again and I'd had enough. I fought, Jamie wouldn't say any of this shit to me, why do I have to put up with it from this cunt. So I punched him. Then we started brawling.'

'Couldn't you have just, you know, left, instead of punching him? Where were you anyway?'

'It was after football. We was at the bar at Anchorians. I dunno. I just lost it. I weren't finking.'

'Do you want a drink?'

Tom picks up the beermat on the table. 'I could murder a Guinness.'

'Coming right up.'

I return with fresh beers.

Tom is scratching his arm through the sling.

'So what happened afterwards?'

'These rugby players threw us out. These big fuckers. Me and Mark rumbled a bit more in the street and then the police came. We both legged it. I hid in a bush in Darland Banks for a couple of hours.'

'What about Mark?'

Tom shrugs and sips his drink. 'Dunno. Ain't heard from him.'

'Never a dull moment with you, is there.' I point at the

sling. 'Is it broken?'

'Nah.'

'You been to the hospital?'

'Nah.'

'What? Did you do that yourself?'

'My girlfriend did it for me.'

'You have a girlfriend?'

'One of many.'

'Yeah right.'

Tom rubs his elbow gingerly. 'It don't feel broken.'

'Mate, go to the hospital and find out.'

'Nah, I can't be fucked with all that.'

'I'll drive you.'

'Honestly bruv, it's fine. I can't move it but it's probably just, like, bruised or whatever.'

'Suit yourself.'

Tom winces as he gets out his cigarettes.

'What else is new with you,' I say.

'Nothing much. Where have you been? I ain't heard from you in a while.'

'I went to London today.'

'Oh yeah? Why?'

'I met up with Alice.'

'Who's Alice.'

'I told you about her. I used to live with her.'

'Oh. Why were you seeing her?'

'She had something to tell me.'

'Pregnant?'

'Yeah... how did you know.'

'What else would she have to tell you.'

'I don't know.'

'So you're gonna be a dad.'

'No. She's not keeping it.'

'Why did she tell you she's pregnant then?'

'Because... it's the right thing to do.'

'Nah bruv. She's trying to fuck with your mind.'

He taps his temple then motions for us to go outside and smoke.

It's still raining. We walk up the street and find cover under the overhang of a building.

'I don't think that's it. She wanted to talk about it.'

'Did she show you the pregnancy test?'

'Of course not.'

'Then how do you know she's pregnant?'

'I believe her.'

Tom shakes his head.

'She wouldn't do that,' I say.

'You know her better than I do.'

'Exactly. You've never met her.'

'Sounds suss, that's all I'm saying.'

'It does sound kinda suss, now that I think about it.'

'Right?'

'Ah fuck it. It doesn't matter either way. I'm not going to see her again. If she calls me again, I won't answer.'

Tom lights his cigarette behind a cupped hand, keeps the flame going for me.

'I'm speaking from experience,' says Tom. 'Lauren tried that shit with me once.'

'Lauren Hitchens.'

'Yeah. She told me she was up the duff. I asked to see the

171

test and she wouldn't show me.'

'But she got pregnant later on.'

'Much later. We'd already stopped seeing each other. She was getting into smack, all that shit, so I left. I went round there to get some of my stuff one day, clothes and all that. I fought she'd be out and I still had a key. She was home though. One thing led to another and we started shagging.'

'As it does.'

'Same thing happened as before. A few months later she told me she was up the duff and I made her show me the test. She just lifted her top up and showed me the bowling ball. Her belly button had already popped out.'

'How often do you see the kid?'

'Xavier.'

'Xavier, right. How often do you see Xavier?'

'It used to be every other weekend. Now he's in care.'

'After the accident.'

Tom stubs out his cigarette on the ground, gets another one out of his pack. 'Yeah.'

'Why can't Xavier live with you though? You've got money. Don't you have enough space for him at your place?'

'Social Services came round to assess my old flat after the accident. They found coke.'

'You idiot.'

'The police got involved. I got two years.'

'You're messing with me. You went to prison?'

'And a fine. Got out last year.'

'Fuck me. You never told me.'

'You weren't around.'

'No, I mean, since I've been back.'

172

'It never came up.'

'Tom, honestly. That's fucked.'

'Yeah. And it weren't even my gear.'

'Whose was it? Lauren's?'

'Mark's.'

'That fucker. And he didn't say anything? He didn't own up?'

Tom shakes his head.

'Let's get another drink,' I say. 'I'm getting angry thinking about it.'

Tom puts his arm around my shoulder as we walk back to the pub. 'It's good having you around again, Sinbad. I'm done with Mark now. For good this time.'

'I can't believe you've been hanging out with him since you got out.'

'I know, it's dumb. But that's it now. Fuck all those cunts.'

'Amen brother.'

We stay until last orders then share a cab home.

Tom's place is first.

He gets out and gestures for me to roll down the window. 'Wanna come up for a nightcap? I've still got some of that weed.'

'I'll pass. Maybe at the weekend.'

'Safe.' Tom slaps the roof of the cab and gives the peace sign.

The cab takes me home.

I pay the driver and leave a drunkenly large tip that I can't really afford.

Stagger across the immaculate lawn fumbling for keys.

I open the door, step into the hallway, flick on the light.

Which reveals Col standing in the kitchen.

'Jesus, you scared me Dad. What are you doing?'

'Where have you been,' says Col.

'I told Mum. London.'

'It's 1 o' clock. Your mother's been worried.'

'Dad, I'm twenty-four years old.'

'This isn't a hotel.'

I notice the good scotch on the kitchen counter.

'I never said it was.'

'She left you a list of jobs to do. You haven't done any of them.'

'I'm not the butler here.'

'You're on thin ice. This better not happen again.'

'Yes boss.'

'Are you mouthing off?'

'No boss.'

'I'm going to bed. Turn the lights off down here when you're finished.'

I nod once.

'Thanks for paying for the psych sessions.'

Col grunts and brushes past me on his way upstairs.

When I hear Col shut his bedroom door I grab the good scotch and take it to the sink.

I take a big gulp and tip the rest of it, about three-quarters of a bottle, down the sink.

Stupid mistake, buying it for him.

As I make my way up the stairs, I realise I can't remember the journey home, can't remember where Mark's house is.

It's already leaked out of my memory.

48

'The psychiatrist was right. I am unfulfilled. I want more. I feel 'entitled' to more. It's embarrassing to admit, but I do.'

'Why is it embarrassing?'

'Because I don't want to sound entitled.'

'What do you feel entitled to?'

'Nothing really.'

'There must be something you have in mind.'

'No, there isn't. I'm just fed up with the whole game.'

'What game?'

'This game.' I make a gesture that signifies everything. 'The game of life.'

I hadn't intended to see the psychologist.

After the psychiatrist recommended the CBT I'd Googled local practitioners and discovered how much they charged per hour.

It turns out only the wealthy can afford to repair their minds on a long-term basis.

Plus I viewed the role of the psychiatrist as that of a kind of a healer for hire and the role of a psychologist -- their less intelligent cousins -- as that of a hierophant or bogus priest.

I wasn't interested in handing my money over to these head-shrinkers.

I'd recently acquired a second-hand copy of 'Modern Man in Search of a Soul' and was going to read that.

But after Alice informed me I could get a few sessions free on the NHS I found someone online who seemed okay. She specifically mentioned in her bio some of the things I was concerned about.

So far though, she's aloof.

Is she sneering at me? Not quite.

Maybe.

Her facial expression is on the cold side of neutral, the warm side of a sneer.

She adjusts her glasses. 'Do you want to die?'

'Why does everyone keep me asking that?'

'I have to ask. You implied you don't want to live.'

'I don't want to die.'

'Do you wish you'd never been born?'

'No. Sometimes. Life is absurd but I'm curious enough to keep going.'

'Why do you think life is absurd?'

'Don't you think it's absurd?'

Unfixable defect.

'I think it's important to have goals. A sense of purpose. Life seems meaningless when you're adrift.'

'I've had goals before and life was still absurd.'

Sisyphus.

Sisyphus on a beach in Costa Rica. Sisyphus happy in Costa Rica.

Sisyphus and Caitlin rolling a rock along a beach in Costa Rica, laughing, experiencing eudaimonia.

'Could you perhaps go back to university? Do a post-grad course? Aim for a career?'

'I wasn't even sure about university the first time around.'

'Why did you go then?'

'Because when you go to a grammar school that's what you're meant to do. We were taught to aspire to the middle-class professions, not those nasty common ones. Who'd want to be a carpenter when you can become an accountant, or a psychologist?'

The psychologist smiles with her mouth.

'I'm half-joking,' I say. 'No offence.'

'None taken.'

I take a sip of water from the plastic cup the psych had given me when I came in. 'Look. Despite being completely point-less, university wasn't actually that pointless. I can admit that. Many of my lecturers and tutors were conceited and boring and lazy, sure, and I had to share houses with embittered Oxbridge rejects who were intellectually insecure bullies. But. I actually fucking loved what I studied and had plenty of free time to read and watch and listen to extracurricular things I'd never heard of or would have balked at when I was younger. It was a good time.'

I try to remember some of the bourgeois things I learned/ enjoyed in Manchester but never think or talk about any more.

'The Divine Comedy', Iranian cinema, Messiaen.

Proust, Plato, Deleuze.

I used to go to the campus library all the time and sink into their big armchairs with the latest editions of Prospect, The Economist, The New Statesman, Foreign Affairs, Private

Eye, New Scientist, The Spectator, among other 'high-brow' publications, which were all stocked in the revolving stand in the foyer.

Left or right, progressive or reactionary, it didn't matter.

When I got my first laptop I watched hundreds of hours of talks and lectures and documentaries. I hungrily sopped up as much as I could, including a lot of cultural references that every 'educated person' is supposed to know.

I slept with a lot of sexy spoiled brats. I got a Trevor Nunn.

It wasn't all cigarettes-for-breakfast and porridge-for-dinner.

'What did you study?'

'Politics.'

'Could you perhaps go into the civil service? There would be plenty of other like-minded, intelligent people there. The work would be challenging, worthwhile.'

'I might have missed that boat.'

'There'll be other boats.'

'Maybe.'

I scratch my beard. Run my fingers through my hair. Check for evidence of more shedding.

'I should've listened to my dad, I reckon. I should've got a trade. It was good advice, really. I ignored him and ended up sitting in a grey office cubicle in Salford, doing grey work for grey money. I should've done a carpentry apprenticeship by day and Open University courses in my spare time.'

'You still can. There's nothing stopping you.'

'Except money. I don't want more debt. To be honest I'd be quite happy as a binman if everyone would just leave me alone. Maybe a little sunshine would be nice, enough money not to starve.

A binman in Costa Rica, tidying up the beach, the sun on my back, a few Costa Rican beers in the fridge at home.

'I'm theoretically equipped to participate in the giant circle-jerk of middle-class life, but I don't belong. I'm not welcome. And I don't really want to be there. I'm an untouchable.'

I wince at how self-pitying I sound.

'There's nothing stopping you from doing whatever you want. You seem overly concerned with what other people think of you.'

'I don't care what other people think, I just want them to leave me alone. I went to university and people thought I was too posh. If I hadn't gone other people would have said I wasn't ambitious enough. Why can't they get on with their own lives. I don't tell them what they should and shouldn't be doing.'

'Are there any particular people you're referring to?'

'No-one in particular. Certainly not my parents. Nor my ex-girlfriend. Nor my old friends. No-one.'

'You can't control other people but you can control how you react to them. We can work on some strategies for dealing with how other people's expectations make you feel. I'd like to see you again next week, if that suits you, Jamie?'

'Okay,' I say.

'Good. See you then.'

'See ya.'

I exit the clinic, a sturdy post-war building that would be completely grim if it wasn't for the blue NHS sign emblazoned at the top-left corner of the front facade.

There's a chill in the air portending early snow. I take my

179

woolly hat out of my (new) backpack and pull it on.

It isn't long before I reach Rochester station.

It's been three weeks since I saw Alice, since I re-started my medication. I see the psychiatrist every other Wednesday and the psychologist every other Friday. There haven't been any astonishing shifts in my outlook or mood, but I am shitting more productively, so the pills must be doing something.

What I actually need to banish my malaise is to move on from my parents' place and see out my twenties with a bang rather than a fizzle.

I knew it would be stifling to live with them again. Knew there was something unnatural about the relationship between many parents and their children, contrary to what the politicians are always banging on about.

The nuclear family: that microcosmic autocratic regime.

It strikes me as an alien and unhealthy concept.

A train arrives and I'm on my way 'home' again.

I get my phone out and check Facebook. Alice has posted photos from our day in London.

There's a selfie of us in the Tate. Someone with the same surname as Alice, maybe a cousin, has commented underneath. 'Gorgeous couple! xx'

I grimace and close Facebook.

I go to spareroom.co.uk and quickly find an ad for a room in a house in Gillingham.

A cis couple called Pete and Jo posted the ad. They look like yuppies. But the room is cheap and the security deposit is nominal.

I post a message to them.

Open a new tab, check Facebook again.

There's a message in my inbox now from Alice.

She says she's paid my share of the security deposit on our old flat. A small windfall. I'll be able to pay my parents back for the psych sessions.

She says she had the PROCEDURE and that she's okay.

She says she's moving in with someone called Felix. They met online and have 'so much in common'.

I'm surprised at how happy I am for her. All the negative feelings I had have more or less shrunk to nothing, as have many of my other feelings.

It was good to meet up with her and it's good we've both moved on.

We weren't meant to be together but that doesn't mean Alice is an awful human being.

We were both so young when we met. Both a bit crazy. I can forgive her for a lot of stuff that happened. Perhaps she'll forgive me too one day.

I don't want to think about the chronology of her and Felix's relationship. She's getting on with her life and that's good; no need to give air to that little envious creature within.

I don't reply though.

49

I'm loading up my Corsa again. Ready to move once again.

I pick up my last box of things in the hallway.

Col's in the lounge, engrossed in Football Focus. Andrea comes into the hallway.

She begins to cry.

'Ah Mum, what's wrong.'

'Nothing. Hormones. Sorry.'

I put the box down again.

We hug.

'I thought I'd have you for a bit longer than this,' she says.

'I know, but it's better if I go now. I don't want to outstay my welcome. And anyway, I'm only going down the road. It's like ten minutes, tops.'

'You can come over for dinner whenever you like.'

'Thanks.'

'What are your new housemates like?'

'I don't really know yet. They seem all right. I met them for coffee the other day and they said I can move in whenever I like.'

'When can I come and see your new pad?'

'Give me a couple of days to settle in. I'll call you.'

'All right love.'

We hug again.

'Col! Jamie's leaving now!'

I hear Col mutter something and make a big deal about getting off the settee.

He ambles into the hallway and folds his arms.

'See ya Dad.'

'Did you clear everything out of the gym?'

'You mean my old bedroom? Yes. I think so.'

I pick up my box of stuff and tap the side.

Col nods.

'Oh, hold on, I nearly forgot.'

I put the box down and take the cheque out of my wallet.

'Here you go guys. For the psych sessions.'

'Darling,' says Andrea. 'I told you not to worry about that.'

'I know, but I got my security deposit back from Alice.'

Col takes the cheque, folds it carefully, tucks it in his shirt pocket.

'This better not bounce,' he says.

I study him to see if he's joking.

He isn't.

I laugh and walk out to the car.

As I drive away I roll down the stiff window and stick an arm out to wave at them.

I peek in the rear-view mirror.

Andrea is still on the doorstep crying and waving.

Col has already gone back inside to watch the rest of Football Focus.

PART TWO

'This town drags you down.'

1

I move west along the A2 to a house in Gillingham with this professional cis couple from spareroom.co.uk.

Pete and Jo.

They're a bit older than me, they have their shit together.

They're a good-looking, go-getting couple in their early thirties with heteronormative hairstyles and heteronormative designer-label clothing.

Pete is an engineer and Jo is an estate agent.

Like me, they're Medwegian.

Unlike me, they're successful and haven't doctored their native accents.

They wanted a lodger to help with the mortgage and have a spare room which was big enough to fit a single bed, nothing else.

The room is almost identical to the shoebox room I just left at Mum and Dad's.

It has a small shelf on one wall, but there isn't space for any other furniture. I have to keep most of my clothes and other stuff in the airing cupboard along the landing, which means my clothes are always warm and smell like freshly washed towels.

Which I don't mind.

Overall it's an okay little sixties terraced house. Quite cosy, and the rent is cheap enough.

There's a small secluded garden bordered by high thuja trees that stand guard like friendly giants.

I feel calm in the garden.

Pete and Jo have a cat called Zeus that happily sits with me out there on a plastic deck chair during the day while I read and smoke.

Still no job.

Zeus is a great cat. A brown and white tabby who walks around like an Amazonian jaguar.

I like his sleepy/bad-ass face and his fluffy chin.

Zeus has a great attitude towards life. He's adventurous, but he also knows how to relax.

Medway, you could learn something from this cat! England, you uptight bastard, you too!

In the middle of the night Zeus jumps onto my bed, struts onto my chest and licks my face with his small sandpaper tongue for a minute or so, then jumps off and leaves me alone until the same sort of time the next night.

I really like it.

Even though my bed is constantly covered in cat hair, even though I could make a new cat out of all the moulted hair, I wouldn't want Zeus to stop his nightly visits.

One day I will do the same to Zeus to pay him back. Will creep up to him while he's sleeping and lick his feline face.

And I will swallow the hair on my tongue with gratitude and a beatific smile and radiance in my soul.

2

So far it's good with Pete and Jo.

I'm feeling okay.

Taking my meds, trying to get fit, using the CBT strategies my psychologist has been teaching me.

The psychiatrist is pleased with my progress and says once I finish my last session with him I'll only have to see the psychologist on a regular basis, and him in an emergency.

I haven't told Pete and Jo about the bipolar.

No need to freak them out.

I pay my rent on time and help out around the joint.

What more do they need from a lodger?

Total sanity?

Come on. Be realistic.

3

Tom Pritchard is also getting fitter.

He's been taking supplements to get 'jacked'.

Has stopped drinking fluoridated water because he doesn't want to have his mind controlled by the government.

If he ever catches me with a tap water in my hand he shakes his head as though I'm going to start goose-stepping within seconds.

Tom plays football every Wednesday night and Sunday afternoon.

He asks me to fill in for his five-a-side team, Geezers F.C., this Wednesday.

The game's at the local Anchorians sports club.

I'm chronically out of practice but keen.

I need the exercise, need the dopamine hits you get from scoring goals.

I dig out my old shinpads and astroturf boots and drive there early to warm up.

The other three players were all part of Tom's and my delinquent squad at school.

Tom neglected to tell me they'd be there, so when I turn up I have to feign pleasure at seeing them all again.

'Oh my dilly dolly days!' says Chino. 'Look who it is!'

Chino shakes my hand, claps me hard on the back.

Darren Bentley comes over to say hello, as does Liam O'Connor.

While we're all stretching I whisper to Tom, 'I thought you weren't hanging out with this bunch of pricks anymore.'

Tom is stuffing his shinpads down the front of his socks.

'Mark's the problem,' says Tom. 'And he ain't here. You're filling in for him.'

'You could've told me they'd be here.'

'You didn't ask. They're fine when he's away.'

'Why do I have to ask you everything? Can't you volunteer critical information for once?'

Tom ignores me and calls the team over for a pep talk.

'Lads, this is a must-win game. We've only got five, so no subs.'

'Can't promise I won't have a heart attack before half-time,' I say.

'If we lose the newbie buys everyone a drink,' says Chino. 'Hope you brought your wallet Sinbad.'

'Don't call me Sinbad,' I say.

'All right treacle, keep your knickers on.'

I smile tightly. 'Who are we up against,' I ask.

'Bunch of Kosovans,' says Liam. 'There's a fucking a plague of them in the area now. This bunch of clowns are top of the table. They're dirty bastards, so watch your ankles.'

The referee blows the whistle and we take our positions.

'Don't stand too close too them either,' says Liam, leaning towards me. 'They stink.'

It's a relatively clean game in the end and we lose 4-3.

I didn't score, but at least my knees didn't give out.

I was worried that they'd burst off, like fire hydrant caps under pressure.

The only incident occurred when one of the other team slid in and took out Darren.

Darren got up and squared up to the guy.

'I'll fucking have you for that,' said Darren.

'Yeah yeah mate. Go cry to your mummy.'

The ref intervened, gave the guy a yellow card. The game continued.

At one point, after Tom had booted the ball over the boundary fence and we were waiting for him to get it, I asked the same guy if he was from Pristina.

'Where?' he said.

'Pristina. Aren't you from Kosovo?'

'No,' he said. 'Istanbul.'

'Oh,' I said.

I offer to give Tom a lift after the game.

'Wanna come by mine for a beer and some Fifa?'

'Fuck yeah!' says Tom.

Pete and Jo are out.

We sit on the floor of the lounge and take off our shinpads.

Zeus saunters in, sniffs the shinpads. I pick him up and tickle his chin.

'Nice place,' says Tom.

'Yeah I like it.'

'Where are your housemates?'

'No idea. Out for dinner maybe.'

'Is that your laptop?'

I nod.

'Giz it here,' says Tom.

I stretch for it and pull it off the footrest.

'I've gotta show you this.'

Tom lifts the lid, starts typing.

He turns the screen towards me.

'This guy's amazing,' he says. 'Tells it like it is. This is where I buy my supplements from. No toxins. They ain't got anything in 'em the government can manipulate ya wiv.'

It's a video on a website called Infowars.org

A stocky, full-faced Texan man called Alex Jones is shouting at the camera from behind a desk.

Ranting about the Democratic nominee, Barack Obama.

Ranting about how everyone on the Left thinks he's going to save the constitution of the United States, save the world.

'They think he's some sorta god!' he yells, with wide eyes, face reddening.

'Does he go for McCain?' I ask.

Tom nods.

'He's certainly forthright,' I say.

We watch for five minutes or so, then this Alex Jones guy switches topics.

He starts talking about chemtrails and government surveillance and how the Earth is flat.

'All right, that's enough for me,' I say.

'No, no, keep watching,' says Tom.

'He's a conspiracy theorist.'

I take the laptop from Tom, close the window.

'Mate, we need to listen to that stuff,' says Tom, bristling slightly. 'There's something in it.'

'I don't go down those rabbit holes.'

'Don't be one of the sheeple,' he says.

'The sheeple?'

'Yeah', the sheeple. The people who believe the main-stream media.'

'I know what it means. No offence, but when you use that word you sound like you're in a cult.'

'The sheeple are the ones in the cult.'

'Okay.'

Tom takes out his phone and looks at it for a while, sulking.

I yawn. 'Wanna play Fifa?'

Tom nods.

We play best of three and Tom wins, which brings him out of his sulk.

'All right,' I say, 'I'm gonna hit the sack. And then go to bed.'

Tom smirks, stands up, stretches his arms above his head. His hairy belly pokes out.

'What you up to tomorrow night,' he says.

'Nothing.'

'Pub?'

I nod.

'Safe,' says Tom. 'I'll give you a tinkle when I've finished work.'

4

I get on okay with Pete and Jo.

They aren't people I'd usually hang around with but they respect my privacy and are always pleasant.

A few little things bug me.

Like, they constantly have the giant, wall-mounted plasma-screen TV on, even if no-one's watching it. Jo's parents will come over and we'll all sit in the front room chatting away and yet the TV will be on.

Or Pete's sister and nephew will be over and even though his nephew is a baby and everyone is focused on him, lavishing him with attention, the TV will still be on.

I'll go to turn it off and no matter what mindless shit is airing someone will say, 'Oi, Jay, we were watching that.'

It's like they're worried that without the background noise of the TV they'll all cease to exist, which might be true for all I know.

Apart from that they're good housemates/landlords.

Once I stopped hiding in my room in the evenings and felt relaxed enough to join them for dinner, I began to feel something like hygge, an untranslatable Danish word I learned recently.

Maybe hygge is a precursor to eudaimonia, I wondered, as Pete put a roast dinner in front of me one Sunday afternoon.

'Thank you, Lord, for this food and fine company,' I said.

'I know I'm a good cook but you don't have to refer to me as 'Lord',' said Pete.

Jo laughed and raised her wine glass. 'Cheers. Here's to our new housemate, Jamie. Thanks for not being a total slob and for paying your rent on time.'

'Thanks for not being shit landlords,' I said.

'It's early days,' she said, and winked.

Jo's lovely.

She can instantly put a person at ease, a trait I'm envious of.

Sometimes, when I'm lying in bed at night, I can hear her and Pete having sex in their bedroom across the landing.

I know it's wrong but I masturbate to the sound of her moans.

Luckily Pete often seems to finish before Jo, and as soon as the moaning stops I lose all interest.

5

During this period many of my dreams are set on unsettling, overlapping terrains where my old life in Manchester and my present life in Medway are surreally confused, conflated.

Are they happening in the past, or the future, or now?

It's impossible to tell.

It feels like all three.

In these dreams loose acquaintances of my who've never been to Medway -- nor will ever come to Medway -- live with me in Medway, have always lived in Medway.

Or else I live with them in their hometowns, which I've never visited and never will.

We go and get breakfasts together at fancy cafes that I can't afford to patronise, then walk along roads that lead inexplicably and impossibly to old haunts in Manchester.

Sometimes the roads lead to Beijing, or Schiele's Dead Cities, or giant steampunk train stations.

To medieval France, Helmand Province, or New Mexico.

To alien rainforests, or strip malls on the tops of mountains in Australia, or Erbil, or Glasgow, or Mongolia, et cetera.

In these dreams I drink inside dark pubs and nightclubs that don't exist, with people I will never see again or haven't ever met. I talk to people I despise as though we're old friends, and to people I love as though they're unreachable strangers.

I keep waking up devastated, alone.

It usually takes a few hours before the hygge returns.

6

I don't put up any posters or photographs on the walls of my room.

I like the room bare.

All I have in there are my books stacked up on the floor along one wall and my electric guitar and amp in the corner. There's a little window at the foot-end of my bed, which I keep open even as winter approaches because I sometimes smoke in there, but also because there's something pleasing about being able to see my breath as I lie in bed, swaddled tight in my duvet.

The view is of the rust-coloured roofs and chimneys of some nearby terraced houses and a thin slice of sky behind them, always grey. Occasionally the air horn of a train echoes across the town as it speeds along the tracks running to and from London.

I spend a lot of time sitting on the bed quietly playing my guitar, amp switched off, noodling The Smiths, or reading, looking up from my book and out the window if I sense a bird has landed on one of the roofs.

In the evenings Pete and Jo often shout up the stairs and ask if I want to come and watch the latest '24' episodes they've recorded on Sky.

I always say no.

7

One evening they knock on my door and come and sit on my bed.

'Jay, we think you need a girlfriend,' says Jo.

'Yeah,' says Pete. 'And we know someone we think you'll like.'

Is it you Jo, I think. Please be you.

'She's a colleague of mine,' says Jo. 'Kim. She's coming over this weekend for dinner. Do you want me to tell her you're interested?'

'Uh, I dunno guys. What's she like?'

'She's a babe,' says Jo, reaching forward and touching my knee. 'And she's super clever. She's like the top seller in our office.'

'And she's got a great personality,' says Pete, stroking his own invisible jumbo-sized breasts.

'Pete!' says Jo, back-handing his arm. 'You're such a div.'

She looks at me again and says, 'You have a lot in common. She likes books as well.'

I put my book face-down and open by my leg. 'What does she like to read?'

'She loves Harry Potter. She's read them all.'

'But they're children's books. What about adult stuff.'

'I dunno,' she says. 'I'll ask her tomorrow. Can I tell her you'll be here though, at the weekend?'

They're both smiling at me with closed mouths.

'Fine,' I say. 'Okay.'

Jo makes a kind of muted squeal and touches my knee again.

Pete winks at me.

They get up.

'Wanna watch 24 with us?' says Jo.

I smile and shake my head. They leave my room.

As soon as I hear the '24' intro countdown pips I slide a hand down my trousers and start masturbating to a series of mental images of Jo and me on my bed.

Saturday night comes around and I'm setting the kitchen table for dinner.

The TV is on even though we're all in the kitchen and can't see it.

Family Fortunes is on. I keep involuntarily tuning in to the 'Ih-ihhhh' of the wrong-answer buzzer and the laughter and applause from the studio audience.

I put out Pete and Jo's crystal wine glasses and the nice set of cutlery.

They're grown-up people; they have all this stuff.

The placemats have watercolour pictures on them of different native birds in their natural habitats.

They were probably Jo's parents' at some point. They look like they're from the seventies or eighties.

I study each one and think about who'd like what.

I give Jo the heron on the riverbank.

Pete gets the azure kingfisher on a branch.

I take the liberty of giving Kim the robin, and I treat myself to the wading redshank.

Pete is at the stove-top tending to a giant pot of chilli 'non' carne. They're cool about my vegetarianism and don't mind having a meat-free meal when we eat together.

It smells nice and spicy with plenty of chilli. The air is thick with heat and steam. My eyes are watering.

I rub them and say, 'That's a spicy meat-a-ball.'

Pete looks at me and says, 'Aw yeah, aw yeah, you love it.'

Jo uncaps a bottle of rosé wine.

Booze flows freely and generously in the house from a source of monthly wine-club deliveries.

There's a wine-rack that never stays depleted for long before the next batch arrives and it's replenished.

It's great.

Jo pours us each a glass of the rosé and we say cheers.

The doorbell rings.

'That'll be Kim,' says Jo, walking out of the kitchen.

Jo and Kim return to the kitchen together.

Jo hadn't lied. Kim is good-looking.

I was expecting some kind of bimbo; she isn't that.

She's not my usual 'type', but what does that mean anyway.

I notice she has intelligent eyes and immediately feel exposed, as though she's gleaning from me all my paltry thoughts, discovering my unfixable defect.

Jo introduces us.

'You're sitting here,' Jo says to Kim, 'and you, Mr Sinclair, are sitting here.'

Kim pulls my chair out for me and, trying to be hilarious, I say, 'Thank you, kind sir. It's rare to meet such a gentleman.'

Jo tuts. 'He's not normally this much of a div, Kimmy.'

Kim laughs, and something stirs in me.

It's a boozy dinner.

We all talk about sex a lot.

Jo and Kim share the job of recounting a story about one of their bosses being caught on CCTV getting a blowjob from a hooker in his office and subsequently getting sacked, which they'd found hilarious because he was a prick.

Each of us ends up revealing when and how we lost our respective virginities.

I tell everyone about how Alice sometimes used to giggle hysterically at the point of orgasm (a humble-brag for Kim's benefit), and how disconcerting I found it.

Then Pete starts to tell us about his and Jo's first attempt at anal sex.

He reveals how messy it had been.

Ih-ihhhh.

Jo stops chewing and glares at Pete. She's gone bright red.

'What, darling?' says Pete. 'It's funny. You've gotta be able to laugh at yourself.'

He reaches over to touch her arm but she pulls it away.

'Why did you have to tell them that,' says Jo. 'That's so embarrassing. I can't believe you told them that.'

She gets up and goes out the back door to the garden.

Zeus appears from somewhere and darts out before she closes the door.

I can see Jo light a cigarette in the dark from where I'm sitting.

Pete looks sheepishly at us. He excuses himself and goes outside too.

Kim and I smirk at each other.

I pour us both another glass of wine.

Kim asks me about work.

'Currently funemployed,' I say. 'I've only recently moved

back to the area and I'm still looking.'

'When did you move back?'

'About three months ago.'

'Shit, and you still haven't got a job? What are you look-ing for?'

'I dunno, anything. I'm holding out for as long as possible, but can't be too picky. I don't have a lot of savings left. Got any ideas?'

'You can earn pretty good money doing what I'm doing,' she says. 'I've done it since I was eighteen. All my mates went to uni and got into debt, but I bought my own house when I was twenty-one.'

I think about my student loan, which I've barely made a dent in since graduating, and imagine myself as a cloud floating over a dark ocean.

'So you got into debt too,' I say.

'Sorry?'

'I'm assuming you have a mortgage. A debt.'

'Well yeah, but it's different. It's an investment.'

'So's an education, apparently.'

More wine.

'What if house prices drop?' I say.

'They won't on my street. They keep going up.'

She makes a gesture with her hand that signifies exponen-tial growth.

'Okay.'

'What, don't you believe me? It's my job to know this stuff.'

'I believe you, but I don't believe the rhetoric. They want us to get mortgages for a reason, don't they. They want us to get into debt. It's a kind of slavery.'

'I agree, kind of.'

'The whole banking system's a racket.'

'Are you talking about that bank? Who was it, RBS?'

'Well, there's that.'

'I think it's wrong they got bailed out.'

'Right? Nothing will change though.'

'Probably not. But there's regeneration in my area.'

'Where do you live?'

'Rainham.'

'Oh yeah? My mum and dad live in Rainham.'

I take out my phone and show her on Google maps where they live.

She takes my phone and scrolls to where she lives. It's only few streets away from Mum and Dad's.

'My mum wants me to buy a place,' I say. 'But there are alternatives. Or rather there could be. Like what they're doing in Utrecht. Did you hear about that?'

'Is that in Holland?'

'Belgium isn't it?'

'I think it's Holland.' She looks it up on her phone. 'Yeah, it's Holland.'

'Okay. Well, they're trialling a Universal Basic Income there.'

'What's that?'

I feel myself go red at the prospect of having to sound posh.

'It's this idea where the state gives everyone, no matter how much they earn, the same amount of money.'

'That's ridiculous. Where would they get the money from to do something like that?'

'Number one, you'd go after all the tax that corporations have evaded. You come down hard on tax evasion. Last I heard there was like 120 billion of owed tax. That would help. If you clawed it all back and invested it properly you could pay for it with the interest alone.'

I pause for another sip.

Kim's eyes have glazed over.

'Number two, you seize all the assets of the millionaires and billionaires who've avoided tax, and dole that out to everybody. Like Philip Green.'

'Who's that.'

'The owner of Arcadia, which is Topshop and BHS and all that. He raided his employees' pension funds so he could buy yachts. You seize his assets and make him and people like him do community service for the rest of their lives, wearing t-shirts that say 'I'm a tax-avoiding, pension-raiding cunt'.

'You've got it all worked out,' she says.

I go red again. 'Sorry. I'm slightly drunk and on my soapbox. This is boring. I have nothing worked out.'

'You're lucky you have those eyes, otherwise I'd be out of here.'

I go cross-eyed and smile a goofy smile.

'Pour me another drink Mr Know-It-All,' she says.

She smiles and proffers her glass and I pour pink wine into it.

I feel her foot against my shin. Something else stirs in me.

Jo re-enters the house. She marches straight past us, through the front room, and stomps upstairs.

Pete, looking beleaguered, immediately follows her.

Their bedroom door slams and Kim and I can hear their voices coming through the ceiling.

I make an 'oh dear' facial expression and begin clearing the plates from the table.

I place the stack in the sink and when I turn round Kim is right there. She places a hand on my chest and kisses me.

Probably to make sure I don't talk about the Universal Basic Income anymore.

Fair enough.

It's a good kiss.

'Where's your room?' she asks.

I lead the way, and we have sex while Pete and Jo are still arguing.

8

In the morning, Kim's gone.

There's a blu-tacked note on the wall above the headboard.

'What's with that cat? It woke me up licking my face. And if you're not prepared to buy your own house, the least you could do is get a decent-sized bed. x'

I rub my lower back and push my hips forward and concede that she has a point.

Her business card, which shows her work and personal phone numbers and her work and personal email addresses, is blu-tacked to the bottom of the note.

Where did she get the blu-tack, I wonder.

What's blu-tack made of, I wonder.

I go downstairs for some breakfast and find an envelope on the kitchen table addressed to me. I open it to find a cheque for £50 and a birthday card inside from Mum and Dad.

It's Andrea's handwriting.

'Dear Jamie, wishing you a very special day. Lots of love from Mum and Dad xxx'

I'd completely forgotten it was my birthday today. Totally lost track of time.

I'm twenty-five now.

I visualise the numbers two and five in my mind's eye. Let them hover there for a moment, waiting for thoughts to form around them.

I feel nothing.

Later on Pete asks about the envelope.

We're on the settee watching TV.

Zeus is on my lap.

'Who was it from,' Pete asks. 'It looked like a card.'

'Ah not exactly,' I say. I scratch Zeus's head and proceed to lie. 'It was an invitation to a friend's wedding. I can't go. It's in Mexico and I don't have enough money.'

'That's a shame,' says Pete. 'Mexico's great.'

'Everything all right with you and Jo?'

'Ah you know,' he says, not looking away from the TV. 'I'll be in the doghouse for a couple of days, but it'll be all right.'

Zeus rolls over, so that I can rub his belly.

'You're never in the doghouse, are you mate,' I say.

Zeus purrs.

'Or the cathouse.'

Pete tuts. 'Lame joke mate.'

I pull a goofy face, but Pete is still watching the TV and doesn't notice.

9

Tom and I are at the pub again, this time The Old Post Office in Chatham.

I had another pointless interview with yet another pointless temp agency and Tom met me afterwards.

We've each become the other's codependent enabler, spending more and more time together drinking and validating our respective poor lifestyle choices.

Tom has already begun to annoy me again. His proclivity towards conspiracy theories and wingnuts like David Icke and Alex Jones is infuriating; his constant braggadocio has worn thin.

It's not all bad though.

Tom has changed since we were younger. He's trying hard to extricate himself from a rotten group. He can still make me laugh.

He just needs more time, and I do have a little more time to give him.

I feel comfortable with large doses of him.

It just so happens that many of those large doses are taken with commensurately large doses of alcohol.

Tom works down the road at a travel agent.

Is pretty good at it, based on his own testimony. He always has cash anyway, and seems to be able to come and go from the office as he pleases.

It's 4pm and we're two beers in.

Tom's arm is no longer in a sling but he still has some bruising around his eye.

I notice his shoulders are broader and his triceps are more pronounced. The supplements must be doing the trick.

'They told me the usual thing, that they didn't have any vacancies currently but they'd call me blah blah blah.'

'Why don't you come and work at my place,' Tom says. 'I could get you a job like that.' He snaps his fingers.

I swig my beer. 'I guess I could try it. I could email you my CV.'

'Do it. It's wicked. The commission's amazing.'

'Ah, sure, why not. I'll give it a go. I'll probably suck at it, but whatever. It's a job.'

'Don't be so negative, bruv. You've gotta believe in yourself. The job's all about confidence.'

I stand up, being slightly tipsy already, and say, 'I am a strong, independent woman who don't need no man. Let's marriage.'

'Sit down you idiot,' Tom says.

We roll cigarettes.

'So what's Kim like then?'

'She's... nice.'

'Is she fit?'

"Fit'? Are you an In-Betweener?'

'Ga, just tell me what she's like.'

'I like her. That's all you need to know.'

'Well that's boring.'

I shrug.

'Better keep her away from me,' says Tom. 'I'm irresistible to women.'

'Obviously.'

'You're really not gonna tell me anything about her, are you.'

'No.'

Tom sighs. 'Okay. So what do you actually want to do then? Like, with your life and all that.'

'I wanna be your dog.'

I make the guitar noises from the song for a bar or two.

Then I throw my cigarette up and catch it between my lips, like a boss.

I raise my eyebrows and widen my eyes and grin. I can't believe I did it. It usually bounces off a cheek or my chin.

Then Tom tries it with his own cigarette. Catches it between his lips too, like a total bloody boss.

We stand up and cheer and hug each other.

An old grizzled drunk in the corner tuts.

When I graduated I'd considered becoming a 'Writer'.

I studied politics but was always scribbling poetry or weird little stories.

Alice read one once and said something like, 'That's actually pretty good. Weird, but good.'

So I had it my head that maybe I could do that for a living.

However, I found poverty didn't help with creativity or motivation, it completely snuffed them out.

The starving-artist-living-in-a-garret thing didn't work for me.

I'd get in from my job at the insurance company, make dinner, then sink a few beers, feeling melodramatic.

Watch TV for a bit then pass out on the settee while Alice tidied up in the kitchen.

It's all I could do. I had no energy to write.

I should've been reading as much as I could, writing a blog, building an 'online presence', getting on with some stories.

But I could only fantasise about writing a book. About what genre I would write in. About the Booker prize. About middle-class characters (doctors, barristers, psychologists, academics) with middle-class angst. About what epigraph I should use, and how epigraphs are pretentious. About the photograph inside the back cover of me looking horrified/handsome. About readers of the book looking at the picture, feeling sad/beautiful/scared.

Or not.

I was aware of multiplicity of interpretations.

Of validation. Of vanity. The letter V.

I was aware of all these things.

If I'd had to describe the situation in, say, forty-eight words I would've said I was stuck in bewildering petit-bourgeois limbo, somewhere between the working class I'd come from and the middle class I was supposed to be a part of now, with none of the 'authenticity' or 'romance' of the former and none of the 'status' or 'security' of the latter.

If Tom had to describe the situation he'd probably have said I was being a posh prick, putting on those 'airs and graces', feeling sorry for myself.

I would probably have agreed with him.

We finish our cigarettes and come in from the smoking deck, rubbing our hands and blowing into them.

I thought I'd escaped the cold by travelling south, but it's taters mate. November is doing what November does in England.

I tell Tom I might study again. That I'm thinking about training as a teacher, or maybe even doing something with more prospects, like law.

Then I remember that I don't have enough money for a law degree, don't want the extra debt, don't have wealthy parents to support me through a series of unpaid internships.

'Actually, forget law. But maybe teaching. Just, something. My psychologist thinks it would be a good idea.'

'You see a psychologist? You a schizo or summink?' says Tom.

'Fuck off.'

Tom rolls his eyes. 'I'm just joshing you fam. Lighten up. Anyway, I thought you said you wanted to be a writer.'

'There's no money in it. I need an actual paying job.'

'Teachers don't get paid much.'

'I know but it would be something.'

'You should write a porno. You'd make loads of money doing that.'

'Not if you were in it. It'd all be over in like two minutes.'

Tom flips me the finger in an elaborate way. I scrunch my face.

'What about your harem,' I say. 'How many girls have you got on the go now?'

'Just the one, for once.'

'What's her name?'

'Zoe.'

'Does she know about Xavier? Have you talked about that?'

'Ah, what's to talk about.'

'Mate. You have a son in care.'

Tom's face darkens. 'Can we leave this alone?'

'Yeah, no, sorry for bringing it up.'

Tom pays for our drinks.

'But surely you should say something,' I say. 'It'll come up eventually.'

'You don't know what you're talking about and to be honest, you're starting to fuck me off a bit.'

'Tom, come on, I'm concerned, that's all.'

'Yeah well don't be. It's none of your business.'

'You're right. It isn't.'

10

I should make my excuses and go home, but I don't.

I'm dubious about what Tom said about Xavier, yet continue the evening because I'm committed to getting drunk.

Lad.

Which is why we end up at The Zone.

Laaads.

Tom eventually softened, and once we were thoroughly trousered he suggested we move on after The Old Post Office called last orders.

I was too weak to say no.

The Zone is banged out, as usual.

This is where Medwegians come for a proper blow-out if they can't afford the taxi to the more 'up-market' Amadeus, which is always.

We exchange our coats for tokens at the cloakroom under UV light and go straight to the bar, sashaying and pushing through all the people on the dancefloor.

We get beer from bottles with tops that come off too easily.

Jagerbomb chasers too.

Why God, why.

We stand at the bar for a while, drinking determinedly.

Round after round after round.

I'm not getting any more drunk, either because I've reached that plateau or because the drinks are more watered down than

I'd thought possible.

I see the lads from Geezers F.C. emerge from a crowd.

Tom sees them too.

I expect Tom to suggest we leave but he actually looks pleased to see them all.

Mark Galbraith is with them. He walks over on his own and embraces Tom in a macho way.

He's also looking more 'jacked'. Perhaps Tom got him onto the supplements too.

Noticing me he says, 'Is that Sinbad?'

I nod at him. 'Long time no semen,' I say. 'How's it going Mark?'

'Good brother.' He slaps me forcefully on the back. Why do these guys all feel the need to do that? He leans on the bar and points at the beer taps. 'What you having?'

'Nah I'm good thanks,' I say. 'I was thinking of heading off actually.'

'Bullshit,' says Tom, putting his arm around my shoulders and shaking me a little. 'The night's just getting started.'

I move most of the relevant muscle groups in my face for a smile.

Mark orders another round of drinks, and I take the one handed to me, and I drink it.

11

The night trudges on.

Tom and I are sitting on stools near the edge of the dancefloor with the Geezers F.C. boys standing around us, trying to look intimidating.

Drum 'n' Bass throbs through the dark club.

Tom and the geezers are openly leching at the handful of women younger than forty. They're ganging up on me with their 'banter'. They quote Guy Ritchie movies at each other, punctuating this with insults about my sexuality, my looks, my poshness.

I'm hanging out with 'Loaded' magazine and his less intelligent friends, 'Maxim', 'Zoo', 'Nuts' and 'The Daily Star'.

Tom is in Mark's alpha-male thrall, despite everything he'd told me about wanting to break free from it.

'So what exactly are you doing back here, Sinbad?' says Mark. 'I thought you were too good for Medway.'

'Ha. Yeah. I went to university,' I say. 'What an awful thing to do. And don't call me Sinbad.'

'Chill out sweetheart, I'm just breaking your little balls.'

'He's a bit precious, this one,' says Tom. 'He can't take a joke. Whatever you do, don't mention his receding hairline.'

The geezers laugh.

'Piss off fatty,' I say. 'The supplements aren't getting rid of that gut, are they?'

'See, I told you,' says Tom, more desperate for Mark's approval than I'd realised.

I tut. 'How's your son, Tom?'

Tom scowls at me.

'Oooh, touchy subject,' says Mark. 'He don't like to be reminded of what he did.'

'What do you mean, 'What he did'?'

'Nothing,' says Mark, smirking at Tom.

Tom gets up and pats himself for his cigarettes. 'If anyone mentions Xavier again I'm liable to get violent.'

'Alright, alright,' says Mark. 'You two need to calm down.' He stands in front of Tom and shadow-boxes him. 'What you need is some pussy. And some coke.'

I face-palm myself in my mind.

Mark pushes Tom towards the dancefloor and marshals the geezers into position.

'You coming?' he asks me.

'I'm going,' I say, and mean it.

'Suit yourself. I guess university made you even more of a poof than I thought.'

Tom snickers at this like a teenage boy in the presence of the school bully.

I frown-smile. 'I... have no words for you.'

Mark imitates me, making me sound posher than ever.

I sigh. 'Be sure to wrap the old chap, guys. We don't want any more accidents.'

'Oi look,' says Mark. 'There's some more faggots over there. Why don't you go and dance with them?'

'Great bantz,' I say, making the a-ok sign.

Mark laughs and walks to the dancefloor, followed by Tom and the geezers.

Mark immediately starts chatting-up a woman; immediately

puts his hands on her person. Then Tom and Mark leave the dancefloor together, whispering in each other's ears.

I notice that when it's Mark's turn to whisper to Tom, Tom tilts his head back slightly, like a beta wolf exposing his jugular in submission to the dominant member of the pack.

I think about howling like a wolf, but grimace instead and make my way to the exit.

I stumble out of the club and into a taxi.

12

Tom texts me at about 3am, half-apologising for what happened while simultaneously blaming me.

I'm awake, have had too much booze, can't get off to sleep. Zeus is dozing at the foot of the bed.

I consider being the bigger person and replying magnanimously, but I don't.

Tom texts again and asks to come over.

- no. i'm in bed.
- please mate. it's important
- no
- i'm getting a taxi now
- wtf. no!
- too late
- wanker
- you love me really

My phone rings.

Zeus briefly opens his eyes, closes them again.

Tom stage-whispers. 'Oi mate, I'm outside.'

'Sleep on the front step.'

'Just let me in you dick.'

I roll out of bed, get a thick jumper out of the airing cupboard. I go downstairs, carefully avoiding the creak on the seventh step, and open the front door.

Tom is hopping from one foot to the other.

'Need a slash,' he says.

I move out of the way and motion up the stairs. Tom bolts up.

'Try not to make any noise,' I mumble.

I creep back up to my room and get under the covers.

Zeus stretches, jumps off the bed, leaves the room.

I hear the toilet flush. Tom enters.

'Fuck man this room is tiny!'

'Pete and Jo are in bed, Tom. Shut the fuck up.'

'Sorry mate, sorry.'

He sits on my feet. I kick him off.

'Sorry mate.'

'Go away, Tom.'

He stands up. He seems 'wired' from all the coke.

'Listen, I'm really sorry about earlier.'

'I know. You said. It's fine.'

'But that ain't why I'm here. Zoe dumped me tonight.'

'At this point in time, I don't care.'

'That's cold fam.'

'I might care once I've had enough sleep.'

'Can I stay here tonight? She kicked me out of my own house.'

'How does that work.'

'I dunno. I'm just gonna lie down here, that cool?'

'There's blankets in the airing cupboard out there.'

'You're a king.'

'Hurry up.'

Tom makes more noise getting the blankets, then hunkers down on the floor.

'We still friends?'

'You need to stop talking.'

'Fine. But I need to know. We all good?'

'Apart from you being the most irritating person in this room, yes, we're still friends.'

'That's all I needed to hear. Night roomie.'

'Fuck you and fuck all of your ancestors.'

Tom laughs.

I pull my pillow over my head and try to sleep.

13

The next morning, a bright Saturday, I awake to Tom's guttural snores.

I step over him, consider farting in his face, decide to spare him.

I go downstairs and put the kettle on. The front door opens.

Jo and Pete come through with bags of groceries.

'Hey guys, sorry if my friend woke you last night.'

'Oh, we didn't hear anything,' says Jo.

'We use earplugs and eyemasks,' says Pete. 'It's the way forward.'

'Ah, that's a relief.'

'Were you up late?' says Jo.

'Against my will. Cuppa?'

'Yeah go on then,' says Jo.

'No thanks,' says Pete.

I help them put the groceries away while the kettle boils.

'I'll transfer some money for this,' I say.

'No rush,' says Jo.

'Oh, Jay, that reminds me,' says Pete. 'The electricity bill came. Can you stick forty quid into my account when you get a chance?'

'Sure can.'

I go to my room and log into my bank account.

Look aghast at my balance.

I've been in Medway for over four months and my savings

have dwindled to an alarming low. I barely have enough to cover my share of the bill.

'Fuck,' I say.

Tom stirs. 'Bruv, keep it down, I'm trying to sleep.'

I grab my pillow and throw it at Tom.

Tom stuffs it under his head and goes back to sleep.

I fetch the phone book and open it on my bed. I ring every pub within fifty miles of Pete and Jo's.

Tom finally gets up and shuffles off to the bathroom.

I get lucky after about twenty calls. I get through to the manager of a local Harvester restaurant and lie profusely about my work experience.

'Wetherspoon's, eh? Which one?'

'In Manchester. I used to live up there.'

'So you know how to pour a decent pint?'

'Yes,' I lie.

'Good. Would you be willing to do some barista training?'

'What would that involve?'

'You know, making artisanal coffee and all that.'

I imagine a Woody Allen character called Arty Zarnle.

'Oh, yeah, right. Sure.'

'Okay,' says the manager, after a (dubious?) pause. 'When can you start Jamie?'

I hang up and open my bedroom door.

'Pete!'

'Yeah!'

'Come here a sec!'

Pete pauses his game of Fifa and comes upstairs. He pokes

his head around the bedroom door. 'All right honeysuckle?'

'You are now the manager of a Wetherspoon's in Manchester. I worked for you between 2006 and 2007.'

'What?'

'I just got a job. I need you to be one of my referees.'

'Oh,' says Pete, entering the room. 'Sure thing. High five.'

We high-five. Pete goes to leave.

'Hang on Pete,' I say. 'Listen, I might not be able to pay my rent on time this month. But I'll make up for it with my first pay cheque.'

'Hey, no problemo amigo,' he says.

'Cheers Pete.'

'It's all good in the hood. We love having you here. We know you're good for it.'

'Thanks.'

'Cup of tea?' he says. 'Actually, hold on.' He looks at his watch. 'It's beer o'clock. Want one?'

I've only been awake for an hour.

'I guess I've got something to celebrate.'

'And I need someone to play against on Fifa.'

I wiggle my thumbs. 'Let me limber up then and I'll meet you on the settee.'

'Did someone say Fifa?' says Tom, from the landing.

'Pete, this is a local reprobate known as Thomas Pritchard.'

'Hey mate,' says Pete.

'Hey,' says Tom.

They shake hands.

'Come on then,' I say, getting off the bed.

'Bring something to pad your boxer shorts,' says Pete, 'because I'm going to spank your little botties.'

224

Pete bends an invisible person over his knee and slaps the air a few times.

14

Jo comes into the living room.

Us boys are fixated on the game.

'I regret buying this for you,' she says to Pete. 'It's all you do now.'

'That's not true,' he says. 'I did a big shit earlier.'

'You're a big shit,' she says.

'Jo, this is Tom by the way,' I say.

'Hi Tom.'

Tom briefly looks away from the screen. 'Hey.'

'Pete, we've gotta go to Mum and Dad's. They're cooking an early dinner.'

'Nooooo!' says Pete.

'Look at that, top bins,' says Tom, clenching his fist in celebration.

'Pete,' says Jo.

'Coming darling.'

He puts down the Xbox controller. 'Enjoy, lads. This isn't over though. I'll be back later to exact my revenge.'

'You wish,' I say.

Pete puts his hand in his pocket, pulls out a middle finger.

'Laters,' I say.

'We won't be too late,' says Jo.

I give her a thumbs-up. Jo and Pete go out to the hallway, put their shoes and coats on, leave the house.

'She's a bit of all right, eh?' says Tom.

'She's happily married,' I say. 'Well, she's married anyway.'

'That's never stopped me before.'

'Aren't you going to try and patch things up with Zoe?'

'To be honest I wasn't that into her. I prefer her sister. That's why she dumped me, in the end. She found text messages.'

'Oh my God, you're a moron.'

'I'm a playa,' he says.

'Not mutually exclusive.'

The final whistle goes and an option to go to extra time pops up on the screen.

'Shall we call it a draw, or do you want me to punish you in extra time?'

'Actually,' says Tom. 'I was hoping you'd give me a lift home. I need to make sure Zoe hasn't changed the locks or anything.'

'You've got a brass neck, you know that?'

'What are friends for.'

'To be exploited, clearly.'

The car doesn't start first time.

'You need a new car,' says Tom, putting his feet up on the dashboard.

'No shit, Sherlock. Get your feet off.'

'What, am I ruining the gorgeous upholstery?'

'Get your feet off or get out.'

'Keep your hair on. You ain't got much left remember.'

'I'm gonna tear yours out and force-feed it to you in a minute.'

'Ooh, kinky.'

On the fourth attempt it ignites, and Tom cheers.

'I can't remember where you live,' I say.

'How can you not remember?'

'Because I've always been completely smashed whenever the taxi's dropped you off. And it's always been dark.'

'You know The Flying Saucer?'

'In Hempstead.'

'Yeah. Just up from there.'

'Cool.'

We drive in silence for a while.

Tom eventually breaks it. 'Seriously, you and me, we're cool right?'

'You're on thin ice.'

'I just get carried away when I'm drinking around those guys. We go back a long way.'

'Forget about it.'

'You're a good mate Sinbad. A real mate.'

'Don't call me Sinbad.'

Tom puts his hands up. 'Sorry, forgot.'

'I heard you saying to Pete you ain't got much money,' he says.

'I just got a job, so it'll be all right.'

'I can lend you some if you need.'

'Should be fine, ta.'

'What's the job?'

'It's at that Harvester. I'll be working behind the bar.'

'Oh yeah, I know it. Sweet. You'll be able to give me free booze.'

'Maybe.'

'Turn right up here.'

'Yes boss.'

'It's that one there.'

'That one?'

'Yeah.'

I stop and pull up the handbrake.

The house is huge, beautiful. There's a brand new BMW parked on the drive.

'Cheers geez,' says Tom. 'I owe ya.'

'You do.' I gesture towards the house. 'I guess travel agents get paid more than I realised.'

'Eh?'

'This house. It's massive.'

'I know, bare huge innit. Got three bathrooms. I've got my own jacuzzi.'

'Maybe I really should come and work at your place. I'd probably end up killing you though...'

'Seriously, if you need dosh, lemme know.' He makes it rain.

'Okay. Whose car is that? Is it yours?'

'Nah... it's Zoe's.'

'Zoe drives a beamer?'

'She's a lawyer innit. She's loaded.'

'Your life is a mystery to me.'

He makes a fake gang sign. 'Playa for life.'

He gets out. I watch him as he goes through the side gate.

Tom looks back at me, waves, shuts the gate behind him.

I stay where I am. I peer through the gap between the fence and the gate.

See the side door open and Mark step outside.

Mark, even taller than Tom, stands over him and appears to threaten him.

Then he stands aside and lets Tom into the house.

I immediately text Tom.

- what's going on. why's mark at your house
- ah, you were always going to find out eventually. he lives with me
- since when
- since i got out of prison
- how did i not know this? also he's the one who put you there
- i know, that's why i live with him. he pays the rent
- i thought you were done with him
- it's complicated
- you were best pals last night
- i said sorry didnt i
- is the bmw his?
- yeah
- why did you lie to me
- i knew you'd get all antsy about me living with mark

I don't reply.

I seethe for most of the journey, gripping the steering wheel tight and arguing with Tom in my mind, but then I switch to autopilot and allow myself to get lost in my Costa Rica daydream.

15

When I get in I turn on the Xbox and start a new game of Fifa.

While the game's loading I nip upstairs and roll a joint with some of the weed Tom recently gave me.

I have a few tokes, blowing smoke out of my bedroom window.

I go downstairs and start playing, but have to stop midway through a game when I start to imagine the little football players as sentient and doomed.

I sense a panic attack coming on, as I imagine myself as an avatar in a simulation, maybe being controlled by some higher dimensional being.

I drop the Xbox controller on the floor and do my botched yoga pose on the sofa until the feeling wears off.

I get a text message from Kim.

- Hello stranger. What you doing later? xx
- i'm a free agent. wanna hang out? xx
- Yes please. Let's go to the cinema. I haven't been in ages. xx
- sounds good xx
- I'll check the times and let you know the plan xx
- okay :) xx

Jo picks me up and we drive to the Strood multiplex near the river.

Inside the foyer we change our minds: none of the films

appeal that much.

'Wanna get something to eat instead?' says Kim.

'Yeah. There's that Mexican place over the road.'

'Yum.'

We're seated by a waiter who looks no older than fourteen. His voice hasn't fully broken.

He takes our orders and leaves us alone for a while.

'They're employing children now,' says Kim.

'He probably has more money than me.'

'Are things getting bad?'

'Actually, I got a job today.'

'What? That's great. What's the job?'

'Barman.'

'That's something at least.'

'Yeah. I start tomorrow night.'

'We should get margaritas to celebrate.'

'You've gotta drive.'

'Just one. When in Rome and all that. Or should I say Mexico City. I'll pay.'

'You've twisted my arm.'

We finish eating.

Kim showed her usual self-control and stopped after the first margarita.

I'm two margaritas and three Coronas in. Ranting a bit. On my soapbox again, complaining about the state-of-the-nation.

'How is it that someone with a double-digit IQ who's been to prison can live the life of Riley, and I can barely afford this poxy chimichanga? I'm all for giving people second chances, but what's that about?'

'Poor little Jamie.'

'I know, woe is me.'

'What does Tom do again?'

'He's a travel agent, allegedly.'

'Allegedly?'

'You should see where he lives.'

'It's quite fancy, right?'

'Yeah. It's in Hempstead. He told me Mark pays all the rent.'

'That's weird.'

'He must feel guilty or something. I know Mark though. He's not the caring, compassionate type. There's something weird going on. I think they're dealing coke. How else could they afford all of it? Mark works at the paint factory in Gillingham Business Park. Tom's a travel agent but has wodges of fifties in his wallet at all times.'

'Maybe I'm with the wrong guy. Is Tom single?'

'Don't even joke about that. His ego's big enough as it is.'

'He's kind of gross, no offence to your friend.'

'He's always got someone on the go.'

'So he says.'

'No, I've seen him at work. It's inexplicable. They fight over him.'

'He must have a big... bank balance.'

'That must be it.'

'Oh well. I guess I'm stuck with you for the time being.'

'I'm a big-shot barman now, don't forget. If you play your cards right I might even contribute my half of the bill.'

'I love it when you flex your financial muscles. It turns me on.'

'Hey, you're only human.'

16

We head to Kim's place.
It's my first time staying over there.

We have to drive past my parents' place. I notice their car isn't in the drive.

'That's my mum and dad's house,' I say, pointing across her.

She slows down. 'Aw, it's cute. I like the little garden.'

'Yeah, they look after it.'

'Should we go and say hello?'

'Ha, funny.'

'What, are you ashamed of me?'

'Other way around.'

'That's mean.'

'I'm just kidding, sort of. Anyway, they're not home.'

'Oh. Another time then. I'm sure they're lovely.'

'They're all right.'

'Do you have any brothers or sisters?'

'One brother. He lives in Perth with his family.'

'In Australia?'

I nod.

'That's awesome. Have you been over there?'

'Not yet. I want to go next year, once I've replenished my savings.'

'I've always wanted to visit Australia. Bit scared of the spiders though.'

'John says you hardly ever see them.'

'Once is more than enough for me.'

'I don't think it's as bad as everyone thinks.'

'Probably.'

She pulls into her driveway and kills the engine.

'Here we are. Welcome to Chez Kim.'

'Mangetout mangetout, mademoiselle.'

Kim's house is nearly identical to my parents' place, typical of the area, but the layout is the mirror-image of theirs.

The stairs aren't against the right-hand wall of the hallway, but the left. To enter the lounge you have to turn right.

It disorients me, and because of the booze in my system, I briefly forget where I am, who I am.

'Come on drunkie, let's get you some water.'

'Got any wine?'

'I don't think you need any more booze.'

'Yeah, no, you're right.'

Kim guides me into the lounge and onto the settee. She carries on through to the kitchen -- again, on the wrong side of the house -- and I notice the bookshelf in the corner, packed with books.

I go over and have a squiz.

The entire Harry Potter collection is there, but there's plenty of other books that aren't Harry Potter. A lot of non-fiction, including dozens of science books, especially to do with dolphins and general marine biology.

Not a celebrity autobiography in sight.

Kim returns with a glass of tap water and puts it on the coffee table. I sit down next to her, close, and put my arm around her. She kisses my shoulder, my neck.

'Are your housemates out?' I ask.

'What housemates?'

'You live alone?'

'Yeah...'

I suppress the twinge of inadequacy that shoots through me and help her out of her clothes.

17

On her way to work the next morning Kim drops me home. I'm hungover, maybe still a little drunk.

'Thanks for letting me stay over,' I say. 'And for the lift.'

'You're welcome.'

'I have a good time with you.'

'Me too.'

'I like you, Kim England.'

She laughs a little. 'I like you too, Jamie Sinclair.'

'I'm gonna get out now before I embarrass myself any further.'

I kiss her then clumsily exit the car. She winds down the passenger window. 'Good luck with the job. Let me know how your first day goes.'

'I will.'

'Hope the hangover doesn't make your first shift too difficult.'

'Nah. I'll sleep it off.'

She smiles, but not with as much warmth as I'm used to. 'All right. See ya.'

'See ya.'

She drives away.

I go inside and get into bed, where I stay until I have to get ready for work.

18

The Harvester is in the suburb of Wigmore, supposedly a 'posh', 'affluent' part of Medway.

When I was a kid Andrea was always talking about how she wanted to live in Wigmore, in a 'detached' house, as opposed to the semi-detached and terraced houses she'd known her whole life.

Well, now her son works there, like a real big shot.

The job pays £5.60 an hour.

A 'living wage', according to the Department of Work and Pensions.

I'm given a quick tour by Bill, the manager.

He's a big, foreheady South Londoner who looks like Rafael Benitez.

He takes me to the kitchen, which is steamy because of the open dishwasher and smells like grilled meat and barbecue sauce.

Two overweight, sweating chefs nod and grunt by way of greeting as they throw cheap steaks onto the open grill, which hisses and sends plumes of smoke through the narrow but wide hatch that looks onto the restaurant floor.

We go there next, where most of the tables are already full, and Bill introduces me to several of the beleaguered waiting staff, who impatiently pause between tables to say hello.

Bill points to the Salad Cart and says, maybe sarcastically, maybe not, 'That's where the magic happens.'

Then there's the actual bar, which will be my domain.

'We're down on staff tonight, so it's just gonna be you and Becky here.'

'All right mate,' says Becky, who's pouring a pint.

'Hi,' I say.

'Let me show you how the till works,' says Bill.

He does that, and gives me a fob which allows me to log in under my own name.

'I'll let Becky show you the rest of the ropes. Any problems, I'll be upstairs doing paperwork.'

He claps me on the shoulder and goes through the door which says 'STAFF ONLY'.

'Welcome to the madhouse,' says Becky.

I smile.

A man approaches the bar and asks me for a pint of Stella.

I look at Becky, who gestures for me to go right ahead.

I grab a glass from under the bar, and pour the man his drink.

19

Over the next few shifts I mainly work behind the bar with Becky but sometimes I'm put in the kitchen to wash dishes or assist the chefs with food preparation.

The chefs are always angry and yelling at the waiters and waitresses.

'Get these dishes out pronto or the steaks will overcook!'

'Who touched my knives! Which one of you muppets touched my knives!'

'Where are the steak sauces! The sauces are supposed to be right here! I put them right, fucking, here!'

I prefer being front-of-house in the bar where I don't have to interact with them as much.

Where I quickly become a hit with some of the regulars because I work hard.

Keep their thirst slaked and don't say too much.

Becky talks to them; I listen.

I like their frequent guffaws and I like when they raise their voices during arguments about football or politics. I like the faint tang of limes and stale beer that never leaves the air behind the bar.

I like the dark wood of the bar and the way all the different spirits are arrayed on the shelves, and the soft light from the wall-lamps above the tables, and the faded William Morris-esque wallpaper.

It's another one of these faux-Noir type pubs.

But it's a place of solace for the regulars, and I like being a part of that.

Back in the kitchen I'm disliked because I'm a 'posh cunt' who earns the same amount per hour as the chefs, except I occasionally receive tips and they don't.

Plus, in their eyes I don't work as hard.

'Bar people never do,' one of the chefs informs me during an impromptu rant while I'm slicing flavourless beef tomatoes.

I tell him that this is both unverifiable and unfalsifiable.

The chef tuts and says, 'Get fucked, princess.'

20

I start to get on well with one bunch of regulars in particular.

Working men and women ranging from their early thirties to late sixties.

Full-blown alcoholics.

They come into the bar every evening, take their positions, drink four or five or six or seven drinks, then go home and drink from their whisky or gin or vodka reserves until they pass out in their armchairs, drooling down their chins.

At the weekends their partners join them.

They start shambling in around midday and are there until closing.

It makes my liver ache watching them drink.

But they're good people. And they're good drunks, most of the time.

I learn about them. Their lives are pockmarked with disappointments and sadness.

They need each other and they need booze.

There's John, who always buys me and Becky a drink when he comes to settle his tab.

His position is the middle of the bar, always standing, never sitting.

He likes that I pay attention to the level of his drink so he doesn't have to ask for a refill.

What I do is plant the next beer in front of him as he finishes his current one. He winks at me and moves straight on to the next beer, nudging his empty glass towards me with his free hand.

He has a beer gut that extrudes further than the ends of his toes.

Pink cheeks, pink neck and a bulbous pink nose.

Grey hair in an eighties-era feathered cut.

I'm jealous. He must be thirty years older than me but has way thicker hair.

It's weird hair, but it's all his own, and I can tell he's quite proud of it.

John always speaks to me warmly and with courtesy. I believe, probably unjustifiably, that he sees me as 'full of potential but down at heel', or something like that.

I think this because it doesn't annoy him when I use 'long' words. He says things like, 'Bloody hell, what does that mean?' and, 'He'll go far, this one,' smiling knowingly at his mates.

It's like he feels firgun for me, an untranslatable Hebrew term I came across recently.

I imagine John can enjoy what he perceives as my intelligence because I'm non-threatening and at a slight remove from him.

We're different people leading different lives. John is a real man, I'm a real dickhead.

We have nothing in common except this bar.

But we show each other respect.

John's son died of meningitis a few years before I started working at the bar.

I found this out because I asked him if he had any children and his eyes welled up.

He told me in a calm, husky voice about the meningitis.

He told me that he found him in his bed one morning.

Had to travel with him in the ambulance, knowing he was already gone.

I said I was sorry.

Because I'm useless at finding the right thing to say to someone who has experienced that level of grief.

John wiped his eyes and pulled out his wallet. He paid his tab and told me to get us both a good scotch.

We clinked glasses and drank to his son, whose name was Aaron.

There's Paula, who looks like Liza Minelli in a Tesco uniform.

She arrives after her shift has finished and sits at the bar drinking half-pints of Guinness, never full pints.

Why, she will not say.

When I asked her she sipped her half-pint, laughed enigmatically, sauntered out for a cigarette.

Her ritual is to have four half-pints before her partner comes by to pick her up.

He arrives at the bar with his haggard face. Greasy black fingernails from working with machinery all day.

He walks in slowly and nods at everyone without saying a word.

Everyone silently nods back.

Paula downs the dregs of her glass, dabs her mouth with a napkin, and they leave together arm-in-arm.

It's the same thing every day. Except at the weekends when he sits next to her and drinks half pints of Guinness too.

They watch the Formula One together, steadily getting pissed.

Go on drinking right up to last orders.

The bell rings and they might crack up at something mysterious.

Kiss each other passionately, with their old tongues.

Stagger out together, cackling.

I still don't know his name.

There's Danny Dyer.

Not the Danny Dyer. His real name is Sean.

But he looks and behaves like the actor, so everyone calls him Danny Dyer.

He's a self-styled 'geezer'. He always has money.

How he sources this money, no-one knows.

But everyone suspects.

I think Danny Dyer tries a bit too hard to seem, well, 'hard'.

He often mouths off about all the fights he's had recently.

It's obvious he's lying.

There's still something likeable about Danny Dyer. Something vulnerable.

He has a laugh that makes people want to be in his company. It's loud but charming; it gives everybody a little boost.

But then he'll start talking about headbutting someone.

I want to sit him down and explain how he needs to relax about all that stuff. How he needs to stop bullshitting, and everything will be okay.

But what do I know?

I'm a man-child who's only recently moved out of his parents' place.

Despite their peccadilloes the regulars are slowly pulling me from my frozen state.

They're somehow able to harness the lambent sadness in their lives and warm other people with its blue flame.

I'm surprised to catch myself thinking this, but it's great to be working once more.

I'm getting fitter. I'm on my feet all the time, sometimes doing twelve-hour shifts. I don't have time to smoke as much.

It's good. I feel good.

Money in my pocket, a home full of hygge, and Kim.

I might have to shunt Tom Pritchard out of my life again at some point – history is repeating itself on that front – but for now, the gravity level is definitely returning to normal.

21

'm eating cereal in the kitchen when Jo and Pete come in and announce they're having another dinner party, tonight.

'Are you around?' says Jo. 'Kim's keen.'

'Yeah, she mentioned it,' I say. 'I have the night off. I could cook. I do a sweet risotto.'

'Do it,' says Pete.

'It's so exciting that you two are hitting it off,' says Jo. 'We can all hang out together here. It'll be like double-dating, but at home.'

'It's early days,' I say.

'Still exciting,' she says, scrunching her nose.

'Are you inviting anyone else?' I say.

'How about your mate Tom,' says Pete. 'He seems like a laugh.'

'Nah, I need to talk to him about a couple of things. We've got some shit to sort out.'

'Oh... too late,' says Pete. 'I bumped into him at Tesco the other day and mentioned it to him.'

'Oh, okay.'

'Sorry -- did you want me to text him and say that it's not happening?'

'You swapped numbers?'

'Yeah.'

'No it's all right. I don't want to cause any drama. It'll be fine.'

'Sorry if I've caused a problem.'

'No, it's all good.'

I finish my cereal, put my spoon and bowl in the dishwasher.

'We're gonna head out and get some things for tonight then,' says Jo.

'I'll come with you,' I say, wiping milk from my beard.

'Cool,' says Pete.

'Hey, I got my first paycheck from the pub,' I say. 'I transferred rent earlier.'

'Wicked,' says Pete. 'You're a legend.'

'We're gonna go to Homebase as well,' says Jo. 'We're thinking of re-doing the upstairs bathroom. Would you wanna help at all? We'd pay you in booze for your time.'

'I know how to tile,' I say, putting my coat on. 'I've done it with my dad before.'

'Awesome,' says Jo. 'Pete's useless when it comes to that stuff.'

'How very dare you,' says Pete, and slaps her arse.

22

We come out of the Homebase at Horsted Retail Park and load up Jo's car with the new bathroom suite.

I announce that I want to get Jo a present. My breath is visible as I talk.

'Cute!' says Jo. 'What are you thinking?'

'You could get her a new toolbox,' says Pete. '20% off here at Homebase.'

'Haw haw haw,' I say. 'I dunno. I just wanted to get her something now that I can afford it.'

'We could go to Bluewater,' says Jo.

Pete facepalms himself. I know what he means.

'It's a bit of a drive,' I say.

'It's only up the M2. I wanted to go there anyway,' she says.

'I guess...' I say.

'It'll be fun,' says Jo.

'That's debatable,' I say.

'Well can we debate it in the car?' says Pete. 'It's fucking freezing.'

'All right, Jesus,' says Jo. 'Why do you have to be so rude all the time.'

'I'm not. It's just cold.'

'He always does this,' she says, talking to me.

'Leave me out of it guys,' I say, putting my hands up.

Pete and I look at each other.

Pete pulls a face and I quietly laugh.

We all get in the car.

Jo drives off too quickly, causing a brief wheelspin.

When the tyres gain traction again Pete and I are pushed back against our respective headrests.

'Babe, I'm impressed,' says Pete. 'You didn't stall it for once.'

'Shut up,' she says.

Jo makes an executive decision and drives to Bluewater.

Pete grumbles about the traffic.

'Seriously, if you don't put a sock in it,' says Jo, 'I'm buying a pair of Jimmy Choos instead of getting you a Christmas present.'

'Yes boss,' he says.

Bluewater is nestled in an old quarry.

The entry road spirals down towards the shopping centre.

It's like descending into the inferno.

Christmas decorations are already up. Around the carpark there are reindeer sculptures made out of iron (?), festooned with fairy lights.

I check the date on my phone.

It's still November.

We emerge from the car park and stand amidst the hordes in the mall.

'I'm getting a burger,' says Pete. 'I'll meet you back here in an hour.'

'Fine,' says Jo.

He disappears into the human traffic. Jo stares after him for a bit.

'What do you think Kim would like?' I ask.

'How much are you going to spend?'

'Like, fifty quid max.'

Jo grimaces. 'Urgh. And there I was thinking we'd be looking in there.'

She gestures towards a high-end jewellery shop.

'Are there any bookshops here?'

'Yes,' Jo huffs. 'This way.'

She drags me by the arm, the Virgil to my Dante, deeper into Satan's lair.

We have to tango through the throng of Christmas shoppers zombulating along the thoroughfare to get to the entrance of a Waterstones.

Along the way I count three zombie families with the parents and children all wearing matching Ralph Lauren polo shirts.

'This'll do,' I say.

'I knew you two would get along. Both bookworms.'

'You coming in?'

'I'm going to pop into John Lewis and get a Christmas tree.'

'Good luck. I'll meet you at our designated rendezvous point.'

I salute. Jo salutes back and walks off.

It isn't long before I find something appropriate.

A large monograph book of recent marine photography.

According to the blurb It's by some famous photographer, though I've never heard of him.

The pictures are beautiful.

I find an armchair in the middle of the store and leaf through the book.

I stop at a picture of a dolphin, a turtle and a school of fish.

It's in the Pacific Ocean, just off the coast of Costa Rica.

I imagine scuba diving there with Kim one day.

Maybe even next year.

Scuba dive in the day, bar-tend at night.

My phone beeps. Jo.

- where are you??

- coming

I pay for the book and leave.

I hum a random song to myself ('Barbarism Begins at Home') to drown out the Christmas song that's jangling out of the Tannoy system.

I count two more Ralph Lauren zombie families along the way.

Have to suppress the urge to drop my trousers and take a shit in the middle of the mall and start throwing it at anyone wearing Ralph Lauren.

Jo's standing near the escalator with a gigantic oblong box.

'Do you think it's too big?' she says.

'Might be actually. We could always forgo the angel on top.'

Pete arrives chewing a Big Mac, his third, he tells us.

'Fuck me is that big enough?' he says, mouth full.

'We were just saying the same thing,' says Jo. 'But I really like the colour. It's a silver one. And they'd sold out of smaller ones.'

'Whatever,' says Pete. 'Let's just get out of here.'

'You're such a grinch,' says Jo.

'I'm with Pete on this one,' I say.

'Remind me never to bring you two with me again.'

Pete and I silently cheer. Jo punches both of us on the arm.

23

I'm tending to the risotto when Kim rings the doorbell.

Jo is still upstairs getting ready and Pete is playing Fifa again.

'I'll get it,' I say.

Pete makes the okay sign without looking away from the screen.

I open the door. Kim looks great, standing there in her favourite coat and a humongous shawl.

'Hey,' I say.

'Hey,' she says, stepping inside and wiping her feet on the mat.

Kim does her little jump-hug.

She always does this kind of leap into me as she grabs me.

I love it.

We kiss. Her nose is cold on my cheek.

'Mmm, that smells good,' she says. 'Can I help?'

'Nah, it's all under control. Why don't you play Fifa with Pedro.'

'Why don't I help,' she says, going cross-eyed.

'Okay.'

'I brought this.'

She holds up a bottle of white wine. 'It's Italian. To go with the risotto.'

'Perfect,' I say, taking it.

She hangs up her coat and we go through.

'Hey Pete.'

Pete pauses his game, gets up to hug her.

'Hello gorgeous.'

He sits down again, unpauses the game. The roar of the crowd resumes.

Kim and I continue through to the kitchen.

'Can you stir it for me for a sec,' I say. 'I just need to get something.'

She picks up the wooden spoon resting on the pan. 'Sure.'

I come back with the book, which I wrapped in brown paper.

'An early Christmas present,' I say.

'What?'

'Just something small.'

'You're sweet.'

She puts the spoon down and I lean across to turn down the heat.

She unwraps it.

'Jamie, that's so lovely.' She turns the book over and reads the back. 'How did you know I like this guy?'

'I stalked you on social media.'

'What?'

'Just kidding. I didn't know you liked him specifically. Lucky guess. I saw on your bookshelf the books about marine biology. I flicked through it in the shop and thought the pictures were great.'

'I really like it.'

'Go and read it. I'll take over again here.'

She kisses me on the cheek and jump-hugs me again. She sits at the table and leafs through the book.

Jo appears. Zeus saunters in behind her.

'Hey lovely,' says Jo.

Kim stands up and they embrace.

Zeus rubs his head against Kim's shin and she bends down to gather him up.

'Smells good Jamie,' says Jo.

I wiggle my eyebrows, stir the risotto.

'When's your mate getting here,' she says.

'With Tom Pritchard,' I say, 'one never knows.'

24

We're already well into dinner when Tom arrives.

He comes in with a six-pack of lager and I can tell immediately that he's a) already drunk/coked up and b) attracted to Kim.

A twinkle in his eyes or something.

I get up to serve him a plate. Tom takes my seat, next to Kim.

'Nice to finally meet you,' he says to Kim.

'You too,' she says.

'Beer?'

'No thanks,' she says, pointing to her wine.

He cracks one open and glugs. I put a plate of the risotto in front of him.

'Cheers fellaaa,' he says. He prods the risotto with his fork. 'Hang on,' he says. 'Where's the meat?'

I roll my eyes.

'It's vegetarian,' says Pete. 'It's good.'

'He's such a snowflake, ain't he,' says Tom, pointing his thumb at me.

'Beautiful and unique,' I say.

'You tell yourself that,' says Tom.

'What the snowflake giveth, the snowflake can taketh away,' I say, reaching across for Tom's plate.

Tom raps my knuckles with his fork. 'I'm just joshing you bruv. It looks good.'

25

For a while the conversation is convivial and light.

Kim shows everyone the book I bought her.

'I didn't know you were into that stuff,' says Jo.

'Actually,' she says, 'I'm thinking about going to uni. I think I need a change.'

'Babe!' says Jo. 'That's amazing!'

'What would you study,' says Pete.

'I was thinking of doing Biology. I got good A-levels, so I wouldn't need to do an access course or anything.'

'What grades did you get?' says Pete.

'I got three A's,' she says.

'What?' I say. 'That's awesome.'

'Yeah. I could've applied to Cambridge. My biology teacher kept going on about it, but I wanted to earn money.'

'Told you she was clever, didn't I,' says Jo.

'You did,' I say, blushing.

'I'm thinking of going to uni as well,' says Tom.

'Really,' I say.

'Maybe we could study together,' says Kim.

'Watch out Sinbad, I think your girlfriend fancies me.'

'Don't call me Sinbad.'

'Why's he calling you Sinbad,' says Pete.

'Don't ask,' I say.

'Yeah,' says Tom. 'I wanna study history. Actually, science and history.'

'Here we go,' I say.

'Except I'd try and set them straight on a few things.'

'Like what,' says Jo.

'Like, first of all, the Earth isn't round.'

Everyone except me laughs, because they think he's joking.

'Secondly, the Holocaust.'

'Tom,' I say.

'What about the Holocaust,' says Pete.

'Like how it probably didn't happen.'

'For fuck's sake,' I say.

'What?' says Tom, feigning innocence. 'When you look into it, you realise that loads of what they tell you at school is bollocks.'

'Did David Icke tell you this?'

'David Irving actually,' he says. 'He went to Cambridge.' He nudges Kim. 'Smart dude. Smarter than you Sinbad.'

'Who's David Irving,' says Kim.

'A well-known antisemite and Holocaust-denier,' I say.

'It ain't like that,' says Tom. 'You always believe whatever they tell you, don't ya.'

'Who's 'they'?'

'You don't think for yourself.'

'Tom, you've watched a few YouTube videos and you think you're some kind of radical free-thinker.'

'I ain't one of the sheeple, that's all.'

'Oh my God, are you still using that word.'

'Get over it.'

'I can only apologise for my friend,' I say, looking around the table.

'You see, this is the problem with people like you,' says Tom, holding his cutlery over his plate. 'You can't stand it when someone has a different point of view. If you ain't the smartest person in the room you get all antsy.'

'You're denying the Holocaust,' I say. 'It's not like we're disagreeing about the latest Tom Cruise movie.'

'Hold on,' says Pete. 'I'm still reeling from the first revelation. The Earth isn't round?'

'Think about it,' says Tom, missing Pete's irony. 'How do you know it's round? Everything you fink you know has been fed to you by the government.'

'But there's pictures,' says Pete. 'I've seen them on Nasa's website.'

Tom shakes his head and laughs at Pete's stupidity. 'They're composites. They're fake. NASA is a joke.'

'The thing is,' says Pete. 'I know the Earth is round, but this is actually a good exercise in challenging what you accept without question.'

'See, Pete gets it,' says Tom. He stands up, triumphant. 'I'm going to the toilet. Scuse us.'

He leaves the room.

'He's a bit full-on, isn't he,' says Jo.

'He's a bit of a penis,' I say. 'Sorry guys.'

'I didn't know you hung out with Nazis,' says Pete, laughing.

'It doesn't necessarily make him a Nazi,' says Kim.

'I'd say denying the holocaust puts him on the Nazi spectrum,' says Pete.

'Maybe we should change the subject when he comes back,' says Jo.

'He's not coming back,' I say, getting out of my chair.

26

I go upstairs and wait for Tom to come out of the toilet.

The door opens and I begin remonstrating with him.

'You need to go,' I say.

'I've only just got here!' says Tom.

'You're embarrassing me.'

'I ain't going anywhere. Pete invited me and it's his house, not yours.'

He pushes past me and goes downstairs.

I go into my tiny room.

I open the window, perch on the sill and roll a cigarette.

Kim comes in.

'Tut tut,' she says. 'They'll kill you eventually.'

'Life is bizarre,' I say. I blow smoke out the window. 'If you'd asked me at eighteen where I'd be at twenty-five, I would never have predicted I'd be living in a cupboard in Gillingham and have a Holocaust-denier as a friend.'

'The risotto was good.'

'Thanks.'

'And you have a hot girlfriend.'

'That's true.'

I put an arm around her waist and pull her closer.

'Would it be all right if I stayed over tonight?' she says. 'I've had too much to drink.'

'I thought you couldn't suffer my tiny bed?'

'You'll just have to spoon me all night.'

'If I have to.'

'Dick.'

She kisses my forehead then takes my cigarette and stubs it out.

'Come on,' she says. 'He's talking about football now. We'll keep him away from David Irving or whatever his name is.'

'Pray for us,' I say.

27

We finish dinner and I begin to clear the table.

Kim and Jo both help. Pete invites Tom to play Fifa.

'Think I'll head off actually,' says Tom. 'I'm clearly not welcome here.'

'I wonder why that is,' I say.

Tom walks out and goes upstairs again. He's been in and out of the bathroom all night.

I roll my eyes and put the wine glasses in the dishwasher.

Tom comes back in, rubbing his nose. 'Thanks for having me over,' he says to Pete. He puts his jacket on. 'I'll have to return the favour some time.'

Pete says, 'That would be great.'

Jo pulls an incredulous face at him.

Tom rubs his nose again.

I say, 'You all right there? Got a bit of hayfever or something?'

'What?'

'Nothing.'

'See you later then,' says Tom. 'Kim, when you've had enough of this prick you know where to find me.'

Kim makes a silent gagging face which Tom doesn't see.

'Bye Tom,' I say.

Tom smirks, then grabs his last two beers from the table and leaves.

'Fuck me,' says Pete. 'Got a bit tense there eh?'

'I'm really sorry,' I say.

'It wasn't your fault,' says Jo.

'Yeah, I invited him,' says Pete.

'He does too much coke,' I say. 'It's giving him brain damage.'

'You think he does coke?' says Jo.

'I know he does coke.'

'Don't worry about it dude,' says Pete. 'He's gone now.'

Kim puts her arm around me.

'I really love my book,' she says. 'I guess I'll have to get you something for Christmas now.'

She pokes my side.

'Get me a new friend,' I say.

28

The next day I check Facebook and find I've been invited to a wedding, the first starring people from my own generation.

An estranged friend from university, Sam, has left me a message replete with hyperbolic adjectives, exclamation marks and kisses.

She and Nathaniel are having a winter wedding in London next month. They've been together since we all lived in halls and have recently re-branded themselves as 'Londoners'.

She's sorry for the short notice but they've decided to get hitched on a whim. It would be 'fab' if I could come along, it says in the message. 'Super lovely' to see me after all these years. 'Amazeballs' for the old gang to be reunited.

She happens to be on Facebook chat so I immediately ask if Alice is going to be there.

- Unfortunately she can't make it babe. She's going to be in the Caribbean with her beau, Felix.

A jealous thought flickers across my mind like a small moth, but I catch it with chopsticks, dispose of it in a napkin.

- ok. i think i can make it. it would be good to see you
- Fab fab fab!!! Sooo happy to hear that babe!!!! Can't wait to see you looking handsome in a suit. Give me your address so I can send an invite!!! xxx
- but you already know i'm coming mate
- I know babe but it's tradition to send out an invitation!!! xxx
- ok. i'll send you it in a sec xx

Kim is still asleep.

I go to the landing and tug out my trusty three-piece suit with the vomit stain.

It's warm from being in the airing cupboard. It's still hideous. I'll have to get a new one.

I perch on the bed near Kim's feet and check my bank balance again.

I've been doing this a lot more lately, hoping with each page refresh that I might finally get a bank error in my favour, as in Monopoly, but there aren't any decent Chance cards in the deck today.

I open a new tab and go to the National Lottery website. I buy twenty pounds worth of tickets for the next draw, hoping the Community Chest pile will prove more lucrative.

I smoke a cigarette and ponder the wedding while Kim sleeps.

Why not just contact Sam right now and say actually, sorry, you can't make it?

It'll be excruciating.

And you'll have to spend money you don't really have.

And weddings are a platform for narcissists to show off.

And it's a vestigial system of transference of ownership of the woman from the father to the husband.

But there'll probably be free booze.

And you morbidly want to find out what all your old friends have been doing these last few years.

I make a deal with myself: I'll go if Kim agrees to go too.

She'll bolster me, make me feel less vulnerable.

I stand up and take the suit downstairs.

Zeus hops off the settee and rubs his head against my leg.

I lay the suit on the floor and encourage Zeus to step onto

it, but Zeus isn't in the mood. He struts off.

I pick the suit up and stuff into the bin in the kitchen.

The jacket sleeves and trouser legs hang over the edge. It looks like a man fell back and got stuck in the bin and then mysteriously biodegraded and disappeared, leaving the suit empty and limp.

29

At the Harvester there are other regulars I don't like so much. Bill schooled me about them before I met them.

He walked me around the bar with a hand on my shoulder and quietly explained their unpleasant quirks and idiosyncrasies.

As their servants we are to bend to their every whim. They spend so much money that if they ever cease to drink there the place would collapse.

'They're a bunch of pricks but we treat them like gods,' said Bill. 'Whatever they want, you give it to them.'

'I will if they have good manners.'

'You will if they don't.'

'That doesn't seem right.'

'That's the business we're in.'

Bill explained about Andy.

I found Bill's assessment to be accurate.

Andy is a bully and a policeman and a Northerner. He's the worst of them.

He treats everyone he interacts with like slime.

Fortunately he isn't someone who props up the bar; his position is at a table over in the corner near a fruit machine, so I rarely have to put up with him for an entire shift.

Andy always arrives late.

At ten pm, more or less to the second.

The bar closes at eleven. He has an hour to get completely shit-faced.

Tonight he arrives at the bar like he's Clint Eastwood. Kicks open the door and swaggers over to his stool.

Day-old stubble on his face; bleary red eyes.

He's of medium height and build, but he seems huge. People shrink when he comes in.

He doesn't say hello or ask for a drink.

No-one is to talk to him until he's ready. That's his thing.

He has to allow the trauma of the day's events to ooze out of him like grease. He's been dealing with the scum of the Earth all evening. They get inside him like demons and he has to exorcise them before he's capable of social interaction.

When he's ready he appears at the bar. Looks at me like I've failed at everything in life.

His red eyes say, 'You better have my Carlsberg ready for me otherwise I'm going to smash your face in.'

He has to have his precious Carlsberg in his precious Carlsberg glass, the one with the embossed lettering on it. He got it free with a crate of Carlsberg once. Brought it in and told the staff to keep it for him and him only.

I make the mistake of asking him why he insists on using it.

'Because it's made for Carlsberg, you fucking cretin!' He slides his index finger up and down the embossed lettering. 'That's why it says Carlsberg on the side!'

He snatches the pint off me and downs it in two or three mouthfuls.

Plonks it on the bar.

I have to refill it immediately. Never mind the other customers who've been waiting longer.

He drinks two or three beers at the bar like that, by which point a few of his fellow police friends have arrived.

They make their way over to their spot with their beers and some whisky chasers, and that's the end of Andy until last orders.

Last orders is a pain in the perineum.

Andy and his coterie are the last and most stubborn customers.

I ring the bell to signal the end of the night. Andy and his friends ignore it.

Which means I actually have to go over to their table.

Which is a demoralising experience.

'Hey Andy, we're closing up now.'

Nothing.

'Andy, we're --'

'I fucking heard you the first time, you thick, balding twat!'

Laughter from the group.

'Okay, well, you didn't answer me so--'

'Are you fucking talking back to me? Walk away now if you know what's good for you.'

I do walk away. Like a younger child telling on his tormentors to the teacher, I get Bill, who deftly coaxes them out of the bar.

30

Bill.
    Bill is an okay manager, though he doesn't have a grasp on what motivates people.

He spent some time in Australia in his thirties and wants to import their 'cafe culture' to the UK.

He wants to turn all the bar staff at the Harvester into baristas. He showed us how to make a proper flat white, how to clean the coffee machine and how not to burn the coffee.

But because Harvester sources shitty beans and provided a shitty machine, the coffee tastes like mud, even though we've all learned the mystic secrets to a good cup.

Bill is always moaning about how we don't appreciate good coffee, how we don't have pride in our work. But the shareholders of Harvester don't have pride in their products or respect for their employees. They buy the cheapest beans available and pay their staff peanut shells, so why the hell would we have pride in our work?

Bill's an idiot.

But he has our backs when it comes to the difficult customers like Andy, so I respect him for that.

He knows how to handle Scott, for example.

Scott owns his own scaffolding business. He inherited it from his dad a few years before and turned it into a large successful enterprise.

He's loaded.

He's good-looking. For a man his age; for a man of any age.

He has a good-looking wife who occasionally comes in and sits quietly at his table while he holds court.

They're the sort of people who are good-looking from all distances. Right up close, far away, and every increment in between.

Scott probably works hard, but he was given a pretty good start in life.

I don't resent people that; I just like it when they're able to acknowledge how good they've had it.

Scott acts like he built the business from scratch, single-handedly. He's a self-proclaimed 'self-made man'.

The term 'self-made' always annoys me because it's a logical impossibility. It's literally impossible to be self-made.

Everyone is part of the dynamic cosmos; each 'individual' is an agglomeration of individual particles, with each of those particles made up of smaller individual particles, and so on, maybe infinitely, in a fractal way, like a Mandelbrot set.

That's the way it seems to be.

Everyone is part of a wider context, is all I'm saying. Everyone is the beneficiary and victim of a million different forces, biological, societal and cosmic. Some people have great hair; others don't. Some people get a free education; others private. Some people are emotionally abused and neglected by their parents; others are given businesses by their dads.

It's mostly down to luck. Because free will is an illusion.

Don't try to deny it.

I'm right, and you're wrong!

Coming from Scott's mouth the phrase 'self-made man' makes me orders-of-magnitude more irritated, since he often bad-mouths vulnerable or marginalised people.

He punches down. He won't criticise the strong, only the weak.

Overweight people because they're breaking the NHS; benefit claimants because they're lazy freeloaders; asylum seekers because they're too cowardly to stay and fight for their own countries.

These are his default conversational topics; there is no nuance to his patter. He's an 'either/or' kind of guy, not a 'both/and'.

I'm not the best person to deal with Scott.

He doesn't take me seriously and there's a hint of menace in everything he says; I often like he could headbutt me at any moment.

Like Tom Pritchard he refers to me as a 'snowflake'. That is, an over-sensitive person who sanctimoniously virtue-signals instead of making meaningful change in the world.

He has a point.

Bill on the other hand is able to silence him. Bill knows him from way back and is able to bring up embarrassing or incriminating details that make him seem like a hypocrite.

And because Bill is huge and can handle himself, Scott can't intimidate him. It's great when Bill chooses to intervene in an argument.

As he does tonight.

It's raucous in the pub.

It's Friday night. Everyone's here.

272

Everyone is pissed, or on their way.

Scott, Andy, Danny Dyer, Paula, John, their respective partners, a lot of their friends and associates, plus sundry drunks, inebriates, pissheads, old soaks, dipsomaniacs, carousers and ne'er-do-sobers.

Everyone has to shout to be heard. I'm pouring drinks non-stop, taking multiple orders at a time, wiping sweat from my brow with my forearm.

Emaciating before their eyes.

Scott's arrogant voice dominates. It isn't particularly deep, but he knows how to project it above the crowd; it seems to ricochet around the room.

He's holding forth on how Polish people come over here and undercut the wages of British workers in the building industry.

'They work like beasts, I ain't saying they don't, but they'll take half what our boys'll take.'

Several of Scott's beta friends nod their assent.

'Hold on a minute,' says Bill, who's helping behind the bar pouring drinks. 'You own your own business. Don't you get to decide how much you pay them?'

'Yeah, but if someone says they'll work at such-and-such a rate, you ain't gonna pay 'em more, are ya.'

'But you're blaming them for undercutting when you could easily pay everyone the same. Base it on their experience and competence, then pick the best workers for the job. Standardise it.'

'You don't understand how it works Billy boy.'

'I think I do,' says Bill.

'How much do you pay your staff?'

'I pay them according to the structure laid out by Head

273

Office. I don't set the wages.'

'So you don't understand how it works.'

'Scott, I don't need to set the wages to know you're a tight-arse.'

Scott goes red. He doesn't like that.

A few people laugh. It's a rare opportunity to watch Scott squirm.

Paula, sitting at the bar, lifts her half-pint of Guinness, sways it involuntarily. 'Hear, hear!' she says.

'Look,' says Scott, ignoring Paula, growing redder. 'The point is, they don't pay tax. They undercut the other boys because they're getting cash-in-hand, which they send back to Poland. Then they claim housing benefit because they declare they ain't earning enough to pay their rent. There's twelve, thirteen of them to a room. They're gaming the system.'

'Scott, you were in here last week boasting that you don't declare all your earnings, so don't give me that shit. And I remember when you were starting out -- you always got cash-in-hand from your old man when he was still here, God rest his soul. Did you always pay tax on that money? Did you fuck.'

'It's different though.'

'Why? Because they're Polish?'

'No, it's just different.'

Danny Dyer has been listening in to all this. He lets out his joyful laugh. He usually spouts similar views to Scott but can't be seen siding with him in public.

'He's got you there, ain't he, you mug!'

Scott glares at Danny Dyer. 'Shut the fuck up, Sean. You know I'm right.'

Scott sips his Stella.

Danny Dyer stands up and squares up to him. 'Say that again.'

'I said shut the fuck up.'

Danny Dyer pushes his forehead against Scott's like a ram.

'Oi!' shouts Bill. 'Enough of that! You carry on like that and I'll bar the lot of ya!'

The two men relax and allow their hackles to lower. They absorb themselves back into their respective groups.

Bill pours more drinks. I give someone their change and take another set of orders.

There's no trouble for the rest of the evening. It's just loud and bibulous.

I make a lot of tips.

And Bill buys all the staff a drink at the end of the shift, to say thanks for our hard work.

31

The next morning I rise early, against my will, to help Pete and Jo do the upstairs bathroom.

They begin chipping at the tiles shortly after 8am. It's like there isn't a wall between my room and the bathroom. It does nothing to mute the noise.

But I'd said he'd help, so I'm soon in there with them, chucking fragments of white tiles into a large bucket on the landing, and eventually come to enjoy myself, the way I do when I feel useful.

Pete sets about removing the toilet.

He takes the lid of the cistern off, and pulls out a white brick wrapped in plastic.

'What's this?' he says.

'Dunno,' says Jo. 'It looks like flour.'

'Shit,' I say.

'What,' says Pete.

'Tom. He's planted it there.'

'Is that cocaine?' says Jo.

I nod.

Jo looks terrified of it. Pete rubs her arm.

I go into my room and phone Tom.

'Fam, you woke me up.'

'We found your package.'

'What package?'

'Don't play dumb. I'm flushing it right now.'

'Whoa whoa whoa, hold your horses. You don't wanna do that.'

'Why not.'

'There'll be... consequences.'

'Consequences. Fuck you. I'm flushing it now.'

'Sinbad, I'm telling you, you don't wanna do that.'

'Don't contact me again.'

I hang up, march into the bathroom.

I unwrap the cocaine, which is compacted like icing sugar, and sprinkle some of it into the bowl. It congeals on the surface of the water and forms a spiral pattern.

Jo and Pete watch me, looking concerned.

'So he's a Nazi and a drug dealer,' says Pete. 'Top bloke.'

'I'm so sorry,' I say.

'You should have told us, Jamie,' says Jo.

'I didn't know.'

'What if the police come over?'

'That's why I'm flushing it.'

'Wait,' says Pete. 'Maybe we should call the police and hand it over.'

I pause. Good point.

But then I say, 'No, I don't trust him. There's no linking it to him. He'll wriggle out of it somehow and we'll be implicated. That's why he stashed it here.'

'I can't believe this,' says Jo.

Pete puts his arm around her.

I sprinkle the rest of it into the bowl, flushing it every few seconds until it's all gone.

32

Later the same day I drive to Mum and Dad's.

Andrea invited me over for a late lunch.

December has arrived and it's a beautiful, vital day. The sort of day that makes you love winter as much as summer.

Except I can't appreciate it because I'm still angry about Tom.

I park across the road and yank up the handbrake.

It feels loose, broken.

'Fuck!' I yell.

Fortunately I'm not on much of an incline. I get out and take a pair of ornamental rocks from Mum and Dad's front garden and wedge one under each of the rear tyres.

I ring the doorbell. Col answers the door.

'Son.'

'Father.'

We shake hands.

Col notices the rocks.

'What are you doing?'

'The handbrake's gone. I didn't want the car to roll away.'

Col gestures for my keys. 'Let's have a look.'

He goes over and leans in to test the handbrake. Gets down on his knees and peers under the chassis.

'Just what I want to be doing with my Sunday off,' he says.

'Dad, I didn't ask you to do this.'

He ignores me. Andrea appears at the door and calls over, 'Everything all right?'

'Bloody handbrake's on the blink,' I say.

'Careful of your back Col,' she says.

Col grunts from under the car.

He gets up and claps muck off his hands. 'It'll probably cost about 200 to replace it.'

'Tits,' I say.

'You should take it to Derek's garage,' he says. 'He'll charge you for parts only.'

'Uncle Derek? I thought you two weren't talking.'

'If you actually bothered coming round here more often you'd know what's going on in this family.'

'You know what,' I say. 'I'm not in the mood for this. You're a fucking prick!'

I take the rocks from under the tyres, march across the road and lob them onto the garden bed. March back and get in the car.

Andrea calls out, 'Where are you going? What's going on? Lunch is almost ready!'

Col is standing in the middle of the road. He shrugs and makes a flummoxed face as if I'm being the ultimate flake.

I pull away and punch the steering wheel, which sounds the horn as if I'm cheerily tooting goodbye after a pleasant visit.

33

When I get in I decide to Skype John, my brother. They're seven hours ahead in Perth so I'll just catch him before he puts his son Max to bed.

'Well well well, if it isn't my little bro. To what do I owe the pleasure?'

I can hear my sister-in-law Nat in the background trying to coax Max to the screen to say hello.

John is sitting in his kitchen, which looks big and modern.

He's losing his hair like me, but he's shaved his head and looks healthy and tanned.

'Hey. Just thought I'd check in. What's going on with you guys?'

'Come on Maxy, it's your Uncle Jamie. Come and say hello.'

Max waddles over to John, who lifts him up to his lap.

'Hey there Max!' I say.

Max goes shy and presses his face into John's chest. I haven't Skyped them in a while and have reverted to being a stranger in Max's eyes.

'Aw, mate, why are you being silly?' says John. 'It's Uncle Jamie. Come on, say g'day.'

'It's all right,' I say. 'He must be tired.'

'Yeah he is a bit. Hardly surprising given how much he's been running around today.' He lifts him up and offers him to Nat. 'Here Nat, can you have him?'

Nat takes him and awkwardly cradles him.

She leans forward and says in her Australian accent, 'Hey

Jay, how's it going mate?'

'Not bad Nat. You're looking well.'

She pulls a face, which becomes pixelated for a moment while the internet tries to keep up. 'Ah, you're kind but I know I look ragged.'

Max is peering at me.

He has dark hair in the same style as Boris Johnson, all over the place.

Nat says, 'Listen I'm gonna take this one to bed. Will say bye for now.'

'Okay.'

'Are you gonna say goodnight, darling?' she says to Max.

Max briefly glances at me, limply waves at the screen, hides his face again.

'Aw, sorry Jay. He's in a funny mood, aren't you mate?' She kisses the top of his head.

'It's okay. I'm in a funny mood too. See you guys.'

They go off-screen.

John whispers to Nat, 'I'll come and help in a minute.'

'He's so big now,' I say.

'Yeah,' says John. 'It's fucking hard work to be honest.'

'I bet it is.'

'Don't leave it too late to have kids. It's too hard when you're older.'

'You're only thirty five.'

'Yeah but thirty-five isn't twenty-five.'

'I won't be having them any time soon.'

'Yeah, Mum told me about Alice.'

'I'm seeing someone else now.'

'Oh yeah?'

'Yeah.'

'Does Mum know? She didn't mention that.'

'I was going to tell her today but I left early.'

'What happened?'

'I was supposed to have lunch at theirs but Dad did his usual and started mouthing off.'

'What did he say?'

'Ah, nothing really. He's just so fucking grumpy. He made a few digs at me and I flounced off. I can't handle it.'

'He was always the same with me.'

'Was he? Why does he do it?'

'You know why he does it.'

'I do and I don't.'

'Why do you think I live here?'

'More money. More sunshine. Nicer house.'

'That's part of it. But there's no way I could have them interfering with Max all the time. Nat's parents are way more chilled out. They live up the road but they know their boundaries.'

'Can I come and live with you for a bit?'

'I've been telling you for months now, you can come and stay any time.'

'I can't afford it at the moment. But I will. Maybe next year.'

'We have a wedding to go to in Bali in April, so don't come in April.'

'Ah, that reminds me. I've got a wedding next weekend. I need a new suit. I'm sorry to ask, but can you lend me some money bro? I can pay you back when I get paid next.'

He sighs. 'So that's why you called me.'

'Yeah. Sorry.'

'Don't tell Nat.'

'Okay.'

'How much do you need?'

'Like, 500 quid?'

'Mate, what the fuck? What kind of suit are you gonna get?'

'I forgot to say. The handbrake went on my car today. It's gonna cost like 200 quid.'

'You need to get that thing scrapped. It's a piece of shit.'

'I need it. The public transport still sucks here.'

'You got PayPal?'

'Yeah.'

'I'll send it when we get off the phone.'

'Thanks bro.'

'It's fine.'

He leans closer to the screen to scrutinise me. 'What's going on with your hair? You're not too far away from a combover.'

I gingerly touch the top of my head.

'Best thing you can do is shave it off,' he says.

'I've got a weird shaped head. Being bald actually suits you.'

He sweeps his palm over his scalp and grins. 'Just do it. It'll make all the difference.'

'Whatever dude,' I say. 'You're not my dad.'

'Haha, funny boy. Listen, I've gotta go. Max is a nightmare to put to bed.'

'Okay. Thanks again.'

'This is a one-off. Get your act together.'

'I know. I will.'

'Love you bro. We should do this more often.'

'We should.'

He salutes me.

I blow him a kiss and hang up, now 500 quid in debt.

I close the laptop lid and light a cigarette.

Pete calls up the stairs.

'Jay! You wanna come to the football?'

'Who's playing?'.

'Gillingham-Fulham! FA Cup! I've got a spare ticket! Jo's not well!'

'Can you two shut up!' Jo yells from their bedroom. 'I'm not well!'

'Sorry Jo!' I yell. 'I'll get my things Pedro!'

'Wicked!' yells Pete.

'Shut up!' yells Jo.

'Sorry darling!' yells Pete.

'Yeah, sorry darling!' I yell.

Jo laughs then starts coughing. 'I hate you both equally!'

I put out my cigarette in a beer can by my bed and go downstairs.

34

I haven't been to a football match in a long time.

A while back I went off sport in general, because it was infantile and atavistic. It had all become too samey, too commercialised, too egomaniacal.

Too pointless, too base.

The latent (manifest) homoeroticism didn't bother me, but the sublimated need for dominance did.

Also, it reminded me of my own failure to make it as a footballer.

Each game I watched brought back the sting of my Sunday League manager's words:

'You don't have what it takes.'

This evening, however, I enjoy the game. It's like comfort food. It takes my mind off Tom.

Pete asks if Tom's made contact.

I shake my head. 'I phoned him to tell him I flushed the stuff. I haven't heard anything since.'

'That's good. Right?'

'I dunno. Hopefully. I don't really see what he can do it about it.'

It's a good game.

For the most part I'm engrossed. I get distracted for a while by a colourful beach ball being batted around the crowd in the stand below us. I watch it on its 'random walk', stochastically bouncing from person to person. No different, really, to a dust particle in a sunbeam.

It reminds me of when I went to see The Flaming Lips years ago and Wayne Coyne crowd-surfed inside a translucent plastic ball.

I imagine a tiny version of myself inside the beach ball, rolling around, screaming for them to let me out.

Then I get back into the match.

Gillingham-Fulham is what's known as a non-local derby, which means even though Gillingham and Fulham aren't geographically close they still share an intense historical rivalry, because a lot of hardcore football fans are morons.

Despite this, the hardcore fans are pretty well-behaved. Pete says he saw some EDL thugs wandering around before the game, but nothing materialises.

I don't see or hear any major rowdiness, anyway.

It starts to snow just before half-time.

Priestfield's giant floodlights illuminate the gentle flurry over the stadium. Perhaps this mellows everyone out.

The Gills play at a higher standard than I've ever seen and they win 3-1, which sends them through to the third round of the cup.

35

We decide to head to The Barge to celebrate. It's dark and freezing but we're up for the walk.

We walk along Gillingham's London-like streets and I feel optimistic, despite the UKIP posters I spot in a few windows.

Maybe things are looking up for Gillingham.

I've grown fond of it lately; I'm starting to see its untapped potential.

I don't care what anyone says: with the first snowfall of the year settling on the roofs of its quiet, under-appreciated houses, it actually looks kind of beautiful.

And The Barge is a genuinely brilliant pub, a fairly rare thing in Medway.

It's a low-lit, low-ceilinged place with lots of dark wooden beams providing skeletal support. It's like you're inside the hull of an old boat.

It has a simple, pretty beer garden which overlooks the Medway estuary. When you sit out there smoking, watching an understated sunset, you can imagine the Dutch fleet sailing in during the 1667 raid on the Medway.

The sailors coming into the pub for refreshment, bringing in the waft of seawater and gunpowder and their unwashed clothes.

The building is probably about as old as that time.

There's a goliath Peruvian bird-eating spider preserved in a glass case above the bar. Real ale. Low frequency of arseholes.

They occasionally do lock-ins if the punters are well-behaved, and at some point the owner will pick up one of the many acoustic guitars lying about the place and invite anyone still awake to play and sing with him until the sun comes up.

It's great.

Pete and I go to the bar. We order a couple of beers and ask for two sets of darts.

I notice an old friend from school, Shaz, sitting at a small table near the back door, texting.

I haven't seen him in years and realise that I regret this; he was always cool.

I go and say hi. Shaz looks up from his phone and smiles.

'Whoa, Jamie Sinclair. It's been ages, man. What's going on with you?'

'Oh you know, this and that. The great mystery of life continues. This is my friend Pete. Pete this is Shaz'

Shaz stands up and they shake hands.

'What are you doing back here?' says Shaz.

'I still haven't come up with a good answer for that.'

'I heard you were all set up in Manchester.'

'Yeah, long story short, I broke up with my girlfriend and moved back here to clear my head. But now I'm starting to feel like this place is getting its hooks into me. What about you?'

He holds up his phone. 'I'm supposed to be meeting my brother but he just bailed on me. I'm leaving for Canada in a couple of days and this is the last opportunity to see him for a while. He's such a dick.'

'Perfect, you can join us.'

A fire is going in the little alcove where the dartboard is and it's cosy. Pete and I remove our coats, scarves, gloves and hats and lay them on a nearby table.

I look out the window. It's started snowing again.

We play a few games of killer then sit down with our drinks.

Someone is playing one of the guitars somewhere, noodling a familiar song.

I take out my tobacco and Rizlas, Shaz his Marlboro Lights. The landlord is extremely relaxed about indoor smoking, despite the smoking ban.

See? What did I tell you. Great.

'So, Canada eh?' I say.

'Yeah, can't wait dude. I'm doing a ski season.'

'I did that a few years ago,' says Pete. 'I went to France though.'

Shaz nods quickly. 'I thought about France. Did you like it?'

'It was awesome,' says Pete.

'Why don't you go travelling Jay?'

'I'd love to but I'm running low on cash. Might do at some point though. You quit your job then?'

Shaz had worked for one of the big banks at Canary Wharf since leaving school and worked his way up.

'Yeah man I just thought fuck it. If you ain't happy you've gotta change your circumstances innit. I'm sick of the commute. And let's just say I'm a little jaded with the banking system right now.'

'Sounds like it's going to be a good thing for you,' I say.

'Another round chaps?' asks Pete.

'Yes please,' I say.

'Yeah, thanks dude,' says Shaz.

Pete goes to the bar, returns with a bundle of crisps as well.

'You should come and visit me in Canada,' says Shaz. 'I'll put you up for a small fee, mates' rates.'

He grins and shoves some crisps into his mouth.

'Thanks,' I say. 'When you going.'

'What's today,' he mumbles. 'Sunday. I go on Tuesday.'

'You all packed and ready?'

'Born ready bruv.'

'A pinky, purply sort of reddy.'

'Jokes, jokes.' He smiles with his eyes and wipes his salty hands on his designer jumper. 'But yeah, I'm basically all packed.' He lights a cigarette, inhales, exhales, taps ash.

'Why Canada?' asks Pete.

'Good snow. Least racist place in the world.'

I say, 'What, after the United Kingdom of Great Britain and Northern Ireland, you mean.'

'Of course, of course. I'm serious though. Come and visit. You can't stay here too long. Things will happen to you.'

'Nothing happens here.'

'Exactly.'

'Yeah, true.' I light my own cigarette. 'Maybe I will visit. It'll be an excuse to get oot and aboot.'

After about three pints we're all on their way to being pissed. Shaz suggests that for old time's sake we go to The Zone.

'Noooo,' I say. 'I was only there a few weeks ago and I promised myself it was the last time.'

'Yeah, no, I've got work tomorrow,' says Pete. 'But you guys go ahead.'

'And I'm supposed to be seeing Kim later.'

'Is that your Mrs? Invite her along too.'

'Could do I guess. Can't we go to the Tap N Tin instead though? The music's better.'

'Yeah all right,' says Shaz.

'Come on Pete. It'll be fun.'

'I know. But I can't.'

I make the sound of a whipcrack.

'Invite your Mrs along too, Pete,' says Shaz.

'Er, Jo's not so keen on Medway's pub scene. And really, I've got work in the morning.'

'To be honest I don't have a lot of money,' I say. 'I should probably go home with Pete.'

'Don't worry about that, I'll pay,' Shaz says. 'Come on, it's Sunday – it'll be free entry. And it's a rite of passage. Whenever you have a last weekend in Medway, you have to go to the Tap N Tin. That's the way it's been since the -- since the fucking Magna Carta.'

'It actually says that in the Magna Carta.'

'Yup, it's like the second or third line in.'

'Have you ever read the Magna Carta.'

'I read it every morning before I go to work.'

Shaz gets up and starts walking towards the toilet. 'I'm gonna bleed the lizard. You call a taxi.'

'It says that in the Magna Carta too.'

'I fucking love the Magna Carta!'

'The Magna Carta is a babe!'

36

Pete reluctantly walks home and Shaz and I get a taxi to the Tap N Tin.

I text Kim but she isn't in the mood.

- Have fun tho. Don't do anything I wouldn't do. XXX
- :))))))
- What does that mean?
- it means i'll see you tomorrow after work xxx
- :))))))

Shaz pays for the taxi and our entry fees, and hands me enough cash to cover my drinks for the rest of the night.

I promise to pay him back but he won't hear of it.

'I got an insane Christmas bonus this year,' he says. 'It's honestly a joke. The bank nearly collapsed a few months ago but we still got paid.'

'In that case,' I say, 'Get me a white wine spritzer, spritzer, spritzer.'

The Tap N Tin is an indie pub and gig venue where I first heard some of the music that changed me.

Once I'd dislocated myself from my old squad I stopped going to the Zone and Bar Rio and discovered the alternative scene in Medway.

I walked through its big, green farm-gate doors, into the

rock dungeon, and that was it. I wasn't the same sixteen-year-old anymore.

I discovered bands that said something to me about my life.

Discovered people who could think for themselves, people who weren't beholden to their respective cliques from high school.

I discovered that I was capable of feeling things that were buried deep within me.

Basically, I became a bit emo.

But it was good.

I saw Billy Childish perform there. Holly Golightly too. The Libertines.

The Tap N Tin was a friend when I didn't have many at school anymore.

It's good to be here again, standing at the bar, talking to a group of students while Felt plays on the jukebox.

Shaz, being a 'ladies' man'.

Me, not.

Sunday night at the Tap N Tin.

Half an 'ecstasy' tablet each, acquired from someone who might've been underage.

Dancing with strangers in the gig room while some local math-rock band outstays their welcome on stage.

Serotonin being created in our bellies.

Me being propositioned by a woman at least fifteen years my senior, who clutches my cock and balls through my trousers, whispering obscene things in my ear with her wine breath.

Staggering outside at 2am, trying to hail a taxi under the railway arches, laughing at very little provocation.

Too many competitors for taxis.

Deciding to walk home instead, 'like we used to.'

After an hour or so arriving at the 24-hour Tesco, smuggling pick 'n' mix in our coat pockets through the checkouts, purchasing cheese and onion pasties to mask our thievery.

Sitting in the middle of a roundabout, eating our food, a bit more sober, a little less skittish from the ecstasy.

When we start walking again it isn't long before someone says, 'Oi, Taliban.'

'Ah fuck it,' says Shaz, looking sideways at me.

'Oi Taliban, why don't you fuck off back to where you came from.'

'Ignore him,' I say.

I look over my shoulder at the guy.

Big dude. Built like a squaddie. Probably recently back from Afghanistan.

Looks as though he could easily take both me and Shaz, pair of scrawny bastards that we are.

We're on a quiet street, kind of near my digs. Shaz lives much further away.

'Can you run,' I whisper. 'We're near my place.'

'I guess,' says Shaz. 'It's a bit icy.'

'Allahu Akbar, Allahu Akbar!'

Shaz stops and faces the guy. 'Mate, I'm not even a practising Muslim.'

'What did you say to me, you black cunt.'

'Shaz, leave it.' I pull on his coat sleeve. 'Let's keep going.'

'No, fuck him.'

'What the fuck did you just say to me, you fucking paki.'

'I said I'm not a practising Muslim, nor am I from Pakistan, you fucking moron. And if you come any closer I'm calling the police.'

The guy comes closer.

I can see his breath coming out of his nostrils, like a Minotaur.

He marches right up to Shaz and lamps him on the chin.

Shaz stumbles back a few steps, slips, falls to the ground.

Isn't knocked out, but looks dazed, sitting with his arms splayed behind him and his legs out before him. His eyes are wide; he blinks slowly a few times.

The guy moves quickly and tries to kick Shaz, but I step in front of him and push him back.

Do this weird thing with both hands out of panic, sort of like jazz hands.

Shout as loud as I can about four times, sometimes mangling the order and pronunciation of the words, 'Fuck off, you coward!'

The guy steps back. He looks at me.

I guess he's on something like speed; he's clenching his jaw and doesn't seem to be able to focus properly on me.

Then he walks off. Goes round a corner, disappears from our lives.

It's weird how it's over so quickly; all that commotion, then nothing.

I tend to Shaz, ask him if he's okay, does he need an ambulance.

'I think I'm okay,' he says, massaging his chin. 'It doesn't even really hurt.'

I help him stand up. Shaz brushes snow from his backside.

I inspect his face.

'I think I'm okay,' he says.

'Looks all right,' I say. 'Maybe go to the doctor tomorrow if it hurts in the morning.'

'Yeah.'

We start walking again.

'This place,' says Shaz.

'I know,' I say.

We get to the junction where we have to go our separate ways.

We hug and say goodbye.

'Come visit me in Canada,' Shaz says. 'Any time. It was good to see you.'

'I will man. I'll hit you up on Facebook.'

'Good.'

'Have a safe flight.'

'Thanks mate. Adios.'

I take out my tobacco and watch Shaz become smaller as he walks away.

I probably won't see him again for many years, if ever.

I light my cigarette as it starts to snow again.

Gillingham really does look beautiful in the winter.

37

ıg to work,' I say. 'And I'm staying at Kim's tonight,
ɔrobably see you tomorrow.'
aying Fifa again. Jo's out.

npleted that game yet?'
ı't complete it. It goes on forever.'
, I was joking.'
;ht.'
dude.'
taters.'
ıy coat on and step outside.
ent snow has melted. Patches of brown slush on the
ı; a few crocuses poking through, awake prematurely
;.
ɪ be dead by tomorrow; the morning frost will
ı.

;et to my car I notice that it's sitting obliquely, slightly
the kerb-side.
'res have been slashed. It looks like they've partially
nd fused with the slushy ground.
the passenger door, put a dent in the panel.
ɔ phone Tom. No answer.
ɪ him, I think.

38

I finish my shift at 11.

Bill, Becky and I do the close-down checklist. We lock the pub behind us.

Bill's wife is waiting for him across the road.

'Thanks guys. Appreciate your hard work. See you back in the fray tomorrow.'

He puts on his woolly hat and crosses the road.

I walk with Becky to the carpark on autopilot, having forgotten about the car.

'Where did you park?' says Becky.

'I just remembered -- I didn't. I walked here.'

'Why?'

'Someone slashed my tyres.'

'Why would they do that?'

'Long story.'

'So you know who did it?'

'I have my suspicions, yeah.'

'Do you want a lift?'

'Would that be going massively out of your way?'

'Depends. Where do you live?'

'Gillingham.'

She hesitates just long enough to betray her reluctance.

'It's okay. I can get the train.'

'How about I drop you at Rainham station? I live pretty near there.'

'That's a good compromise.'

We arrive as the level crossing barriers are coming down.

'Better get a move on,' says Becky. 'That's your train.'

'Thanks mate, I owe you.'

'All good.'

She waves and drives off. I sprint to the platform.

It's only one stop to Gillingham.

I exit the station and start walking towards the high street.

I check my watch. The Red Lion will still be open – they have a late licence.

One whisky, then home.

It's more or less empty in there, as usual.

I sit at the bar and sip a good scotch paid for with borrowed money. Cheers, John.

The bell goes for last orders.

I order a second whisky, down it.

I stand up and put my scarf and coat on.

The door swings open.

From the corner of my eye I can tell it's a group of blokes roistering in.

As I adjust my scarf I feel a tap on the shoulder.

I turn round to see Tom, Mark and the Geezers F.C. gang.

'Want a lift home?' says Tom.

'I'm good thanks,' I say.

I try to walk past them, but Mark puts a hand on my chest and brings me to a halt. 'It wasn't a question,' he says.

They bundle me out of the pub and push me to the pavement.

I try to get up but a brutal kick to the ribs puts me down again.

More kicks.

I ball myself up and wait for it to be over.

Eventually Mark hauls me up by the lapels.

'Forty fucking grand you flushed down the toilet!'

This cracks me right in the sternum, harder than any of their kicks.

'I don't know what you're talking about.'

'You do, and you're gonna get it for me by the end of the month.'

I laugh.

Mark punches me in the mouth.

I can taste blood.

I scrape my teeth along my tongue, spit out a red globule.

'It ain't funny. Get me my money or you're a dead man. Simple as that.'

'How do you expect me to do that? I earn less than six quid an hour.'

'You're a clever boy. Went to university, didn't ya? You'll think of something.'

He lets go of me and pushes me backwards, causing me to land on my backside.

'End of the month,' he says. 'Meet us here, closing time.'

He leans down and claps my cheeks. They all walk off.

Tom looks back at me and smirks.

I give him the finger, then lie back on the cold pavement, forty thousand five hundred pounds in debt.

(Let's not even think about my student loan, which accretes interest every day, like stalactites to a cave ceiling.)

39

The next day I finally ask Kim to be my 'plus-one' for the wedding.

We're sitting on her bed, naked and comfortable.

I'm not expecting her to say yes. She does though, and I'm grateful. She'll be able to mitigate the stress of seeing everyone again. She has a knack for chilling me out.

She's so unpretentious that it's hard to stay uptight around her.

She's able to unpeel my armour, which paradoxically makes me less vulnerable.

I'll need her company. I'm more anxious than I've been in a long time.

Old friends can have that effect on a person.

'I need to get a new suit tomorrow,' I say. 'Wanna help me choose one?'

'We'll talk about the suit in a minute,' she says, gingerly stroking my face. 'First I want you to tell me what really happened.'

'I already did. I got jumped on my way home from work.'

'Yeah, but that's not the whole story. Who was it?'

'I told you, I don't know. Just a bunch of teenagers.'

'Was it Tom?'

'Why would Tom do something like that?'

'I don't know. You two haven't been getting along. He seemed weird when he left after dinner the other week.'

'It wasn't Tom.'

'Fine. You're not gonna tell me. But you need to let me take you to the hospital.'

'I'm okay.'

'No, you're not.'

'All right, Mum.'

'Do you want another black eye?'

'Ooh, kinky.'

'Come on, get dressed and get in the car.'

'I really don't want to go to hospital. It looks worse than it is.'

She sighs. 'If you die in your sleep from a concussion, I'll kill you.'

40

With my car out of action and Kim's car in for a service, we catch an early-evening train up to London.

The plan is to go to Oxford Street tomorrow morning before the wedding to get a suit.

I'm flush with borrowed cash.

We'll stay over again tomorrow night and see a play together on the Sunday.

I'm determined to forget about Tom and Mark and the cocaine and the money.

Things are going well with Kim.

Owing forty thousand pounds to a drug dealer isn't going to sour it.

We connect to the tube at Victoria and check into a bed and breakfast in Islington.

We have sex, then go to a nearby pub where I've arranged to meet some of the old Manchester set.

Before we left the room I weighed myself on the scales in the ensuite.

A scarecrow with a little beergut; slabs of alky fat slapped around my midriff, raw chicken fillets on a wire frame; crow-pecked, talon-torn jacket with frayed sleeves, bunches of straw poking out; patches on my knees.

I'm down to 10st 4.

It's a gentrified pub, horribly busy.

I instantly want to sit on the polished concrete and hug myself, gently rocking back and forth.

Back in the day this would have been a no-go area frequented by gangsters. Now it seems like everyone is either a yuppie or a hipster or worse, a hybrid of both: a yupster.

There's a restored penny farthing hanging from a wall. A cis couple is playing Guess Who at their table. Mumford and Sons is on the jukebox.

People seem pleased and relaxed about all of this.

I feel doomed.

'Hey, look,' says Kim, pointing towards one corner of the pub. 'There's a table. I need the loo.'

'Cool, I'll hold the fort,' I say.

She gives me her purse to hang onto and I slide between a pair of yupsters and take an iron garden chair with a tatty cushion.

I look around the pub, eavesdrop on conversations.

I hear bloated egos fighting for prominence. People signalling their status and their self-perceived importance to their acquaintances by talking about their jobs and bragging about how busy they are.

Londoners.

Busy, busy Londoners.

So many of them talking in this strange, stilted way, trying to sound posher than they are. I hear one person pronounce 'land' as 'larned', as though it's the past participle of a made-up verb, 'to larn'.

'We larned in New York on Friday.'

I vow only to use my native Medwegian accent from now

on. The idea that I might ever have sounded like these people makes me nauseous.

Kim and I have already had a couple of drinks when Dan, Lucy and Emily turn up together.

I lived with them in halls, had once been pretty close with them all, but I don't feel much when I see them except for cold adrenaline swilling around my stomach.

Emily notices me first. 'Oh my gourd, Jamie Sinclair! So good to see you!'

She's another one who speaks in this weird way.

'You too, Emily.' I stand up, hug her awkwardly.

I force myself to make eye contact with the other two, hold up a hand in a frozen wave. 'Hi Lucy. Hi Dan.'

Lucy and Dan take turns to shuffle towards me; they hug me and high-five me respectively.

They all look healthy and successful.

They're wearing an array of sanctioned designer labels. Superdry, Gorman, Matthew Williamson, Paul Smith, Levis, Ray-Ban, Nike.

They look like they've spent a lot of money on their haircuts, possibly hundreds of pounds between them. If I were to shave off their hair and stuff it in a satchel I could take it into a letting agency and put down a deposit on a flat.

The girls are wearing pearl earrings and have expensive-smelling perfume on.

I'm wearing clothes that I've had since I was twenty-one. I have a scraggly beard, and my hair...

A sliver of my former self, I'm like a piece of undifferentiated flesh sliced off the person I used to be which has since become conscious, sentient, semi-alive in its own right.

'How'd you get the black eye,' Emily asks.

'I got punched in the face by a drug dealer because I flushed forty thousand pounds-worth of his cocaine down the toilet.'

'Ha ha. What really happened?'

'I... walked into a lamppost.'

'Great timing. You're going to look funny in the wedding photos tomorrow.'

'Yeah, Sam'll be annoyed, probably. I'll have to stand at the back. Speaking of whom – is she still coming tonight? I haven't seen her in ages.'

'Yeah,' says Dan. 'She said she'll be here a bit later though.'

'Cool,' I say.

I introduce Kim to the group.

She says hello and gets talking to them, genuinely unashamed of her own Medwegian accent. I watch them silently evaluating her

'How did you two meet?' asks Lucy.

'I work with one of Jamie's housemates,' says Kim. 'She set us up.'

'Oh how sweet!' says Lucy.

Kim looks uncomfortable, but lovely.

'And that's in Kent, right?' says Dan.

'Yeah,' I say. 'I moved back earlier this year. To, uh, Medway, where I grew up.'

'Medway,' says Emily. 'Is that near Tunbridge Wells?'

'It's a world away from Tunbridge Wells,' says Kim.

'Wait, I've heard of Medway,' says Lucy. 'Isn't that where chavs originally came from?'

She laughs.

Dan laughs.

Emily laughs.

Kim and I do not laugh.

'Sorry,' Lucy says. 'No offence guys.'

'None taken,' I lie.

'No, but seriously, do you see many chavs on a daily basis?' says Emily, leaning forward in her seat. 'Do they walk around in their Burberry caps, mugging old ladies?'

'Yeah, do you see a lot of twelve-year-olds out with their babies?' says Lucy.

'Hahahahahahahahaha, hilarious,' I say. 'Let's all laugh at poor people. When did you become such snobs?'

'Oh come on,' says Lucy. 'We're just having a bit of fun.'

'You've always had a good sense of humour,' I say.

I excuse myself for a cigarette.

Kim comes with me.

'I thought you said they were your friends,' she says.

'They were,' I say.

When we come back Lucy and Emily are talking about who they would like to sleep with more, Justin Timberlake or Robert Pattinson.

They talk about Sex and the City and New York – how they would live in Williamsburg or Brooklyn or Manhattan, but not Queens.

Dan's on his phone, looking bored.

Emily announces to no-one that lots of the guys at this pub have great beards.

Lucy looks around and nods. I look around too and notice

that lots of them do indeed have great beards.

There's a brief lull in the conversation. Drinks are sipped. I'm already tipsy.

'So Jamie,' says Dan, putting his phone away. 'Sam tells me you're working in a bar these days.'

'Yeah,' I say. 'It's going all right. I'm treading water, but it's fine.'

'What do you do Dan?' asks Kim.

He runs his fingers through his obscenely well-maintained hair. 'I'm a film producer.'

He says this like he's a big deal. Like we're in the presence of a celebrity.

'Oh yeah? What kind of films,' Kim asks, looking impressed.

'Commercials mainly. But I'm trying to get funding for a short film I've written.'

'You make propaganda then,' I say.

'What?'

'You make adverts, yeah?'

'Yeah...'

'Who do you make adverts for?' asks Kim.

'We've done stuff for BMW, Nike. Oh, we just finished a project for Coachella in the States.'

Again, like a celebrity.

'So you make propaganda,' I say, slurring a little.

'What are you talking about.'

'You make propaganda that supports capitalism. The ideology of capitalism. You're a propaganda merchant. You spin dreams. You channel your energy into convincing people to buy things to keep the system going. You're like an evil wizard, casting spells that get everyone to think the same thing at the same time, to buy the same things, to keep the status quo intact.'

'This is going to be a fun conversation,' he says, looking handsome and evil.

I continue anyway. 'That's what you do though, isn't it. Let's be honest. You trick people into buying shit during Coronation Street. You're a volunteer in the Ministry of Propaganda, which doesn't officially exist and yet we know it does because it's staffed by people like you who believe you're being creative and cool.'

'I can't help being cool,' he says, pretending to be ironic.

'People over the age of 25 who care about being cool are tragic,' I say hypocritically.

'Whatever Jamie. Haters gonna hate. You're just jealous.'

'You're a sell-out.'

'You're drunk.'

I imitate his voice. 'You're drunk.'

'Oh my God, you're actually a prick.'

'Oh my God, you're actually a prick.'

'Listen, fuck you Jamie, you loser.'

'No, you listen, take Coachella. Everyone knows it's for sell-outs. It's for musicians who'll happily take a pair of...' I look at Dan's shoes. '...Nike trainers or whatever for a bit of publicity, not thinking about how much power they're giving to these corporations or how they were made in a factory by slaves. You're complicit. You're making the world shitter. Art's supposed to offer people an alternative, not bolster the established ideology. You're a courtier for Moloch. Maybe, Dan, you are Moloch.'

'Why don't you have another drink,' says Dan.

'Moloch! Solitude! Filth! Ugliness!' I shout,

channelling Ginsberg.

Kim intervenes. 'Hey, Jay, let's go, yeah? I think it's time to call it a night.'

'Nah, I'm good. I wanna stay here. I wanna hear what Lucy and Emily have been up to.'

I look at them in turn. 'Come on. Tell me all about how vacuous you've become. You look like you've both become tremendously vacuous yupsters.'

'What the fuck is a yupster?' says Dan.

'Shut up Moloch. Come on you two, tell me how this happened. You used to vote for the Green Party. Once upon a time you would've balked at coming to a place like this.'

'Someone's got a chip on their shoulder,' Emily mutters.

'It's more chip than shoulder, really, isn't it,' says Dan.

I can feel myself reddening. 'Look, I'm sorry,' I say. 'We didn't come here to get abused, that's all. I'm sorry.'

I look at Kim. She's gripping the sides of her chair and her shoulders are hunched.

'You're the one hurling abuse, Jamie,' says Emily.

'Yeah,' says Lucy. 'It didn't take long for his inner chav to come out, did it.'

I glower at her. She says this with such snottiness that I can't help myself: I chuck the dregs of my beer into her smug face.

It's a reflex. As it is when Dan puts me in a headlock.

As it is too when I grope for something on the table, find a tall glass of gin and tonic, and smash it over Dan's head.

Dan's grip loosens; I wriggle out from the headlock and push him away.

He falls limply to the floor.

Emily screams. Lucy's face is wet with beer as she screams.

Kim jumps out of her seat and steps backwards.

There's blood and glass everywhere.

I lean back in my chair, grip it so as not to slide off, watch everything unfold before me like a play.

Surrounding people are cleared out of the way by a couple of bar staff.

Dan, on his back, seemingly unconscious, tended to by another staff member who says she knows first-aid, armed with a cloth and antiseptic spray.

She orders one of her colleagues to call an ambulance.

Then a bouncer, this great, hefty immoveable object of a guy, catches me off guard.

He yanks me out of my chair and twists me into some kind of death-grip.

This is interactive theatre now, with audience participation.

My cheek is pressed to the wet floor.

I can smell gin and cucumber.

The bouncer holds me there for a moment. I try to move but I'm helpless.

I can see a thin section of the bouncer's pale, hairy calf between his Doc Martin boot and the hem of his black trouser-leg.

The bouncer effortlessly hauls me up, drags me through the bar and chucks me out onto the pavement.

Nearby smokers step out of the way.

Sirens wail in the distance somewhere.

Kim runs out and helps me up.

'Let's go,' she says, her breath visible because of the cold. 'I'll hail a taxi.'

'No, I want to walk for a bit. Clear my head.'

'You're too drunk. And they're calling the police.'

'I'm fine.'

'I'm not. I'm going back to the B&B.'

'Suit yourself.'

'Come on Jamie, this is stupid.'

'Says the person who reads Harry Potter.'

She looks at me in a way that leaves me completely undone.

She hesitates for a minute, then walks away, resolute, and disappears round a corner.

I make to jog after her but stumble and almost fall into the road.

The smokers chuckle at me.

I right myself, give them the forks, dig out my tobacco.

An ambulance appears.

It mounts the kerb and two paramedics get out and jog into the pub.

I watch through the window as they tend to Dan, who's awake now and clutching his head.

Lucy and Emily help him up to a chair and one of the paramedics dabs his head with a cloth.

I turn around and spark up.

Watch groups of 'revellers' on the other side of the street join the queue of a nightclub until a bus pulls over and obscures them.

Then I see a police car out of the corner of my eye.

Two police officers get out and walk towards the pub.

Sam, the bride-to-be, suddenly appears alongside them. She spots me.

'Jamie! Yoo-hoo! Jamie! It's me!'

The bouncer who threw me out comes to the door and points me out to the police officers.

I drop my cigarette and leg it.

One of the police officers shouts, 'Oi! Get back here!'

I hear Sam call out to me but her words are unintelligible as they blend with the sounds of the street.

I sprint across the road.

A black cab beeps at me and a car coming from the other direction has to do an emergency stop.

I push through the people disembarking the bus.

Someone calls me a twat.

I run up a side street, go round another corner and emerge near Angel Station.

I'm puffed out but I carry on running up the road for a bit until I find a busy-enough pub.

I march straight to the back and into the toilets.

Find a vacant cubicle, lock it, sit down, wait it out.

41

After about half an hour I emerge from the cubicle.

I splash my face at the sink.

There's some graffiti on a wall tile by the hand dryer, drawn with marker pen.

Inside a small cartoon television are the words, 'Change your life not the channel.'

On some adjacent tiles there's a picture of a cock shooting out jizz at Space Invader-style craft lined up in rows above it.

Towards the ceiling someone has scrawled, 'The more I think about it the bigger it gets.'

I place my hands beneath the nozzle to activate it.

It turns off prematurely.

I move my hands like I'm jiggling a giant pair of testicles suspended in mid-air.

The dryer comes back on.

I repeat this process like eight times until my hands are dry, all the while trying not to vomit.

I go to the smoking area out back.

There are three or four lively groups of people.

I roll a cigarette with too much tobacco in it and with the Rizla inside out.

It keeps unpeeling and I have to relight it constantly.

I totter between the groups of people, taking in great big lungfuls of smoke and exhaling audibly.

I splutter and go into a coughing fit.

I hawk up some phlegm and launch it over the wooden fence on one side of the deck.

Someone from one of the smoking groups says, 'Oh for fuck's sake, gross.'

I go back inside.

Order a good scotch then stagger over to a vacant booth.

I get a text from Sam. It just says, 'Emily told me what happened. Not impressed.'

I try to call Kim, but she doesn't answer.

Try again but this time it goes straight to voicemail.

I text her something mawkish and apologetic, then proceed to get absolutely annihilated.

42

I'm woken up by a woman forcefully shaking my shoulder.

'Come on mate, time to go. We're closing.'

'Where am I?'

'Jesus Christ.' She raises her voice slightly and speaks more slowly. 'You're in The York. In Angel. Come on mate.'

I look up at her, then rest my head on the table.

'Alexa, can you give me a hand? He's a dead weight.'

Alexa comes over and the two women hoist me out of my seat and set me on my feet.

'Sorry,' I say. 'It's okay. I'm going.'

My coat sleeve is damp with beer and my head is filled with concrete.

'We'll call you a cab. Where do you need to get to?'

I slide the address of the B&B out of my wallet and hand it to her.

'I'm really sorry,' I say.

I pay the cab driver and go up to the room.

I find a note from Kim blu-tacked to the mirror in the bathroom.

Where does she keep finding this blu-tack?

Does she keep a ball of it in her handbag or something, just in case?

'I'm sorry for leaving but I can't be with another alcoholic. I did it once before and it nearly killed me. Here's some money for the room. Take care. Kim x'

I tug the note from the mirror and peel off the blu-tack.

Alcoholic?

That's a big word.

Bit melodramatic, I think.

I roll the blu-tack between my thumb and middle finger, flick into the bin next to the toilet.

Pick up the money and shove it into my back pocket.

I regard myself in the mirror briefly but feel too much litost, an untranslatable Czech word I learned recently, so I have to look away.

I turn off the light and shut the door behind me.

Get undressed, almost tripping over my trousers in the process, and climb into bed, which is still unmade from our love-making earlier in the evening.

43

At least I don't have to buy a new suit any more.

I skip the wedding and use some of the money John wired me to get breakfast and a Bloody Mary.

On a side street I find a small pub with a chalkboard on the pavement advertising its breakfast menu.

I step inside and approach the bar.

The barman takes my order and while he's mixing the drink I try to call Kim again.

Nothing.

The barman puts the Bloody Mary in front of me.

I gulp it down and order another.

I finish my food and decide to walk the long way from Islington to Victoria, on a kind of derive, like a flaneur.

I haven't been to London in a while (since I went with Alice, in fact) and it's mild enough to justify a stroll.

I go East.

I drift through the chartered streets, a pencil in the hand of an artist doing automatic drawing, illustrating an improvised story.

Reclaiming the city somehow, stripping it of its intended purpose.

I'm a trespasser among the inscrutable buildings, the inscrutable people.

I go through labyrinthine alleys and passages, find my way into courtyards and squares and gardens, all of them strangely quiet despite being in the middle of the city.

Places which can shelter you, provide safe haven, anonymise you; or else absorb you against your will, and nullify you.

To access certain places in London you have to be invited in, which is to say you need a certain amount of money.

But my footfalls at the Inns of Court, Threadneedle Street and Paternoster Square subvert this notion in the tiniest of ways.

I will never work in The Gherkin or The Lloyd's Building, but no-one can stop me loitering in their purlieus, bringing down the average bank balance.

These are some of the many dens of Moloch and I'm suddenly here, on an improvised mission, to defy him in my own way.

Moloch is the genius loci of these places, something to be overcome.

He's been worshipped instead of vanquished; thus, despite refined appearances, the prevailing culture is maladaptive, diseased.

I can smell the sickness in the air.

It gets into my lungs, into my heart.

It makes me small.

At St Paul's I go South and cross the river via the Millenium Bridge, buffeted by the crosswinds.

I stop in at the Tate Modern, but don't get much further than the gift shop.

I pick up a pair of green 'therapy glasses' which are on sale.

'Green for feelings of peace, love, harmony and relaxation.'

I pay for them, put them on and leave the gallery.

When I get to Borough I stop at a library to get out of the cold for a bit.

Been walking for nearly two hours.

My cheeks are red, my lips are chapped.

I skim-read the newspapers that are laid out on the large, low coffee tables, still wearing the therapy glasses.

More bleak news.

An explosion at a school in Baghdad, twelve children and two teachers killed.

In Mogadishu a male suicide bomber disguised as a woman blew himself up at a graduation ceremony for local medical students.

Chelsea and Man Utd more or less neck-and-neck in the Premier League, with Chelsea looking to go ahead in their game against Everton this afternoon.

Tiger Woods repentant after yet another woman claimed to have had an affair with him.

The glasses do nothing to make me feel better.

I take them off and leave them on the table for someone else.

I leave the library and go West along the river.

Past Shakespeare's Globe and down to the rocky littoral area near the Southbank.

There's a guy making sand sculptures on the small patch of grey sand.

I approach him and we get chatting.

His name is Karim.

He's from Algiers and waiting to hear from HM Border Force about his immigration status.

He's a medical student struggling to get a visa.

He got evicted last month for complaining about the damp in his flat. Now he's homeless.

I spend an hour or so down there watching Karim sculpt.

He's working on an elephant.

It's incredible.

Honestly. Unbelievably good.

There's a strong smell of seaweed in the cool air, with the occasional whiff of sewage interfering. The temperature has markedly dropped.

I sit and rest against a large, slightly moist rock, my teeth and jaw and ears aching with cold.

I arrange my over-sized scarf over my nose so that my breath can heat up my face, and I stretch my woolly hat as far down as it will go until it nearly reaches the bottom of my ears.

Karim is wearing fingerless gloves.

I'm wondering how he's still able to move his fingers to sculpt when this guy shambles up to us.

Another homeless guy, except he's clearly been homeless for a lot longer than Karim.

He's wearing an oversized football manager's coat.

Chelsea, circa 1998.

He's filthy and bedraggled.

Nose and lips blistered and red from the cold.

He stands near us, watching Karim cupping his hands up and down the elephant's trunk.

He asks for some money.

I find a fiver in one of my pockets and hand it to him.

He grunts something then slumps to the floor a few metres away.

He starts talking, sort of to us and sort of to himself.

It's like my money activated soliloquy-mode.

He mumbles that he was in Iraq, and I realise we're about to get a glimpse of the horror.

He says, "I saw a pregnant woman shot in the stomach."

He says, "I saw a human head in the middle of a bombed-out street."

He makes a limp chopping gesture near his throat to indicate the decapitation.

Mindless killing, mindless violence.

He says, "I can't sleep anymore."

He tells us more about Iraq.

We listen.

Then he gets up and walks away.

Karim and I sit quietly for a while.

My own problems suddenly seem pathetic and minuscule.

44

I need caffeine and something to eat.

I ask Karim if he wants something.

He shrugs and nods.

I go up the steps to a cafe near the Southbank Centre and get a couple of overpriced paninis and some coffee.

While I'm waiting for my order I try to call Kim again.

Still no answer.

When I return Karim is on his knees arranging a thin, tatty piece of crimson cloth over the sculpture.

He hears me approaching and glances over his shoulder.

Holds a hand up to halt any further progress from me.

'Wait there,' he says.

'What's wrong.'

'Nothing. Just wait.'

I put the coffee and food on the ground.

I hug myself and jump up and down on the spot.

London is a shard of ice lodged in England's belly.

Karim eventually unveils his creation with a flourish.

'Tada,' he says, moving aside and turning round to face me.

The elephant is finished.

It has a sad, aged face.

But it's extremely accurate and true-to-life.

'What do you think,' says Karim. 'Do you like it.'

'It's very good Karim. You're a talented man.'

He dusts away some excess sand from one of the eyelids.

I pull out a few pound coins from my back pocket and chuck them into the flat cap near Karim's feet, which creates a small clink as they hit the other change in there.

'Thank you sir,' he says, bowing his head briefly.

'You're welcome,' I say.

I hand him his coffee and panini.

'Thank you,' says Karim.

It starts to drizzle.

Above us a train groans and judders across the gigantic Hungerford Bridge towards Charing Cross.

I shake hands with Karim and say goodbye.

Continue West along the promenade, which is bustling with tourists resisting the increasingly foul weather.

Huddled together like penguins, they clutch their umbrellas, trying to make the best of it.

45

It's all over with Kim.

She's stopped replying to my messages.

The last one I got from her was filled with so many home-truths that I almost went completely insane.

Good old cognitive dissonance kicked in though, and rather than admit she was right and attempt to improve myself as a human being, I sent her possibly the most obnoxious message I've ever sent since owning a mobile phone, and that did it for our relationship.

I immerse myself in work, trying to rack up as much cash as possible to pay off my debts.

Ha.

After a week off I'm back at Harvester for some long, late shifts.

I mainly work with a new bar person called Sarah.

Becky left while I was gone. Sarah stepped in like a champion, and we quickly got a good little system going.

Sarah's only nineteen but she's smart and hard-working.

Systems are important in service jobs and ours is working well.

We seem to operate telepathically.

It makes the shifts go quicker.

We're able to serve more people.

We intuitively understand each other's strengths and adjust our work patterns accordingly.

I change the barrels.

She changes the top-shelf spirits because she's taller.

We both move quickly and agilely around the bar.

She gets on with the good regulars as well as I do.

She's funny, doesn't take herself too seriously.

She's able to handle the abuse from the chefs, and gives as good as she gets.

But the following weekend she doesn't come into work.

Maybe she went off to uni or something.

I struggle after she leaves.

There's no-one else like her.

46

My other colleagues at the Harvester are an eclectic bunch. Some of them are okay, others not so much.

There are a few who've been there for years and years.

Then there are the more itinerant.

I work with dozens of students, most of whom only work for a few of days before moving on.

They usually get waiting jobs in the restaurant.

Stay until they become sick of the rude customers who are too stingy to tip properly.

Disappear to another low-paid job, to be replaced a few nights later by someone else.

The chefs are making it harder and harder for me to enjoy the job.

I have to spend more time in the kitchen because the restaurant is down on prep staff.

If it's quiet in the bar I'm expected to help the crazy chefs.

Usually I load/unload the dishwasher or cut up vegetables.

I have a constant film of moisture across my face from the sweat and steam intermingling.

Have a constant stream of loud nonsense entering my ears from the chefs' mouths.

They are obnoxious and racist and stupid.

The shifts drag on and on, and my kneecaps ache from standing up all day.

I get in from work when Pete and Jo have already gone to

bed. I crack open the first beer and walk around barefoot on the cool shingle outside the back door to massage my feet.

Grab an ice pack or two from the freezer.

Lie on the settee and arrange the ice packs on my knees.

Fall asleep like that.

Wake up fully clothed at 4am with stiff kneecaps.

Somnambulate upstairs to bed.

Have dreams about being in the kitchen, with the chefs, huge and aggressive and dumber than ever, yelling at me to work harder, and Mark Galbraith standing nearby, staring at me and dragging a finger across his throat like a cartoon pirate.

47

Deadline day arrives and I have three hundred and sixty-two pounds to my name.

I'm a little shy, but maybe Mark will cut me some slack.

I decide to phone Tom, who as it turns out is still another one of Mark's minions.

Maybe we can talk things out.

All I get is an abrasive beep and an automated message telling me that the phone's been disconnected.

I go on Facebook to see if Tom's online.

Tom's Facebook feed is littered with links to David Icke videos, multifarious anti-Muslim articles and memes decrying Political Correctness. There's a feature-length video about the unfair vilification Tommy Robinson of the English Defence League.

I scroll down for ages.

He's been posting this sort of stuff for months, with the only comments below the posts coming from the Geezers F.C. boys and a few other people I don't know.

I click on the name of one of them which takes me to their profile.

There's a link on his feed to a Kent Messenger article, underneath which he's written, 'Fuck the police!'

The article reports a drug raid on a house in Hempstead.

Four people were arrested and charged with the possession and sale of ten kilos of cocaine (street value two hundred thousand pounds), including Mark Galbraith and Thomas Pritchard, who both have previous convictions for drug offences.

Just like that, my little problem vanishes.

It would have been nice to say some final words to Tom.

For all his failings, he's been my closest acquaintance for almost a year.

But his time finally came; it was meant to be like this.

He'd tried to improve himself, but he hadn't tried hard enough. He was too stupid not to get caught. He was too weak, and this is what happens to the weak.

I walk down to the local shops, involuntarily smiling, and withdraw twenty pounds. I buy a pack of expensive beer and a tandoori vegetable pie to celebrate, picturing Mark and Tom shivering in their cells.

When I get home I crack open a beer in the kitchen.

I let the bottle-top spin on the laminate floor like a coin while I drink to Lauren Hitchens.

48

One of the chefs has been at the Harvester for ten years and is functionally illiterate.

Twenty-seven years of age and can spell his name and little else.

T-R-O-Y.

Apparently there's a 'literacy crisis' in Medway.

The local paper reports it all the time.

Such-and-such a percentage of kids leaving school can't read or write properly, and the teenage pregnancy rate is allegedly the highest in Europe.

The heroin addiction rate too.

But I think about how it doesn't matter that Troy can't read or write.

He can do his job.

I don't like the chefs but I have to give them credit for their work ethic.

Troy is a steak chef and one of the other chefs reads the tickets to him.

This other chef takes the piss out of Troy's illiteracy, but they have their own little system and rarely mess up anyone's order.

I've worked maybe half a dozen jobs in my life and haven't needed to be particularly literate for any of them, even though they'd claimed to need people with a minimum of a grade C in GCSE English.

Some of the employers had even had the audacity to advertise for graduates.

Troy has an embellished union jack tattoo on his calf muscle and a Chelsea F.C. crest on his bicep.

He has a Liam Gallagher monobrow and tooth decay that makes it look like he has masticated liquorice stuck to his gums.

I hate listening to him.

Troy hates blacks and Muslims and Pakis and the Polish. He tells me this whenever he can.

But Troy never stood a chance in this life.

His mum, Susan, guaranteed that.

She comes in occasionally to give Troy his lunch. (He still lives with her, of course. He'll never leave.)

I hardly speak to Susan, but when I do it makes me singularly depressed.

She owns a golliwog keyring for which she's fashioned a miniature noose to tie around its neck.

A golliwog!

A noose!

She's proud of it.

She visibly enjoyed how uncomfortable it made me the first time she showed it to me.

I noticed it on the bar once and asked her why she had it.

She jingled her keys in front of me and said, 'I keep it for good luck.'

I handed her a port and lemon. She pretended to lynch the golliwog and started cackling.

Troy laughed too, and I had to look away from that mouth of his.

49

People from school sometimes drink at the Harvester.

I notice that this always motivates me to move on and find something else.

I'm worried what these people might think about my situation.

It's pathetic.

'I've been to university and I'm a barman,' I think.

Then I think: 'Yeah, so what, you actually kind of like this job, most of the time.'

I constantly imagine arguments I might have with these people whose opinion should've meant nothing to me.

One time a couple of guys from my old form class come in.

Aaron and Matt.

They say hi, order drinks and go and play the fruit machines for a bit.

When they come back to order more drinks we start to reminisce together about school.

About teachers and the dumb, funny shit that happened in class.

They aren't rude to me. But they're distant somehow.

I don't want to see these people anymore, and guess they hadn't expected to see me back in Medway.

Especially not in this capacity: I fucked off years ago to university – what was I doing back here?

I think they tacitly believe I'm an interloper in their town, just as I believe they're interloping in my own life.

I sense a low-level tension that infuses me with a vague dysphoria.

50

Christmas is nigh.

I say goodbye to Pete and Jo and walk to work for another long evening shift.

My car's still fucked.

Too busy, too poor to get it fixed.

The money John lent me disappeared all too quickly on booze.

At least I'm doing my ten thousand steps every day.

Are you?

On my way I slip on the icy ground, flat onto my back.

The wind is shunted out of me and I can't move.

I lie still until I can breathe again properly.

I can smell the snow on the ground by my head.

Can smell a distant bonfire too.

Someone's garage roof is bearded with multicoloured Christmas lights.

I try to feel 'Christmasy'.

Try to summon the excitement I had as a kid about snow and Christmas lights.

But it disappeared a long time ago. It's too lost, too far away to make it back.

Eventually I haul myself up from the ground.

I'm near the church Mum used to take me and John to when were kids, and can faintly hear a children's choir singing inside.

The sound of their voices is muted: absorbed and flattened by the snow.

When I finish my shift, I take the empty stool next to John.

He asks me why I'm so dirty.

I tell him what happened.

He chuckles.

He buys me a whisky.

Jona Lewie's 'Stop the Cavalry' starts playing.

The lights on the plastic Christmas tree in the corner seem to flash in sync with the song.

'Cheers Jamie,' John says as we clinks glasses. 'What are you doing tomorrow? Will you be going to your parents' place or something'

'What's tomorrow?'

'Christmas Day, you numpty!'

Completely lost track of the date.

All the twelve-hour shifts have warped my sense of time.

I have no plans for Christmas; haven't seen my parents since I stropped away all those weeks ago.

I smile dumbly at John and say, 'Oh yeah.'

John chuckles again and pats me on the back.

All of my shadow selves concertina out of me.

All my selves from parallel universes that exist invisibly alongside me: an eternal paper chain of me suddenly appears.

I see the infinite number of ways I could be better, the infinite number of ways I could be worse.

Bill appears behind the bar.

He's holding his phone and has tears in his eyes.

'What's wrong, Bill?' says John.

'It's Paula,' he says. 'She passed away this evening. The cancer finally took her.'

One of the more recent regulars, a woman whose name I don't know, starts howling.

John walks behind the bar and hugs Bill.

Some of the other regulars come to the counter.

'The next round is on the house,' says Bill, patting John on the back.

John stays behind the bar and helps to serve drinks as everyone else assembles at the counter.

He hands a scotch to Bill, who gulps it in one.

I get back there too and start pulling pints.

'To Paula,' says John, and everyone raises their glasses.

I feel as though I'm inhabiting someone else's body, someone else's life.

spend Christmas day on my own.

Mum and Dad flew to Australia on Christmas Eve to be with John and his family, and Jo and Pete are with their respective families.

Andrea sent me a text as she and Col were about to take off from Heathrow.

- mum, what the hell, why didn't you tell me you were going away
- I tried to, but you wouldn't answer my calls. We wanted to take you as well xx
- and anyway, aren't they coming over in next year?
- Yes. But we wanted to see our grandson at Christmas, if that's okay with you. xx
- how can you afford it? i thought you were struggling
- Our finances are none of your business, young man. Happy Christmas. Xx
- yeah, you too, mum xx

It was true I'd ignored her calls.

The last time I'd spoken to her she was complaining about the rainbow flag one of their neighbours put up in their window, in solidarity with those trying to get same-sex marriage legalised.

'But you have a St. George's cross in one of your windows. Why can't they have a flag as well?'

'It's just not the same thing, Jamie.'

'It's better, in my opinion.'

'I think they're attention-seekers. No-one has a problem with them being gay or anything, but...'

'It sounds like you have a problem with them being gay...'

'Why are you always so argumentative?'

'I'm not being argumentative. I have an opinion that's different to yours. Just like them.'

'Let's agree to disagree, shall we?'

'Ok.'

I'd decided to go 'phone-free' for a couple of weeks, mainly to wean myself off Facebook again.

Tom and Mark were no longer a problem, but I wanted to keep a low profile nonetheless.

I also wanted to avoid any blowback from the night with Emily, Lucy and Dan.

It had been lovely.

I reactivate my account and log in now though.

Andrea has posted photos of them all, with little Max often centre stage.

Christmas on the beach. Barbecued prawns. Sunglasses. The Indian Ocean.

She and Col look happy.

I sip the Belgian beer that Jo and Pete gave as a present and voyeuristically scroll through other people's feeds, their Christmas photos, their seasonal good wishes to one another.

The nut roast I cooked for myself, more or less untouched, goes cold on the floor.

I watch old Christmas movies until I fall asleep, drunk, on the settee.

52

I leave the pub against my will.

Not because I get fired.

I simply stop showing up.

I ignore my ringing phone, ignore the beeps notifying me of voicemails, until Bill gets the idea and stops trying to contact me.

I hadn't meant to leave like that.

I was doing okay at the pub.

I was in a good routine; was almost out of debt; was making plans for the future again.

I'd nearly paid my brother back.

Tom and Mark were a distant memory.

But one morning I woke up and the so-called 'black dog' was with me.

No. It was more like a black demon, a weightless, shadowy form that became dense as dark matter once it possessed my body.

I couldn't face anybody -- couldn't face doing anything -- so that was that, and I became financially precarious once again.

A week of lying in bed.

The curtains have been shut the whole time.

Pete and Jo assume I have the flu.

They intermittently come to check on me, bring me cups of tea.

I leave them all on the floor at the side of my bed.

Before long little mould flowers appear on the surface of the beige liquid in each cup.

Little mould flowers appear on my mind.

53

A few weeks later I'm feeling slightly better and go on the hunt for another job.

It's the New Year.

2009.

This is when I realise I have to rely on my labour to survive.

If I don't work I fall over the edge.

I've used up the generosity of my parents.

I can't go and stay with them again -- we'd kill each other.

And they're hard-up themselves. They have little in the way of savings. I found out they paid for their Australia trip on credit.

My own savings would barely keep me afloat for longer than a week.

I think about the dole but I'd heard it takes ages for the money to come through.

I have to work.

54

I manage to get a post as a teaching assistant in a primary school in Gillingham, which pays the minimum wage of £4.85 an hour.

I still have vague plans to become a teacher so I reason that working in a school isn't an entirely hare-brained idea.

I'm put in the reception class from day one – the smallest kids in the school.

Some of them can't go to the toilet by themselves yet.

It's a culture shock, and smelly.

They grow on me though.

I admire how raw they are.

They're young enough not to have been transmogrified by what educational theorists call the 'doxa' of the school system.

Which means they still say and do unselfconscious, liberated things.

Such as randomly breaking into dance whenever they feel the calling.

Showing me their latest wobbly tooth like it's a huge deal.

Handing me funny/frightening drawings, with no preamble or explanation.

Cheering and hugging my shins when I arrive at their classroom in the morning.

Judging people only by how friendly/entertaining they are.

They are consistently brilliant and, despite my best self-sabotaging efforts, I'm happy at work.

55

After I've been there a few weeks and have gotten to know t he class, one of the little girls, Mia, climbs over everyone else on the carpet while the teacher, Mrs Winterbottom, is in the middle of a story.

Mrs Winterbottom pauses to give Mia a look which conveys, 'What on Earth do you think you're doing?'

I silently gesture for Mia to sit down.

We've bonded and she listens to me.

A few of the other kids giggle.

One of them rolls backwards for no reason.

Another one gets up and goes to the kitchen in the home corner, maybe to rustle up some breakfast for everybody.

Mrs Winterbottom snaps at him to get back on the carpet right away.

She's going to start yelling in minute, I can sense it.

They're small but they know how to get her raging.

Oblivious to all this or else insouciant, Mia clambers over the other kids to where I'm kneeling down, gets right up close to me and whispers directly into my ear canal, sotto voce with warm breath, 'You're my favourite one.'

And that's nice.

That makes me feel good.

The trouble is, I've started drinking every day.

At least once a week I pull a sickie and catch the train to Rochester.

Go to one of the tiny, dark, Tudor-looking pubs on the high

street near the castle and stay there until I'm supposed to have finished work.

One afternoon I have so much to drink that when I walk out of the pub I spray vomit all down myself and onto the pavement.

A man walking past laughs and yells out, 'Fucking lightweight!'

But usually I don't get quite as drunk as that.

Usually I leave the pub around 6pm to get something carby and proteiny to eat, go back and have a couple more beers, then catch the train home.

Where I sleep.

I sleep so much, have so many troubling dreams.

I really like the job though.

I like much of the staff, like the kids.

It's damn hard work, but when I actually turn up I get a lot out of it.

56

A boy called Ethan is playing a game of chess with me.
It's lunchtime.

Ethan punched a child in his class this morning and is therefore in the Responsible Thinking Room with me, some other teaching assistants and four or five more kids who've had to forgo 'outdoor play'.

It's part of my job description to look after children with complex behavioural needs during the main lunch period, even though I and many of the other Teaching Assistants are unqualified.

Ethan is eight.

He can barely make it through his sight words but he's already pretty formidable at chess.

'Checkmate!' he yells.

He whacks my king off the board with his queen.

'Oh man, you did it again,' I say. 'Have you been practising?'

'Yep,' he says. 'I beat my dad all the time.'

He grins at me.

A new top incisor is beginning to poke through the gum next to the over-sized adult tooth already in place.

'I'm not surprised,' I say, omitting to mention that I know Ethan's dad is AWOL and has been for several months. 'Want to play again?'

'YEAH!' he yells.

A teaching assistant called June comes over to the table.

'Hang on,' she says. 'It's time for your meds sweetheart.'

'Aw, but I want to play another game.'

'After your meds,' says June.

Ethan knows the drill.

He hops off his chair and runs over to the makeshift kitchen area.

June retrieves his Ritalin and the accompanying tracking sheet from an out-of-reach cupboard.

Ethan fiddles with some mugs on the draining board.

He picks one up and pretends to drink from it.

'Mmm I love coffee!' he yells.

He does a weird little dance.

'Indoor voice please, Ethan,' says June.

She places a tablet and plastic beaker of water in front of him.

Ethan grips the coffee mug with his teeth so it looks like a kind of muzzle on his face.

He picks up the tablet.

June takes the mug from his mouth and sets it down.

'Jamie love, could I get your autograph here please?'

I nod and walk over to them.

Ethan makes a big deal about swallowing the tablet.

He lets it sit on his tongue for a while then tries to manoeuvre it to the back of his mouth with quiet gags.

He finally swallows it and grimaces.

I sign the sheet to say that the medication has been administered.

'That shit tastes disgusting!' yells Ethan.

'Ethan, we don't swear in here,' I say.

'Can we play chesk now?'

'Chess,' I say. I look at my watch. 'We've got ten minutes. Reckon you can beat me in that time?'

But he's already over at the table, setting up the board.

I join him and swap his knights and bishops around.

'No,' says Ethan. 'They don't go that way.'

'Yeah,' I say. 'Knights are colder than bishops, remember? Castles are coldest, then knights, then bishops.'

'Oh yeah,' says Ethan.

A kid named Kane, about the same age as Ethan, comes over to watch.

'Can I play?' says Kane.

'Sure,' I say. 'You can be black.'

I go to get out of my seat.

'No!' yells Ethan. 'I want to play you!'

Kane frowns.

'I want to play,' says Kane, sulkily.

'C'mon, let Kane play,' I say. 'He's better than me and you need a tougher challenge.'

'No!' yells Ethan. 'No! No! No! No! NOOOO!'

'Ethan,' says June from across the room. 'That's not how we talk to each other, is it. Calm down or I'll have to take you to Mrs Hopkins.'

Ethan scowls.

'How about Kane and I team up then,' I say. 'Us v you. I need his help. Pull up a chair here Kane.'

Ethan turns away and folds his arms. 'This is a stupid game and I'm not playing anymore.'

You speak the truth, I think.

I look at Kane. 'Can I play you afterwards?'

Kane nods sweetly.

'Thanks Kane.' I tap Ethan on the shoulder. 'All right, let's go grumpypants. Kane has kindly agreed to wait.'

Ethan ignores me.

I look at Kane and shrug.

'You're a fucking dickhead Ethan,' says Kane.

Before I can do or say anything to defuse the situation, Ethan turns, stands up, picks up the chess board, and hurls it at Kane.

The pieces scatter everywhere.

Kane spends the remainder of the afternoon in the sick bay with an ice-pack on his forehead.

I play chess with Ethan every lunchtime for the rest of the week.

57

Skiving off again.

I overslept because I was out again last night.

I text Anne, the SENCO, saying I've got that thing that's going around.

- Get well soon love. This is what working in a school does to us!

I go to one of the Tudor pubs on Rochester High Street not long after noon.

It's just me and a few older inveterate drunks.

I'm reading the news on my phone when the local MP walks in.

He recently defected to UKIP from the Conservatives.

He has a small entourage of staff with him and they sit at a corner booth behind me.

They're having an impromptu meeting about a speech the MP is giving later at the Guildhall Museum.

One of the staffers is urging the him to make a reference to the prehistoric lineage of the people of Medway.

I eavesdrop. Fucking morons, having a meeting like this in public.

'You can stand next to the axe they have on display. It's 200,000 years old.'

'Why would I do that?'

'Because it's symbolic. We can press the issue of, you know, immigration and the EU.'

'What does it have to do with immigration?'

'It's palaeolithic. It makes a statement that says, 'We were here first.''

'I see. And who are 'we' exactly?'

'Sir, you know what I mean.'

'Do you realise the British have more in common genetically with people of the Basque country than they do the Vikings, Anglo-Saxons and Celts?'

'No...'

'No. So if we're ever going to get out of Europe we need to know our fucking history.'

'Fine, but I still think it's a powerful symbol.'

'Drop it. I'll stand in the foyer where I usually stand.'

I finish my drink and decide to go into the second-hand bookshop along the road.

They have a lot of good stuff in there. My kind of stuff.

The owner's cool.

Over the months he's recommended several things to me that weren't on my radar but turned out to be great.

The shop has that second-hand bookshop tang of old sweat and dust.

Endless books all squeezed together on wonky shelves and bookcases that crisscross the rooms.

It's like someone has pressed pause on an avalanche of books and frozen them in time.

Like it would all come crashing down on you if you pressed play.

It's beautiful.

I'm in the Politics section, wondering if I should get Clinton's autobiography.

Just to see if I can stomach reading that raping sociopath's putrescent, deluded prose.

Another teaching assistant from the school walks in.

My stomach drops.

Is she skiving off too? Will she recognise me?

I haven't been working there that long. She probably doesn't know who I am.

I pretend to read Clinton.

'Oh, hi Jamie,' she says.

Damn.

'Hi...'

'Carly. I work at Greenslade.'

We shake hands, which I find weird and slightly arousing.

'Oh, that's right, yeah, sorry. I haven't been working there that long...'

'That's all right. Is it your day off today?'

'Um, yep.'

I wonder if she can smell the drink on me.

'Cool, mine too. You work in Lilian's class, don't you?'

'Yep, but it's Mrs Winterbottom to me.'

Carly laughs. 'Yeah, she's not a first-name-terms kinda gal, is she.'

'Not really.'

'Are you going to buy that?'

'Have you read it?'

'No. I... probably wouldn't though.'

'Are you more of a Bush girl?'

'Ha, no. But I'm not a Clinton girl either.'

'Me either. I was briefly tempted to see what he had to say for himself.'

'It will be non-apologies for all the things he did wrong and shameless trumpeting of all the things he thinks he got right.'

'You're right.' I shove Clinton back onto the shelf.

'What are you up to now,' I ask.

'I need a few books for my course.

'What are you studying?'

'Primary Education,' she says.

'Ah, makes sense. That's why you're working in a school. I've seen you with the kids. They love you.'

'Oh, I don't know about that. But yeah, it's good to get experience. You get to observe a lot. Do you want to be a teacher?'

'Me?' I say. 'Nah. I mean, I've thought about it, but I don't think I could handle it.'

'I think you'd be a good teacher.'

'Oh, really? Thanks. I'm not sure I'd have the patience.'

'You're good with the kids.'

'It's easy to be popular when you're not telling them to hand in their homework.'

'You smile a lot. They tell you on the course that's a bad thing, but I don't believe it. A lot of our kids don't see adults smiling very often at home.'

'I bet.'

'It's true, unfortunately. All right, listen, I better get on. I've got two assignments due this week and I'm starting to freak. Nice running into you.'

'Yeah, you too,' I say. 'See you tomorrow?'

'Yep, see you then, bright and breezy.'

However.

I don't see Carly the next day.

I oversleep again, this time by about an hour and a half.

The black dog/shadow demon is back in town. The little flowers of mould are on my brain again.

There was no forewarning.

I'm too ashamed to call in sick again, so I leave the school, like I did the Harvester, silently.

58

A couple of days later, I'm making toast in the kitchen. I've been crying again.

For most of the morning I was on the verge of tears, then I eventually broke and howled like the black dog.

The front door opens and closes.

Jo comes in and drops her handbag on the dining table.

'Oh, hey, wasn't expecting you to be here,' she says. 'You chucked a sickie?'

'Sort of,' I say.

'What's wrong babe? You okay?'

'Yeah, it's all right. My grandad died.'

'Ohh, babe. Sorry to hear that. Were you close to him?'

'Pretty close.'

'Oh, come here.'

She hugs me and I sob into her shoulder.

'When's the funeral?'

'Not sure yet.'

'Right,' she says. 'Sit down. I'm gonna make us some tea and we're gonna have a duvet day on the settee. I'll even play Fifa with you.'

'How come you're home anyway?'

'I'm working from home. I'm not in the mood for clients today.'

'Fair enough.'

'Go on, put the Xbox on. I'll put the kettle on.'

I listlessly destroy her at Fifa and then lay the controller on the floor.

'I still don't get it,' says Jo. 'It's a stupid game.'

'Yeah,' I say. 'It is.'

She taps me on the shoulder. 'I saw Kim this morning.'

'Oh,' I say.

'She looked sad.'

'Well, I was an arsehole.'

'I think she's crazy. You two were great together.'

'Did she tell you what happened?'

'I haven't seen her. She's been off sick for a while.'

'Is she okay?'

'I think so. I'm catching up with her on Friday.'

'Tell her I'm sorry.'

'What did you do?'

'I'll let her explain.'

'I'm sure she'll forgive you.'

I make an 'I don't think so' face.

'We'll see. I'll put in a good word for you.'

She stands up and stretches.

'You're a better boyfriend than Pete.'

'Ah, don't say that.'

'It's true though. Do you know what he got me for Christmas?'

'No.'

She leans down and picks her controller off the settee, the pink one.

'This.'

'Fucking hell Pete.'

'I love him and everything, but I'm not happy.'

Now it's her turn to cry.

I stand up, nonplussed, and hug her.

After a little while, she kisses my neck.

'Whoa, wait.' I pull away.

'Oh shit,' she says. 'I didn't mean to do that.'

'It's okay.'

I walk to the kitchen and start doing the washing up, just for something to do.

She comes over and stands nearby.

'I won't tell him if you don't.'

'Okay,' I say.

'I'm just so sick of it,' she says. 'He never makes an effort anymore.'

'Why don't you tell him what you want.'

'I have. He tries hard for the next week then it's back to normal again.'

'I'm not a relationship expert. I have no idea how to make one work.'

'Nor do I,' she says, and starts crying again.

Zeus wanders in and rubs his head against her shin.

She sits on the floor and rubs his belly.

He rolls over to indicate that he loves it, and she carries on rubbing him, quietly crying, while I dry glasses with a tea-towel and put them in the cupboard.

59

I go back to my psychologist.

Force myself, somehow.

She's sitting at her desk, her computer monitor showing my medical history.

I always feel that she wishes I weren't there.

From the moment I walk in it's like my presence is anathema to her.

'So, Jamie, it's been a while. What can I do for you.'

I shift in my seat, sit on my hands.

'Um, I'm not feeling well again.'

'Well obviously. What's the matter?'

'I'm depressed again.'

'Why do you think that.'

'Google told me.'

'Google isn't a doctor.'

'I know. That's why I'm here.'

She's actually sneering at me, no doubt about it this time. 'So... give me more to work with. What made you Google 'depression'?'

'I have bipolar disorder. I didn't need to Google it. I just know.'

'But you said you Googled it.'

'I was being facetious.'

'Ok, so what are your symptoms?'

'I've been sleeping a lot --'

'That isn't necessarily a symptom of depression. Remember

we talked about your need to focus on your diet.'

'I know, but I hadn't finished.'

She seems impatient. 'Go on.'

'I've been unmotivated. I keep leaving jobs because I'm too tired and depressed to go into work.'

'Again, these aren't necessarily symptoms of depression.'

'I know. But again, you didn't let me finish.'

She ignores me. 'I've been thinking you should see a nutritionist. I can recommend this person.'

She scribbles on a notepad and tears off the top leaf.

'Based in Rochester. They're very good. I'll print off a referral for you.'

'Thank you,' I say, shutting down.

Just as I'd started to feel combative I instantly feel sluggish.

The increased gravity is back.

It's like I have narcolepsy: I've exerted some energy and am immediately spent.

The psych prints the referral letter and places it on the desk.

She sighs through her nose. 'Jamie, can I say that, the thing is, happiness is not a given. It's not something that just happens. You have to work at it. You have to focus on the things you have the ability to control. Have you been exercising? We talked about that last time as well. '

'Not really...'

'You see, there's something you can control. And what about intellectual pursuits. Have you thought any more about something you could get stuck into?'

I think about the book I haven't started.

'Not at the moment.'

'Again. This is something else you can control. Goals are

360

crucial. Why don't you go on a cookery course, for example. Learn a language --'

'I can already speak fluent French.'

This may or may not be entirely vrai.

'Well learn Mandarin then.'

'Why?'

'Because it will give you a purpose, a goal to work towards. Do it for its own sake.'

'I like to write.'

'Okay.' She reflects on this information. 'Which authors are you influenced and inspired by?'

I nearly say Bukowski and Hunter S Thompson, but think better of it.

I pick a know-it-all, middle-class writer.

'Sebastian Faulks,' I lie.

'Ah yes, he's terrific. Have you read 'Engleby'?'

I shake my head.

'It's excellent. Worth a read. And I suggest you look into his working habits, his routines, his work ethic. Try to emulate him as much as you can.'

She seems pleased with her own advice.

I nod and half-smile.

'What about friendships, Jamie. Do you have a healthy social life?'

My reflex is to say yes, of course, but then I realise this wouldn't be vrai, either.

I think of Kim.

Tom Pritchard.

Deb.

Dan, Lucy, Emily, Sam.

Shaz, in Canada.

Lee, still in Manchester.

My school friends.

All the people I'm disconnected from and all the different reasons for the disconnections.

I still have Pete and Jo, though.

Still have some hygge in my life, for now.

I grimace and tilt my head to the side briefly.

She regards me. 'Have you ever heard of the phrase 'failure to launch', Jamie? It applies to members of your generation, the so-called Millenials. It's quite common. It strikes me that you're deeply unfulfilled.'

'You're not the first person to tell me that.'

'Hmm. Try to seek out things that engage your interest, and go from there. In the meantime, I recommend seeing the nutritionist.'

She moves the mouse and looked at my file on the monitor.

'It says here you're a ten-a-day man. Are you still smoking?'

I nod.

'Well you need to stop that. I have some literature on nicotine replacement therapy somewhere.'

She opens the desk drawer and pulls out another leaflet, puts it in front of me.

'Thanks,' I say, ready to fall to the floor, get all foetal, sleep.

'Okay, ' she says. 'I think that will do for today. Goodbye Jamie. See you again soon. Don't leave it so long next time.'

She puts out her hand for me to shake. I pick up the smoking cessation leaflet.

Stand up slowly, walk out, leave her hanging.

I approach the receptionist.

'That'll be two hundred and fifty pounds,' she says.

'What? I get my sessions free on the NHS.'

'You used your last free session last time.'

'I'm sorry but I don't have the money,' I say.

She sighs.

She taps at the keyboard.

'All right, Mr Sinclar. I'll put it through this time. But next time you'll have to pay.'

'Really? That's nice of you.'

She smiles thinly and looks at her screen again.

'Thanks,' I say.

She doesn't reply.

Right, well. No more psych sessions, then.

I come out of the surgery feeling like a drugged snow leopard.

A proud, solitary creature, constantly moving to find its next meal, but with a poison dart in its neck, about to collapse under the sedation.

And I look more like a mangy stray cat than a snow leopard, with my patchy hair, crumbling teeth, and skin that feels warm and clammy, like a chamois leather.

I shamble toward the nearest pub.

Have to cross the A2 via a footbridge.

The old Roman road, connecting London and Dover.

I pause on the bridge to imagine all the people, all the traffic that has passed by in both directions over the centuries.

Cars now, in this era; horses and carts in the past; all those people – the various groups and the solitary wanderers: Roman tradesmen finishing a day's work; Saxon merchants heading to market; Norman tourists; Medieval pilgrims –- all of them heading to places that wouldn't have existed in quite the same way as each new day, hour, second passed.

I envision a talking Medieval friar.

'Places transform unnoticed, Jamie: tiny little metamorphoses constantly occur at the electron-microscopic level, which you don't think about when you're zoomed out as we are and looking at things such as buildings as though they aren't reconfigurations of stardust; when you're looking at a street and you still call its polarised destinations by the same names despite the millisecond-by-millisecond shifts of unending sub-atomic matter; when you're looking at a brain and can't see that its mind has been denatured by something it thought was good for it.

Because the truth is there is only one day.

We chop up our existence into calendars and timetables, when it's really just (no, not just – it's something greater) a swirling, permanently changing maelstrom within one colossal, sublime moment.'

I watch the traffic below.

The monk has disappeared.

It would be so easy to jump over the railing.

Splat.

All over.

I don't want to ruin anyone else's life though, so I continue walking, assailed by grisly, gargoylish thoughts that harass me for the rest of the journey.

60

Drunk, moist-eyed, shivering, I amble up the garden path. I enter the house and find Pete on the settee.

I know something's wrong because the TV is off.

I see Pete's been crying.

'All right?' I say, slipping out of my coat.

'Not really. Jo left earlier. It's over.'

'Oh, mate, I'm sorry.'

'Thanks. It was a long time coming.'

I don't know whether to stay standing or sit down.

'Is there any chance you might be able to, you know, reconcile?'

'No... I don't think so. I went too far this time.'

'I know what that feels like.'

Pete smiles, then starts crying again.

I sit next to him and put an arm around him, give him a squeeze.

'Do you want to go out? Get some fresh air?'

Pete shakes his head and sobs.

'It'll be okay,' I say, because I'm an idiot.

I rub Pete's back then go to the kitchen to put the kettle on. I stare out to the garden while it boils. I make the tea, take one to Pete.

'Thanks mate,' says Pete. He sips his tea then says, 'Listen Jay, I've got some bad news. I'm going to sell the house. Jo wants me to do it, and I think it's the right thing to do.'

'Oh,' I say. 'I understand.'

'I don't know when it'll happen, but I'm going to put it on

the market tomorrow.'

'Okay.'

I physically feel all the remaining hygge leave the room, leave my heart. My heart collapses like a paint can in the vacuum of space.

I rub Pete's back again and go upstairs.

I open my laptop and log onto Facebook.

In my feed there's a post from the Kent Messenger.

A sinkhole yawned open on the field of the school where I used to work.

The thing was twenty metres in diameter.

The accompanying photograph shows a couple of students in their hockey uniforms, holding their hockey sticks like guitars, peering over the edge, and a member of staff facing the camera, looking concerned.

According to the post the fire service was called and the perimeter of the hole was cordoned off.

No-one was hurt, no-one fell in, but the school was closed while they set about filling in the hole.

If it had appeared fifty metres south a huge portion of the school's main building would have been devoured by it.

Zeus nods the bedroom door open and hops onto my bed.

I gather him up and lick the top of his head.

PART THREE

'And everybody's got to live their life.
God knows I've got to live mine.'

1

Just before Pete and Jo sold their place I moved to a new housing association development at Chatham Dockyard.

I saw it advertised online and applied for it thinking I wouldn't stand a chance. But my name came up and I moved in at the start of the Spring.

I've been here for a year; haven't had a job the whole time.

The gravity is strong. The shadow demon is here again. My words have been greyed out once more.

It's a small two-bedroom place, basically appointed, but it's a good location.

There's a new university campus nearby.

The public transport is better.

It's a part of Medway where the regeneration seems to be making a difference.

Twenty years too late, but it's happening.

I spend my days sleeping, reading, applying for jobs, and volunteering at a local allotment.

I need a housemate.

With the little bit of housing benefit and the jobseekers' allowance I'm getting, I'm afloat.

Ends are being met, but it's precarious. A housemate will make things a lot easier.

I like living on my own, but it's time.

I'd very nearly moved to London instead.

Its gravitational pull had been working on me.

London – sprawling, greedy London – subsumes everything at its periphery, so its periphery is constantly expanding.

Sidcup, formerly of Kent – you belong to London now.

Ilford, formerly of Essex – omnomnomnomnom.

Medway's next, I can feel it.

Where will it stop? Scotland? Wales? The Isle of Wight?

To me London was the great whale which would indifferently gobble me up like plankton and indifferently shit me out.

I knew I wasn't up to life in the capital, and didn't know whether to feel relieved or disappointed in myself.

So I'm based near the famous Dockyard.

They don't build ships here anymore: it's meant to be a tourist attraction now.

There's a museum which celebrates the area's maritime heritage.

You'll learn that HMS Victory was built in Chatham.

The Fighting Temeraire was also built in Chatham.

It was an important dockyard in its day.

Its closure in the eighties ripped the guts out of the local area.

It was like the north of England when all the mines closed.

Col's brother, my uncle Derek, lost his job as a shipwright when the dockyard closed down, and he never forgave Thatcher for it.

He was so enraged when Col voted for the Tories at the next election he didn't speak to him for over a year.

Along the esplanade there's Dickens World, a tacky, themed attraction centre which commemorates the time when Dickens lived in Medway as a youth.

There are a few shops nearby and some chain restaurants, and they've built new homes and a new school on St Mary's island over the bridge.

They used to dump nuclear waste on that island; hence all the children born since the millennium are freakishly strong and have glowing green eyes.

But the gentrification has started and you can see that the council has put some money into the area, even if it is misguided.

2

I spend the morning at the allotment, planting veg and digging weeds, knees in the wet earth, the smell of herbs on my fingers, then walk home to apply for more jobs.

I trawl the internet.

Monster.com.

Indeed.com.

Reed.com.

LinkedIn, Gumtree, Adecco.

I've signed up with them all, made profiles for them all.

I've exaggerated my skills, my education, my work ethic – I've done everything I can, but there's nothing for me.

I want to be up at Darland Banks, under the pale blue moon, listening to the wind.

I want to become the wind.

I want to become an elm tree, producing irresistible sap for woodpeckers, with the wind blowing through my branches, making my leaves and my perfect flowers dance.

I want to become a bee and pollinate the perfect flowers of an elm.

I want to lick the sap from a woodpecker's beak.

I want to devour a woodpecker whole.

But here I am, on my laptop, on my couch, in my flat, in Medway.

I sign up with a yet another new temp agency and keep my fingers, still fragrant with allotment basil, crossed.

About an hour later someone from the new agency phones me and asks me to interview in London.

Wasn't expecting that.

Moloch has called, and I've answered.

The economy is bouncing back!

Jamie Sinclair is bouncing back!

Thank you Moloch!

Thank you for your infinite generosity and care and humanity!

Moloch, you fucking legend!

3

I still need to get my car fixed.

It's still parked outside Pete and Jo's old place. It's been rusting there for over a year while I've been rusting in my flat.

I haven't needed it, haven't had the money to fix it up, so I haven't bothered with it.

But if I get this job I'll need to drive to Chatham train station to catch the train into London.

Uncle Derek's garage isn't too far away from where I live so I stop in.

I haven't seen Derek for a few years but when he sees me he greets me warmly.

'Jamie my lad! What a pleasant surprise!'

'Hi Derek. How's tricks?'

He pats my back and takes me through the small workshop to his office.

We pass a mechanic working on an old Escort that's raised on a hydraulic lift.

There are two other cars further back each with wheels missing.

It smells of engine oil and rubber in there.

I'm envious of the mechanic and how engrossed he is in his work.

Envious of his knowledge, his purpose, his status as a worker.

'What can I do for you sunshine?' says Derek, wiping his hands with a rag.

I sit in a tatty swivel chair and Derek perches on his desk, which is covered in hand-written invoices and spare parts.

'There's a million things wrong with my car.'

'You still got that Corsa?'

'Yeah.'

'Where is she?'

'Parked outside my old place in Gillingham. I walked here. If I got it towed in would you be able to look at it?'

'Course. I'm pretty busy though so it might not be till next week.'

'That's fine. That'd be great, thanks.'

'I know someone who could tow it for free.'

'Really? That's awesome.'

He nods. 'Cuppa?'

'Yes please.'

Derek goes over to the small kitchenette area, wipes more grease from his hands with the rag and flicks the kettle on.

He goes back to his desk perch.

'How's your dad?'

I laugh. 'Oh, you know. Same old Colin.'

'You see 'em much, your folks?'

'Not really.'

'Why not?'

'They're hard work, Derek, you know that.'

'Don't be too hard on them. They're good people.'

'I know, but...'

I look at the floor briefly, look around the office.

A mechanic leans into the room and says, 'Del, Mr Evans is here about the Rover.'

'Cheers Steve, on me way.'

He hops off the table and pats me on the shoulder. 'Back in

a bit. Finish the tea would you, there's a good chap.'

I go over to strain the teabags.

I think about the argument between Derek and Col when Derek had come over for dinner one evening a few years back.

I was back from uni one weekend.

The conversation had ineluctably turned to politics and Derek ended up storming off.

It was around the time the Dockyard was being transformed into what it is now and everyone had something to say about it.

Derek and Col were simultaneously lamenting and celebrating the Dockyard's fate, agreeing but somehow contradicting each other at the same time, winding each other up.

Col had a habit of saying that Derek remembered the Dockyard with pinko goggles; Derek would always obligingly take the bait.

This time was no different.

'Col, I ain't saying it would have been the best place to work – you're twisting my words.'

'It sounds like you're romanticising the place to me. It was grim. Don't forget that.'

'I know it weren't the dream job or nothing, and granted, after the Falklands there weren't the need to build warships no more. But people need meaningful work, something to feel connected to. I haven't had that since.'

'You were miserable there.'

'I weren't miserable.'

'You were.'

'Look, whatever, I'm just saying, it was a fucking terrible idea to shut it down like that with nothing to replace it. Nothing worthwhile. The whole area became sort of... sort of injured. It still is. All we have left is the Pentagon Centre and a knackered old high street.'

'Yeah, you say that, but we all know the world and his wife are here now, and it'll only get worse with our borders wide open to Europe.'

'Why do you have to lick the Tories' aresholes so much? Why can't you admit, just for once, that maybe they ain't done such a good job for us.'

'And Labour have done so much better, have they? You forgotten the Three Day Week? Enoch Powell was right, is all I'm saying. He was right on the money.'

'You're an ignorant dickhead, Col. That's such a warped way of looking at things. It don't even make sense! There ain't that many immigrants here anyway--'

'Not that many immigrants?' Col paused and looked incredulously at me and Andrea. 'The man's delusional!'

'Well, okay, but the ones what do live here are cleaning things, and mending things, and fixing people. Just look at my garage. Szymon's my best worker!'

'Szymon's probably on housing benefit and sending it back to Poland.'

'Bigot.'

'I have a right to be a bigot in my own bloody house!'

Derek got up and left at this, and we didn't see him again until Andrea forced Col to get on the phone and apologise.

Derek re-enters the office.

'Tea's on your desk,' I say.

'Cheers.'

He lifts the cup and slurps.

'Listen,' he says. 'I've gotta sort something out. What's your phone number?'

He passes me a notepad and a biro and I scribble my number on it.

'Ta,' he says.

'Business good then, I take it?'

'Pretty busy today,' he says. 'Could be better, could be worse. Mustn't grumble.'

'I'll get out of your hair then. Let me know when's good to bring the car in. No rush though.'

'Okay sunshine. I'll give you a tinkle soon.'

He leads me out of the office and onto the forecourt.

The sun's come out. I shade my eyes with my hand.

'Good to see you Jay. You looking after yourself?'

'Yeah, you know,' I say. 'Keeping it fast, keeping it loose.'

'You need money or anything?'

'No,' I lie.

He looks at me askance. 'Hmm, just like your old man. Too proud to ask for help.'

He draws his wallet out of his back pocket and slides out a couple of twenties.

'Here,' he says. 'I'm sure I've missed the last couple of birthdays.'

'No, Derek, it's fine, really.'

'Just take it,' he says, and gently pushes me away.

'I'm only gonna give it back to you when you fix my car!'

'As if I'm gonna charge you for that,' he says.

'Thanks Derek...'

He turns and goes back inside, waving with his back to me.

4

There's something I don't like about the word 'London'.

The way it sounds: it's like a low-pitched bell with a strange timbre.

It sounds odd, jarringly antiquated.

I can't figure out precisely what it is, except that it seems unsuitable for the city I believe it to be; the word should've evolved along with the place itself, but hasn't done so, which unsettles me.

Londinium, Lundenwic, London.

Why has it fixed itself there, at that end-point?

What does this say about the city?

Maybe it says that London deserves Boris Johnson as its mayor...

I have a sense of impending doom about working there.

This manifests itself physically with night terrors and sleep paralysis

experiences.

I wake up in the middle of the night, unable to move. Can sense an 'evil' presence on its way into my room.

I try to yell out but only a tiny, bleating noise comes from between my closed lips.

I try to wiggle my little finger.

If I can just move it a little bit it will break the spell.

Eventually I get there, just in time, before the evil descends upon me.

For the next few days I feel like a slightly different person.

One night the hag is sitting on my chest.

I wake up because there's something heavy on me.

In my drowsy state I forget where I am and think I'm still living at Pete and Jo's.

I think the weight on me is Zeus.

But there she is.

This demonic crone, leaning towards me, looking me in the eyes and smiling like she's going to devour my balls.

This time I manage to yell out.

She disappears.

Am I awake now?

Pete comes into my room, bleary eyed.

'Dude, what the fuck,' he says.

'Sorry Pete,' I say, leaning on my elbows, sweating. 'Nightmare.'

'Oh,' says Pete, scratching his armpit. 'Do you want to come and sleep in Mummy and Daddy's bed?'

Before I can respond, I look down and see that Pete's dick is poking out of his boxer shorts.

Pete also looks down.

'It's a dick only a mother could love,' he says.

He collapses to the floor laughing hard.

I laugh too, until my cheeks and jaw ache.

Then I really do wake up.

5

The new job is with an expanding start-up media company called LiteSpeed, based in Holborn.

I'm a 'Digital-Content Provider'.

I don't know what that means.

All I do is update their website and look after their Twitter account.

It's a stupid job.

At the interview with the temp agency, the recruitment consultant said the company were looking for someone who 'cares about their colleagues and loves the work they do.'

I told them everything they wanted to hear and started the following Monday.

I had to fill out a medical questionnaire on my first morning.

The answer to everything was a resounding no.

Heart issues? No!

Diabetes? No!

Mental health problems, including but not limited to anxiety, depression or bipolar disorder? No! No! No!

(Imagine if I'd said yes to this last one. It would have been the same as admitting to having a criminal record.)

I'm earning the big bucks now.

£8.50 an hour.

I'm like a modern Dick Whittington on mood stabilisers, ready to make my fortune.

6

My manager, Chris, is seen as a rising star in the company. He's a narcissist.

An actual, full-blown narcissist, and possibly a sociopath.

Or maybe he's merely a common-or-garden douchebag.

Either way, he has no problem airing his personal life and his Machiavellian schemes in the office for anyone to hear.

It's part of his shtick.

He seems to get away with it because he's charming.

He's able to bend people to his will with his disarming humour and charisma.

It's hollow, transparent, manipulative behaviour.

He wouldn't be out of place as a Cockney character in a Brett Easton Ellis story.

He has perfect hair and looks as though he was once a member of a boyband before all the creatine warped him out of shape.

One hundred per cent of his conversations are about himself, which I have to concede is quite impressive in some respects.

But it's still annoying.

Luckily he's not a micro-manager. He leaves us alone most of the time, and I can put my headphones in and turn the volume right up whenever he pauses his work and begins a story about his sexual rapaciousness or the latest professional enemy to be vanquished.

7

On Friday evenings the majority of my floor migrates to the yupster bar across the road from our building on High Holborn.

Chris tells anyone who'll listen about his sex life, then goes to the toilets to take cocaine.

Once he's had enough coke and booze he usually takes his shirt off and shows everyone how his abs are coming along.

Usually puts someone in a headlock, gives them a noogie and says, 'I love you, you ugly cunt!'

It's during one of these Friday night drinking sessions that I get to know one of the senior project managers in my team.

Lydia.

I notice her putting Chris in his place and go over to talk to her, on the pretext of some made-up work thing.

She has the self-trimmed bangs, expensive Ray-Ban tortoise-shell specs, and she's wearing a Bo Ningen t-shirt which she sports at least once a week (traditional office attire is banned at LiteSpeed).

She seems witty and I'm attracted to her.

'What I like about Chris is his humility,' I say.

'He's the best at being humble,' she says.

'Better than you, better than I.'

'The best of all time.'

We have a couple of drinks together, and when I go to work the following Monday I feel less anxious, because I have an ally now.

8

It isn't long before we start seeing each other.

It becomes a regular thing for one of us to send an email at about four o'clock wheedling the other into leaving work early to go for a drink.

After a couple of weeks of this we end up getting a cab back to her place following one of our heavier drinking bouts, and we become lovers.

It's clear from the start that we're destined to fail as a couple.

We immediately fall into a teenage kind of dynamic where we try to undermine each other all the time.

I'm regressing: I know I should be looking for someone more mature with their shit together.

Someone to be happy and invisible with.

Instead I've found an adversary masquerading as a friend.

She's a middle-class white woman who believes her eye-watering privilege is diluted by her gender.

Someone who speaks with Received Pronunciation and has done since she learned how to speak.

She blames the patriarchy for everything bad that happens to her, and describes consensual sex as a kind of 'invasion' of the vagina by the penis (as opposed to a suffocation of the penis by the vagina).

Sometimes I can't believe she's a real person. Some of the stuff she comes out with. It's almost funny.

She drinks Kombucha every day and goes to yoga classes with a view to becoming a yoga teacher at some point, 'maybe next year', and attain 'enlightenment', which to her isn't the Buddhist definition, but a kind of local celebrity where she's the coolest/'wokest' person in her peer group.

She wears Nike trainers, only uses Apple tech products, reads Hipster Runoff secretly/unironically, and identifies as 'gluten-free' despite not being a celiac.

She has a tendency to become desultory and spiteful after a few drinks: as she gets drunker she skips from topic to topic, waving her cigarette around, swaying in her chair, interspersing her soliloquies with insults.

She refers to men as 'males', rather than using the word in its adjectival form.

She performs frequent character assassinations on her female colleagues.

But she's bright and funny, and when I trap her in my 'male gaze', as she calls it, I find her extremely attractive.

I know I'm heading for the rocks, but I can't help myself.

She's hot, and I'm lonely.

At least I'm earning good money!!!!!!!!!!!!!!!!!!!!!!!!!!!!!!!!!!

9

One evening we're sitting at a table under the awning outside the yupster bar.

As usual the place is full of people who work in our building.

They're spilling out onto the pavement and into the road.

Drivers beep their horns as they speed through High Holborn.

The people standing in the road briefly step up onto the curb as a vehicles fly past, then drop back down into the road again.

They will happily risk their lives for a drink.

Lydia is trashing one of our colleagues, Veronica.

'The way she comes over to my desk like a fucking cat, trying to mark her territory. I feel sorry for her. She's too fat to be alpha. And I know those aren't real Manolo Blahniks she's wearing.'

A guy emerges from the bar carrying three pints of beer in triangle formation.

As he tries to manoeuvre through the crowd someone jogs his arm and some of the beer spills on Lydia's shoulder.

'Nice one mate,' says Lydia. 'Thanks for that.'

The guy completely ignores her, grimly persevering towards his own coterie.

Lydia glowers at him like he's a rapist who's gotten off scot-free.

She slips off her coat, dabs it with a napkin to soak up some of the wet, drapes it over the back of her metal chair.

'You know that guy works with Manny Hague,' I say, gesturing towards the beer-spiller. 'He earns about fifty grand a year as a consultant, which means he sits in meetings all afternoon up in the canteen and gets to work from home on Fridays.'

'He probably sits in his front room with his curtains drawn wanking to punishment porn all day.'

'That's what I'd do.'

'What, you'd watch punishment porn?'

'No, but I'd definitely wank a lot.'

'You're both wankers, that's why.'

'Hey, he's a different species to me. Don't lump us together. I have a technique all of my own.'

'Really. Explain.'

'A good magician never reveals his tricks.'

Lydia pulls a face and gestures for a cigarette.

I take out my tobacco and fling it across the table to her.

As she's lacing the Rizla with tobacco she says, 'The Italians have this word, Sprezzatura. It suits you well.'

'What does it mean?'

'It means 'studied nonchalance'. Males are very good at it.'

I'm not sure whether she's being wry or spiteful; it's hard to tell the difference this early on in the evening.

'Isn't Sprezzaturra a brand of coffee?' I say.

'Everything's a brand of coffee these days,' she says in a goofy voice. 'It started with Moby Dick and Starbucks and will end with Jesus and Satan hugging each other because they both love coffee so much.'

'Coffee will heal the wounds of the world.'

'That's the power of coffee,' she says, in the same goofy voice.

'The only downside is that Jesus will be a coffee snob when he comes back. It happens to the best of us.'

'Yeah he'll be like, "Yuck, this isn't single-origin, is it. And it's too hot. You scalded the beans."' She mimes throwing the coffee in a barista's face. "Do it again, bitch, and this time use the Colombian roast, otherwise no-one gets into heaven."'

'Satan will be his own personal barista,' I say. 'He'll do sensational latte art. A frustrated artist who can only express himself in foamy milk.'

'He'll draw a cock-and-balls on Jesus' flat-white when he isn't paying attention. When Jesus is talking to one of his many groupies.'

'Jesus will be like, "Oh Satan, you cad. Now you must clean the same coffee machine for all eternity. Don't fuck with me. I am Jesus. I am cool."'

'One day I will have dominion, Jesus! I'm Satan for fuck's sake. Fucking Satan.'

'Nononono, look at my groupies, dumdum. Behold them with thine eyes. They are sexy and they're hot for me. I am a stud-muffin. You are merely barista. I have a good beard, a handsome beard. You have a bad goatee. I am Jesus. You will breweth coffee for me every morning. Sometimes in the afternoon too if I'm feeling sleepy. No more cock-and-balls, Satan! Wait. That doesn't sound right. Cocks-and-balls?'

'I'm not sure,' she says.

'I'm drunk.'

'I'm Jesus.'

We light fresh cigarettes.

Lydia gets up to go to the toilet, leaving her lit cigarette in the ashtray, smoke curling off its tip in pretty, stochastic movements before being buffeted by the breeze.

A lot of our conversations go like this.

Like many people we work with, Lydia is rather partial to

the cocaine, so there are always plenty of toilet breaks when we drink together.

We hardly ever develop a topic, let alone finish one.

She doesn't dwell on the chain of death and exploitation from Colombia to London, or doesn't care.

Nor does she care about the credit-card debt she's racking up, because her father looks after that.

I still fancy her though.

10

She comes back from the toilet looking furious.

A guy standing at the bar tried to chat her up.

'Did he touch you?'

'No, but he he was so full of himself. Like if only I were to have a drink with him I'd drop my knickers.'

'I can go in and say something if you like.'

'Eurgh, men. You're apes.'

Lydia is a 'fourth-wave' feminist.

She tells me this while we're having yet another conversation about my male privilege (as though I'm personally responsible, as a man, for the poor behaviour of the guy at the bar, and all those other guys).

Being fourth-wave should mean she talks about the equality of all humans, and the intersectionality of various dominance structures affecting different marginalised groups in society.

She does not do this.

All she does is talk about men being apes. Men being stupid. Men being monsters.

All men.

I suspect she had some sort of issue with her father growing up, but she's very cagey whenever I ask about her parents.

At first I don't mind listening to the abuse – she's fundamentally right. Women across the globe have it harder than men, anyone can see that.

But I happen to know that Lydia went to private school,

had her university tuition fees and accommodation paid for by her parents, and has her credit card bill paid off every month by them too.

She drunkenly let slip one night that she even had a maid growing up.

I therefore find it difficult to take her seriously.

'Lyd, do you mind if we talk about something else? I get it, but let's move on.'

'Oh, darling, are you feeling beleaguered?'

'Little bit.'

'It's hard being a straight white male, isn't it darling.'

'I'm straight, white and male. You're straight, white and middle-class. You're the one who should check your privilege.'

'That's ridiculous and you know it.'

'It's not – you're waaaaay more privileged than I am.'

'You need to stop being aggressive.'

'I'm not.'

'You are – you're clenching your jaw.'

'I'm… not.'

When Lydia talks about the suffering of women the first person I think of is Lauren Hitchens.

I think of Kim England.

Ayaan Hirsi Ali.

Of the rape culture in India.

Of the girls kidnapped by Boko Haram.

Of women in Saudi Arabia not being allowed to drive.

Of my mother and my late grandmother.

Lydia never talks about people like this.

It's almost as if she doesn't really give a shit about anyone except herself.

'I just can't understand, Lyd, why you're the one lecturing me about suffering, a woman with a £900 Mulberry handbag -- a 23rd birthday present from your parents, I might add -- and a £200 a week cocaine habit.'

'So that makes it all right for men to harass me whenever I go to the toilet?'

'Maybe if you cut down on the coke you wouldn't have to go to the toilet so much.'

'You're such a pig sometimes.'

Lydia is a woman who would call someone like Lauren Hitchens a chav, so fuck her.

In my view class is the biggest problem, especially in London, and if you could solve that you could solve more or less everything else.

Full of self-righteousness, I tell her as much. I even claim that I'm more of a fourth-wave feminist than her.

She snorts.

'No, seriously, think about it. Tackle the problem of scarcity once and for all and everything else will follow,' I say.

'As a male you would say that. You're deflecting attention from the pay gap.'

'They're selling t-shirts in Topshop now that say 'This is a feminist.' They've co-opted feminism and turned it into a brand. Young women are wearing those t-shirts thinking they're empowered.'

'Which only proves my point.'

'But we have a common enemy,' I say. 'We want the same thing.'

'My only enemy is you.'

'I can't tell whether you're being wry or not.'

'I can't tell whether you're a misogynist or not.'

'You can't call everyone you disagree with a misogynist.'

'When you stop hating women I'll stop calling you a misogynist.'

'I'm not a misogynist. I've read Camille Paglia and Germaine Greer, and agree with them!'

She tuts. 'Germaine Greer is second-wave and transphobic. She's a dinosaur. She doesn't even have Twitter. And Paglia doesn't know it but she hates women too.'

'I don't know about all that. But I do know I don't hate women. I just think it's outrageous for you to tell me you're hard done by. You've led a charmed life.'

'You know nothing about my life. And I think you do hate women, but it's casual and under the radar, which is more sinister in a way.'

'More sinister than, say, a wife beater or a rapist?'

'There isn't much difference.'

My jaw clenches.

'You're clenching your jaw again,' she says.

'No I'm not.'

I try to stop but can't.

She smirks. 'Males do that when they know they're wrong but can't admit it.'

'Now you're being a misandrist again.'

She rolls her eyes. 'Allan Johnson says, "Given the reality of women's oppression, male privilege, and some men's enforcement of both, it's hardly surprising that every woman should have moments when she resents or even hates men."'

I want to win the argument and put Lydia in her place.

Fuck Allan Johnson and his pandering to this juvenile gender-war bullshit.

My chest is tight with anger.

Then I realise that Lydia is carrying around a lot of pain and I'm being a complete imbecile, have always been an imbecile.

All I say is, 'That's fair enough, actually.'

Lydia turns slightly away from me and puffs her cigarette.

Chris staggers over to us. He lifts his shirt, strokes his perfect abs.

'Get a load of this,' he slurs. 'Lydia, come here darlin', touch me. I'm so ripped right now.'

'Fuck off, Chris,' she says.

'Oi, don't be like that love. I'm just trying to do you a favour. I'm fit as fuck.'

He laughs with his tongue out and nudges her shoulder with an elbow.

He strokes his abs again and yells out, 'Who wants another drink then! Come on you losers, I'm getting a round in! The milky bars are on me!'

A few of his beta-chimp followers organise around him.

Chris approaches one of the other women in his team and pinches her arse. The woman turns away from him and makes a face at someone else in the group.

Lydia raises her eyebrows at me.

'That's our manager,' she says. 'He earns 60k a year and is on the fast-track programme to directorship.'

I avert her gaze and roll another cigarette.

I'm often hungry at work.

Hungry and tired.

I get headaches, I'm tetchy, I'm sluggish.

How come I haven't been fired yet?

I have no idea.

I can't think properly half the time and make mistakes all day long.

I have to fold my arms across my stomach to stifle the growling.

I get the Sunday Night Blues so bad that I can't sleep, and spend each Monday in a fugue state, barely making it through the day awake.

I'm poorer than ever.

I've fallen into my overdraft for the first time since being a student.

I checked my online balance this morning and there it was in red font, with a little minus sign in front of the figure.

I'm getting the train from Chatham.

I sit next to other dejected people staring out the carriage windows, resigned to their fates. People who look like they've tried and failed to psych themselves up for another day.

People getting incrementally more impoverished by going to work.

People unable to pursue anything artistic or creative because they've got to work at least forty hours a week just to cover the rent.

My season ticket costs £300 a month, plus there's my monthly Oyster card which costs another £100.

My rent (inc. bills) is £350 a month.

After tax, National Insurance and student loan repayment I earn £900.

I can't afford breakfast. Nor do I have time for it.

Door-to-door it takes me on average two and half hours to get to work, though it's usually slightly quicker on the way home.

I have to leave my flat at 6.30am to guarantee a parking space at the station (a space which costs me another £100 a month).

I get to my desk at 9am -- as long as there haven't been any delays to the various services -- slightly sweaty and out of breath.

Start doing my list of tedious tasks until about 10, when I need to go downstairs for a cigarette.

Now before you get on your high horse about my smoking habit, let's do the sums.

A 12.5g packet of tobacco plus rizlas and filters costs me five quid and lasts at least five days.

I'm an addicted but relatively light smoker (<10 a day).

That's roughly £30 a month.

I did manage to quit for a few months but the dirty weed called me back to her.

Cans of Stella are a quid each from my local off licence, or six for a fiver; let's say I spend £30 a month on these.

That leaves £-10 for food and whatever else a human is supposed to do with their life before they vanish out of existence forever(?).

Which means I can't always guarantee full cupboards or a full fridge.

I can afford two out of three meals a day: I opt for lunch and dinner.

Smoking temporarily staves off the morning hunger, and gets me out of the office for a few minutes each day.

Don't worry, I'll probably die before you will!

12

So yeah, I'm in my overdraft again.

I really need that housemate.

I get on the phone to someone at the housing association, who gives me the okay but tells me I'll have to find someone myself.

Fine by me.

I put an ad up on spareroom.com; the same afternoon Jade calls.

He seems fine on the phone, except he says he's from Tunbridge Wells.

I nearly decline him on that basis but think better of it.

The housing association approve his references the same day.

I text him this, and ask when he can move in.

- Saturday alright?
- sure is. see you then :)

He turns up with his belongings in a VW camper van. To the untrained eye he's a hippie.

He has longish blonde hair like a Californian surfer and several years' worth of ratty festival wristbands on his wrists.

But when I get talking to him over our first cup of tea together I discover that he has plans to become a millionaire on the stock market, 'like my dad'.

That's why he's studying business and finance at the local university.

I have to bite my tongue. I don't want to argue with him; I've only been living with him a couple of hours.

I change the subject, make more tea.

13

We end up getting on pretty well.

He has a similar enough sense of humour to me, makes an effort to get to know me.

Despite his hippie appearance he's clean and tidy.

Despite his avaricious ambitions he's not a complete twat.

We each do our chores without the need for a roster or any passive-aggressive post-it notes on the fridge.

Plus my financial burden is gradually being eased.

He'll sell out one day and start wearing Hugo Boss suits, but until that day comes I'm happy to live with him.

We're in the kitchen when he suggests we invite some people for dinner.

He's leaning against the counter, eating a bowl of cereal.

I'm washing up.

I ask if I can have my parents over.

'Yeah man, it'd be good to meet them.'

I've been avoiding Mum and Dad for weeks. Months actually.

But I feel happy to invite them now that I have a job and I'm not on the dole anymore.

'Can I invite Imogen?' he says.

'Who's Imogen?'

'My girlfriend.'

'Sure thing.'

'You got a girlfriend?'

'Yeah. Sort of.'

'Ask her too.'

I tip the dirty water from the bowl into the sink and run the tap to clear the bits of food from the plug. 'Okay,' I say.

Everyone's free for a mid-week dinner.

I offer to cook my famous baked mushroom risotto.

Jade's girlfriend Imogen turns up first.

We get chatting in the kitchen, and it turns out she can do a fantastic impersonation of Tony Blair.

It's unbelievable -- she sounds just like him, captures his mannerisms perfectly.

I did ask Lydia to come but she finds it difficult to leave London.

'It's so far away,' she'd said. 'It makes more sense to go to mine.'

I couldn't be bothered to argue.

14

Jade and Imogen are setting the table when the buzzer goes.
    I let Mum and Dad in and dart into the toilet quickly.
When I come out I introduce everybody.
Andrea wants a tour of the place.
'Why. You've been here before.'
'No, Jamie, we haven't.'
'You're kidding. Of course you have.'
She shakes her head, tight-lipped.
'Okay. Sorry. Let's go.'
I show her around. It takes two minutes.
'It's lovely,' she says.
'Could do with a fresh coat of paint throughout, but it's fine for us.'
'We got you a housewarming present.'
'Oh, thanks.'
'Colin, where did you put it?'
Col leans behind the settee and retrieves a large indoor plant.
'Cool!' says Imogen. 'A philodendron.'
'It is indeed, Imogen!' says Andrea. 'You know your plants.'
Imogen nods sagely.
'Thanks guys,' I say.
'Your dad chose it,' says Andrea.
I take it from Col and puts it on the kitchen counter.
'It's great Dad.'
Col smiles with his mouth closed.
'It has care instructions just here, on this,' says Andrea.

She partially removes the triangular card that's wedged in the soil.

'It'll only need watering once a fortnight,' says Col. 'Otherwise you'll kill it. It's warm in here. They like to be quite dry.'

'I really like it,' I say. 'I'll look after it.'

15

I take the risotto out of the oven and place it at the centre of the table.

'Smells great Jamie,' says Imogen.

'Is that thyme?' asks Andrea.

'Yeah,' I say. 'Queen of the herbs. From the allotment I volunteer at. So are the courgettes.'

'Looks delish,' says Jade.

'I put balsamic vinegar in. Baking it deepens the golden colour.'

I give everyone a serving of risotto, pour water into glasses, get wine and beer for whoever wants it.

'There's salad too,' I say. 'Help yourselves.'

'Is this it?' says Col.

'What do you mean?' I say.

'Isn't there any meat?'

'Just ignore him,' says Andrea, touching my hand.

I feel my chest tighten but manage to swallow the anger like hangover vomit.

'Cheers everyone,' says Jade. 'Good to finally meet you both.'

'You too,' says Andrea.

'Cheers,' most of us say.

Andrea asks about Lydia.

'She's busy,' I say.

'We'd love to meet her. We were getting worried about you, weren't we love.'

'I'm not saying anything,' Col says. He makes a camp limp-wrist gesture.

Jade and Imogen laugh.

'Dad, they say that homophobic people are more likely to get aroused by gay porn than anyone else.'

'Jamie!' says Andrea, 'That's disgusting!'

'What's disgusting?'

'Don't talk about that stuff while we're eating.'

'You brought it up.'

'I did not.'

'Okay.'

'It's delicious Jamie,' says Jade with his mouth full. 'Really good.'

'Thanks,' I say.

'So, ah, there's an election coming up,' says Imogen. 'Have we all decided who we're voting for?'

I make a face to say, 'Change the subject,' but Imogen doesn't notice.

Col says, 'If you don't vote for David Cameron you're an idiot. He's going to sort out the mess that one-eyed Scottish idiot has gotten us into. He undersold all the gold!'

'And he's old, covered in mould -- don't tell me you weren't told,' I say.

'What?' says Col.

'Nothing.'

'I'm voting Conservative,' says Jade. 'Don't get me wrong, I have nothing against Labour, but the Tories seem to want to help people who want to help themselves.'

'If the Tories had their way you wouldn't be living here,' I say.

'Jade, I don't mean to be rude or anything, but to look at you I wouldn't have thought you'd vote Conservative,' says Andrea.

'There's more to me than meets the eye Mrs Sinclair,' he says.

'No, there's less,' says Imogen, quoting Seinfeld and inadvertently speaking the truth.

'Oi cheeky,' he says.

'Do we have to talk about politics,' I say.

'Politics is important!' says Andrea. 'You of all people, a politics graduate, should take an interest in it.'

'Mum, I do take an interest in it, I just don't want to talk about it right now. War by other means, and all that...'

'He's just sore because he knows that Labour are going to get a drubbing,' says Col.

'I don't vote Labour.'

'Doesn't vote Tory, doesn't vote Labour,' says Col. 'Who else is there?'

'UKIP,' says Jade, half-joking.

Imogen snorts.

'That Nigel Farage is a smart guy,' says Col. 'But his party's too disorganised. He's the only one with any brains, which is a shame. He says what we're all thinking.'

'He doesn't speak for me,' I say.

'No-one speaks for you,' says Col. 'If Karl Marx himself were running for office you wouldn't be happy.'

'No, I wouldn't, because I'm not a Marxist. I mean, he was right about alienation, commodity fetishism and the perils of social stratification, but just because I agree with everything he says it doesn't make me a Marxist.'

'Who are you voting for then Jamie?' says Imogen.

I swallow my mouthful of food. 'I'll probably vote Lib Dem,' I say.

Everyone bursts out laughing.

16

I quickly make an enemy at LiteSpeed.

One of the project managers, this guy called Hamish.

I don't work with him every day but he gave himself the role of copyeditor-at-large, which means the website falls under his unauthorised auspices.

No-one asked him to do it. It's just something he wanted to put on his LinkedIn profile.

So we occasionally have to liaise about some perceived grammatical error he wants me to correct on the website.

He considers himself a guardian of the English language, a kind of linguistics maven.

He has this arch, smirking demeanour, a permanent fleer on his face, and prides himself on what he once described to me, apropos of nothing, as his 'extensive vocabulary'.

He thinks he's charming and witty but everyone else thinks he's a pretentious wanker.

I imagine he has books by Umberto Eco and Derrida and Martin Amis prominently displayed on his bookshelves at home, which he started years ago but never finished.

Like many people who like to correct other people's grammar, Hamish has a limited intellect.

By huffing and puffing about the multifarious grammatical misdemeanours he witnesses on a daily basis Hamish is able to kid himself into believing he's intelligent.

He challenges me on some petty grievance he has with one

of my sentences.

He's leaning over my shoulder, pointing at his screen, lecturing me about split infinitives with his coffee breath.

'Didn't you cover this at university?' he says.

'I did, and I learned that split infinitives matter in Latin, not English. It became fashionable in the nineteenth century to apply Latin rules of construction to English, and people like you have been erroneously correcting people ever since.'

'Just change it, Jamie. It's ugly.'

'No. It doesn't affect the meaning of the sentence.'

'I'll do it myself when you've gone home then.'

'And I'll change it back. If I do it your way it'll ruin the rhythm of the sentence.'

'You're not writing poetry, Jamie.'

'Nor would I want to.'

'You're using a Stradivarius to hammer in nails.'

'You're not David Foster Wallace, Hamish. He could say that stuff because the boy could write. People like you who know all the rules of grammar but have nothing beautiful or worthwhile to say are like people who can read music but can't play an instrument. Fucking useless.'

'You're butchering our great language!'

'Get a life, Hamish.'

17

make Hamish look foolish in front of other people.

This is unforgivable.

He's standing by my desk again.

Behind us Yemi and Lydia are talking.

Yemi is from Hackney and uses a Hackney dialect.

'Has that guy responded about the conference?' says Lydia.

'I arksed him if he's gonna attend,' says Yemi, 'But he hasn't got back to me yet.'

Hamish turns around, horrified.

He interjects before Lydia can reply to Yemi. 'Excuse me, Yemi, can I ask you, how do you spell 'ask'?'

Yemi gives him a look but doesn't say anything.

'It's a, s, k, isn't it. Not a, r, k, s. So why do you pronounce it that way?'

Yemi kisses her teeth. 'Shut up Hamish. I wasn't even talking to you.'

'It's just so jarring,' says Hamish, and shudders.

I clap slowly.

'Well done Hamish,' I say. 'Once again you've managed to publicly display your profound ignorance of the history of the English language.'

Hamish sniffs. 'Really Jamie.'

I swivel in my to chair to face him. 'Yeah. Before 'ask' was pronounced 'ask', it was pronounced 'ax'. Then at some point in the seventeenth century people randomly started saying something like 'ask', and it evolved from there. So in a way, Yemi is

409

using what was a literary variant of the Old English word, and you're asking her to use a non-standard form.'

Yemi and Lydia laugh.

Hamish goes red.

'Why are you such a twat, Hamish?' says Lydia.

'It's all in the name,' I say. 'Most people called Hamish are twats.'

'That's true,' says Yemi. 'I went to school with someone called Hamish. He was a fucking twat as well.'

Hamish skulks off. We all laugh at him.

I carry on working, a lot more productively than usual.

18

Hamish sends me and my team an email about some bullshit policy update.

It's written in his overly formal, pretentious style.

I spot a spelling mistake.

Just a typo, but come on, Hamish. One should punctiliously proof-read one's emails before hitting send, shouldn't one?

I click 'Reply All' and cc the director of the company, Hamish's line manager, and anyone else I've seen Hamish sucking up to.

I paste a link to Dictionary.com with the correct spelling of the word, and hit send.

Lean back in my chair with my hands behind my head and wait for Hamish to come over and bollock me.

19

Now Hamish tries to undermine me whenever he can.

He finds out I've seeing Lydia and begins to flirt with her to annoy me.

Lydia flirts back, also to annoy me.

I don't care though. I'm drunk most of the time.

Which is ultimately why I get fired. I'm pushed before I get a chance to jump.

I'm sacked for 'chronic lateness, being intoxicated during working hours and for not performing [my] duties in a way that the company considers acceptable'.

Chris is no longer my boss. He's been promoted already, in accordance with the Peter Principle.

Chris's replacement, Graham, is the one who sacks me.

Graham is an ugly, passive-aggressive coward with halitosis who speaks as though it's the directors of the organisation themselves who are angry with me, rather than he himself.

That's why he always refers abstractly to 'the company', either in person or in the many stiff emails I receive from him, when he's really expressing his own views about my conduct.

'The company prefers it if its employees arrive on time to work.'

'The company prefers it if you let someone know when you're going to the toilet.'

'The company feels disappointed when you don't contribute in the team meetings.'

It happens when I come back from a long lunch one day.

I haven't actually had that much to drink. Two pints, maybe three.

But they've gone straight to my head.

I log onto my computer and see an email from Graham asking me to join him in Meeting Room C along the corridor.

I lock my computer and amble to the meeting room. As I open the door I trip over my own feet and fall into the room.

Graham and Hamish are sitting at a large conference table which has nothing on it except a single corporate-looking telephone.

I look up at them from the floor. They're staring at me with undisguised contempt.

'All right, cunts?' I say.

I'm escorted from the premises and will likely never see either of them again.

20

It won't be long before Lydia and I break up.

Since I left LiteSpeed we hardly ever see each other.

I have little incentive to schlep into London any more and Lydia rarely leaves the capital.

She says she'll make an exception for the Dickens Festival in Rochester, which is coming up soon.

I manage to tease her away from London with the promise of fun and frolics at the jewel-in-the-crown of Medway's social calendar.

She's resistant at first but I wear her down.

'I hate Dickens,' she says.

'No you don't. You hate the idea of Dickens.'

'Either way, it sounds shit.'

'It is shit, but in a good way.'

'I wanted to go to yoga though.'

'You can still do your yoga. We'll go afterward.'

She groans. 'Fine. But you're paying for my train ticket.'

'I don't have a job remember.'

'I'm not going then.'

'Chill out. I already took the liberty.'

I retrieve the tickets from my wallet and hold them out before her. 'Pick a card, any card.'

She takes a ticket and holds it over her eyes like a small mask with no holes. 'Is it fancy dress?'

'Only for the people participating.'

'I might dress up anyway.'

'Go as Little Dorrit.'

'What would I have to wear?'

'I have no idea. Something Victorian and workhousey.'

She claps her hands quickly. 'Ooh, I'm excited now.'

'My housemate's coming too. He'll probably bring Imogen.'

'What are they like?'

'They're cool.'

'I seriously doubt that.'

'Yeah, no, not cool cool. Just cool. As in, they're not cunts.'

'That's a low bar.'

'It's higher than you're used to. I've met your friends, remember.'

'Ooh you're a wicked man, Jamie Sinclair.'

'Wicked wicked? Or just wicked.'

'Just wicked.'

21

Lydia's friends are insufferable.

Oxbridge-reject types who like to pretend they're working class.

They use London slang ironically, even though they've spent zero time with people who use London slang unironically.

Lydia has them over for dinner the night before the Dickens festival.

We sit around her high-ceilinged front room in Tufnell Park, nibbling olives and vegan cheese.

They talk all evening about their respective food allergies, ailments and bowel movements.

They're so boring that their identities can only be expressed by what foods they can and can't eat, what makes their shits more liquid than usual, what makes them feel 'bloated', etc.

Apart from Lydia, none of them drinks or takes drugs. They're some of these puritanical millennials I've heard all about.

I sit silently in an armchair, soaking myself to stupefaction, listening in.

A guy called Josh or Noah or Francis asks me if I want some of the vegan cheese.

I try to answer, but the words won't come.

'Oh my God, he's so drunk,' says Josh, or whatever-the-fuck his name his.

I giggle a bit and start doing facial exercises to loosen up my tranquilised lips.

'What are you guys going to be like when you get cancer?'

I say, eventually, interrupting the continuing hypochondria-cal conversation. 'Or like, Crohn's disease or something? If lactose-intolerance makes you this anxious, I worry about your resilience when one of you gets the Big C.'

No-one answers. They all look at me like I'm a weirdo.

'Seriously, I'm worried for our generation,' I say. 'There are Nazis out there, and we're in here wringing our hands about gluten.'

Lydia goes red with silent fury. 'And you're going to stop the Nazis, are you, pissed as a fart and skinnier than my grandmother?'

'I'll take 'em,' I say. 'I'll take the lot of 'em.'

'Go back to doing what you do best, Jamie.'

I try to answer but again, but again, no words come.

I sip my drink while they continue talking about the quality and consistency of their faeces.

22

On the morning of the festival, Lydia is in her bedroom getting ready for her yoga class.

'Why don't you come with me,' she says.

She has a towel on her head and a towel around her body. I'm still in her bed.

'Yeah nah,' I say.

'You need to do some exercise.'

'I'd rather go for a run.'

'But you won't.'

'My statement is still true though.'

'Why are you so dismissive of yoga?'

'It just seems... I don't know. I don't understand it.'

'What's to understand?'

'Why do you do it?'

'It helps me feel, like, balanced in my body.'

She holds her hips briefly.

'What does that even mean.'

She glares at me. 'Are you being wilfully obtuse?'

'Maybe,' I say. 'Ga, I don't know. A bunch of uptight middle-class white women in Lorna Jane active wear being competitively spiritual. It seems narcissistic to me.'

'Anyone who exercises is narcissistic to you. Just because people take care of themselves, doesn't make them narcissistic.'

'What's a chakra? In empirical terms – what it is? What's it made of?'

'Not everything has to be explained empirically.'

'Okay, touchy.' I tap her side of the mattress. 'Can't you just come back to bed for a bit?'

She ignores me. She pulls out two pairs of yoga pants from the chest of drawers and holds them up for my inspection.

'Which looks better?' she says.

I point to the pair in her left hand. 'You look great in those.'

'You think so?'

'Babin',' I say. 'Hot spice.'

I kiss the tips of my fingers and flick them out, the chef's gesture to signify 'delicious'.

She tuts and rolls her eyes.

She holds the pants against herself and twists from side-to-side, looking at herself in the mirror.

23

We get off the train at Rochester and walk along the high street arm-in-arm.

Hundreds of people are out and about, dressed up as chimney sweeps, Artful Dodgers, Fagins, Nancies, Magwitches, Micawbers, Pickwicks, Miss Havishams, Scrooges and so on.

Shopfronts have been altered to look more Victorian.

Bunting crisscrosses above the street, fastened to the eaves of the buildings and the street lamps, which are authentically Victorian anyway.

There's a boisterous carnival atmosphere.

Somewhere a brass band is playing.

People are laughing and talking theatrically in character.

Children are playing in the street and the alleys. Some of them are probably pickpocketing their own parents.

'Jade's at the Jolly Knight,' I say. 'He just texted to say they're out in the beer garden.'

'Great,' she says, pulling a face.

'You didn't have to come.'

'I'm here now aren't I.'

'Here but not present.'

'Oh darling darling darling. Don't be a bore.'

'Okay, I'll be super interesting. Here's a riddle for you. What's got four letters, sometimes nine and never five.'

'True.'

'Have you heard that one before?'

'No.'

'You're joking. That was so quick.'

She shrugs. 'What's got two thumbs and needs some coke before she falls into a coma?'

I move behind her and prod her shoulder blades with my thumbs.

'This guy,' I say.

I massage her shoulders a little. 'No coke today though, if only because I can't guarantee the quality of anything from Medway.'

'Good job I remembered to bring my own then, isn't it.'

She pats her handbag and hunches her shoulders to indicate that the massage is unwelcome.

'Good job,' I say. 'Bloody. Good. Job.'

Jade and Imogen are sitting at the back of the beer garden, right next to the cathedral.

'Hey guys,' I say. 'Sorry we're late.'

'All good,' says Jade. 'Just enjoying the sunshine out here.'

'Lyd, this is Jade and Imogen.'

Imogen stands up to greet her and Lydia kisses both her cheeks like she's at Paris Fashion Week.

Jade shakes Lydia's hand.

'Pleasure darlings,' says Lydia. 'Now, I just need to pop to the little girls' room.'

'It's just inside the back door there,' says Imogen.

Lydia scrunches her nose to say thanks then minces inside.

I take a seat.

'Nice to finally meet her,' says Jade.

'Yeah. Drinks?'

'Go on then. Want me to come with you?'

'Nah it's all right.'

When I return to the table Lydia is on her phone and Jade and Imogen are studying the festival programme.

'So, did you wanna go and watch the performance in the castle at 2?' says Jade. 'It's Little Dorrit, apparently.'

He places a finger on the relevant section of the programme.

'Ha, Lyd was going to come dressed as her, weren't you.'

'Mmm, sorry?'

'Never mind.'

Lydia puts her phone away. 'Sorry, had to update Facebook.'

'With what?'

'You'll just have to see for yourself, won't you.'

'Jade was saying there's a performance of Little Dorrit.'

'I'm getting quite comfortable here,' says Lydia. 'It's actually really nice.'

'I told you,' I say.

'You tell me lots of things darling.'

'I'd like to go,' says Imogen. 'We brought picnic stuff.' She lifts up a large wicker hamper.

'Nice,' I say. 'All right, here's the plan. One more round here, then we'll walk up to the castle grounds via the off licence.'

'Sounds good,' says Jade.

'Oh yeah, Imogen,' I say. 'Can you do your Tony Blair impersonation for Lydia?'

'Oh,' says Imogen. 'Now?'

'Yeah. Tell her about the importance of reading Dickens.'

'Okay,' says Imogen, sounding exactly like Tony Blair. 'Our top priority is education, education, education. At a good school children gain the basic tools for life and work. But they should also read Dickens, Dickens and more Dickens.'

Jade and I are crying.

Lydia scrunches her nose, gets back to scrolling through her phone again.

24

ydia and I are in a tailspin, but I'm meeting her parents for the first time this afternoon.

They invited us over for Sunday lunch and Lydia doesn't want to go alone.

That's the only reason she asked me.

As we're walking up the path to their front door Lydia orders me not to mention how amazing their house is.

'Why not?' I say.

'Because it's vulgar,' she says.

I do though. I can't help it. Their house is amazing.

This huge Georgian place up in Hampstead, right near the Heath.

Her father answers the door.

He leads us through the hallway and into the atrium (they have an atrium) and the first thing I say is, 'This place is amazing!'

Lydia refuses to have sex with me for the rest of the week.

25

Friday night.

We're heading to this flat in Whitechapel.

Lydia knows some musician called Jack who lives there.

We take the tube from Tufnell Park.

Copies of Metro and the Evening Standard are strewn on the seats.

I leaf through a Metro and read a disturbing article about campaign donations to the major political parties.

I imagine getting spit-roasted by Moloch and Paul Dacre.

The article below disturbs me even more.

A sinkhole appeared on a building site not too far from Lydia's place.

Three workers were injured and are in a critical condition.

'Babe, this is our stop,' says Lydia.

We get off, ascend on the escalator, tap our Oysters, walk through the barriers.

'What are you thinking about?' she says. 'You look miles away.'

'I'm thinking about the ground swallowing me up,' I say.

She sighs. 'Oh God, please don't embarrass me tonight.'

On arrival at the flat I presume all the inhabitants are on the verge of a mental collapse.

It's a sleazy little crack den. Hideously bleak.

There's rubbish everywhere, cat shit from phantom felines in the corners, and there's no furniture anywhere except the two bedrooms off the narrow hallway, where there are only beds and cheap clothes rails laden with unwashed clothes.

The whole place smells like a mixture of damp, rotting food and cannabis.

None of the lights has a shade. There are only exposed bulbs, queasy yellow light.

There are these terrifying, nihilistic paintings resting on the floor against the walls in the hallway.

I can't look at them for long. They make me even more frightened and depressed than usual.

Most of the people in attendance seem to be taking the concept of being 'cool' very seriously, despite the majority of them being over the age of 25 – still an arbitrary cut-off point for 'coolness' in my mind.

It isn't the kind of party where you greet everybody as you enter.

We walk into the lounge.

No lightbulb at all in here. Just an empty fitting.

There are a few people slumped on the floor, backs resting against the walls, only partially illuminated by the street lamps outside.

House music is coming from an iPhone and a speaker on the white mantelpiece, which is flaking and spalled.

I grin at them all.

They stare at us. None of them says hello.

Lydia struts past them as though they're beneath her (to impress them and thereby increase her social esteem).

She's in her element.

It's set to be a loose night.

I feel like I could cause trouble at some point if I don't eject myself from the situation early enough: I haven't eaten anything since lunch, and the couple of beers I drank at Lydia's before we left have gone to my head.

I take our cans of beer out of my backpack and put them in the filthy bath which is full of other alcoholic beverages and ice.

I grab a couple of already-cold cans of Stella.

Lydia takes hers and goes to say hello to Jack, who's in the tiny kitchen.

I follow her, silently hatching my escape plan while admiring her body, feeling confused and sexist for being attracted to my own girlfriend.

Jack is leaning against the fridge talking to Pete Doherty from The Libertines. Not someone who looks like Pete Doherty from The Libertines.

The actual Pete Doherty from The Libertines.

I say, 'You're Pete Doherty!'

Lydia groans and face-palms herself.

Pete Doherty smiles and nods quickly in his skittish way.

He shakes my hand and doffs his porkpie hat.

Jack shakes my hand too.

'Jamie,' I say. 'I'm here with Lydia.'

I gesture to Lydia.

'Hi,' says Jack, somehow making me feel like a fool.

Lydia gives Jack a peck on the cheek.

She shyly waves and semi-curtsies at Pete Doherty, his majesty.

Pete Doherty mock-shyly waves back.

He taps Jack on the shoulder and indicates that he's going out to smoke.

There's a little window which leads to a fire escape and up to the roof. Jack nods and says, 'I'll be up in a minute man.'

Pete Doherty from The Libertines climbs through the window and disappears up the fire escape.

'How's it going Lyd,' says Jack.

'Not too shabby mate,' says Lydia. 'Can't believe he's here. Have you been playing with him?'

'Yeah,' says Jack. 'We're supporting Babyshambles at the moment.'   'Amazing, amazing,' says Lydia.

Jack nods like it's no big deal. 'Thanks for coming guys. Help yourself to anything you want. We've got hors d'oeuvres and everything.'

He points to the kitchen sink.

There are bags of red Pom Bar piled in there, spilling over onto the crusty draining board.

'Haha, cool,' says Lydia, earnestly.

'Thanks, don't mind if I do, I'm starving,' I say. 'I love the ready salted ones. It's like eating a handful of transitional objects.'

Jack smiles then turns to Lydia, who's looking at me like I just groped someone.

Lydia and Jack are immediately engrossed in conversation.

I munch Pom Bar and slurp my can of Stella.

The three of us are the only static people in the kitchen.

Others come in and out all the time, mainly to access the fire escape.

A couple of girls in their late-teens come through, pausing

next to me to roll cigarettes.

One of them says, 'There's so many hot guys here tonight.'

The other one says, 'Yeah, and I heard Pete Doherty's supposed to be coming later.'

'He's up on the roof,' I say.

They turn to me.

'Do you know him?' one of them asks.

'Yes,' I say. 'He's my son.'

They both sneer. One of them tuts.

They put their cigarettes in their mouths and climb through the window, holding the front of their skirts down so as not to flash anyone as they kick their legs over the ledge.

I go to say something to Lydia but she and Jack are snorting cocaine off the kitchen counter.

Jack finishes his line, stands up straight, throws his head back.

He turns to me and proffers the little straw.

'Want some?'

'Nah thanks,' I say. 'It's not my thing. Someone died to get that up your nose.'

Lydia says, 'Now now, don't get on your high-horse darling. You'll happily hang out with Mandy if she's around.'

I shrug and pout innocently. 'MDMA gets made in student chemists' bathtubs. Pablo Escobar has nothing to do with it.'

'I don't have any Mandy on me,' says Jack. 'But if you go through to the back room you should be able to, uh, source some there.'

'Right-o,' I say. I make a clicking noise with my mouth, make a finger gun, fire it.

I imagine turning the gun on myself.

Imagine myself as a bullet and Lydia as the gun, firing me

into my own mouth, through the back of my skull, out the window and into the London night.

Jack turns and does another line.

I put my empty beer can in a box full of other empty cans.

'Might go and mingle,' I say.

'I'll come with you,' says Lydia.

She moves closer to me and puts a hand in my back pocket.

The last time she'll ever do that.

Jack rubs his septum.

'Cool,' he says. 'I'll see you sweethearts later on. Make yourselves at home, yeah?'

He touches Lydia's elbow and climbs out onto the fire escape.

26

Lydia takes my hand and leads me through the flat.

We find the guy we're looking for in one of the bedrooms.

He's sorting out vinyl records that are stacked against the wall.

He pulls one out and holds it up to us.

'Mind if I put this one on?'

It's The Smiths by The Smiths.

'Go right ahead,' says Lydia.

Lydia and I sit on Tracy Emin's unmade bed.

The guy puts the record on the turntable and lowers the stylus. He and Lydia then make a transaction.

He hands Lydia some foil which she unfolds.

We all rub the MDMA crystals into our gums.

Lydia and I lie back on the bed and listen to the music with our eyes closed.

It kicks in pretty quickly.

Lydia and I get up involuntarily and start dancing to the music, which by now has become something I haven't heard of.

The guy is our own personal DJ.

He picks the perfect song every time.

Everything else melts away: pure bliss courses through us.

I pull Lydia close to me and kiss her neck.

She puts her arms around me.

I suddenly feel extremely horny.

Lydia too.

We don't care that the guy is there.

We're beholden to other forces; he's in his own universe.

Lydia and I kiss and start undressing each other.

The guy is oblivious to us.

I push Lydia back onto the bed and part her legs.

Lately Lydia banned me from going down on her because she said my ego got more out of her orgasms than she did, but right now she wants me to. Moments later, Lydia is on top of me.

At one point I slip out and she has to put me back in.

As she does this I get a strong niff of something terrible.

I feel paranoid, worried that it's something coming from my body.

'Can you smell that?' I ask.

'What?' she says, with her eyes closed.

'That smell. What is it.'

'I can't smell anything. Wait. Yeah I can. What the fuck is that.'

She climbs off me and we both stand half-naked on the bed, trying to locate the source of the stench.

Then I discover what it is.

The streak of cat-shit on her thigh.

The streak of cat-shit on my shin.

'Wait there,' I say. 'I'm going to get some tissues.'

Lydia follows my gaze.

I go to get up but she pushes me back onto the bed.

She runs out the room with tears in her eyes, into the bathroom next door.

I hear the squeak of the shower tap and the white noise of the water against the shower curtain.

I use my boxer shorts to wipe the noisome shit off my leg

and stuff them into an old pizza box next to the bed.

I put my trousers on.

Gather up the bedsheets and chuck them at the foot of the bed.

Start whistling along to the song that's playing.

I manage to hit a high note I've never been able to hit before.

I whistle the note three or four more times before the magic leaves me and I can no longer reach it.

The DJ carries on dancing, happy to be alive.

27

Lydia and I text each other intermittently for about a month after the party but then one of us doesn't respond and before long we quietly uncouple.

I still haven't got another job since leaving LiteSpeed.

I'm back on the dole, drawing housing benefit again.

I have to sell stuff.

I drive all over the Medway towns.

I sell dozens of my books to the second-hand place in Rochester.

I sell CDs at a Cash Converters in Chatham.

The same Cash Converters also gets a ring my parents gave me for my eighteenth birthday, my electric guitar and the accompanying amp.

I drive up Chatham Hill to Gillingham.

Sell a bunch of clothes at a vintage place on the A2 and give the rest, including the vomit suit, to an Oxfam down the road. I keep only the warmest items and a few basics.

I want to sell my car too, except I'd probably have to pay to have it scrapped.

I condense my worldly possessions to a pile that can fit inside an old backpack Pete lent me which I'd never returned.

I'm so thin now that I could probably squeeze myself into the backpack too, if I wanted.

28

I deactivate my Facebook account once again, determined never to reactivate it.

I do it on the day I wig out completely.

I return from the off licence with a few cans of Stella and fire up the laptop. I put on some music and spend a couple of hours drinking and smoking and peering into the lives of people I haven't seen since I left school.

I look up Kim but can't find her.

Perhaps she's deactivated her account, though it's more likely she's blocked me.

I look up Alice, then Lydia, but it's the same thing.

I watch 'David After Dentist' on YouTube.

I watch the 'Tra La La' song, a weird video featuring some Russian dude.

Then I put on 'Claire de Lune' by Debussy and search for Caitlin Gilberthorpe.

I immediately see she's engaged.

At the top of her timeline are three pictures of her and her fiancé looking happy and healthy, with comments below from various friends and family congratulating them.

I want to believe these photos, like everyone else's photos, are a facade.

I've seen it so often on Facebook: the holiday smiles, the baby pictures, the post-half-marathon posing, the persistent chirping, the motivational, life-affirming memes, the close-up shot of the ugly diamond on the ring finger -- all calculated to convey the best impression of a person.

But I know there's stuff roiling beneath the surface: neuroses, bitterness, insecurities, melancholy.

I want to believe that Caitlin is secretly miserable, hiding behind these pictures.

But I can see that she really is happy.

It's plain enough. She's on her way to eudaimonia.

I scroll through her entire timeline.

She doesn't seem to use Facebook all that much. She rarely puts photos up of herself -- she's usually tagged by others.

There are few clues to how she is doing at work, or where she's been on holiday, or who she votes for.

She's quietly getting on with her life with dignity.

The pianist rolls through the final bars of 'Claire de Lune'.

I nearly post a comment underneath one of Caitlin's photos.

I type out a long message, check its spelling and grammar, remove clichés and platitudes, add pretty imagery and sincere sentiments.

But I refrain from pressing return. I highlight the text and delete it.

I open a new Word document and start typing.

The context changes but stays the same.

One cacistocracy makes way for another.

David Cameron is elected in a landslide and rapidly starts selling weapons to Libya, continuing Tony Blair's legacy of doing sensational business in the Middle East.

More and more people are flocking to Bluewater to buy expensive brand goods on credit while the high streets of the

Medway towns rot.

1.5bn of the Earth's inhabitants are members of Facebook, which collects our private data and sells it to the highest bidder.

Ronald Reagan once said in an inaugural address, 'We seek the total elimination one day of nuclear weapons from the face of the Earth.'

He also said in a State of the Union speech that 'A nuclear war cannot be won and must never be fought.'

The nuclear non-proliferation treaty is currently being ignored by every single one of the nuclear powers, with all nine countries maintaining, expanding or upgrading their stockpiles.

In the middle of the night, in Poland and Austria and Germany, neo-Nazis deface the shop-fronts of businesses run by immigrants.

In England, the English Defence League and UKIP are growing in confidence.

Boris Johnson, a well-known pathological liar and racist, continues to be mayor of London.

Alex Jones currently has 2m followers on YouTube.

Barack Obama, our Lord and Saviour, sends more and more drones to bomb Yemen into the Gulf.

David Cameron says he loves The Smiths.

While all this is happening, I sleep.

I deactivate my Facebook account and close the laptop once the song ends. Put on my shoes and coat.

It's June but it's still cold.

I've been in Medway for almost two years.

I don't know what time it is but it's dark when I step out of my building.

Medway is asleep, save for a few taxi drivers and anyone who might have been at The Zone.

I start walking.

I walk for hours.

Walk all night, maybe.

Can't be sure.

I have another panic attack.

Wake up in the morning somewhere outside Tonbridge to a stranger Good Samaritaning me into their car.

29

The stranger drops me at my place.

'Are you sure I can't call someone for you,' she says as I unclick my seatbelt.

She's frowning concernedly.

'Quite sure,' I say, using my poshest accent. 'Thanks so much for the lift. Can I give you some money for petrol?'

'Wouldn't hear of it,' she says.

She smiles and touches my forearm briefly.

'Thanks again,' I say, and get out.

Before I enter my building I walk over to the river.

I sit on a bench and watch a pair of small sailboats drift out to sea.

Ketches, maybe. I read that word somewhere.

Mini Sydney Opera Houses, floating along, like Cubist representations of boats, white triangular sails imbricating, jagged, serene.

Weirdly glamorous for the River Medway.

Sailing from Chatham to St Tropez.

Maybe onward to Costa Rica.

It's a cool morning, but sunny.

A few people are out and about along the esplanade.

'Why do protons spin the way they do?' I think. 'Not how. Why.'

A pigeon waddles nearby, occasionally pecking at crumbs on the ground.

'Why are there rules of nature?'
'Why are there protons?'
I stand up and walk to my flat.

30

Jade is out.

I get a glass of tap water and sit on the settee for a few minutes.

I go to the bathroom and splash my face.

Take out my beard clippers from under the sink.

Plug them in and begin shaving my head. Number one all over.

Clumps of wispy brown hair fall to the floor.

I run the clippers through my beard as well, followed by my eyebrows.

When I finish I slap my bare cheeks until they go red.

I slap them at least a hundred times.

I have a shower.

When I get out I don't look in the mirror. I dry off and put my dressing gown on and go to my bedroom with my glass of water.

Take out my lithium carbonate from the bedside cabinet.

I have four unopened packs. I've dutifully collected the prescriptions but ceased taking them a couple of months ago.

I take a pack and pop out all the pills from their little foil blisters.

Twenty-eight in total.

I array them on the cabinet in a single line.

Eat them one by one, swallowing each with a small gulp of water.

Not too long after that, a sinkhole opens up in my mind, and everything falls into it.

31

The last time I saw my brother John before he left the UK, Col and I had an argument.

A big one.

And Col got arrested.

I blame the house itself for the argument.

It's too small.

It's not tiny, exactly, but it feels smaller than it is.

As soon as I step through the front door into the narrow, wall-papered hallway I feel this pressure.

I feel this pressure at my temples.

I instantly slip into a bad mood, and it's only a matter of time before someone says something that sets me off.

This time it was Col who started it.

Perhaps it was Andrea.

Or was it me?

We were having dinner and no-one was saying very much.

I took out my tobacco and started to roll a cigarette.

Andrea tutted, asked me not to do that at the table. 'I thought you were going to give up,' she said.

'When I'm twenty-five, Mum. Right now I'm just getting into the swing of it.'

'You might as well roll up a five-pound note and smoke that instead,' she said.

'Not really,' I said. 'A pack costs about five pounds, and I probably get about forty out of a pack. So really it would be like rolling up twelve pence and smoking that, if you could find a way to do it.'

'When did you become so clever,' she said, smiling with worry.

Holding up the cigarette I excused myself from the table to go and smoke outside, but Col vetoed this.

'Sit down,' he said. 'We haven't had dessert yet.'

'I understand,' I said. 'But as a free citizen of this fine democracy I'd like to exercise my individual agency, if that isn't an absurd statement, being as it is applied to the matter of a personal addiction, and insofar as we have such a thing – free will being so spurious and illusory a concept. I'm electing to have one now, between courses. Because once I've had this I'll be so much funner, Daddy-o. I'll be so much the funner, brillianter conversationalist over the trifle, believe me, once I've had this.'

'Sit down,' Col said again. 'We've cooked for you. You can at least have the bloody courtesy to sit down with us for an entire meal.'

'Correction: Mum's cooked for us.'

'True, but your dad's actually a very good cook,' said Andrea. 'Aren't you love. He does a terrific tuna and pasta bake.'

Col ignored her.

'Just have your bloody fag later,' John said.

I took out my tobacco pouch, stuffed the unfinished rollie into it and slumped into my chair like I was thirteen again.

I smirked at John.

John rolled his eyes, said nothing.

'And you can wipe that look off your face,' said Col, 'Or I'll wipe it off for you.'

I involuntarily snorted with laughter.

Col started going into one.

'Oh, you think it's funny, do you?'

I shrugged like a teenager.

'You don't show us respect anymore.'

He was glaring at me.

'You make it seem like that's my fault,' I said

Col wiped his mouth with a napkin. 'Ok then,' he said. 'Tell you what. Get out. If you're going to be like this, get out.'

I looked at John, then at Andrea, then at Col, perplexed.

'So I can go and have my cigarette? All this flipping and flopping, Dad. It's making my figurative head spin figuratively.'

'You know what, you pretentious git?' Col let his cutlery fall from his hands to his plate; the noise made everyone jump. 'You can fucking piss off back to Manchester where you ponce off the taxpayer and talk your poncey shit all day long. I won't have you mocking us like this. Not in this house. Go on. Off you go.'

I sat there, flummoxed, as Col's voice got louder.

'I said get out. Come on, time to leave, sunshine. Welcome outstayed. Go on, if we're not good enough for you. Fuck off out of my house.'

Andrea said, 'Colin, you don't need to talk to him like that.' She kept her hands in her lap.

'It's alright Mum,' I said, standing up again. 'Our procrustean overlord has spoken. And I'm a-gagging for this fag. I'm a-digging this here cig.'

I patted my back pockets. 'Ah shit. Anyone got a light? As-tu du feu?'

Well this really did it, didn't it.

This really got Col's gears.

This really ground his goat.

The camel's back was unequivocally broken, because this man now well and truly had the hump.

No-one speaks French in his house.

Col smashed his plate off the table and clattered upstairs.

There was lot of cursing and crashing and banging.

I could hear that he was in my old room.

'What the Dickens,' I said. 'What the Chaucer.'

John sat back in his chair and rubbed his forehead.

I left him and Andrea at the table.

Watched Col from the bottom of the stairs.

He was shouting, tipping out the contents of a drawer.

It was all tumbling down to where I stood.

A few years earlier it would've been me he was chucking down the stairs, but by then he knew better.

Bits of old stationery and my A-level essays.

Micromachines.

A small man-of-the-match football trophy.

Love-letters from an ex-girlfriend.

Sci-fi books.

A deck of Top Trumps.

'You're not welcome here anymore! You are now trespassing on my property! Take all this shit back with you. And don't ask me to help you move it! Don't you dare ask me to help you move it! You can sort it yourself. Not my problem anymore!'

When the drawer was empty he disappeared, still heaving, into his and Andrea's bedroom behind a slammed door.

It was utter carnage at the bottom of the stairs.

All of my stuff was disarrayed there like a broken mind.

When Andrea came into the hallway she started sobbing.

The telephone rang.

John joined us, holding the phone. 'Mum. It's the police. They said they're coming to speak to Dad. Something to do with his work. He's not to leave the house.'

Col came downstairs quietly and let the police officers take him out to their car.

When the policewoman clicked the handcuffs onto his wrists, she did it apologetically, almost tenderly it seemed, like she didn't want to break his wrists, or his spirit, or his heart.

We watched from the lounge window as she ushered Col to the police car and protected his head as he got into the back seat.

To me he didn't look like my dad as they drove him away.

He looked grey and sad and helpless.

John put his arm on my shoulder.

Then he hugged Andrea.

A week later he and Nat and eleven-month-old Max flew ten thousand miles to the other side of the planet.

32

Andrea, Col and John pick me up from Medway Maritime Hospital.

I'm wearing about fifteen layers of clothes, all of which Andrea grabbed from my drawers at home.

I shuffle out with them through the dark car park, past a couple of elderly women sitting on a bench and a drunk man walking into A&E with a paramedic by his side.

The drunk man yells, 'I have rights! You can't do this to me!'

He's allowing himself to be escorted in by the paramedic.

He's holding a battered old teddy bear.

The automatic doors open and the paramedic waves the drunk man in.

'This is bullshit!' he yells. 'Fucking bullshit!'

He stops and tears the head off the teddy.

It comes off in a few yanks with ripping sounds.

The man throws the bear's head over his shoulder.

The paramedic picks it up and gently guides the drunk man into the waiting area.

33

Col drives us home.

We each take off our coats and hang them on the stand in the hall.

Andrea hugs me, rubs my arm.

'I'll put the kettle on,' she says.

'I'll help,' says Col.

John and I walk through to the lounge and find Nat and Max playing with Sylvanian Families on the floor.

Thomas the Tank Engine is on the TV with the sound low.

'Here they are,' says Nat.

She stands up and squeezes me.

'What are you playing at you silly duffer.'

'Sorry,' I say.

'Don't be sorry,' she says. 'It's great to see you.'

She gives me another squeeze.

John comes in and Nat kisses him on the cheek.

Max is warily looking up at me from the floor.

I sit next to him and pick up a tiny squirrel in a flowery dress, move it to the front door of the little house, the front facade of which is open on a hinge.

'Knock knock, can I come in?' I say in a squeaky voice. 'It looks nice and warm in there. Can I play with you?'

Max picks up another squirrel in red trousers and says, 'Yeah, come in! Pway turtles.'

I look up at Nat for help.

'Ninja Turtles. He loves them.'

'Oh, yeah, Ninja Turtles, I know them well. Can I be Michaelangelo?'

Max nods.

'I Leonardo.'

'Let's get some pizza,' I say.

I sit there with Max pretending the tiny squirrels are Ninja Turtles eating pizza.

Andrea and Col come through with tea on trays for everyone.

I stand up and take one from Col.

'Cheers Dad.'

'Biscuit?' says Col, offering me a bourbon from the tray.

I take one and stuff it in whole.

We all take seats on the armchairs and settee and watch Max play for a bit.

'That's some house,' I say.

'Colin and Andrea bought it for him,' says Nat. 'He left his ninja turtles in Perth and was beside himself without any toys.'

'We took him to Toys R Us and he chose all this stuff,' says Andrea.

'He's a very lucky boy,' says Nat.

'That's what grandparents are for,' says Col.

'I remember all this from when I was a kid,' I say.

'You used to love them,' says Andrea. 'You had a lot of toys.'

'I know. I was a very lucky boy too.'

Max waddles over.

He puts the Michaelangelo squirrel on my leg and says, 'Pway now.'

'Uncle Jamie is drinking his tea,' says Nat. 'He'll play with you in a bit.'

Col gets out of his seat and picks Max up.

He holds him aloft, pretends to drop him.

He blows a raspberry into his tummy.

Max squeals with delight.

Col looks happy.

Nat checks her watch. 'Actually it's time for your dinner Maximus,' she says. 'Johnny, can you grab the bag please darl?'

She goes to get up but Col puts a hand on her shoulder.

'It's all right love,' he says. 'You stay there. John and I will sort it.'

Col carries Max into the dining room and John follows.

'Dad's in his element,' I say.

Mum smiles. 'It's so lovely to have you all here. Colin and I have been excited for weeks.'

'We've been looking forward to it too,' says Nat. 'We were worried how Max would go on the flight but he was good as gold.'

'It's so lovely to have you here,' Andrea says again. 'We've missed you so much.'

I doze off in the armchair.

I wake up to the chatter of everyone in the dining room setting the table for dinner.

I yawn and stretch; I get up and go through to join them.

'Hey love,' says Andrea. 'Hungry? We're about to have some chilli. Dad made it vegetarian for you.'

'How long was I asleep?'

'Only an hour or so. We didn't want to wake you.'

'I might go for a walk,' I say.

'All right darling.'

'I'll have a cigarette first.'

'Okay,' she says.

'Is Max in bed?'

'Yeah,' says John, laying out cutlery. 'He was pooped.'

I roll a cigarette, go out to the garden.

Col follows me out.

'Can I have one of those?' says Col.

'Really?'

'I'll have one every now and then,' he says. 'Can you roll it for me?'

I roll a cigarette for my dad.

'Let me show you something,' says Col.

He leads me to the bottom of the garden.

'I've been growing some veg,' he says. 'Look at the size of this lettuce.'

He chuckles at how massive it is.

We quietly smoke for a bit.

'Listen,' he says. 'I know we've had our differences. But I want you to know that Mum and I are here for you.'

'Thanks Dad. That means a lot.'

'I'm serious. We'll help you through this thing.'

He has tears in his eyes.

I have awkwardness in mine.

'I didn't realise what was happening with you. You've been so distant, I didn't know you were at crisis point.'

'Dad, it's okay, it's not your fault.'

I pat him on the back.

Col takes my hand, holds it for a moment.

I nearly yank it out of his hand and punch him in the face.

Not because I'm angry with Col – not anymore – it's just a

reflex which I have to suppress.

'You know, when all that stuff happened with me, I was completely oblivious. I had no idea what was going on in my own head.'

Col releases my hand and sits on the bench next to the shed.

'The first time I realised something was wrong was on one of my days off. A Tuesday, I think. Or was it Wednesday? Doesn't matter. It was my day off, and I came down here with my cup of tea to have a look at the wisteria here.'

He reaches up and feels one of the lilac petals.

'I sat here on the bench to look at them and before I knew it, nine hours had passed. Nine hours, Jamie. I'd lost the whole day. Your mum came in from work and I hadn't moved at all since she left that morning. I had to admit then that something wasn't right. Something wasn't quite right. But there wasn't anything I could do about it. Not a bloody thing. I was conscious of it but completely paralysed. Not physically. Not exactly physically paralysed. Up here, I mean.'

He touches his temple, looks at the wisteria again.

'You know, I used to have long hair before it started to fall out. Like this. Down to here.'

He gestures with a gentle chopping action to a point just above the nook of his elbow.

He lets his hand rest there.

I sit down next to my dad.

'I've always loved this garden,' I say.

'Me too,' says Col.

We sit together on the bench without saying anything else, just us two, and stay like that for, oh, who knows, a while.

34

I come out of the toilet and John's waiting for me on the landing. He's holding an old coin.

'Remember this?' he says.

He hands it to me.

It's a silver Roman coin that he'd found on a school trip.

He'd had the wherewithal to keep the discovery to himself so his teachers couldn't confiscate it.

I pinch it, turn it from obverse to reverse.

It has the head of Claudius on one side and a Latin inscription that neither of us can read on the other.

'This should *be* in a *museum*,' I say, channeling Indiana Jones.

'Ssh, don't tell anyone,' says John.

'It's probably worth a lot of money.'

'It is. I looked it up online. But I'm going to take along to the Guildhall tomorrow.'

'Really?'

'Definitely,' he says. 'Well, definitely maybe.'

'Our coins haven't changed much since these,' I say. 'What's that about.'

'What did the Romans ever do for us,' says John.

'Haw haw haw. G.K. Chesterton said that England doesn't just have Roman ruins, it is a Roman ruin.'

'Dude, G.K. Chesterton was a religious zealot, so what did he know.'

'He was a genius.'

'I know, I know, I'm just joking. Didn't I put you onto him

in the first place?'

'Probably. You put me onto a lot of things.'

'Why don't you come with us to Perth,' says John. 'I'll pay for your flight. You can stay with us for as long as you want. I've cleared it with Nat, she thinks it's a great idea.'

'I don't know bro. It would put Jade out.'

'Who's Jade?'

'My housemate.'

'Jade's a big boy.'

'I feel like I owe him. He was the one who found me.'

'I know, but he'll understand, given the circumstances.'

'I'll think about it,' I say.

'Don't take too long. We leave next Thursday.'

'When's this wedding?'

'Saturday, but we can skip it if you want us to spend time with you.'

'No, you should go. I'll be fine.'

'Okay.'

I motion for us to go downstairs. 'I'm going for a walk,' I say. 'Wanna come?'

'I'll pass. I'm pretty wiped.'

'Listen,' I say. 'I haven't forgotten. I still owe you that money.'

'I know you do you little shit. Did you get the car fixed in the end?'

'Yeah, Uncle Derek sorted it. I will pay you back.'

'Don't worry about it.'

'I will though.'

John punches me lightly on the arm.

'How is Uncle Derek these days? I should try and see him before we leave.'

'He seemed well actually. You should stop into his garage. He'll be stoked to see you.'

'Maybe I will. Hey, that suit for that wedding you went to. Did you get a good one in the end? Maybe I could borrow it. I've got another fucking wedding in Bali to go to after we fly home. I've been to eight weddings in the last two years.'

'Oh yeah, it's sexy,' I say. 'I got a lot of compliments about it. It wouldn't fit you though.'

I puff out my cheeks.

'Dick,' says John.

John nods at the coin. 'Give it here then.'

I put it in his hand.

'Heads or tails,' he says.

He flips it in the air, traps it on the back of his hand.

'Tails,' I say. 'Fifty per cent of the time, fails.'

John puts the coin in his pocket.

'We'll never know what it was,' he says.

'I'm comfortable with that.'

Just then a fly lands on my head.

I raise a hand to slap it.

It flies away.

'Hair looks good,' says John.

I rub my shaved head.

'Seriously, it suits you. You look like Neo from The Matrix.'

35

I put on my scarf, coat, gloves and woolly hat.

'Are you sure you're going to be okay?' says Andrea. 'Can you take your phone with you?'

'Got it here,' I say, patting my back pocket. 'I won't be too long. I just need some air.'

'Call me if you want me to pick you up.'

'Thanks Mum.'

I close the front door behind me.

I look at their neat little square of lawn.

I look up and down their street, the street on which I grew up.

I start walking.

I wonder where the people are now who lived here when we were kids, the ones I played football with on the green up the road.

I used to live near so many friends, but they're all disparate now.

I think about how it would be extremely odd if we all lived that close to each other as adults.

It would be good though, to see them all.

As I turn down an alley saudade materialises in the middle of my belly.

From there it courses through my whole body.

The street lamp ahead of me flickers, casting jittery, pale light into the alley.

I walk all the way down to The Cricketers pub, 'The Cricks', which is next door to a Norman church called St Margaret's.

I pause outside the pub, looking up at the church's fragile-looking tower for a while.

The bouncer on the door asks if I'm coming in or not.

I shake my head.

I walk over to the fence separating the pub's car park from the churchyard, keeping my eye on the church tower.

I climb over and land next to a grave overgrown with weeds and grass.

Clap dust from my gloves.

I find one of the pathways that intersects the graves and walk around, peering at the fading names on the headstones.

I try not to step on the graves.

It's so dark.

There's a street lamp which could illuminate the churchyard if it weren't for the looming chestnut trees lined up along the far, southernmost wall, blocking it out.

I carry on creeping around the place, making sure to keep to the pathway.

I soon recognise a name on one of the headstones on which a patch of moonlight is resting.

Howard Grist
1984-2009

I went to primary school with Howard and saw on Facebook that he died in a car accident last year.

We weren't really friends and I didn't know him very well, but I remember something about him from what must have been our third or fourth year at school.

I'd been getting into individual fights with these boys for a few months, but one time they ganged up on me.

Really laid into me.

They'd finished beating me up behind the free-standing wall in the corner of the playground and I was curled up in a ball, crying.

It was Autumn and I had wet leaves from the ground stuck to my face.

Howard came over to help me up.

I shouted at him to leave me alone and batted him away, but Howard waited until I'd calmed down, then pulled me up and took me to our teacher.

I don't think I ever really spoke to him after that.

We both grew up and went our separate ways, and I hadn't run into him at all since.

I become aware of the muted sounds of the pub from where I'm standing.

I read the rest of the inscription on Howard's headstone and then I decide to leave, exiting the churchyard the way I climbed in.

I walk into The Cricks, trying to maintain a veneer of equanimity as the bouncer lets me through.

I text Mum and Dad while I stand at the bar waiting to be served.

The pub is packed.

In the corner a man is setting up the karaoke machine.

He holds the microphone up to his lips and says, 'Testing, testing, ein zwei, ein zwei.'

He taps it a couple of times and says, 'Shit, it's broken. It's in German.'

A few people nearby laugh.

'I think I have another one here somewhere,' he says, looking around himself. 'A Czech one too, Czech one too.'

I smirk as the bartender hands me my drink.

I go out to the smoking deck.

No-one else is out there.

I sit on a stool and look once more at the church tower, and I drink to Howard Grist.

No, that's not quite true.

I drink to Medway.

THE END